"Enchanting, visceral, and twisty, *Bloodleaf* is a phantasmagorical wonder that will keep you guessing until the very last page."
—Laura Sebastian, *New York Times* best-selling author of *Ash Princess*

"Smith weaves together mystery, adventure, and a reimagined fairy tale in this bewitching debut. An irresistible, spellbinding story."
—Rebecca Ross, author of *The Queen's Rising*

"Romance, danger, and magic make for a winning combination that will keep readers glued to the pages long after bedtime."
—*School Library Journal*

"A multifaceted scheme, mistaken identity, and a simmering romance will keep readers riveted and dying to know how it all unfolds. . . . An excellent choice for fans of smart, independent female leads, intriguing fantasy worlds, and a race against the clock to defeat evil."
—*Booklist*

"The plot is breathlessly fast, complete with creepy spirits, a satisfying romance, and complex but clear political twists and turns. . . . Political, romantic, magical, timely, yet also traditionally appealing."
—*Kirkus Reviews*

"A riveting read . . . rife with surprising twists. . . . This novel is a well-developed page-turner that will have fans of both the fantasy and mystery genres rushing to finish."
—*The Bulletin*

"Debut author Smith explores the power of sacrifice in this darkly romantic reimagining of the Brothers Grimm's 'The Goose Girl.'"
—*Publishers Weekly*

Bloodleaf

CRYSTAL SMITH

HOUGHTON MIFFLIN HARCOURT
Boston   New York

* * *

hmhbooks.com

The text was set in Bembo Std.

The Library of Congress Cataloging-in-Publication data is on file.

ISBN: 978-1-328-49630-0 hardcover
ISBN: 978-0-358-24225-3 paperback

Manufactured in the United States of America
DOC 10 9 8 7 6 5 4 3 2 1
4500792434

To Jamison and Lincoln—
Guess what? You're the best.

And to Keaton—
I love my you.

✳

The City of

ACHLEV

Corvalis Manor

The Tower

The Castle

City Square

The Stein and Flagon

Ebonwilde Forest

Nihil Nunc Salvet Te

Tomb of The Lost

Tunnel
Entrance

Aurelia's
Hut

Kate's
House

Sahlma's
Apothecary

PART ONE
RENALT

The gallows had been erected in the shadow of the clock tower, partly so that the spectators could witness the executions without the nuisance of sun in their eyes, and partly so that the Tribunal could keep its killings on precise schedule. Order in all things, that was the Tribunal's motto.

I held my cloak tight around my chin, keeping my head down as the crowd converged in the square beneath the clock tower. It was a chilly morning; breath was billowing from my mouth in wispy clouds that rose and disappeared into the fog. I scanned right and left from under my hood, wary.

"Good day for a hanging," a man next to me drawled in a conversational tone.

I glanced quickly away, unable to meet his eyes for fear he might notice mine. It wasn't often that a person was determined to be a witch by such a trivial trait as the color of her eyes, but it wasn't unprecedented.

A murmur rippled across the crowd as two women were prodded up the stairs onto the platform. Accused witches, both of them. The first woman's shackled hands shook so hard, I could hear the clink of her chains from my distant spot in the throng. The second, a younger woman with a sad face and stooped shoulders, was perfectly still. They were both dressed in rags, dirt caking their sallow cheeks and clinging to their matted hair. They'd probably been isolated and starved for days, long enough to turn them desperate and feral. It was a calculated tactic; if the accused witches seemed subhuman and unhinged onstage, it not only quelled the reservations of the scrupulous few who might doubt the Tribunal's practices, but it also made for a more entertaining show.

The man who'd spoken to me sidled in closer. "Fantastic fun, these hangings. Wouldn't you agree?"

I tried to ignore him, but he leaned in, repeating quietly, "Wouldn't you agree, *Princess?*"

Startled, I found myself staring into a pair of purposeful, umber-colored eyes flanked by an unsmiling mouth and a cocked eyebrow.

"Kellan," I said in a heated whisper. "What are you doing here?"

He set his jaw, shadows collecting in the hollows beneath his copper-brown cheekbones. "As I am supposed to be guarding you, perhaps you can tell me what *you* are doing here and answer my question and yours at the same time."

"I wanted to get out."

"*Out?* Out to this? All right, let's go." He made a grab for my elbow, but I snapped it back.

"If you drag me away now, it will cause a scene. Is that what you want? To draw attention to me?"

Kellan's mouth twisted. He had been appointed as a lieutenant to the royal family's regiment at fifteen and assigned as my personal guard at seventeen. Now twenty, he was long since oath-bound to protect me. And he knew the only thing more hazardous to my health than standing in the middle of a crowd of agitated witch haters would be alerting them to my presence. Though it pained him to have to do so, he relented. "Why do you even want to be here, Aurelia? How can this possibly be good for you?"

I didn't have a reasonable answer for him, so I didn't reply. Instead, I nervously fiddled with the charm bracelet at my gloved wrist; it was the last gift I'd ever received from my late father, and wearing it always had a soothing effect on me. And I needed serenity as the black-clad executioner arrived, followed by a Tribunal cleric who announced that the great Magistrate Toris de Lena was taking the stage to officiate.

Toris was a commanding presence in his starched collar and stiff black Tribunal coat. He paced in front of us, holding a copy of the Founder's Book of Commands to his chest, the very picture of somber regret.

"Brothers and sisters," he began. "It is with great sadness we gather today. We have before us Madams Mabel Lawrence Doyle and Hilda Everett Gable. Both have been accused of practicing arcane arts, and both have been tried and found guilty by fair tribunal." Around his neck hung a vial of red liquid. He raised it so all could see. "I am Magistrate Toris de Lena, bearer of the blood of the Founder, and I have been selected to preside over these proceedings."

"I don't understand," Kellan was saying quietly by my ear. "Is this some challenge you've put to yourself? Come stand in the midst of your enemies? Face your fears?"

My eyebrows knitted together. Being arrested and tried and publicly executed was a very acute fear of mine, but it was only one black horse in my vast stable of nightmares.

"My people are not my enemies," I insisted even as a fist-pumping chant burgeoned around me: *Let them swing! Let them swing!*

Right then I saw a dim shadow pass in front of the younger lady—Mabel—and pause next to her. The shadow flickered at her feet, gathering form from the morning mist until it became starkly clear. The air grew even colder in the square as the spirit pulled heat and energy into his cloudy form. It was a young boy, no more than seven. He clung to the skirt of the shackled woman.

No one touched him. No one even looked his way. I was likely the only one who could see him. But Mabel knew he was there, and her face shone with something I could not name: perhaps pain, perhaps joy, perhaps relief.

"I know that woman," Kellan whispered. "Her husband used to come through Greythorne, selling books, at least two or three times a season. He died last year, one of those who caught that awful fever that went around the first part of winter. Him and a son, too, I think."

I knew Mabel too, but I couldn't risk telling Kellan that.

The tower clock showed it only a minute away from the hour, and Toris's florid speech was winding down. "It is your time to speak," he said to the women as the executioner situated a rope over their heads and around their throats. "Madam Mabel Lawrence Doyle, you have been tried and found guilty by fair Tribunal for the distribution of illicit texts and for attempting to raise the dead through use of magic and witchcraft, in defiance of our Book of Commands. By the blood of the Founder, you have been condemned to die. Say your last words."

I stiffened, waiting for her to point a finger at me, to call me by name. To bargain for her life with mine.

Instead she said, "I am at peace; I have no regret." And she lifted her face to the sky.

A familiar scent drifted around me: roses, though it was too early in the season for them. I knew what it meant, but when I looked right and left, I saw no sign of her. The Harbinger.

Toris turned to the second lady, whose whole body was shaking violently. "Hilda Everett Gable, you have been tried and found guilty by fair Tribunal for attempting to use witchcraft to harm your son's wife, in defiance of our Book of Commands. By the blood of the Founder, you have been condemned to die. Say your last words."

"I'm innocent!" Her voice rang out. "I did nothing! She lied, I tell you! She lied!" Hilda pointed her bound, shuddering hands at a woman near the front of the audience. "You liar! You liar! You'll pay for what you've done! You'll—"

The clock struck the hour, and the bell reverberated across the multitude. Toris bowed his head and pronounced over the sound, *"Nihil nunc salvet te." Nothing can save you now.* Then he gave a nod to the executioner, and the floor dropped out from beneath the women. I let out a cry, and Kellan pulled me into his shoulder to muffle it.

The bell tolled nine times and fell silent. Their feet were still twitching.

Kellan's voice was gentler now. "I don't know what you thought you'd see here." He tried to turn me away to protect me from it, but I twisted from his grasp. Even though being near a transition from life to death always made my stomach turn, I had to bear witness. I had to *see*.

Mabel's body had gone completely still now, but the air around her shimmered. It was a strange thing to watch a soul extricate itself from its body, slipping out from the grotesque shell the way a fine lady might step from a muddied, cast-off cloak. When she emerged, she found her son waiting and she went to him. In the instant they touched, they were gone, moving from borderland into whatever lay beyond, out of my sight.

It took longer for Hilda to die. She gagged and spluttered, her eyes bulging from their sockets. When it did happen, it was an ugly thing. Her soul tore itself from its body with what would have been a snarl, if there had been any sound. Hilda's specter lunged at the woman she'd pointed at in the crowd, but the woman did not seem to notice. Her attention was on the sloppy sack of bones swaying at the end of the gallows rope.

"Would you like to claim your mother-in-law's body?" Toris asked the woman.

"No," she said emphatically. "Burn it." And Hilda's ghost silently screamed, dragging her intangible nails across her daughter-in-law's face. The woman paled and put her hand to her cheek. I wondered if Hilda's rage had given her spirit enough energy to exert a real touch.

I didn't envy the daughter-in-law. Hilda would probably remain in the borderland indefinitely, following her betrayer, silently screaming, clouding the air around with her hate. I'd seen it happen before.

"Let's *go*, Aurelia," Kellan said. He used my name instead of my title; he was becoming distressed.

The crowd was starting to get raucous, pushing forward as the bodies were dragged down from the stage. Someone next to me gave me a hard shove, and I stumbled forward toward the cobblestones, putting my hands out to catch my fall but coming down hard onto my wrist instead. I wasn't down for long, though; Kellan was already lifting me to my feet, his arms circling me like a protective cage as he forced our way out of the mob.

My hand went to my empty wrist. "My bracelet!" I cried, straining to look over my shoulder at the place where I'd fallen, though the ground could no longer be seen through the mesh of bodies. "It must have broken when I fell—"

"Forget about it," Kellan said firmly but kindly—he knew how important it was to me. "It's gone. We have to *go*."

I slipped from his grasp and turned back into the crowd with my eyes on the ground, pushing when I was pushed and shoving when I was shoved, hoping for any glimpse of my bracelet. But Kellan was right; it was well and truly gone. He reached me again and this time held fast, but I didn't want to fight him anymore; the whistles had begun to blow. Within minutes the Tribunal's clerics would be marching on the gathering, rounding up any who seemed to lack the requisite enthusiasm for the cause. There were two new vacancies in the Tribunal's cells, and they were never left empty for long.

✴

It wasn't more than an hour later when I found myself standing in the beam of my mother's antechamber skylight, staring at the half-finished confection of ivory gossamer and minute, sparkling crystals—thousands of them—that would soon become my wedding dress. It would be the most extravagant costume I'd ever worn in all my seventeen years; the Tribunal's influence in Renalt extended even to fashion. Clothing was meant to reflect the ideals of modesty, simplicity, and austerity. The only allowable exceptions were marriages and funerals. Celebration was reserved for the events that curtailed one's opportunities to sin.

The dress was my mother's wedding gift to me, every tiny stitch done by her own hand.

I touched the lace of the one finished sleeve and marveled at its fineness before reminding myself how unhappy I would be the day I had to wear it. Every day brought the occasion closer and closer. Set for Beltane, the first day of Quintus, my wedding was now little more than six weeks away and looming large on the horizon.

Sighing, I straightened and went through the door into the next room, ready for battle.

My mother was pacing on the other side of her table, skirts rustling with each restless stride. Our family's eldest and closest adviser, Onal, sat straight-backed in one of the parlor's less comfortable chairs, sipping her tea with pinched brown lips and a carefully cultivated disdain. At the sound of the door, my mother's blue eyes whipped toward me, all of her anxiety loosed at once, like the snap of a bowstring.

"Aurelia!" She used my name like an epithet. Onal took another slow sip of her tea.

I thrust my hands into my pockets. The gesture was supposed to make me look sheepish and repentant, of which I was neither. But this whole thing would be over faster if Mother thought I was remorseful.

"You went to town alone this morning? Have you lost your mind?" She lifted a stack of papers and shook them at me. "These are the letters I've received this week—this week!—that call for you to be investigated by the Tribunal. Over there"—she pointed to a separate pile of paper, two inches high—"are the possible threats against you that my informants have gathered since the beginning of this month. And here"—she pulled open a drawer—"are the more poetic and fanatical predictions of your demise we've been sent since the beginning of this year. Let me read one to you, shall I? Let's see . . . all right. This one contains a very detailed methodology of how to determine if you're a witch. It involves a sharp knife and a thorough examination of the underside of your skin."

I didn't have the heart to tell her about the severed kitten's head I'd found in my closet last week, laid out alongside a poorly scrawled country prayer to ward against witches; or the red x's that were scratched on the underside of my favorite saddle, an old hex meant to make a horse go mad and turn on its rider. I didn't need to be reminded of how much I was hated. I knew it better than she did. "They want to peel my skin off?" I asked lightly. "Is that all?"

"And burn it," Onal supplied from behind her teacup.

"One week until you leave," Mother snapped. "Can't you manage to stay out of trouble until then? I'm sure when you're queen in Achleva you'll be able to come and go as you please. You can go into the city and do . . . whatever it was you went to do today."

"I went to a hanging."

"Stars save me. A *hanging*? It's like you *want* the Tribunal to come after you. We're very lucky we have Toris there on the inside."

"Very lucky," I echoed. She might think Toris, the widowed husband of her favorite cousin, was the crown's trusted ally keeping the Tribunal in check from within, but I'd never be convinced that he didn't enjoy the part he played up there on the gallows stand.

"Aurelia," she said, taking stock of me, head to toe. I knew what she saw: a tangle of pale hair and eyes that should have been blue but weren't, not quite, erring more on the side of silver. Outside of those attributes, I was not particularly unpleasant-looking, but my peculiar traits and tendencies made me stand out, made me *strange*. And Renaltans were suspicious enough about me simply because I existed.

I was the first Renaltan princess born to the crown in nearly two centuries—at least, the first who hadn't been given away in secret at the hour of her birth. It was my duty to fulfill the treaty that had ended the centuries-long war between our country and Achleva by marrying Achleva's next heir. For 176 years our people believed that the lack of girls born to the royal family was a sign that we were never to truly align ourselves with the filthy, hedonistic Achlevans. Proof of our moral superiority. My birth shook their faith in the monarchy, the king and queen who had the gall to first have a daughter and then keep her.

Sometimes I agreed with them.

A knock at the door broke the tense quiet. Mother said, "Bring him in, Sir Greythorne."

Kellan came through first, looking around and then giving a wave behind him.

A man stepped out from behind Kellan. He was dressed in crushed velvet the color of a twilit sky, with a golden sash crossing his chest and fastened by a brooch in the shape of a three-pointed knot. In his ear winked a rakish ruby stud; on his finger shone a silver signet depicting a spread-winged raven. He had a shock of gleaming black hair, untouched by the silver that should have accompanied his age. Startlingly colorful, he was like a lone stained-glass window in a world made up of plain leaded panes.

He was an Achlevan.

2

Mother peered behind Kellan. "You weren't followed?"

"No."

"The guards on the grounds?"

"Dismissed. We have perhaps an hour before the new guards come to replace them."

"The room guards?"

"Taken care of."

Mother introduced the elegant stranger. "Aurelia, this is Lord Simon Silvis. Brother-in-law to Domhnall, king of Achleva, and uncle to Valentin, prince of Achleva. Welcome, Lord Simon, our honored guest." She kissed him on each cheek.

Startled into shyness, I averted my eyes, suddenly fascinated with the tiny glass grapes and silken leaves at the foot of a nearby candelabra.

"Hello, Aurelia," he began, "so glad to meet you again."

"Again?"

"You were a baby the last time. Still quite small. I barely even got a look at you, though, as your mother wouldn't let you out of her arms, not for anything."

"Things have changed since then, I'm afraid. Now she can't wait to see me off and away."

"And who can blame me?" Mother scowled. "I've asked Simon to be your escort into Achleva. He knows the best route for travel. He will take you across the wall and—finally—to Valentin's side."

At the mention of my future husband's name, I lowered my eyes. About Valentin I knew precious little outside of the handful of stilted, stuffy letters we were forced to exchange when we were still children.

Simon said, "You're nervous about it, aren't you? The marriage."

The questions came out of my mouth in a torrent. "Is he really sick? Bedridden and half-blind? Did his mother lose her mind trying to care for him?" I tried to reel the words back in. "No, no, I'm sorry. I'm being insensitive."

If the bluntness of my questions ruffled him, it didn't show. "I know the prince very well," he said carefully. "I've known him his whole life. I hold him in high regard, the same as if he were my own son. Valentin has not had an easy life, to be sure. But he's an honorable, determined person. His infirmities are hardly noticeable when compared with the scope of his character. He will make a good husband for you, and someday a good king."

"Then he is not ill? Not mad like his mother?"

A shadow crossed his expression. "My sister had a difficult life and she left us too soon, but she wasn't mad. Let me assure you, her son is a worthy soul. And these anxieties you have . . . don't be surprised to find that he shares them. It may be that you have more in common than you think."

My doubts were not assuaged. "Yes, of course. I can only imagine what they say in Achleva about me."

"They hardly know anything about you except your name and that you will be their queen."

"They don't think that I'm a witch?"

"A witch?" His face blanched. "Your Renaltan superstition . . . claiming to worship the Empyrea and yet damning anyone with gifts that could only ever have been given by that Divine Spirit."

"'The arcane, polluted power of witches, who use animalistic rituals and blood sacrifice to commune with the dead, is in direct conflict with the Divine Light of the Empyrea,'" I recited.

Simon gazed at me for a long moment. "That came straight from a page of your Founder's Book of Commands, didn't it?"

"It's the truth." Even as I said it, I hoped I was wrong. I'd sullied my hands with enough blood and magic that if it were true, I was already certain to be damned.

He took a seat beside me and leaned forward in earnestness. "No. No, the truth is that there is power in our world and it has many forms and many faces but no designation of good or evil outside of the intent of the person wielding it. Look at me. Do I look evil to you? Because I am a practitioner of blood magic."

My eyes darted to his palm, where it was easy to see the scars crisscrossing it.

"Enough of this," Mother said. "We haven't time for lessons or arguments right now. Thank you for coming, Simon. I know you must be confused by this furtive meeting when you deserve a royal welcome, but I saw a rare window of opportunity and hoped we could use it to make good on the offer you extended us all those years ago. Do you know of what I speak?"

"I remember the offer." Simon was grave. "And it still stands. But things have changed quite a lot in seventeen years, Majesty. I was younger and stronger. As were you. And your husband was still alive. We need three willing participants. Myself and two more."

"I would be one, and Onal has agreed to be the other."

"Agreed to what?" I asked. "What are you talking about?"

"Your mother wants me to work a spell on your behalf," Simon said, "One that, while not guaranteeing your safety, would ensure you a better chance of long-term survival."

"We have an hour," Mother said. "Is that enough time?"

"It should be."

"You can't be serious. Spellcasting? Even just *talking* about it is dangerous," I said. "If word got out, it could get you—all of you—*killed*. The Tribunal—"

"Doesn't know." Onal lifted her chin to peer at me from beneath her spectacles. "Nobody knows about this except the people in this room. Of all of us, you should be the last to take issue with the use of a little witchcraft."

I chewed my lips. Everything I'd ever done, I'd done alone. The consequences if I were caught would be mine and only mine. "It isn't worth it," I said. "Not for one person." Not for *me*.

"I need a piece of cloth," Simon said. "Something that is tied to Aurelia. Do you have a kerchief, my lady? A scarf?"

"Can you use this?" Mother went to her desk and pulled out a square of silk, bordered on one side with a silver, embroidered vine.

It was fabric from the cuff of my wedding dress. With a guilty pang, I realized she must have taken it apart after the hundredth time I'd told her I hated it.

"That will do." He spread the fabric out in front of him and slowly began tracing a pattern across it with his finger.

My curiosity got the best of me, and I sat down next to him at the table. "What kind of a spell is this?"

"It's a binding spell," he said, continuing the pattern. "A spell to connect our three lives—Queen Genevieve's, Onal's, and mine—to yours." His golden eyes were solemn. "After it is complete, our lives will shield yours."

"I don't understand."

"It means," Mother said, "that you cannot die until we also have died."

Kellan was taking short, impatient strides across the room. He probably hated this; he had no love for superstition. Kellan didn't believe I was a witch. He didn't believe in witches at all. He was solid and practical, possessing a deep trust in the things he could see and touch but naught else. So it surprised me greatly when he burst out, "Can there not be a fourth? If this spell puts lives before the princess's, would it not be even better protection to add one more?"

"Only three," Simon said. "Three is a sacred number; the only way to strengthen it would be to add multiples of three. Six, or even better, nine. Are there more out there we'd be willing to trust with this secret? Who'd tie their lives to Aurelia's?"

"No," Kellan said, looking at me. "There's nobody else." It was true, but it hurt to hear him say it. He considered me for a moment before continuing, "But I am strong, and I know Aurelia. It is my job to protect her. Couldn't I take your place in the spell?"

"I follow a very strict set of rules when I practice magic. I must be a part of the spell; drawing blood from others is permissible only with willing participants and when the executor of the spell shares the bloodletting. Were it not for that, I would let you take my place." He was thoughtful. "But as you said, you are young and strong."

"Onal already has many years behind her—"

"Are you calling me old, Lieutenant?" Onal asked shrewdly, drumming her long, brown fingers against her weathered cheek. "I may not have as many years ahead of me, young man, but I don't live a dangerous life. I may live a hundred years; you may die in combat tomorrow."

"Kellan," I added reluctantly, "you don't even believe in these things. In spells and witchcraft."

"He doesn't have to believe," Simon said. "The magic exists whether he believes in it or not."

"I don't believe," Kellan said, "but I want to do it. For you."

"So sentimental," Onal snapped. "Fine. You can have my place. Not as if I wanted to die for Aurelia anyway."

"Die for me?" It was such a ridiculous notion, I almost laughed. "No, no . . . Simon didn't say that. He just said you'd die *before* me. So as long as you are all alive, so will I be, too . . ." I trailed off, marking their solemn expressions with growing dismay.

Simon said gently, "If we do this spell and you are at any time injured to the point of death, one of us will die in your place and their drop of blood will fade from the cloth, until we are all gone."

My chest began to constrict. "I don't want you—any of you—to die in my place. My life isn't worth all three of yours. And why do we have to keep this treaty anyhow? It's been two hundred years. Nobody cares anymore."

Mother spoke first. "Fulfillment of the treaty is the only way to get you to Achleva."

"Renalt is my home. My people—"

"Want to *kill* you," Mother finished.

"They wouldn't," I argued, a bitter taste on my tongue, "were it not for the Tribunal."

We'd had this discussion many times before, but never to any avail. To my mother, the Tribunal simply *was;* implying that it could be dismantled was like calling for the sky to be pulled down from the heavens, or begging for the dispersion of all the water in the oceans. It could not be done.

"Achleva needs you, too, Princess," Simon said. "There are many forces at work against the monarchy. Domhnall may be petulant and prideful, but we have to keep him on the throne until the prince can inherit. For now, we at least have a tentative balance. But I'm afraid that if Renalt reneged on the treaty now, there would be little to keep the steward lords from making plays for the crown at the expense of people's lives."

"You'll be safe in Achleva," Mother said. "We just have to get you there."

Simon beckoned. "Give me your hand."

I reluctantly removed my gloves and placed my upturned palm in his. He paused, taking in the sprinkling of thin, white scars that crisscrossed it, before drawing a new line with his knife. As the blood began to well up from the cut, he put the bowl beneath my hand to catch it.

"Now repeat what I tell you, word for word. 'My blood, freely given.' Say it."

"I thought blood magic doesn't require incantations." I swallowed. "I mean . . . that's what I've heard." *Stupid.*

He gave me a sidelong glance, eyebrow raised. "Is that so?"

I shrugged. "A rumor, I guess." To cover, I added, "My blood, freely given."

"Good." He held a bandage against my palm, to stanch the flow. "We'll fix it up better once we're done. This will have to do for now."

He placed the knife in my hands and folded my fingers over it. Then he reached into his breast pocket and retrieved a velvet purse. He tugged at the drawstrings, and three clear, strangely cut stones tumbled into his palm. "These stones are called luneocite." He held them out for me to see, but I already knew what they were. The Tribunal called them spirit stones. To be caught in possession of them was the same as a direct confession of witchcraft—probably the quickest way to earn yourself a rope necklace for the next spectacle in the square.

He placed the stones in a large triangle in the center of the room, and the air felt suddenly charged, like the atmosphere of a lightning storm. Simon placed a bowl in my other hand and then guided me into the center of the stones. As I stepped over them, they gave off a momentary flash of blue-white and then dimmed back down. Lights were darting in front of my eyes, and my ears were buzzing, the silver knife and bowl growing warm in my hands. "Luneocite is rare and precious, and can only be found in seams beneath the ley lines—the paths the Empyrea traveled when she descended from heaven to journey across the earth. Luneocite is, in many ways, the crystalized remnants of her power. We use it like a prism, to enhance our spell, and as a boundary, to contain the magic within our designated parameters."

He stood at one of the luneocite points of the triangle, and my mother and Kellan took their places at the others. The buzz in my ears became a breathy hum—almost like a distant whisper.

"Go to each of us in turn. Draw some blood from our palms and drip it into the bowl, just the same as I did for you." Speaking to Mother and Kellan, he said, "As she does this, you must say, word for word, 'My blood, freely given.'"

We all nodded in assent, and I took two steps toward my mother. She calmly opened her palm, not even wincing as I drew the knife across it. As her blood dripped into the bowl, mingling with mine, she said, "My blood, freely given."

The whispering whir in my ears grew louder as I moved to Simon. He held out his long fingers, and I made the cut. "My blood, freely given," he said with determination.

I faltered on my way to Kellan. There were lights zigzagging across my eyes, colliding and converging into vague shapes.

"Something's wrong," I said.

"We're toeing the border between the material and spectral planes," Simon said. "There might be some discomfort. Push through it."

I took the final steps to face Kellan. He held my gaze, and focusing on his face allowed me to ignore the feathery, hissing voices that no one seemed to notice but me. The sound carried with it a cold foreboding that made my hands shake. *Aurelia.* I heard my name in the hum. *Aurelia . . .*

"Aurelia." Kellan held out his palm, and my knife hovered above it. "It's all right," he said. "Do it."

"No," I said, lowering the knife. As I did, the sounds faded. "I'm sorry, but I can't."

"We need to finish this!" Mother cried. "We need to—"

"It's too late," Kellan said, leaving me to look out the window. "The guards are already returning. Our time is up."

"Get her out of here," Onal barked, "so we can clean this up before someone comes and sees it. My neck is too delicate for a rope."

"Act as if nothing has happened," Mother directed. "There's a banquet tonight to welcome Simon to our kingdom; you will attend, Aurelia, but only after you've spent a good long while in the sanctorium considering your improprieties. We need people to see you in humble worship. We need to let them witness your devotion to the Empyrea. To see you being normal."

"So pretend," Onal sniped, smiling.

I couldn't even muster a decent glare at her as Kellan led me away.

3

While the rest of the castle was preparing a feast for our royal visitor, I adjourned to the alcove where the royal family went to worship in elegant seclusion. Indeed, it seemed that while the Empyrea demanded humility and simplicity from her worshipers, her own tastes ran more toward the lavish and opulent. The sanctorium was draped in silk and satin, trimmed with gold, and lined on each side with tufted velvet chairs. Polished marble columns rose to a concave ceiling painted to look like the night sky, with smiling cherubs flitting merrily among the constellations as dark, devilish figures stalked them from below. The painting was supposed to represent our human impulses, the righteous ones above and the immoral ones below, but I always thought it misrepresented the truth of things: Sins were welcoming and charming, like the cherubs. And with their bared teeth and hungry eyes, the devils looked alarmingly like the fervid mobs that frequented Tribunal rallies.

I was far more afraid of those who hated sinners than I ever was of sin.

After letting the door close tight behind me, I turned the lock and lifted the brocade curtain to the inner sanctuary, where a hundred white candles glimmered from golden candlesticks. I lit one of my own and placed it beside the altar. I knelt, murmured a hasty apology for the desecration I was about to commit, and then shoved the marble altar stone aside. With the interior of the altar exposed to the air, I gathered the first layer of my skirts to access the pocket tucked among my petticoats and removed the small spell book I had hidden there. It was meant to be used in a trade with Mabel Doyle, but I guessed I'd be keeping it now.

I paused guiltily, hand on the cover. I should have realized something was wrong that morning when Mabel didn't meet me for our usual monthly exchange of witchcraft lore. I'd waited for ages outside her bookshop before leaving in frustration, not knowing that I'd be watching her hang beneath the clock tower less than an hour later. We weren't that well acquainted; because of the illicit nature of our dealings, we kept our interactions to a minimum. I never knew she had a family, or that she'd lost them. But looking at the books she'd traded with me in the last few months—spirit possession, necromancy, communication with the dead—I wondered how I'd missed it.

"Clever," said a voice from the shadows beside me. "Blasphemous and a bit impertinent, but clever."

"Blood of the Founder," I swore as I jumped back from the altar, nearly toppling a candelabra. "How did you get in here? I locked that door. I swear I did."

Simon gave a soft chuckle and lifted his hand to show a droplet of blood on the tip of his finger. "One of the first spells I ever learned: how to go unnoticed, even when you're standing right in front of someone. I draw the blood and then use a recitation to focus the magic. *Ego invisibilia.* I am unseen. I followed you pretty easily. So, just how long have you been using your time in confessional to study"— he reached into the altar and grabbed the nearest volume— "'a blood mage's foolproof method to ensure a successful soybean yield'?" He clicked his tongue. "I hope you didn't waste any blood on this one. It is likely a fake. Blood magic doesn't heal or grow things."

"What in the name of the Holy Empyrea made you think it was a good idea to sneak up on me and scare me half to death?"

"'But blood magic doesn't require incantations.' Your words. Or rather, the words of the great third-century blood mage Wilstine." He reached into the altar and retrieved another book, a leather volume I'd tied with a ribbon to keep the yellowing pages from escaping the decaying binding. "When I was in training, my teachers made me memorize it. They, too, believed that the use of incantations was more of a distraction than a control. It was an unpopular theory among many of the older mages, however—they did *so* like their arcane chants. Made their demonstrations to the public more impressive, I think. Swirling robes, long white beards, bulging eyes, invocations in an indecipherable language . . . very memorable and awe-inspiring."

Tentatively, I said, "But you used incantations today."

"I did. I do. Partly to keep the memory of my teachers alive." His hand went to a chain around his neck, but I couldn't see the attached pendant, tucked as it was behind his golden sash. "And partly because I find that the words help me focus. Blood magic is rooted in emotion: the faster your heart beats, the faster your blood pumps. Pain, pleasure, fear, passion—anything that heightens your emotion can be used to increase the strength of your spell. But therein also lies the trouble. It's easy to lose your grip, let the magic overtake you. Concentrating on the correct pronunciation of archaic phrases helps to orient me, to keep me grounded. Over time, and with practice, it gets less necessary to rely on such things. Magic becomes more instinctual and easily accessible. More hazardous, too; it's like a dam on a river—you can take it down slowly and carefully and choose what direction it flows, but if you aren't careful, you can bring the whole dam down on top of yourself." He shook his head. "Needless to say, it is very dangerous to use blood magic without training, no matter how well read you are in Wilstine."

Embarrassed, I tucked my hair behind my ear. "I do read a lot, but I don't . . . I mean, I have *tried* a few things, but never anything . . ."

He pursed his lips and turned my fidgeting hand over. I'd left my gloves in my mother's chamber. In the window light, it was easy to make out the dozens of thin scars on my uncovered skin.

"Tell me," he said, "how *did* your soybean crop turn out?"

I grimaced. "In all honesty, I never had an occasion to try that one."

He laughed. "It wouldn't have worked, but it would have been fun to see you try. No, blood magic won't grow soybeans. That's better suited to another type of magic entirely."

"Feral magic?" I guessed.

"Indeed. I see Vitesio's *Compendium de Magia* there in your collection. It's an excellent overview of all three magic disciplines. Good to know you've read that, at least."

"I have, cover to cover. The problem is, there isn't much left between the covers."

He picked it up and thumbed through the sparse pages. "Disgraceful," he said. "Someone has *amputated* eighty percent of the book! This is practically incoherent."

"Most of my books are like that. The Tribunal's regular purges of witch-friendly reading material are thorough. I'm lucky that any of these books made it at all. Most of what I know, I've gleaned over years, from snippets."

In frustration, he slammed the book shut. "Lesson one: Magic is that thing that makes trees and animals and plants and us different from rocks and dirt and water . . . it is the spark. Spirit. Life. Whatever you want to call it, it is power. That said, there are three prevailing methods of accessing this power. The first is called *sancti magicae,* high magic. Practitioners access it through meditation, prayer, spiritual communion with the Empyrea. It gives them visions of the future, the ability to move objects with their mind, sometimes the power to heal. Renalt's famous queen, Aren, was an anchorite of the highest order before leaving it to marry into the Renaltan monarchy. The second is called *fera magicae,* or feral magic. It is mostly herbology, divination, transfiguration . . . it's the magic of nature. Of growth. Of cyclical order and balance. Our namesake king, Aren's brother Achlev, was a mage of this order. And the last is *sanguinem magicae.* Blood magic. Magic of passion and sacrifice. Probably the most powerful and destructive of them all. Before he swore off spells and became Founder of the Tribunal, the third sibling, Cael, was a blood mage, and one of great power. The three of them together were very powerful, in their day. *Triumviri,* they were called by the Assembly at that time. The best in their fields."

I listened in silence as I used his simplistic explanations to fit disjointed pieces of my scavenged knowledge together. "I never knew that about them."

"How could you?" Simon said, casting a dour glance at my piecemeal library.

"Wait," I said, "did you say lesson *one?*" I asked hopefully, "Does that mean there might be a lesson two?"

Simon gave a low whistle. "Your mother, when she wrote to me and asked me to come, said that you were 'dangerously unconcerned with the precariousness' of your position. I begin to see that that was not an exaggeration."

"She's wrong," I said. "I know exactly how precarious my position is."

"And you collect magic books and practice blood spells anyway?"

I shrugged, frustrated. "The Tribunal terrorizes this country— *my* country. If they view witchcraft as a weapon, I must learn to wield it against them"—I swallowed hard—"before they can use it against me." Or others, like Mabel and Hilda. I pushed all thoughts of their deaths down deep, twisting my guilt and sorrow into the taut coil at my center.

Simon was making a face. "Lesson two: *witchcraft* is a coarse term. The Assembly, fallen though it is now, never allowed its usage. The word *witch* refers to untrained, undisciplined practitioners— especially those who willfully ignore the Assembly's statutes, which were established for the safety of all, mages and the magicless alike."

The Assembly of Mages—it had waned in power for many years before it finally fell. I was too young to recall it myself, but I grew up hearing stories about the grand, glorious festivity in Renalt that had accompanied the news of its demise. It was an occasion often remembered and remarked upon with nostalgia, a source of fond anecdotes to exchange in good company. *Where were you when you heard the news? Remember the fireworks? The dancing all night in the streets?*

It wasn't until I was much older that I realized that what everyone was celebrating was death. Death to people with magic, like me.

"What happened to the Assembly?" I asked. "What *really* happened?"

A shadow crossed Simon's expression. "A lesson for another day, I think."

"So you'll really teach me?"

"When you stepped into the triangle during our spell, the luneocite stones flashed. An indication that you're already somewhat attuned to the power. But magic—blood magic, especially, can be grueling to learn and painful to practice. With the Assembly gone, I've long wanted to pass my knowledge on to another generation, but the last time I tried to take on a novice, I am afraid it did not end well. What you experienced within the triangle today was just a *breath* of what's in store. I must ask you honestly: Are you sure you're up to the task?"

"Yes," I said. "Absolutely, yes."

"All right, then. I'll teach you—just on a trial basis, mind you, and only after we're back in Achleva, after the wedding. Until then, I think it would be wise if you abstain from magic completely. That way we can start fresh. *And* you won't be dead."

"Both good things, I suppose." I paused. "Are you not going to lecture me about revenge? Tell me that after becoming Achleva's queen, I should just let my grudge against the Tribunal go?"

"Dear me, no," Simon said. "The Tribunal is an abomination. I can think of no greater legacy for a queen of two nations than to rid the world of that organization for good."

I sat back, speechless. For the first time in my life, I was looking *forward* to my wedding. "I've never thought of it that way."

"It won't be easy, mind you. And Achleva may not have the Tribunal to worry about, but we have our own troubles." The corners of his mouth sagged, and I began to see those troubles etched in the creases framing his lips and eyes, easily mistaken for laugh lines. "I'm hoping that, while I'm here this week, I can look into some things that have been disconcerting me back home in Achleva."

"What do you think you can discover in Renalt? Renaltans can't even cross Achlev's Wall without . . ." Trying to be delicate, I waved my fingers up and down. When his eyebrow shot up, I said, "You know. Burning to death?" Our histories were full of horrific illustrations of Renaltan armies dying in large swaths trying to breach Achlev's Wall. Prompted by the writings of the Tribunal's Founder, Cael, Renalt tried for three hundred years without success, until the marriage treaty allayed the aggression between our countries, if not the underlying enmity.

"Renaltans don't have to cross our wall to influence what goes on behind it," Simon said. "I want to figure out the reason for the sudden abundance of Renaltan coin in circulation with ours, merchants forging new trade deals with coastal Renaltan ports that would never have received them before . . . Hallet Graves, de Lena . . ."

I stiffened. "De Lena?"

"Do you know Toris de Lena?"

"He's a Tribunal magistrate. I can hardly picture him welcoming Achlevan ships to his port unless it somehow furthered his ambitions."

"Perhaps his ambitions include gaining influence in Achleva."

A dreadful thought. I catalogued the information: Toris de Lena, magistrate, bearer of the Founder's blood . . . making secret trade deals with Achleva? "Well, if you find out *anything,* let me know," I said. Toris's voice was ringing in my ears. *Mabel Lawrence Doyle, you have been tried and found guilty by fair Tribunal for the distribution of illicit texts and have been condemned to die . . .*

Maybe adding a bit of tarnish to Toris's sterling reputation would be my parting gift to Renalt. If the truth was bad enough, it could cost him a place at the magistrates' table. Or, even better—it could gain him one in a cell. Or on the gallows stand.

Maybe this time Toris had put the rope around his own neck.

4

When I got back to my room following my time "in worship," my maid, Emilie, was already there, sweeping up what looked like bits of broken glass. She had a round, rosy face and was probably a year or two younger than me, though she was just as tall. She'd been working for me for several weeks now, which was quite a long while, considering that I went through waiting maids like the dancing princesses of my childhood storybooks went through shoes: they rarely lasted more than a day. Occasionally I'd come across my former maids elsewhere on the grounds, mucking out horse stalls or emptying chamber pots or removing entrails from chickens in the kitchen yard. I'd march past them, head always high until I was out of sight. Sometimes I'd cry, knowing they preferred chamber pots and entrails to me, but only if no one was around to see.

"Begging your pardon, m'lady," she said, hurrying to finish sweeping glass bits off the floor. "I'd hoped to have this done before you returned."

"Let me see," I said.

Reluctantly, she held out her dustpan. Amongst the pieces of glass was a large rock painted with ward symbols. It bore a single word: *Malefica*. An old word, most often interpreted nowadays to mean *witch*. I'd seen it a couple of times in the torn remnants of spell-book pages, or scribbled in archaic notes in the margins. In all those sparse mentions, however, it never felt like a description. It always seemed more like a name.

Apparently, someone thought the moniker suited *me*.

"I've already arranged to have the window replaced, m'lady," Emilie said. "I'd hoped to at least have this cleaned up before you got back in, so you wouldn't have to . . ."

"So I wouldn't have to see it?" I frowned. "Have there been other things you've fixed up before I got to see them?"

She looked at me shyly from under her lashes.

"There have been?"

"I didn't want to frighten you, m'lady. Just the work of pranksters and superstitious villagers. Nothing to be worried about, I'm sure."

Emilie scurried to put the stone and shattered pieces of glass out of sight while I situated myself by the broken pane. My private inner room had a good view of the barracks and the stables, so I spotted Kellan easily. He was leading Falada, an exquisite white mare, across the yard to the round pen. I observed them wistfully. The Greythorne family and their horses were renowned, and Falada was a rare Empyrean, perfectly tempered and trained. Kellan had raised her himself from the time she was a foal. Watching them together, I found it easy to believe that the divine Empyrea would have taken such a form when she came to earth, as we'd been taught. There could be no nobler, more beautiful creature in existence.

I should have been glad that Kellan had a moment to get out and ride her before returning to duty for the banquet that evening, but I was jealous instead. As if sensing the brush of my thoughts against him, Kellan turned his head up to my open window, and, seeing me, he gave a salute. Then he mounted Falada and reined her away.

"What would you like to wear to the banquet, m'lady?" Emilie opened the wardrobe wide to let me inspect my options.

"You choose," I told her, as I always told my waiting maids. The girl surveyed the dresses with enthusiasm, sweeping a gown of green satin from its hook after less than a minute of looking. I was surprised, seeing her holding it out for my approval, that it wasn't black. The other waiting maids never chose anything but black.

"You don't like it?"

"No, no, I do . . . just . . . what made you pick that one?"

"Emerald was my mother's favorite stone," she said, lifting my day dress over my head before helping me step into the gown. "She had an emerald ring that looked just this same color of green. She always told me that it's a stone of wisdom and foresight."

"Does your mother know very much about stones?"

The girl was threading the laces of the bodice. "She did, yes, m'lady, before she died. She liked those twisty knot braids, too. She taught me a few fancy ones." She lifted a section of my hair. "I think it would look nice. Would you like me to try?"

I shrugged. "Why not? Your mother . . . she must have been young. Was it the fever epidemic last winter?"

"Not fever, no. She was burned for a witch four years ago."

I felt the coil at my center tighten. Emilie couldn't be more than fifteen or sixteen—which meant she was only eleven or twelve at the time of the execution. Motherless and alone at that bewildering brink between girlhood and womanhood . . . I couldn't imagine what it must have been like for her. And Emilie's mother was just another of the countless number of men and women killed for the practice of witchcraft. Innocent or guilty of the charges, it didn't matter; I raged at the unfairness, the vicious *pointlessness* of the loss. "I'm sorry," I murmured, my voice tinny. I didn't know what else to say.

"As am I." She stepped away to give me a look-over. "She was a good person," she said, quieter. "What they call witches—most of them are just regular people, nice people. The evil ones are those that hunt and hurt others, witch or no."

I snagged her hand and held it. "Thank you," I said. It was a brave thing to say aloud, even to someone like me.

✳

Most days I took my meals alone in my rooms. Not because I had any particular aversion to eating with my brother and mother and the rest of the court but because of the dead man at the bottom of the staircase that led to the banquet hall.

The stairs were steep, and his fall down them must have been terrible, because his neck was bent at such a deeply unsettling angle. Shades like him were often pinned in place by the memory of their traumatic death, burdened with a compulsive need to share it, even reexperience it . . . And if he touched me, I'd be forced to watch it happen again. Often the spirits' memories were so vivid that I could not distinguish them from reality. I relived them as if they were happening to me in real time. And right now I could not afford to collapse, blind and screaming, in such a public place; I'd be dragged away to the gallows before I ever hit the floor.

On days like this I was forced to pass the ghost on the stairs or use the only other route to the banquet hall. As I took my first step inside the kitchen doors and the buzzing energy of the staff stuttered to a halt, I wondered if I might have been better off risking the stairs.

I lifted my chin and made my way past the plates of steaming meat pies and platters of roasted duck that were waiting for their florid entrance. I didn't flinch even as the servants stared. They could think me strange, but I'd never let them think I was apologetic about it.

When I came into the hall, the dinner guests were all steeped in conversation and so did not seem to notice my entrance from the service door. Kellan was nearby, though, waiting without comment. He never asked me about my peculiar habits anymore. He'd decided long ago that I was the product of my circumstances, that if it weren't for my betrothal to the prince of Achleva, no one would have thought twice about my strange habits and weird eyes and I'd have never developed these evasive routines. If I told him about the broken-necked man on the banquet hall stairs—or the purple-faced girl beneath the surface of the lily pond, or the bleak-eyed woman who paced the west wing parapet—he'd probably think me mad.

Kellan guided me to my place at the head table. He looked polished and powerful in his gold-and-ivory uniform and cobalt-colored cloak, the ceremonial costume of the ranking guard. I chewed on the inside of my cheek and made an effort not to notice how one of his corkscrew curls had escaped the rest and was now dangling fetchingly against his brow.

"You're not wearing black," he observed. "I didn't know you owned dresses of other colors."

"I don't always wear black."

"I suppose you're right. I think I saw you in gray once."

I wasn't sure if I should smile or glower at him, but I didn't have to choose. He took his place behind my chair, back to being a guard now that we were in full view of the waiting guests. Formality was something he could take on and off like a mask: one moment he was the heart-strong boy who'd laughingly taught me to ride when I was fourteen and friendless; the next he was the stern and practical knight, in whom I could entrust my safety but never my secrets. I loved the first one—in a discreet and delicate way, known only to myself—but I was thankful for the second. Seeing him so distant, so rigidly severe, made it feel like maybe I wouldn't be losing as much.

"All rise for Queen Genevieve and Prince Conrad." A ripple went across the room as everyone scrambled from their chairs to pay respect to the entering queen and crown prince. Conrad had his arm linked with Mother's, leading her with a dignified tip of his chin, though he was only half her height. He'd never enjoyed the spotlight, preferring books to banquets and arithmetic problems to people, but his posture was proper and steady—he'd been practicing, I could tell. He was even smiling a little. Now only months away from his seventh birthday, he looked like a small copy of our father with his golden hair and blue, blue eyes. At least, he did until he saw me and his smile wavered and disappeared. He gave me a polite nod.

We used to have a game in which I'd tie a colored ribbon someplace he would see it—on a door handle, or the branch of a tree, or a staircase spindle—which meant that somewhere nearby I'd hidden a prize or a treat. The color of the ribbon told him where to look: yellow for up, blue for down, red for north, green for south, purple for east, orange for west. Black meant it was within ten paces and hidden from view, white meant it was within twenty paces and in plain sight. When he found his prize, he'd hide one for me using the same rules. It was an excuse for me to spoil him, really. I showered him with candies and riddle books and little toys I had to sneak out to the marketplace to purchase. When his hands were busy, he found it easier to focus during lessons and lengthy state functions, so I got him puzzle boxes, tiny gyro spinners, a ring that concealed a small compass, and— my favorite—a walnut-size figurine made of metal and magnets, with parts that could be twisted and rearranged into the shape of a half dozen different animals.

It was our own secret pastime, and I reveled in it. While it lasted.

But it was inevitable that Conrad would eventually cross paths with the whispers about me. It was clear that somewhere in the last months he had heard the rumors, understood them, and begun to believe them. He didn't trust me anymore, and I knew it was only a matter of time before that distrust soured into something worse. I could hardly bear it, and so I coped the only way I knew how: I avoided him.

After my mother and brother were seated, the rest of us followed, and soon servants were scurrying around us, filling goblets and lighting candles. The seat to my left was unoccupied; it was my father's chair, and would remain empty until Conrad ascended the throne. The seat to my right was where the toothless, doddering marchioness of Hallet usually sat, too senile to speak to me (or complain about me). But the marchioness was not in attendance; her seat was instead occupied by a man in an austere black Tribunal coat.

"You look lovely, Princess," Toris said. "That color suits you."

"Thank you, Toris," I said through a tight smile.

He absently straightened the place setting, his rings—of which there were five on each hand, one for each finger—glinting. Mother said he'd been an academic once, a man with an unquenchable curiosity for history, who'd traveled far and wide collecting myths and artifacts, who had won her cousin Camilla's love with his humor and wit. Losing his wife changed him, Mother said. But I remembered Camilla well; she was sweet and kind and lovely as a summer's day. The Toris of my memory was exactly as detestable as the one currently straightening the silverware into precise and even parallels. If ever there had been a different version of this man, it was gone before I was old enough to recall it, long before Camilla died.

When the seafood fork was exactly one inch from the soup spoon, he said offhandedly, "I saw you this morning, dear Princess, somewhere you shouldn't have been." He leaned forward on his arms and turned a stare on me. "You're getting rather reckless, don't you think? You'd do well to be more careful."

"I already heard this lecture from my mother."

"You should listen to her. A great woman, your mother."

I felt my lip curl. In the eight months between Camilla's and my father's deaths and my brother's birth, Toris insinuated himself into my mother's circle. Weren't they both grieving spouses? But everyone knew there was more to it than that; because Renalt's crown could only be passed to a male inheritor, our position would have become instantly precarious if the baby was a girl. To remain in power, Mother would be forced to marry, and marry quickly. Toris was the logical choice. Everyone said so.

I was thankful every day that Conrad turned out to be a boy. With a son to inherit, there was no need for Mother to marry; indeed, doing so might weaken Conrad's royal claim. Conrad's birth saved me from a lifetime with Toris as stepfather. Or king. I didn't know which one would have been worse.

Toris was looking at me with his most concerned, paternal expression. "Because of my position inside the Tribunal, I have been able, at your mother's behest, to steer them away from you on more than one occasion. Now that these last two cases, Mabel Doyle and the other—Harriet, I think it was?—have been resolved, I've little doubt I'll have to concert my efforts on your behalf once more."

"Hilda," I murmured. "Her name was Hilda."

"Why would you remember her name?" He looked down his narrow nose at me. "That is exactly the kind of thing that makes people wary of you. Your sympathies are suspect. Be warned, it's only a matter of time before I run out of Hildas to distract them with." A smile crept across his face. He'd convicted a woman who was almost certainly innocent, and he wanted me to be thankful that he'd done it, and would do it again. I gripped the stem of my goblet so tight, my fingernails bit into my skin. Hilda would haunt her daughter-in-law, but I shared the blame in her death.

"Lisette arrived today and should be along shortly," Toris said, cheerily changing the subject. Quietly, so Kellan couldn't hear, he said, "She has been so very anxious to see Lieutenant Greythorne again. She has a particular fondness for him, I'm told."

It was a special talent he had, to send a needle straight into my heart through the tiniest flaw in my armor. It wasn't that Lisette cared for Kellan that way—I sincerely doubted she did—but that Toris knew I did. I took a breath. Well, I now knew a few of the chinks in his armor, too.

"I thought that maybe, now that you're letting Achlevan ships into your port, she might set her sights on a nice, burly Achlevan sailor. You'd make a fine grandfather to a whole brood of sturdy Achlevan pups."

"Aren't you a wonder?" he asked, eyes narrowing into half-moons while the smile remained frozen on his face. "Not afraid of anything, are you?"

I'm afraid of marrying the sickly prince of Achleva. I'm afraid of never seeing my mother or brother again. I'm afraid of the Tribunal. I'm afraid that Kellan protects me only out of duty. I'm afraid of the ghosts that lie around every corner. I'm afraid that someday soon I'll be joining them in the hereafter. I took another drink. "Not anything."

He brushed his suit coat and leaned back. "You should be. The wolves howl, Aurelia, and there may come a time when I will no longer be able to hold them back."

An oily little smile played on his lips, making it clear that he was looking forward to it.

5

stared at him, but his malicious smile had already been smoothed away. Toris stood and straightened his coat. "Looks like my daughter has just arrived. Good evening, Princess."

Lisette de Lena was at the top of the staircase, decked in a crimson gown that set off the rosy glow of her cheeks. Her hair gleamed gold in the lamplight. When we were children, people used to remark how alike we looked, though I always knew such comments were more for my benefit than for hers. If a painting of Lisette was left out in the elements for a few weeks, it *might* fade into something that looked a bit like me.

We were best friends, once.

She paused at my brother's chair to furtively slip him a piece of chocolate, rewarding his eager smile with a stealthy wink before moving in my direction.

"Your Highness." She addressed me coolly as she approached. "And Lieutenant Greythorne," she added, holding out a gloved hand, "always a pleasure."

Kellan gave a quick bow. "My lady." I gave a slight tip of my head. It was all the politeness I could muster.

A twitch of her lip was the only slip in her composure. "Well, good to see you both," she said sweetly. "Now if you'll excuse me, I really must go say hello to Duke Northam. His poor, dear wife, Agnes, just lost her father, and I need to find out if she received the flowers I sent."

I'd already stopped listening. Simon had entered and was being seated in a place of honor on the other side of my mother, beside my brother.

Had I made a mistake, letting Toris know I was aware of his dealings with Achleva? *The wolves howl, Aurelia,* Toris had said. *And there may come a time when I will no longer be able to hold them back.*

Who were the wolves? The Tribunal? The townsfolk who thought I was a witch? The ones who hated me simply because they didn't want our country to be united with Achleva? Enemies were all around me, living and dead. I didn't want to die—I still had too much to do. An idea began to form in the back of my mind, a sort of contingency plan should things take a turn for the worse.

"Excuse me, Princess, your glass—"

A young man in servant's livery was standing over me with a jug of wine. I jumped at the sound of his voice, knocking my goblet right out of his hands. Red liquid splashed across my bodice and into my lap.

"So sorry, my lady," the young man mumbled, trying to dab at the spreading stain with his cloth.

"No, no, don't worry," I said, shoving his cloth back into his hands as I rose. "I'll just . . . I'll just . . ."

People were staring at me now. Kellan, my mother, Conrad. And from the other side of the hall, Toris.

"Princess," Kellan said, taking a step closer. "Do you need assistance?"

Mother had risen, and she rushed over, taking me by the arm. "If this is acting normal, it needs improvement," she said in a harsh whisper.

"This was the work of a clumsy serving boy," I said coldly and quietly, "not some plot I hatched to get out of dinner."

"Go change your clothes and come right back," Mother ordered. "You're making quite a spectacle of yourself."

Kellan came up behind me. "Would you like me to escort you—"

"No," I snapped. Then, with my chin up, I marched across the banquet hall and out the other side in my red-stained green satin. Even the gentleman-ghost of the stairs dared not cross me, for he retreated into the shadows as I passed.

Alone in the hall, I made a rash decision. If I wanted to take my well-being into my own hands, this might be the only chance I'd get. So instead of turning toward my room, I went the other way and followed the darkened corridor until I came to the large oaken door of Onal's stillroom. I took a pin from my hair and jammed it into the lock until it clicked and the door gave way easily.

It had been years since I'd been inside this room, concocting healings and potions under Onal's watchful eye so that my father and I could deliver them to the poorest corners of the city. "We do not rule," he'd say. "We serve. Renaltans do not swear fealty to us; we swear it to them." It wasn't just words, either; that's how he treated them, and they loved him for it. Somehow he'd get the sickest, the hungriest, the most destitute among them to laugh at his jokes, to tell us their stories, to let us sit at their tables. He was teaching me to love them, but he was trying to show them they could love me, too. The kingdom was supposed to pass from father to son, but as far as he knew, I might be his only child, and it would fall to me and my Achlevan husband to rule both kingdoms together.

Asking Renalt to accept an Achlevan king . . . to live under a joint Renalt-Achlevan banner . . . Father knew that such a feat could be accomplished only if I had earned the people's respect and loyalty.

I thought, for a long time, that I had.

Nothing in Onal's stillroom had changed since then, really. The chamber was lined on every side with shelves of many-colored bottles and jars, all herbal tonics and remedies distilled by Onal's own hand. The little rhymes I'd created to help me remember the names and uses of each herb were running through my head. *Cocklebur is the cure for winter colds and shivers. Bluebell stops the swell of headaches, fits and fevers* . . .

I lit one of the worktable lamps and tried to shake the irritating snippets of rhyme away. They were a punishment then, and they were a punishment now. That was the requirement: I was allowed in Onal's special rooms with all their mysterious bric-a-brac if I learned the name and use of each herb in her store. And there were *hundreds*. I never made it through all of my lessons, though; Father's death changed everything. I tried to carry on as he did, but I was young and heart-sore; I didn't last long without him. After the hundredth time a door was slammed in my face with the accusation of *witch* behind it, I gave up altogether.

Despite the passage of time, most of the items on the shelves were recognizable. Feverfew could be used as a tincture for bruises or an infusion for the treatment of swollen joints in the elderly. Witch hazel for bowel complaints. Primrose for muscular rheumatism. White willow bark: useful as a tonic for the convalescent, to help them gain strength. Water soldier, for healing wounds. Each one was familiar, unmoved from its place on the shelves, bottles and vials all arranged in straight, single rows.

The worktable was crowded with glass alembics and copper retorts, bottles and beakers and flasks of all sizes, looming in the dark as if in a cursed cathedral. I tried to ignore the pounding of my heart as I ran my hands underneath the table. Aha! There it was. The key.

Onal always accused me of being absent-minded, head in the clouds. I'm sure she never realized how closely I'd watched her during those days spent in her tutelage. When she didn't think I was paying attention, she'd take this little key to the back wall of the room, move aside the bottles and jars on the third shelf from the top, and then fit the key into the tiny slot in the wall behind them. I repeated each step, and as I turned the key, the panel gave way. Behind it was a small metal box.

I removed the box from the wall, brought it to the table, and lifted the hasp. Inside was a carefully carved wooden block with three thimble-size cutouts. The first two were empty, but the third held a miniature glass capsule and, inside the capsule, a treasure. It wasn't hard to make out, even through the distortion of its glass-and-water encasement. A petal of pure white, shaped like an arrow or a spindly heart, no bigger than my thumbnail. A petal from a bloodleaf flower.

Most in our land knew of bloodleaf—the vile poison that only grows on old battlefields or other soil upon which blood has been spilt—but no one ever spoke of the bloom. I'd seen mentions of it in only a few of my altar books. A magical flower. A miracle cure. Said to be able to heal nearly any wound, stave off any fever—but bloodleaf bloomed only when blood was shed a second time and spread across those thirsty, loathsome leaves. Which meant that for every one life saved by bloodleaf flower, two have already been lost.

The number of murders in our country, one of the books said, was cut in half when possession of the bloodleaf flower became illegal and retribution for being caught with it was swift and severe, usually involving the separation of one's head from one's neck.

But that book was printed long ago, and no one ever spoke of the bloodleaf flower anymore. Still, I understood why Onal kept this locked away behind a hidden panel in the farthest corner of her still-room floor.

There used to be two capsules, I remembered, touching the second empty space before gingerly removing the last one and holding it up in the dim light. That second one disappeared the night they brought my father's body home in a casket. Onal must have used it to try to save him, but she should have known better. All the accounts agreed: bloodleaf flower cannot bring someone back from the dead.

It's wrong to steal, I thought as I traced the shape of the petal through the glass. But it was wrong for Onal to have this in her possession, and *she* didn't have people desiring to examine the underside of her skin. Without Simon's blood ritual, this would have to be my safety. And at least this way no one had to die in my stead.

I pocketed the capsule and returned the empty box to its spot behind the third shelf. I had just moved the bottles back into place when I felt a gust of cold air. I turned to see the window above the table bang against its frame. Had it been open when I came in?

Shivering, I picked up the lamp from the desk and went to pull the window shut, snapping the latch down to keep it secure. The breeze was gone but the cold remained. And something else—the faint smell of wild roses.

Prickling apprehension gathered at the base of my neck and crawled across my back and down my spine. I tried to swallow but my mouth had gone dry. Fear collected in my throat like sand. My gaze slid down to the table in front of me, where a string of colored gems dimly gleamed from their fantastical settings: emeralds burning in the belly of a twisting dragon, topaz winking from the feral eyes of a gryphon, sapphires studding a mermaid's tail, garnets and rubies glinting along the feathers of a carnelian-eyed firebird's wings, diamonds encrusting the flanks of an opal-winged horse, the Empyrea.

It was the bracelet my father had given me. Trembling, I reached for it. I examined the golden links until I found the crushed clasp that had allowed it to slip from my wrist. It was definitely mine, the very one I'd lost that morning, I thought forever, in the press of the crowd.

"Are you here?" I whispered.

Then the lamp went out.

6

whirled around.

It was *her*. The woman who'd haunted me as long as I could remember, lurking on the periphery of every tragedy I'd ever known. I called her the Harbinger, because she appeared only when death was near.

She wasn't quite like any of the other spirits I sometimes saw, who were simply faded versions of their former selves. She was made of shadow and smoke, visible but intangible, bending light and color into her shape like a water droplet on a windowpane.

Other ghosts clamored to get their hands on me the instant they knew I could see them—but not the Harbinger. She'd only ever touched me once.

I was ten years old at the time. Father was gone on a weeks-long expedition to tour our coastal lands with Toris and Camilla, while Lisette stayed with me and my mother, who was feeling poorly, at the castle. We'd spent several days holed up in my room with books of romance and adventure, though the romance was more Lisette's fare than mine. I even let her read several of the stuffy, formal letters

I received twice yearly from my betrothed, Valentin. It was my opinion that they were detestably boring and likely dictated by a tutor, if the rumors about Valentin's lack of wits were true. But Lisette had become enraptured with them, reading one after another with eyes aglow.

"Have you replied yet?" she asked when she was done, clutching the letters to her chest.

"Not if I can help it," I said, wrinkling my nose. I was always too busy helping Onal in her workroom and Father in the city to be bothered with such an unpleasant task.

Lisette gave me her most reproachful look. "Oh, Aurelia, you can't just leave him hanging! You must write back at once."

I said, "You can do it for me, if you like." And she did so with great relish, even signing my name at the bottom and sending it off with a messenger before we went to bed that evening.

That night I had a terrible dream of my mother trapped and dying in a room full of smoke and flame. I woke to find the Harbinger hanging over my bedside, icy hands on my cheeks, sharp fingertips digging into the soft flesh beneath my eyes.

I bolted out of bed with a strangled scream. Lisette stirred. "Aurelia? What's the matter? Aurelia!"

I was already tearing down the hall, praying that what I'd seen was nothing more than an awful, vivid dream.

It wasn't. I arrived at Mother's antechamber to find smoke billowing from beneath her parlor door, which was locked. I tugged furiously on the searing knob to no avail, just as Lisette tumbled into the room after me. "Aurelia?"

"The letter opener!" I cried. "By her stationery! Quickly!" I could see the flicker of flames under the door. Lisette fumbled at the desk, coughing into her nightdress sleeve while I tried to break in by throwing my body against the barrier.

"Found it!" she cried, and I yanked the opener from her blade-first, hardly noticing the way it bit into my skin or the red stain that then crept onto the lace of my nightgown sleeve. I shoved the implement into the keyhole the way all the heroes in my adventure books did it, but it was a losing battle. The blood made my hands slick—too slick to allow me the leverage needed to make it work.

I put my palms and forehead to the impenetrable wood, sobbing. My mother was going to die, and despite the Harbinger's warning, I was helpless to change her fate. Emotion welled up inside me—anger, frustration, fear, guilt, sorrow—pressing against my heart until something inside me burst and all my rage and regret rushed free, like water from a broken dam. That's when I knew. I *knew* what I needed to do. I could use blood. I could use magic.

I began to mutter a haphazard sort of a spell. Most of my incantation was a mash of broken phrases and my own repeated exhortation to the fire itself. *"Ignem ire, abeo, discedo, recedo . . ." Please don't take my mother. Please don't take my mother . . . "Ignem ire, concede, absisto, secedo . . ."*

"What are you *doing?*" Lisette asked in horror, backing away. "Aurelia, stop! Stop," she begged.

Something I said must have worked, because I felt the fire respond. I felt it in my hands. In my veins. In my heart. And when I knew I had it in my control, I gave it a hard push. I thought of water; I wanted the fire to drown.

That's when the guards came and found me staring dully at my hands in a smoke-filled room. They broke down the door, and my mother was found surrounded by blackened curtains, coughing from smoke but untouched by flame.

Lisette was looking at me with wide, terrified eyes. "What did you do?" she whispered. "Where did it go?"

"I don't know," I told her, dazed. "Away."

The next day we woke to the sound of a city in mourning. *The king is dead! The king is dead!* The story was horrific: King Regus and Lady Camilla had been standing on the dock of the port of de Lena when they were overtaken by a sudden, massive firestorm that devoured everything in its path. Ships, shops, people . . . everything. Toris was the lone survivor, and he emerged from the maelstrom with the ardent belief that the deaths of his wife and king could be attributed only to the work of witches.

I tried to speak to Lisette at her mother's funeral, but she wouldn't respond, wouldn't even meet my eyes. She and I both knew I was to blame for what happened to her mother and my father, even if we didn't understand quite how. Toris joined the Tribunal shortly thereafter. I spent every waking minute for months listening for the sound of boots outside my door, convinced that it was only a matter of time before Lisette confessed and they came for me. But they never did.

Lisette kept my secret. I resented it sometimes, knowing that with a single word she could bring the axe down on my neck. Perhaps she wanted just to forget it, or perhaps she wanted to use the knowledge of my wickedness for political gain in the future. I had no way of knowing, and the uncertainty was a torment.

There was some light in the darkness, however. My brother was born. I grew older. I met Mabel Doyle and began trading for magical texts. I began experimenting, ever so cautiously, with the power I'd glimpsed inside myself that night outside my mother's bedroom door.

I saw the Harbinger dozens of times after my father's death, her appearance always a portent of misfortune. Often I could sense when she was nearby before I glimpsed her. She observed me constantly, and though I always had the feeling that she wanted something more from me, she never touched me again.

Now she stood immobile in the still air of Onal's room. A circlet of silver rested on her brow. Beneath it, her eyes, black and bottomless, fixed on some point behind me.

My fingers curled around my unlit lantern and the broken bracelet. "You were there in the square today, weren't you? I felt you nearby." I'd seen ghosts affect objects in the material world before, in fear or anger or desperation, but for her to bring me my bracelet was astounding.

Her eyes clapped on me, and I felt shock roll through my bones from my crown to my toes. Steeling myself, I slid a foot closer. "I've been looking for you."

She waited.

"You can see things before they happen, can't you?" I swallowed. "Tell me, please . . . is it only death that you see?"

She didn't move.

"I'll be leaving here soon," I said conversationally, though my voice was trembling. "Going to a country I don't know. Marrying a man I won't love. And that's only if someone doesn't kill me first." I gathered my courage. "So I want to know . . . can you control what you see in the future? And if you can, will you tell me what you see in mine?"

She took a dragging step forward. Then another. My lungs burned as I held my breath. Ice crystals were forming in the air around me. I forced myself to exhale, my breath a white cloud. When it cleared, she was standing only inches away. Her bony fingers were suddenly wrapped around my face, her thumbs digging into my eyes like cold daggers.

My vision changed. Instead of the Harbinger's face, I saw the lights of the banquet hall. My mother was on the dais, Simon Silvis beside her. This was his introduction to our court. But he wasn't standing tall; he was doubled over, hands around the shaft of an arrow in his chest. Blood on his hands. Blood on the floor.

I came out of the vision with a cry.

There was a pounding on Onal's door. "Aurelia!" Kellan called from behind it. "Aurelia, are you there? Aurelia, answer me!"

The door swung open as the Harbinger released me, vanishing in the gust like the flame of a candle, leaving nary a wisp of smoke behind her.

Kellan was frantic. "You weren't in your room—I was calling and calling. Then I heard you yell. Aurelia . . . ?" His eyes tracked down to the bracelet in my hands.

"The Achlevan," I said distantly. "Simon. He's going to die."

In a flash, I was past Kellan and halfway down the hall in a full run.

✳

I burst into the banquet hall with the force of a hurricane. "Simon!" I shouted. "You're in danger! You have to watch out!"

Fretting guests began to rise from their chairs, but I pushed through the clamor to the dais, where my mother was standing, a look of livid disbelief on her face. Simon was beside her exactly like I'd seen in the vision, and I swept toward him.

"Listen. Listen! I know this sounds strange, but you have to believe me. Something's going to happen to you, something soon. You have to—"

But his eyes shifted from my face and fixed on some point behind me. With one jolting movement, he pushed me away from him and I stumbled on the stairs, looking up just in time to see the arrow fly from the back of the hall and land square in his chest. The person wielding the bow was the same boy who'd caused me to spill the wine on my dress—his features were contorted into a mask of rage and disgust.

Lowering his bow, he cried, "Death to the witch! Death to all practitioners of the dark—" But his war cry was cut short by the sleek shaft of metal that appeared in front of him, protruding from his belly.

Kellan freed his sword from the boy's body and strode toward me, while I turned back in horror to the bleeding man on the dais. Mother had grabbed Conrad and was turning him away from the grisly scene, covering his eyes with both hands.

I crawled toward Simon, but Onal had beaten me there and was already bent over him, assessing the injury. "It didn't get his heart, I don't think."

"Wouldn't matter if it did," Kellan said, removing the arrow with a swift yank and pressing a cloth firmly against the wound. "Look at the shaft. The thing has been coated in bloodleaf poison." He tossed it away. "He's as good as dead."

"As good as dead is not the same thing as dead," I said, clutching Kellan's shoulder. Simon didn't deserve to die this way . . To Onal I pleaded, "Can't you do something?"

"I would if I could," she said.

"This is my fault." The cold realization dawned on me. If I hadn't seen the Harbinger's vision, I wouldn't have come back to the banquet. If I hadn't come back to the banquet, the vision would never have been fulfilled. "This happened because of me."

If he died, there would be no one to teach me how to use whatever strange power I had inside me. The Tribunal would go on with its endless executions, Renaltans would go on masking their fear with hate, and I would have to add another name to the list of those whose lives were lost or plundered by another of my great mistakes.

There was only one acceptable outcome: Simon could not be allowed to die.

Setting my jaw, I pulled the knife from Kellan's belt and drew it across my palm, a slim second cut paralleling the one from the unfinished ritual. When the blood began to well up, I let three drops fall onto Simon's chest.

"What are you doing?" Kellan said angrily. "Aurelia, stop!"

"Ego præcipio tibi ut . . . uh . . . heal. *Curaret!"* I struggled to find the right word. "I command you to heal. *Heal!"*

"I know what you're doing," Onal said, "and it will not work! Stop now, child, they are watching!"

I looked up and found a hundred pairs of eyes on me and my upheld hand, dripping blood. But I didn't have time to care; Simon's eyes were going glassy and rolling into his skull. His rattling breaths were slowing.

Onal was right; it wouldn't work. I could feel it—the magic was resisting. Blood magic wasn't used for healing; that's what Simon had said.

I pulled out the glass capsule I'd hidden in the folds of my gown —wine stains commingling now with blood—and broke the seal.

"Where did you get that?" Onal gasped. "Aurelia, no—"

But I had already poured the contents—water, petal, and all— down Simon's throat.

"What have you done?" she whispered.

7

"Will he live?"

"Yes," Onal said, pacing in front of the settee Simon had been transferred to in my mother's study. "He'll live."

"Please don't be angry," I said, though I knew I deserved every drop of her wrath.

"Angry? Angry doesn't begin to cover what I'm feeling at this moment, you stupid, stupid girl."

"I saved his life, did I not?"

"You broke into my rooms! You stole something most precious—"

My mother had put Conrad to bed in the adjoining chamber and now sat anxiously by the fireplace. "That petal was meant for you, Aurelia," she said. "We were going to send it with you. And now it's just . . . gone."

I struggled to find words. "I'm *sorry*. Can't we just buy another? I know they're rare, but Onal got hold of them somehow . . ." I trailed off. The idea that we could waltz into the marketplace and purchase a bloodleaf petal was so absurd, it was laughable.

I'd made a mistake. A terrible mistake.

"Sorry?" Onal shrilled. "I acquired my bloodleaf petals when my sister was stolen away from our house during the night and we found her murdered the next day in the forest. I lost my sister but harvested bloodleaf flower. Who would you be willing to sacrifice to gain another?"

I directed all my anger at myself toward Onal instead, to avoid having to fully accept my own idiocy. "But you wasted one yourself, did you not? You knew that bloodleaf petals don't work on someone who's already dead, and yet when my father—"

"You *fool*. How *dare* you compare us? I took care of your father from infancy. I loved him like he was my own child, my own heart. It was useless for me to even try to bring him back. He'd been dead for days when they brought him to us. But I *did* try. I had to. Because I *loved* him. And I will never get that petal back, but I don't care. But you . . . you steal my last petal and immediately waste it! How long have you known this man? Less than a day!"

"That arrow was meant for me! I couldn't let him die. And if he, as an emissary from Achleva, were to die in our court, it could have been blamed on us. It could have meant war . . ."

"War may have come—it was a possibility. But what you have done has made the danger to you a certainty," Mother said gravely. "We're all in danger now."

Kellan entered, wiping sweat from his brow. "The halls are quiet for the moment, but the Tribunal magistrates have already begun to gather. I suggest we get Aurelia away, before word about the banquet spreads further." He put his hand on the pommel of his sword. "Maybe my family can take her in, just for a little while?"

"And what will your family do when the Tribunal arrives on their doorstep, bloodthirsty mob in tow?" Onal had always been imposing, but now she was like a prowling, angry cat. "As they will, undoubtedly, now that there is an entire hall full of witnesses to Aurelia's witchcraft." To me she said, "Mark my words: they will come for you, they will kill you, and they will kill anyone who tries to stand in their way."

"This isn't how it was supposed to happen," Mother said. "This isn't how it was supposed to be." Her eyes were glistening. "We never finished the ritual, and the bloodleaf petal is gone. I can't just send you away with no protection, no assurance of your safety."

From the settee, Simon's voice came in a bare whisper. "We can finish it."

"You're awake," I said, amazed. "It really worked."

He groaned as he pulled himself to a sitting position. Looking down at his bloodstained clothes, he said, "How was this accomplished? The last thing I remember—"

"You took an arrow to the chest. And when Aurelia's blood spell didn't work, she used a bloodleaf flower petal on you," Onal said in a cool, clipped tone.

"Stars above." His bewilderment quickly changed to determination. "The ritual. We have to finish it now. Does the bowl still hold our blood? Bring it out. And the cloth and the knife. Put everything back the way it was."

"But you said I shouldn't—" I protested.

"Forget what I said. I think we can agree that things have changed since this afternoon."

The stones were rearranged into the triangle, and Mother, Simon, and Kellan took their places at each point, though this time Simon's arm was draped across Onal's bony shoulder for support.

"Right where you left off," Simon prodded.

"No," I said strongly. "I've already told you: I don't want this. I refuse. No one else is going to suffer in my place."

"Aurelia." Kellan opened my fingers and closed them around the hilt of the knife. "Do it. You have to do it." He held my gaze and I felt my breath catch.

"No, Kellan. I don't want—"

But even as I spoke he forced the knife in my hand down against his own palm. Through gritted teeth he said, "My blood, freely given."

"Quickly now!" Mother commanded. "Take the bowl to the cloth."

Stunned into submission, I stepped into the very center of the triangle.

"Three drops," Simon said. "Repeat after me. *'Sanguine nata, vita et morte.'*"

One drop fell from the iron bowl and spread on the white fabric. *"Sanguine nata, vita et morte."*

"Again."

Another drop. *"Sanguine nata, vita et morte."*

"Again!"

The last drop. *"Sanguine nata, vita et morte."*

"Tertio modo ut ab uno vitae. Ligat sanguinem, sanguinem, facere," said

Simon. "Three lives now tied to one. Bound by blood, by blood undone."

The stones flared up once more, and then all went quiet.

✳

We laid the remnants of the spell away quietly; no one dared to interrupt the silence until the door to the next room creaked open and Conrad's small face peeked out from behind it. "Mama, I can't sleep. There are too many lights."

Mother went to him, placing her hands soothingly on his cheeks. "What lights, my dear?"

"The ones outside. They keep getting brighter."

She moved past him to the window. Beyond the glass, hundreds of glowing orbs were bobbing in the blackness, moving past the castle gate and across the grounds. Her hand moved to her mouth.

"Tribunal." Onal's voice was cold. "They're marching on the castle."

"They wouldn't," Mother said.

"They are."

A heavy knock came from the other room. Toris's voice was muffled through the thick wood. "Genevieve! My queen—they're coming."

Kellan threw the door open, and Toris rushed inside. Breathlessly, he said again, "They're coming. Not just for Aurelia. They're going to overtake the castle. Everything."

"A coup?" Kellan's hand was on his sword.

"It's me they want," I said, trying to keep my voice steady. "If I let them take me, they'll leave everyone else alone."

"You know we can't do that, Princess," Simon said. He was right. If I gave myself up, the Tribunal would kill me. And when it didn't take—and someone else died in my stead—they'd just kill me again and again until all four of us were dead.

"Then I'll leave. I'll go now, today, to seek asylum in Achleva."

"That won't stop them from trying to overthrow me," Mother said.

"You can come with me. We'll be safe inside Achlev's Wall. Renalt tried for three centuries to get past it without any success."

"I will not abandon Renalt to the Tribunal, Aurelia."

In my desperation to learn magic to undo the Tribunal, I'd brought them down on *all* of our heads. I struggled to reconcile with that fact. "But if you stay . . . and what about Conrad?"

"He can go with us to Achleva," Toris said. "I can ensure his well-being."

"With *us?*" I gave him an incredulous glare. "Surely you don't think you are coming along."

He ignored me and addressed my mother directly. "Lisette is already waiting in her carriage. We will meet her in the carriage house in one hour. The Tribunal has blocked every exit from the grounds; only I can get us past them in safety. The clerics on guard know me. They trust me. And they won't question my desire to distance my only daughter from the violence that is about to take place." Toris placed his hand on his chest, over the vial of blood he wore around his neck. "You are well hated by your people, Princess. You should take advantage of what kindnesses you are offered. This is your only chance."

"My people hate me because you told them they could. That they should. You and your stars-forsaken Tribunal."

"I may be a member of the Tribunal," Toris thundered, "but I am loyal to the crown. When my betrayal is discovered, I stand to lose everything. My fortune, my friends, my good name . . ."

"How devastating for you," I said flatly.

"One hour," Toris said, upper lip curling. "The carriage house. Don't be seen."

"I'll get them there," Kellan said. "The prince and princess both."

Toris left with a slam of the door.

My mother busied herself taking my wedding dress down from the dress form, folding it carefully, and tying it into a linen parcel. After a moment of watching her, I turned to Simon. "Is there a way for us to get across Achlev's Wall without you?"

"Yes," he said slowly. "You must be invited into the city by someone of royal descent, of Achlev's direct line. I brought with me three of those documents: one for you, one for a maid, and one for a guard. Anyone else will have to turn back or wait in the encampments outside the wall for the king to issue another invitation for them."

"That's all we need," I said. "One for me, one for Conrad, and one for Kellan. Simon, could you stay here, with my mother? As a blood mage, you're the only person who can offer her any kind of defense. Please. You just tied your life to mine. There must to be something you can do to protect hers."

He frowned. "I might be able to seal us in these chambers, but I can't guarantee how long it will last. If the seal fails at all, the Tribunal could still get in and then . . ." He didn't finish the sentence. We knew what would happen then.

"Do what you have to do."

He brought out three envelopes from his jacket pocket, sealed with the three-pointed-knot symbol of Achleva's flag.

"These will get you across the wall," he said, handing them to me. "May the Empyrea keep you."

"And you."

"We need to hurry," Kellan said. "There's no time to waste."

"Mama?" Conrad asked with glistening eyes.

"Be brave, my prince," she said to him. "You're going away, just for a little while. But Aurelia will take care of you; don't you worry."

He cast a disbelieving gaze at me, and I squared my shoulders to keep from flinching.

Mother presented me with the parcel containing my wedding dress before taking me in a formal embrace and saying in her queen's voice, "Travel safely, my daughter. I love you and will miss you terribly." She touched her lips to my cheek, and I heard her whisper as she shoved something else into my hand, "Keep this with you always. It is a gift. We've protected you with our lives. I'm trusting you to protect Conrad's with yours."

It was the silken square, now blemished with three circles of blood. A reminder of how much those closest to me were willing to give up to keep me safe.

"Aurelia," Kellan said urgently. I turned and looked at him. At Simon. And finally at my mother. If the Tribunal were to overthrow Mother, I was the only hope of returning our family to the Renaltan throne. I needed to keep Conrad safe. I needed to become queen of Achleva. And once I had the power required, I would return to Renalt and reclaim what was rightfully ours.

Throat constricting, I said, "I will."

It wasn't until I was down the dark passageway that I realized I'd forgotten to tell her that I loved her too.

✳

The passageway led out to the Kings Hall, lined on either side with ceiling-high portraits of twenty generations of Renaltan royalty. Beneath their stoic gazes we dashed—Kellan, Conrad, and I—as distant, angry shouts seeped through the walls. We rounded the corner to my chambers to find the door ajar. Pressing a finger to his lips, Kellan drew his sword and pushed it open.

It had been ransacked. Everything that I owned, everything I ever considered mine, was scattered across the floor. The tapestries were torn, the wardrobe overturned. My bed was upended and snapped down the center, jagged slats reaching into the air like the ribs of a long-wrecked ship. Scrawled across every wall were the words *Malefica, malefica, malefica*. Witch, witch, witch.

"Gather what you need as fast as you can," Kellan said. "We've got to get out of here."

"There's nothing to gather," I said. "Everything is gone."

There was a scraping sound as a large piece of my fractured desk was moved aside. Kellan brandished his sword and Conrad ducked behind him, but the face that peeked out was a familiar one.

"My lady?" Emilie asked timidly. "Princess, is that you? Are you all right?"

I helped her from her hiding place. "Are you?"

"I hid when I heard the other servants coming. It's a wonder they didn't find me." She shivered. "The things they were saying about you, my lady . . ."

"They'll be back," Kellan said. "We must go now."

"Wait!" Emilie said, "They'll find you for sure wearing that color. There must be one of your others in here somewhere . . ." But the closet door was hanging crookedly on its hinges, the dresses it still held were slashed and torn, and the rest were gone, likely looted. There was nothing still wearable inside it. She picked up a scrap and then immediately put it down. "Trade me clothes," she said, determination on her face. "We're about the same size. They're looking for a princess in a bright green ball gown. They won't look twice at a servant girl."

"That's a brilliant idea," Kellan said. "Do it. Quickly."

"No," I said firmly. "It's too dangerous. Think of what your mother went through—"

"It's because of my mother that I'm offering," Emilie said, face aglow with fervor. "I was helpless to save her; I am helpless to avenge her. But I can do this for you."

Speechless, I put my hand on her shoulder. She said, "If anyone can make the Tribunal pay, it's you. Maybe if I help you today, you can someday return and make it right for us all."

"Hurry!" Kellan said. "The crowd is moving."

I worked with clumsy fingers to extricate myself from the green dress, handing it to Emilie when I finally succeeded. "Find a safe place and lock yourself in. Tell them I did it," I told her as I pulled her simple shift over my head. "Tell them I forced you to give me your dress. Say whatever you have to. Make them believe it."

"Yes, my lady," she said as I helped her do up the laces on the stained gown. She smoothed out the fabric. "I've never worn anything so lovely."

"Someday I'll pay you back with a better one."

"It's a deal," she said, and removed her yellow headscarf, situating it on my head and shoving my recalcitrant hair beneath it.

"Emilie," I said under my breath, "I won't forget this. I won't let you down."

Kellan, at the door with Conrad, waved me to follow him. Time was running short.

"Wait!" I said before leaving. "In the pocket."

Emilie pulled out the broken bracelet and handed it to me. On impulse I found the dragon charm—emerald, like her mother's favorite stone—and yanked it from the chain. Pressing it into her hand, I whispered, "Thank you."

She nodded, clutching the charm, a token of her mother and my promise to avenge her.

We made our way back to the Kings Hall. Kellan went to scout out the way ahead, but not before situating Conrad and me behind the tapestry across from the portraits of famed King Reynald on one side and his trusted second-in-command, Lord Cael, on the other. The Founder of the Tribunal.

I peered out from my hiding place, and the rigid man in the painting stared coldly back at me: cornflower eyes; square, chiseled chin; sandy hair slicked back into a ponytail at the nape of his neck. *There once were two brothers and a sister, the most promising mages of their orders, who gathered one day to cast a spell* . . . The stories all began the same way. The middles matched up as well: everyone agreed that the sister, Aren, died during the fateful spell. The endings, however, varied wildly: Some say Aren killed herself. Some say Cael saw evil in her and knew he had to protect the world from it, performing the first witch execution on his own sister. The version written in the Founder's Book of Commands and upheld by the Tribunal as immovable truth, however, says that she was murdered by her older brother, Achlev, and that Cael died nobly in her defense, using every last drop of his blood trying to save her. The book's account had it that the Empyrea was so moved by his bravery and selflessness that she chose him to return to earth and become her emissary, spreading her joy and light to all. He woke from death, whole and pure and charged with a holy mandate: found an organization to purge the world of all magic.

This is because of you, I thought, accusing Cael. *You and your Tribunal and your cursed Book of Commands.* There was speculation that his body was too pure to decay, and that it was hidden away somewhere in the mountains, encased in a glass coffin, as fresh and youthful as the day the Empyrea first called him to do her work.

Wherever the Founder was, I hoped he was rotting.

Conrad whimpered beside me, and I awkwardly placed my arm over his shoulders, trying not to notice the way he shrank beneath my touch. "It'll be all right," I whispered to him.

"How do *you* know?" he retorted in a creaky voice.

Kellan appeared and motioned to us. We followed him down a set of service stairs, pausing as a group of people searching for me went by below, laughing and describing what they'd do to me when they found me. We scrambled backwards, Kellan standing protectively over us until they'd passed. "We have to go that way," he said. "Hurry!"

We weren't quite to the next set of stairs when we heard a man yell, "Halt! Wait!"

We stopped. My heart beat a thundering, out-of-rhythm pattern. I looked up to see the shape of a billowing green dress disappear around the corner of the adjoining corridor. The searchers roared past us after her.

"Emilie," I whispered.

"She's given us a distraction. She's given us time."

We took the stairs two and three at once and flew from the service entrance into the herb garden. I swept Conrad up and held him as we dashed across the open courtyard to the carriage house, where Lisette's horses were already harnessed to the carriage and Toris was positioned in the driver's seat.

"You're late," he said. "Let's go."

Kellan helped Conrad into the seat next to Lisette, who fussed over him. "Look at you, love. So brave! Now, there. Don't cry. I'm going to make sure nothing happens to you."

I slumped into the opposite corner, pulling my arms into myself.

Kellan mounted Falada and reined her next to the carriage. "We're ready."

The driveway to the castle gate was long, winding alongside the courtyard where a pyre had been erected. The simmering mob congregated at the foot of the stacked wood, torches waving erratically as they chanted, *Burn the witch! Burn the witch!*

At the gate we were stopped by men in Tribunal coats. "No one is going in or out until we locate the witch."

I hunkered down in my seat and concentrated on the faded floral pattern of Emilie's dress. *Please don't look in,* I prayed.

Toris's voice was clipped and commanding. "I am Lord Toris de Lena, magistrate and bearer of the blood of the Founder. My daughter is inside this carriage, and I will be escorting her away from this violence. Do not make me wait any longer, I pray." His tone went low and flat. "You will regret it."

There was a pause, and then the sound of the iron gate opening. I gulped and held my breath, turning from the window as we went through. Before I could release the breath in relief, the Harbinger was suddenly next to me in the carriage. She was there and then she was gone, like a puff of smoke.

As the gate began to creak closed behind us, I heard the clerics call out to one another in excitement, "Look at that! They got her!"

"Thank the Empyrea, the witch will burn tonight!"

The carriage was picking up speed, but I flung open the door sash, emitting a strangled, animal sob when I realized what it was I saw.

They were forcing a girl up onto the pyre. A girl in an emerald gown.

"No! Stop!" I shrieked. "Stop! We have to go back!" But if Toris could hear me over the pounding hoofbeats, he wasn't listening, and he didn't slow down.

I climbed frantically out onto the carriage step, ready to jump and run back, when Kellan and Falada came galloping up from behind. He wrested me from the carriage step and pulled me up onto the horse with him.

"It's too late now; you can't go back. She made this sacrifice for you. It was a gift. A gift, Aurelia! You can't waste her gift!"

I wept into his cloak as we turned the corner, and the only thing I could see from beyond the city rooftops was a towering orange flame reaching toward the sky.

8

It was nearly a fortnight later when we reached the edge of the Ebon-wilde. We were sodden, sore, and miserable after a parade of difficult days spent slogging through Renalt's meandering back roads, sleeping in marshy gullies, and eating whatever Kellan could catch. Grouse and gnarled old field hares if we were lucky, rodents if we weren't. The Tribunal must have figured out they'd burned the wrong girl; after a few close calls with their scouts, we gave up fires as well and were forced to scavenge to eat. Mostly pennycress and wild clover, as it was too early in the season for much else. We were carriageless now, too, after ours sank up to the sash in spring mud and could not be pulled free. Kellan had wanted to try longer, but I insisted otherwise; I could see that ours was not the first party to find calamity in that spot, and I did not fancy joining the sallow, bloated spirits hopelessly clawing at the mire. We were fortunate it was only the carriage we lost. Many others had not fared so well.

I marked the passage of days with tired resignation more than fear; it was now the first day of the month of Quartus, four weeks from my wedding day.

Morale was low for all but one. Toris seemed to get more and more cheerful the farther we traveled, often whistling an old Renaltan folk song to himself. When we first sighted the forest on the horizon, he even started absently singing the words.

Don't go, my child, to the Ebonwilde,
for there a witch resides.
Little boys she bakes into pretty cakes,
Little girls into handsome pies.
You'll know her by her teeth so white,
Eyes so red and heart so black,
But if you see her, child, in the Ebonwilde,
You won't be coming back.

He was about to launch into the second verse, about a cursed and headless horseman, when I could take it no longer and snapped, "*Please*. No more."

He flashed his teeth in an irreverent smile, but the singing stopped. The whistling, however, did not. It continued for the duration.

That night we camped just outside the tree line, not far from the bank of the River Sentis, and made our first fire in days. Kellan had caught a collection of perch with a long thread from the frayed hem of Lisette's dress and a hook fashioned from one of her earrings. She protested mightily about being deprived of them until the fish were off the fire—after that she made no more noise. It was our first decent meal since Syric.

Conrad ate quickly and fell asleep with his head on Lisette's lap.

He'd barely said two words to me the entire journey, and he cried often—big, round tears that slipped quietly down his cheeks only to be hastily wiped away before anyone could notice. But he never complained, despite the wearying travel and the sting of being deprived of his mother and home for the first time in his young life. I burst with the urge to reach out and comfort him, but I never did; he had Lisette for that. I watched her carefully move him from her lap to his bedroll, tucking a blanket tightly under his chin before lying down herself. They fell asleep swiftly.

Toris took first watch that night and left for a better vantage point not long afterward.

Kellan and I were alone. He settled a fur blanket around my shoulders. "Toris will watch the first half of the night, and then I'll relieve him."

I gave a halfhearted nod, my thoughts far away.

"Aurelia," he said, sitting next to me, "stop thinking about it."

"Emilie died because of me. I *can't* stop thinking about it."

He took my hands. "It wasn't your fault, Aurelia. None of this was your fault."

I looked intently at his hands on mine, then at his face. "After everything, you can't really believe that."

"Of course I do. I *know* you."

He knew the version of me I wanted him to see, because I was too afraid that revealing my real self would change his opinion of me. There was a hard knot in my stomach. I'd never wanted to have this conversation with him, but my mind was punishing me with never-ending images of a girl in a green dress burning to death on a witch's pyre. I was tired of maintaining the illusion of innocence, even for Kellan. "You think you do, but you don't."

"I know you better than anyone. You're stubborn and . . . and maddening and amazing. You're brave but reckless; you have no sense of self-preservation whatsoever." He smiled at the ground. "You care about people. You hurt when others hurt, even if you try not to show it."

He gave me a look of composed determination. "I wish you knew," he began. Then he checked himself, faltering, and started again. "I wish you understood what you mean to me." He placed a tentative hand on my cheek.

I wasn't distracted. "You saw what I did at the castle. In Syric."

"Aurelia, I don't—"

"Tell me what you *saw*," I ordered.

He was shaking his head. "Simon was dying and you said some things and . . . what else do you want me to say?"

"I want you to look me in the eyes and explain to me how you can believe that I am innocent. You were there. You witnessed it firsthand."

"You'd been through some extreme events, the pressure got to be too much, and . . . you've been conditioned your whole life to believe the lies told to you and about you—"

"They aren't lies!" I shouted, standing. "None of it has been a lie. You want the truth? I am exactly what they say I am." I took several long breaths. "A witch."

His face was blank, utterly unreadable. I waited for some sign that he understood, that he believed me, but none came.

"I see ghosts, Kellan. I see them everywhere. How do you think I knew what was going to happen to Simon? It was because a spirit showed it to me. These visions are not superstition. They are real and terrifying and I've lived with them every day of my pathetic life." I gulped as guilt and shame snaked around my throat and tightened. "And yes, I did cast a spell to try to save Simon, and it wasn't the first time. It was a mistake to do it in front of all those people who already loathed me, but you know what? I might be glad I did it. I hate what happened to Emilie, but I'm glad about what has happened to me. Because I don't have to pretend anymore. I don't have to wonder anymore what you'll think of me when you finally realize the truth—"

Kellan took me by each shoulder, stopping to hold me in his brash gaze for an instant before bending his head down to kiss me. He *kissed* me. And in spite of everything, I squeezed my eyes closed and fell into it. Kellan's arms were around me and his lips were pressed hard against mine, and for a moment nothing else in the universe mattered.

Then the kiss broke, and he murmured against my cheek, "You are not a witch, Aurelia. You're just a girl who's had the weight of the world on her shoulders for too long. We are not in Renalt any- more. You can let those fears and superstitions go. You can let all of it go. Renalt, Achleva . . . everything. You and I, we can go wherever we like, be whomever we like. Just say the word, and I can make it happen."

My heart thudded heavily. "You want me to run away?"

"Yes," he said without hesitation. "Run away with me. We'll put all of this behind us. Forever."

I was struggling to comprehend. Just . . . leave? "What about my mother, my brother? Renalt?"

"With you gone, I'm sure everything will go back to normal for them. Conrad can go home, your mother can again secure the throne . . ."

"And the Tribunal can carry on killing thousands more innocents with impunity. Is that what you're saying?"

"It's just the way things have always been, Aurelia. All I care about is what happens to *you*."

My fluttering heart became suddenly still. I was instantly and acutely aware of every point of contact between us: my hands on his chest. My cheek brushing his. His arms crossing my back. I began to pull away, untangling myself from him, until I had completely withdrawn and he stood agape, empty-handed and disarmed.

"Aurelia. Look at me."

I wouldn't look. I didn't want him to see what was written on my face. It wasn't just his hand-wave dismissal of my most intimate confession; it was his belief that things just *were*. That the Tribunal was a simple fact of life, like the tides or the changing of the seasons. That the continued murder of hundreds was an acceptable exchange for the safety of one. Me.

That was one idea I would never be able to accept. Never. If that was the cost for a life with Kellan, it was a price I could not pay. And with that realization, my secret hopes were whipped away like autumn leaves on a winter wind. I stepped farther back, deepening the physical divide between us to mirror the one I felt in my heart.

"Aurelia."

I kept my head turned away and gazed at the fire and the forest looming behind it, a black velvet shawl draped across the white, hard-angled shoulders of Achleva's distant mountains. I said, "Everything you've seen, everything you and I have been through, and you still don't understand."

"Have you been listening at all?" He came between me and my view of the forest and sky, his eyes narrowed and full of feeling. "I'm trying to tell you I love you, Aurelia."

"You can't," I said leadenly. "You don't know how."

"What can that possibly mean?"

"It means that when we get to Achleva and you have been assured that I am safe and settled, I will dismiss you from your duties and you'll be able to return to Renalt. Stay in the guard, or don't. Marry, if you like." I felt my composure slipping. "I hope you do."

He said nothing more; he just turned and walked away, down past where Lisette and Conrad were sleeping, and out into the tall, starlit grass of the border fields. It wasn't long before I couldn't see him anymore and I collapsed onto my bedroll, anguished and alone.

Good, I thought. *The only person I can hurt now is me.*

9

The dream was vivid. I was standing at the edge of the forest, watching a pale light between the trees. I squinted to make out what it was, heading toward it without consciously moving my feet. I was a moth drawn to a flame; I knew nothing good could lie beyond, but I was pulled toward it anyway.

The light was Toris's lamp. He was several hundred feet inside the tree line, hunched over, face obscured by the shadows into something that barely resembled him. I shrank behind the trunk of a large tree and watched as he took the blood of the Founder from the cord around his neck, unstopped it, and let the liquid drip onto his face. One. Two. Three drops. Then he put the relic back inside his shirt.

Toris stood slowly, and for a minute his face looked all wrong, as if his bones had rearranged themselves in unnatural ways. He was muttering under his breath, words both foreign and frightening. I could feel the power in them. This was blood magic. He had used the Founder's own blood to enact a spell. And judging from the heaviness in the air, an unpleasant one.

The dream shifted suddenly, throwing me into a chaotic jumble of upsetting images: a flash of blue fabric. A hand on a knife. And Kellan's visage, contorted in pain as Toris went to strike.

I came out of the dream with a choked gasp, clamping my hands over my mouth to keep from screaming. I saw the Harbinger for less than a moment, but the skin of my arm was marked a chill blue from her hand.

Scrambling from my bedroll, I grabbed a leather satchel and began stuffing it with whatever I could get my hands on.

Kellan was brooding by the fire with his back turned away from me, listlessly poking it with a long stick. I scuttled over to kneel at his side. "Kellan." His name was sticky on my tongue. I tried again, shaking him. "Kellan!"

He finally turned toward me. His sullenness was startled away by my distress.

"What's wrong?" he asked, his hurt and anger ousted by the keen sense of urgency he'd honed in his five years as my guard.

"We have to go. Just us and Conrad. Now. It's . . . it's Toris. He's doing magic. Blood magic. In the woods, he . . ." I trailed off, suddenly aware of how ridiculous it sounded accusing a devout Tribunal magistrate of witchcraft. But I knew the Harbinger had not misled me. I knew I'd seen true. How could I make him believe me, especially now?

I took him by his shoulders. "I know how it sounds, but listen to me. I don't care if you believe anything I've told you up to this point, but you *must* believe me now. We have to leave, immediately. Please, Kellan. I'm begging you. *Trust me.*"

He searched my face and then said, "All right, Aurelia. I trust you."

We seized what we could, and Kellan secured the satchel to Fala-da's saddle. I mounted my horse as Kellan grabbed the still-sleeping Conrad and held him tight as he swept onto Falada's back.

Lisette stirred when she heard Conrad's frightened crying. "What's going on? Aurelia? What are you *doing?* Aurelia! Let him go!"

We broke for the forest with Lisette's shouts echoing behind us. "Father! Father! They've got the prince! They're getting away!"

We bolted past Toris as he was running toward the campsite. A lantern swung from a chain in his hand, painting his face into an angry mask of light and shadow, not unlike his face in my dream. Over my shoulder, I watched him barrel toward the other horses and mount the first one he came to. Lisette had to jump out of the way or be run over.

We urged our horses forward as the trail turned into sharp switch-backs, climbing higher and higher into the trees. Toris was on our heels, close enough that I could hear the sound of his taunting whistle to the rhythm of the horse's hooves. *Don't go, my child, to the Ebon-wilde, for there a witch resides . . .* But our horses were sure and strong; we were gaining ground. I allowed myself some hope that we would make it out of this.

The hope was short-lived.

The path made a sharp turn to the right and ran along the sheer edge of a gorge, the powerful River Sentis rushing below. It was a treacherous road, rutted and narrow, with parts that had long ago given way to weather and time and collapsed into the river, leaving long, jagged scars along the remaining edge. On the other side of the road, the forest loomed. Somewhere within its incomprehensible darkness, a wolf howled. My horse jumped and skittishly stamped her feet at the sound. When it came again, she reared up with a frightened scream, hooves slashing wildly against the air.

I couldn't hold on, and I tumbled from my saddle as she surged forward and bolted into the cover of the trees.

I rolled to my knees, dirt and tears stinging my eyes, every bone aching. Ahead on the trail, Kellan pulled Falada around.

"Go!" I shouted. "Don't wait! *Go!*" If the Harbinger's vision was correct, Kellan needed to get as far away from Toris as possible. But to my dismay, he turned Falada around. They were riding back.

Toris was now upon me. He swept down from his horse with balletic grace and advanced on me, twirling his knife with a grin. I put my hands up. Kellan reined Falada in.

"Let me go!" Conrad shouted, twisting from Kellan's grasp.

"Enough of this," Toris said. "Let the boy down, Lieutenant. Now."

Jaw tight, Kellan helped Conrad down first, then dismounted.

"Be careful, Magistrate," Kellan warned. "Don't do anything you'll regret."

Another rider emerged from the trees. Lisette's hair had come unpinned and was flying around her face in a mad cloud. She climbed down from her horse. "Let Conrad go," she said in a careful, cajoling manner. "You don't need to hurt him, Aurelia."

"What? I'm not—"

With a frightened sob, my brother shook off Kellan's grasp and hurtled into her arms. "He was right," he said. "They tried to take me. Just like Toris said."

"I didn't want to believe it either," she murmured. "But I've got you now."

"No, Conrad!" I cried. "I would never hurt you. You have to know that! I would never—"

"Lies." Toris was circling me now. "We know all about your treason. Your alliance with Simon Silvis and the plot to kill the heirs of two kingdoms: your brother. Your betrothed. Thank goodness we came along with you, or you might actually have gotten away with it."

Kellan came to my defense. "He's lying, Conrad. Don't—"

"The prince has seen enough," Toris said. "Get him back to the campsite, daughter. I'll take care of these two."

"Wait! Don't take him. No—" I felt the point of Toris' knife between my shoulder blades.

Lisette helped my brother onto her horse, casting a look of pitiful disappointment at me from over her shoulder before riding away with him, back the way we had come.

"Now, then," Toris said, knife raised. "I'll be needing the documents, if you please."

"I don't know what you're talking about." At that moment I didn't.

"Come now. Simon Silvis wouldn't have sent you to Achleva without a way to cross the wall. The documents. Now." His knife pressed a little harder into my back and marched me to my horse; the blade had breached the fabric of my dress. One wrong move and it would break the skin.

I pulled the parchments from my satchel. "This is what you want?

I'll give them to you. But only if you bring Conrad back to me and let us all go in peace." From the corner of my eye, I saw Kellan carefully advancing.

"Conrad does not want to go with you," Toris said. "He hates you, in fact. You don't have many friends, do you, my dear?" He tilted his head. "It hurts you greatly to lose even one, doesn't it?"

He moved fast, ducking underneath the swing of Kellan's sword and grabbing him from behind before yanking his head back and laying the knife against his neck. Hands up, Kellan relinquished his hold on his sword.

"I wish I didn't need the invitations, but I do. Magic can be so irritating. That's why the Tribunal's work is so valuable; it keeps things orderly. Now. Give me the documents. I will not ask again." A drop of blood left a thin trail down Kellan's neck.

I swallowed and considered . . . then held the parchments over the river chasm. "Put the knife down or they are gone for good."

"We're not negotiating here."

"Put it down," I stated, stronger.

Displeased, he loosened the knife from against Kellan's neck. I stepped slowly forward and laid the documents down on the ground by the cliff's edge. The knot-stamped seal shone dull red in the moonlight. Toris dragged Kellan with him, and only released his hold on him to swipe up the invitations.

I dashed into Kellan's open arms. From over his shoulder, I could see Toris's smirk return as he deposited the acquisitions into his jacket pocket.

"There!" I cried. "You have what you want! Now let us go, like you promised!"

"I never promised any such thing."

And with a quick flick of his wrist, Toris sank his knife into Kellan's side.

Kellan collapsed against me. I staggered beneath his sudden weight. "Kellan!"

My knees buckled too close to the drop-off, and I clawed at his cloak to keep from losing my grip on him. I held on desperately as his eyes glazed over and he teetered at the brink.

With one last guttural cry, I dug in my heels and wrenched the cloak with all my strength, but the clasp gave way and his body plummeted over the edge and disappeared.

I gaped at my hands, wrapped up in the cobalt fabric that was now flapping empty in the wind. The only sound was the distant roar of the river far below and my own shallow breathing. The darkness had swallowed Kellan whole. He was gone.

Toris grabbed me by the wrist, yanking me around to face him. His knife, still coated in Kellan's blood, was poised beneath my chin. He was calm as he explained. "It was always going to end badly for you. You had to have known that."

My blood ran as cold as the icy river, crystallizing my grief into hatred. "You want to keep Renalt free from Achleva so much, you'd kill me for it?"

"It is for a *united* Renalt and Achleva that I strive. There will still be a wedding. A princess will still marry the prince. *You* just won't be around to witness it. Lisette was always better suited to the role anyway."

So that was it. Lisette would go to Achleva in my place, and I would die here.

"And Conrad?"

"Collateral. We need him to keep your mother in line. And unlike you, he's proven himself valuably malleable. It will be an easy story to sell." He made his voice sound urgent and distraught. "'Don't you see, little prince? We need to stay undercover to figure out the identities of your sister's coconspirators. The queen's *life* hangs in the balance!'" He laughed and brought the knife in closer.

I wanted to close my eyes, but I didn't. Let Toris see my face, my eyes, as the life went out of me. Perhaps Simon's blood charm would work and another's life would be taken instead of mine—an option I couldn't bear to think about—but in case it didn't, I wanted to die angry. Vengeful. I wanted to become a ghost so that I could terrorize him every single day of the rest of his life.

"No hard feelings, Princess," he said. "You're just not part of the plans."

His hands were deft, and the slice he made from one side of my throat to the other was tight and clean. But I didn't feel the knife. I didn't feel anything.

His stroke had been absorbed by another.

The Harbinger had materialized in the air between Toris and me—he'd cut her neck instead of mine. But her throat already bore a gash; his could do her no harm now. He dropped his knife, flinching as if he'd been stung. "Aren?"

He saw her. He knew who she was. His gaze was wild and confused, looking from her to me and then back again.

She blinked out as quickly as she'd appeared.

I wrapped my hand around the vial of blood at his neck and tugged; the cord gave way with a twang as I hurled my shoulder into his chest and knocked him backwards to the ground. Then three long strides brought me to Falada's side, and I swept onto her back, the way Kellan had made me practice over and over again. Still clutching the Founder's blood, I wound my hands into Falada's long mane and dug my heels against her side.

She sprang forward without hesitation, her lithe legs pounding the damp, black earth of the Ebonwilde, carrying me away into the welcoming darkness.

10

We are not here. We are unseen. We are not here. We are unseen.

 I chanted Simon's cloaking spell long into the night, well after the blood I'd drawn to cast it had dried. When I was forced to stop and rest or risk falling, unconscious, from Falada's back, I murmured it into the darkness while I huddled for warmth in Kellan's cloak, listening to the mournful cries of wolves in the distance. *We are not here. We are unseen.* After a while I could no longer tell if I was saying the words out loud or if they were just a chorus going round and round in my head. *We are not here. We are unseen. We are not here. We are unseen.*

 When I woke, I did not know at first how much time had passed. Inside the Ebonwilde, there was very little difference between day and night. What light there was was dim and gray, just enough to see the bloodstained slit in the fabric of Kellan's cloak, marking the path of Toris's knife, right before Kellan fell.

 He *fell.*

 Kellan. My best friend. My guard. My protector. The person who loved me, and—oh, Empyrea!—whose love I had *rejected . . .* he was gone.

The noise that came out of me then was an unholy cross between a wail and a groan, and I shook there on the forest's leafy floor, clutching at his cloak knotted in my fists. I rocked back and forth on my knees, coughing and sputtering between sobs, certain that this is what it felt like to drown.

Falada nudged me tentatively with her nose, and through bleary eyes I saw what had gotten her attention: a fox was watching me from the trees. She was impossibly still, with flame-colored fur and eyes like golden discs.

I got to my feet, my breath still coming in rapid, staccato gasps. "He was good," I told the fox. "He didn't deserve this."

She regarded me for another long moment, as if trying to make up her mind about me. Then she bolted back into the forest, gone as quickly as she had come.

The fox's appearance jolted me back into reason. I was lost in a forest. If I stayed where I was, I'd die—from hunger, or cold, or a creature with more malevolent intent than the fox. I owed it to Kellan to save Falada. I owed it to Kellan to save myself. I had to keep moving.

But which direction? I was suspended between two impossible destinations. On one side was Achleva. I knew now that Toris was headed there with a plan to pass Lisette off as me, to have her marry the prince and upset the entire monarchial line. On the other was Renalt, where Simon and my mother were—hopefully—still holed away, safe from the Tribunal closing in around them.

I couldn't go announce myself in Achleva. Toris and Lisette had my brother in their possession and had convinced him I was guilty of conspiring against Renalt and Achleva both. If Conrad corroborated their claims of identity, whether through complicity or coercion, I had no way to prove otherwise. I'd face a charge of treason for even making the assertion.

I couldn't go to Renalt, either. Simon was keeping my mother safe for now, but if I showed up on their doorstep, the Tribunal would waste no time fixing the mistake they'd made when they killed Emilie. And endangering myself meant endangering Simon, my mother . . .

I took out the bloodcloth, running my fingers over its surface. The three circles of blood remained, but one of them—Kellan's— had faded to the point of being nearly invisible.

A third choice emerged: keep going. Find another way to get inside Achlev's Wall. Stay hidden from Toris and make my plans from the shadows.

It was about more than just me now. Whether I liked it or not, the fate of my nation was wrapped up in every choice I made from here on out. A cut had been made in the center of my life. I'd left behind the *before* and now had to face the *after*.

I took a step. Then another.

I'll always consider that decision—to move instead of lying down to die in the Ebonwilde—my first victory.

As I went along, the only breaks in the monotony of the forest were little sightings of the Harbinger. She'd appear and vanish in the space of a breath, always just ahead, always out of reach. Whether Falada and I were following her or she was following us, I was never certain. But as the time drifted past—one day? Two? I couldn't tell—and my hunger and exhaustion began to toe the edge of delirium, the sight of her became a point of clarity upon which I could fix my attention.

Despite all, Falada never faltered. She carried me through that long darkness and across the edge of the Ebonwilde, stopping only when the trees suddenly broke and revealed the city in the distant basin below, as if she, too, was stunned at the reminder that others existed in the world.

Eons of glaciers had carved out the bowl and left the cobalt-blue water of the fjord, flanked on every side by rocky peaks. At the center of it all, where the mountains and forest and fjord water converged, stood the fortress city of Achlev. Storm clouds hung low and thick over the basin, but there was a perfect circle of clear sky above the city, as if the storm was circling an invisible barrier, angry at being denied entrance.

This was the famed Wall of Achleva—spelled to keep the uninvited from ever passing through its gates, and the reason Achleva's capital city had never fallen in all the long years of war with Renalt. It was as if King Achlev had hewn it straight from a mountain and reassembled the stones as tightly as they were cut. Fifty feet tall and at least fifteen feet thick, the wall stretched in an unbroken ring over the crags and hollows and across the narrowest width of the fjord. Behind those unassailable walls was a complicated series of gray towers and steep turrets. The tallest of them stood in the center, pricking the circle of bare sky like a rapier. This was a place meant to endure even the worst assault.

It was a place built to withstand armies and ages.

It was dusk when Falada and I finally made our approach. There were fires dotting the outskirts of the wall, travelers' camps, mostly. People, I guessed, who'd been ejected from the city and those who'd yet to be invited in. They clustered around the fires in threadbare blankets, and I shrank underneath the weight of their gazes as I dismounted Falada and led her past them.

"You're a long way from home, aren't ye, miss?"

The speaker was a man of late middle age, tall and thick, with gray-tinged stubble growing in unkempt patches across his ruddy cheeks and chin. He stood, a hammered tin cup in hand.

"It's none of your business where I'm from," I said.

He grinned, revealing a row of yellow teeth spread across his gums in irregular intervals.

"You look tired and hungry, miss. Here, here, come sit with me. Rest. Have a drink." He clamped a fleshy paw around my wrist.

I was staring at his offending hand and wondering which would be a more effective way to decline his invitation—kicking him in the groin or gouging out his eyes—when a raucous laugh came from nearby.

"Go ahead, Darwyn. Put the lassie on your lap. Get friendly. I'd pay a gold sovereign to see what happens when Erda comes back and sees it. Maybe this time she'll get yer other ball." The man was pulling down papers tacked to the wall every few feet and gathering them into a pile in his arms.

Darwyn released his grip on my wrist. He said defensively, "It was just a nick, Ray. Erdie didn't mean it. I still got both my balls."

"For now," Ray replied, tugging another paper down with a laugh.

Darwyn glowered at him and went back to his place next to his fire, self-consciously crossing his legs.

"Thank you," I said to my would-be rescuer. "Mr. . . . ?"

"Thackery. Raymond Thackery." He shifted his pile of papers into one arm and rubbed his close-shorn white hair with his free hand. "Darwyn isn't even the worst of 'em, miss. This place is crawling with the unseemly, who'd do a lady harm if given the chance."

"And you, Mr. Thackery?" I asked tenuously. "Are you one of them?"

He barked another laugh. "Gonna get right down to it, aren't ye? I could say no, but there's no real way to tell, is there?"

"Please, sir. I just need someplace to rest, just for a little while. And some food and water for my horse."

"Nothin' comes for free, miss. I won't try to peek beneath yer dress like ol' Darwyn there, but I ain't in the habit of feeding every stray that comes along, neither. You got any money?"

"No, I don't. Sorry."

He gave a nonchalant shrug. "Too bad. Best keep moving, then. Unless . . ." He scratched his chin. "Your horse. Is she an Empyrean?"

My eyes narrowed. "I'm *not* selling my horse."

Another paper came off the nail with a yank and joined the stack. "I'd give you a fair price, seeing as how she's in such bad shape. The girl's half-dead."

"No. Not for any price."

"Everybody has a price. I'd sell my mother for the right price." He shrugged again. "But she's a scheming harpy, so the price would probably end up being pretty low. Too bad for you, though. I've got fresh straw in my stable, and I was about to sit down to some vegetable soup." He put his back to me.

"Wait!" I fumbled in my pocket and pulled out my charm bracelet, twisting off another charm. "Would this work?" I opened my fingers to reveal the topaz gryphon, rearing on its hind legs, claws outstretched and curled tongue extended.

He raised an eyebrow. "Well, now. I suppose that would suffice." In a blink he'd snatched it up and hidden it away in the ragged folds of his clothing. "This way now, miss."

He led me past several other camps, gathering papers as he went. "Royal decrees," he said, sensing my curiosity. "King Domhnall issues a new one every few days and has them posted everywhere, in and out of the city, generally demanding thanks for things he didn't do and praise for traits he doesn't possess. Every time, we think his proclamations couldn't get stupider . . . until the next one." We stopped at a ramshackle structure of sticks and twine propped against the side of the wall, a few thin skins draped over the top. "I use 'em for kindling, see. Only thing ol' Domhnall is good for: starting fires." He crouched next to a smoking fire pit, crumpling the stolen decrees into balls and chuckling to himself as each new one smoldered and caught flame.

"This is your stable?" I asked with chagrin. "And what is that smell?"

"Oh, that." He knelt next to the fire and pointed above his head. "That's just ol' Gilroy."

I cast my eyes upward to see an iron cage creaking high above our heads, chained to a hook on the wall's battlements. A gibbet. And inside, a jumble of bones and moldering flesh that had once been a man. My stomach heaved painfully, too empty to yield any relief by retching.

"Gilroy was a friend of mine," Ray said, giving the remains a deferential tip of his cap. A ghostly face peered out from between the bars, returning a salute that Ray would never see. "Got on the wrong side of His Majesty. Beat him fair and square in a card game. Next thing any of us knows . . ." He drew his thumb across his neck. "Gilroy kind of deserved it, though. He should never have gone to the Stein and Flagon. It's Domhnall's favorite whorehouse; everyone knows that. And he definitely shouldn't have sat down to a card game with the brute, no matter how slobbering drunk he was. But nobody ever accused Gilroy of being a genius."

Gilroy's ghost made a crude hand gesture at him from the confines of his cage above.

"Oh, well," Ray said. "At least with Gilroy around, nobody tries to encroach on my territory. And he serves as a good reminder."

I still had my hand over my nose. "Of what?"

"Of the fragility of existence, of course. And that King Domhnall is a bastard who reacts to losing a game of cards by executing the winner and then immediately issuing a decree banning cards altogether." He stood and shoved a bowl of something into my hands. "There. Eat up."

The soup was little more than tepid water and a few bobbing chunks of what might have been vegetables once. "Thank you," I said with as much sincerity as I could muster, and led Falada to the rickety stall.

At least the straw was relatively clean, as Raymond promised. I took a few sips from the bowl and let Falada have the rest as I ran my hands over her white flanks. "That's a good girl," I murmured. "You have served me so well. Kellan would be proud of you."

The sound of his name aloud struck like a dagger in my heart, and I finally succumbed to the grim cocktail of exhaustion, rage, and bitter grief. With my back to Achlev's Wall, I sank into the straw, buried my face in my knees, and closed my eyes.

PART TWO
ACHLEVA

It was still dark when I woke to the sound of voices outside the stall. The first belonged to Raymond Thackery, but the second was younger, clearer.

"She's real pretty, I tell you what," Ray was saying. "A little bit bedraggled and dirty, but real pretty. Long hair, nice legs. A little skinny for my tastes, but probably a decent ride, I'd say."

"I want to see her before I pay you a thing, Thackery."

"I know your tastes, Zan. She's exactly what you're looking for, I swear."

I cast around in the dark for something—anything—I might possibly use to defend myself, eventually prying one of the knobby sticks from the wall with a prayer that its removal wouldn't bring the whole structure down on top of us. When the door of the stable opened, I was blinded by the glare of a lantern.

"Not an inch closer!" I raised my stick, squinting into the light. "Don't you dare touch me."

"You? You think he's here for you?" Ray burst into hooting laughter. The other person, the man he'd called Zan, lowered the lamp until his face was bathed in the yellow light, and I was startled at the sight of him. *Simon?* I thought. *How could—*

But it wasn't Simon, of course. This man was taller, younger . . . probably only a few years older than I was, twenty-one or twenty-two at the most. His eyes were not brown but green, and his face was leaner. He was less well kept, too; his dark hair was ruffled and windswept, long enough to brush the collar of his leather jacket and the loose linen shirt underneath. But despite that, his clothes were well made, like Simon's—the work of a skilled tailor. And perhaps most telling of all, he wore a ring in the shape of a raven, wings outstretched. The Silvis signet, I was sure of it.

He cocked his head, eyebrow raised. "You can put your . . . uh, *weapon* . . . down," he said. "It's not you I'm here for." He looked meaningfully at Falada.

"I already told him, she's not for sale."

He turned to Ray. "Can you give us a minute?"

Ray nodded and walked away, still snickering to himself.

"All right, let's skip all the simpering and sighing. I *am* purchasing your Empyrean, and I will pay whatever you ask. I'm not in the mind to negotiate; simply tell me your price and we can get on with it." The young man took out a pouch, heavy with coins, and waited for my response.

"There is no price," I said through gritted teeth. "She is not for sale."

"Really?" He put his coins away. "How long has it been since you had something to eat?"

I lowered my stick just a little.

"Your hands are shaking," he continued. "There are dark circles under your eyes. I'd say it has been at least two days, maybe three, since you've had a meal. I know you didn't try Ray's soup, because you gave it to her." He nudged the empty bowl, licked clean by Falada, with his boot. "Probably for the best; I have little faith in Mr. Thackery's culinary skill." He took me in, examining my stark Renaltan servant's dress. "Tell me, what is a Renaltan girl doing in the travelers' camps? No companions, half-starving, sleeping on a pile of hay in a dirty stable . . ."

I gave him the same answer I had given Ray. "None of your business."

"You have to know that you won't survive long without money. Or shelter. Or rest." He approached me carefully, like I was a cornered, feral animal, and slowly removed the stick from my fingers.

I decided the biggest difference was in the mouth. Simon had an easy smile, but Zan's lips were like cut glass, artfully shaped but severe. "I can provide you with what you need," he said.

"She's not mine to sell," I stated, trying not to think about how it would feel to fall asleep in a clean, warm bed with food in my stomach and no terror scratching at my door.

"You stole her?"

"No! No, I didn't—I just . . ." I took a breath. "She belonged to someone I . . . I love. Loved," I corrected myself, and the coil inside my chest tightened, just a little. "He died."

He took a step back, studying me.

"I won't sell her. I'll starve first."

"And what about her? Will you let *her* starve? Is that what your dear departed love would have wanted?"

I didn't have an answer.

He gave a deep, haggard sigh. "We'll continue this conversation tomorrow morning, after you've eaten and slept and can reason properly again. Come along." He took ahold of Falada's reins and led her out of the stable, while I scrambled behind them.

"What are you doing? Where are we going?"

"There's an inn on Canal, not far from High Gate. It's quiet and clean—I expect you'll find it quite comfortable."

"I can't cross the wall."

The corner of his mouth quirked up, just a little. It was the first hint of a smile I'd seen on him, and I didn't think I liked it. It didn't look natural on his grim face. "I've got it covered."

I knew I shouldn't trust someone whose motives were so obviously counter to mine, but if I was going to be of any use at all in taking Toris down, I had to get inside the wall *somehow*. I looked again at the ring on his hand—silver, and bearing the symbol of a bird with a widespread, open wingspan. Just like Simon's. I decided to trust him, for the moment.

Raymond Thackery chased us down. "What about my payment?" he asked. "Services were rendered."

"Here," Zan said, pulling out a small stack of folded papers, dotted with wax and stamped with the Achlevan seal.

Thackery counted them and said, "There's only nine here. You promised ten."

"I'm keeping this one," he said, "as a fee. The horse came with some baggage, as you can see. Count yourself lucky. The prince was in a generous mood to issue ten invitations at once. He might not give me as many next time."

"There might not be a next time. King's been sniffin' around, wonderin' who's been making invitations and handing 'em out to the riffraff—"

"Consider me warned," Zan said, cutting him off. To me, he said, "Let's go."

"Invitations?" I asked as we walked.

"Ray is a smuggler," Zan explained. "I use my connections inside the royal family to get him blood-marked invitations issued by the prince so he can sell them to the highest bidder, and he lets me know when he comes across something I might find interesting. In this case, you. Or rather, your Empyrean."

"Her name is Falada."

"And what is your name?"

"It's . . . Emilie." It was an impulsive decision, to give her name as mine. I'd wear it like a cilice; it would hurt, but at least I wouldn't be allowed to forget her.

Even in the middle of the night, Zan made his way around the outside of the wall with a deftness that suggested he was well acquainted with its unsystematic layout. We zigzagged through the hive of encampments and clapboard hovels spaced between the occupied gibbets, of which there were many.

"Where are we going?" I asked Zan.

"High Gate," he said. "You'll know it when you see it."

He was right; there was no mistaking High Gate when we came to it. Rising at least twenty feet over the already colossal wall was a gatehouse, flanked on each side by a barbican and crowned by a polished sculpture of three majestic horses, stamping and rearing, mouths open in silent, defiant screams. They gleamed white in the moonlight, perfect copies of Falada herself. I had to look back at her to remind myself that she was flesh and blood and they were not.

"Empyrean horses are incredibly rare and very highly valued in Achleva," Zan said. "It is absolutely imperative that we get yours to the stable before anyone else sees her."

"You're afraid someone might buy her before you can?"

"Not exactly."

Beneath the statue, a swarm of shades clamored at the gate. They varied in opacity; some were fully formed, almost real enough to touch, and had likely met their ends in the last several years. The oldest spirits were but tattered threads of their former selves, caught like flies in a web at the place of their demise. They all had one thing in common, however: a network of blackened veins standing out against their pallid skin.

Zan gave me an assessing stare from over his shoulder. "I should warn you. Even with the royal blood-marked invitation, the crossing is likely to be . . . uncomfortable."

Made sense, considering going without one seemed to turn a person's veins into charcoal.

Zan passed me the invitation. "I'll go through first. When you get to the borderline, break the seal on this parchment and place your hand over the prince's mark. After that, you'll step onto the border, holding the invitation in front of you, like this." He demonstrated. Then he reached for Falada. "Animals can cross without incident. I'll take her through first."

"No," I said. "She goes through with me."

He gave an irritated sigh. "Fine. Just . . . well. Good luck." He turned on his heel and walked underneath the portcullis without pause or any further comment. On the other side, he put his hands in his pockets and waited.

I wondered if, when I stepped onto the borderline, I'd find that the invitations were fake. He could let me burn to a crisp and take Falada like he wanted.

But what did I have to lose?

Without breaking his gaze—partly to convince him of my fearlessness, partly to keep from making eye contact with a crowd of spirit spectators, who were all now watching to see if I'd soon be joining their ranks—I broke the wax seal and unfolded the parchment. In black ink, the words were carefully lettered: *This blood, given freely by Valentin de Achlev, hereby grants the bearer of this document passage into the city of Achlev, across the Wall, and through the Gates.* Beneath that, a rust-colored drop of blood had been drawn into an approximation of the three-pointed knot. With a deep breath, I pressed my fingers against the symbol and then, parchment held in both hands, stepped under the portcullis.

At first I felt nothing. But slowly the blood mark began to streak out across the page in cobwebby tendrils, disintegrating the paper into ash as it went. And it didn't stop at the end of the paper; the red lines simply twisted and coiled onto my hands. I fought the urge to scream as searing heat struck across my skin and dug, needle-like, beneath it, boring into my flesh, my bones, my blood, until the whole world was laced with pain and red heat. I closed my eyes and let it overtake me, allowing the magic to circulate inside until I was nothing but burning, molten light.

And then it was over. I took two stumbling steps and fell to my knees on the other side of the borderline with a gasp. Falada followed behind, nonchalant. If the same thing had just happened to her, she didn't show it. "Blood of the Founder," I muttered through heaving gulps of breath. "You bastard."

Zan's mouth was screwed to one side. "I told you it would be uncomfortable. The gates are spelled against foreign blood. It's an incredibly powerful magic—it gets inside you. It *tests* you. Now imagine what it might be like if you didn't have the prince's mark to shield you."

I shuddered, glancing back in sympathy at the sad lot of spirits who hadn't.

"On the bright side," he said amiably, "you only ever have to do it once, unless someone in the royal family revokes your invitation." He helped me to my feet. "The inn is this way," he said. "We've got to hurry. The sun will be up soon."

I took a faltering step forward but had to stop for fear I'd fall again. My legs were weak and unsteady. Zan grumbled impatiently and put my arm over his shoulder. "This is not how I wanted to spend my entire night."

I said icily, "By all means, go on your way and leave me and my horse to ourselves. We were doing just fine."

"Were you, now?" Zan said. "And that's why, at our introduction, you greeted me with a cudgel?"

I glared at him, wishing I still had a weapon at hand.

We went several more blocks in silence, keeping to the shadows beneath the windows of the black-timbered buildings lining either side of the street. A figure stepped out from a side alley, taller than Zan by at least a head and taller than me by two. He put down his hood, revealing a face of deep sable complexion and solemn expression.

"You shouldn't have gone past the wall alone, Zan," the man said in an exasperated rumble. "You know you can't—"

"I'm sorry, Nathaniel, but time was of the essence." Zan hastily dumped my arm from his shoulder. "I had to go as soon as I got Thackery's message. He was right, too; it *was* an Empyrean."

The man, Nathaniel, eyed me. "And this is . . . ?"

"A complication." Zan tossed him Falada's reins.

"My *name* is Emilie," I said irritatedly, turning to Nathaniel. "Your employee is greatly lacking in manners."

Nathaniel snorted to smother a laugh, while Zan went sullen.

"I'm afraid you have that the wrong way around. He is my body-guard and swordsman." Then Zan amended, "My friend, too, of course."

I shot Nathaniel a sympathetic look. "You must have your work cut out for you. I've known him less than an hour, and I already want to kill him."

"It's a taxing job," Nathaniel said.

Zan ignored us. "We'll have to house her in an inn's stables tonight. The horse, not the girl. Though she does seem to have a fondness for sleeping in stables." I glared at him. Unruffled, he continued, "I'll talk to the innkeeper about getting her something to eat and providing her with a place to sleep for a day, maybe two."

"I'm not selling you my horse," I said again.

Zan gave me a patronizing smile. "We'll talk more tomorrow."

12

It is to my great discredit that I slept so peacefully, alone in my tiny room at the inn. For those hours, with food in my belly and a pillow beneath my head, I forgot about everything. Kellan, Conrad, my mother . . . I even forgot the feel of Toris's knife at my throat and the fathomless darkness of the woods.

When I finally woke in the late afternoon, I was pleased to find that a basin of water had been laid out for me, and I knelt with reverential gratitude at the lavender-scented pool. The water was cool and wonderful. I scrubbed my skin pink and lathered up my hair with a chunk of homemade soap that smelled of mint and vanilla and rosemary.

After I was dressed, I assessed the few belongings I'd brought with me, stashed in my pockets and bodice and the pack from Falada's saddle. I took inventory: one bracelet, broken clasp. Charms: a ruby firebird, a sapphire-tailed mermaid, and a diamond-and-opal winged horse. A bloodstained square of silk fabric, two drops dark and copper red, a third so faded it was almost imperceptible. The linen parcel that contained my incomplete wedding dress. And then a vial of blood on a cord, supposedly derived from Cael, the Founder himself.

The last thing I removed from the bag was a bundle of gold-trimmed cobalt, Kellan's cloak. I rubbed the fabric between my fingers. It smelled like him, like summer-sweet grass and windswept hills and the sun setting against a wide, dusky sky. I spent the better part of an hour furiously scrubbing it clean of the bloodstains as if the effort could also erase my memory of how they got there. Soon the water was tinged brown and my hands—as well as my heart—were cracked and raw.

I took the rest of the afternoon to collect myself and gather my things, numbly placing them one by one into the safe darkness of the pack. Then I made myself stand and face my reflection in the room's cloudy mirror, letting my breath out slowly as I relaxed my features into well-practiced composure. In negotiations, my father used to say, emotions were best left in check or they could be used to your disadvantage. When I saw Zan again, my face would be as blank and unreadable as a new piece of parchment.

Before I went down to retrieve Falada and leave the sanctuary of the inn, I removed the firebird charm from the bracelet. I had no intention of selling Falada to Zan, but he *had* helped me, and I couldn't let such a debt go unpaid. I owed too much to too many, and the weight of my dues sat heavy on my shoulders. Better to not add to the sum.

The interior of the stable was dark save for thin threads of sunlight coming through the slats of the roof and the light from the door. It smelled of damp hay and old leather, so much like Kellan's stable at Greythorne that I had to swallow hard to rid myself of the lump forming again in my throat. I went from stall to stall, listening to the horses softly nicker at my passing.

I came to the end of the stable. Then I pivoted on my heel and walked the length of the building again.

Falada was gone.

When I heard the crunch of footsteps on the gravel, I didn't have to turn to look to know who it was. "You took her." It wasn't a question.

Zan said, "I don't expect you to understand."

"I understand that you saw her, you wanted her, and then *you took her.* Where is she? Sooner or later I'll find her, and—"

"You won't find her," he said. "Please know that she's safe and secure in my care. Here, I've got your payment ready. I think you'll find it very generous. More than enough to establish yourself in Achleva: secure permanent lodging, pay for food and expenses while you find suitable employment. It should last you for a couple of months at least, maybe several if you're frugal." He held out a leather purse.

"I don't want it," I said.

"You need it."

Ignoring the coin pouch, I took his other hand and thrust the firebird charm into it.

"What's this?"

"Payment for the room, and the food." I pushed past him, out of the stable and into the inn courtyard.

He grabbed my elbow. "I can't take this," he said.

I looked from the firebird to his face. The likeness to Simon was even more obvious in the daylight.

"You'll have to." I shook his hand from my arm. "This way there can be no argument that what you've done was some kind of transaction. You *stole* Falada. Remember that when you put on your silken finery and parade around on her back so all your friends can stand in awe at your great fortune." There was a bitter edge in my words. To myself I muttered, "I was wrong to trust you. You're nothing like your father."

Zan's eyes narrowed. "And *what* do you think you know about my father?"

"You're Simon Silvis's son. You wear the same signet. And how else would you have such close access to the prince that he'd provide you with stacks of blood-marked invitations to sell in the camps? You're his cousin." I lifted my chin. "You look exactly like Simon, too. That's where the similarities end, though. He was kind and you're a bastard."

"You *met* him? When? Wait!"

I had already exited the courtyard and was trying to disappear into the din on the street, just like I'd so often done back in Renalt. But Zan was not deterred. "Emilie!" he called. "Would you just *stop?*"

I did stop, but not because he told me to. Nathaniel stepped out in front of me, as impassable as Achlev's Wall. His arms were crossed in front of him like a mother about to reprimand a child, but his dour expression wasn't directed at me; he was looking at Zan.

Zan said breathlessly, "She knows my father."

"She *what?*"

"Simon."

"Simon . . . your father." He cleared his throat. "Okay . . . how?"

"She met him in Renalt before coming here." To me, Zan said, "Please, Emilie. You have to tell us how he is. We've heard all kinds of rumors . . ."

I'd made a mistake. I never should have said anything. It was a bread crumb: small and seemingly insignificant, but if I dropped too many, Toris could follow them right back to me. And then he could finish what he'd started before the Harbinger intervened.

She was here now, too, standing still among the tumult of the market. With my attention on her, she turned and walked away, toward the castle and the jutting tower behind it.

"Well?" Zan was asking. "What do you know about Simon Silvis?"

I shook myself, coming back into the moment. "Nothing. I know nothing."

"We need to find another place to have this conversation," he told Nathaniel. "Pick her up if you have to."

Nathaniel moved in but won my nastiest glare. "Don't even try," I warned.

They herded me to a side street without any prying eyes, and Nathaniel went to stand watch while Zan questioned me, pacing in front of me while I leaned, arms folded, against the brick. "It's been several weeks since we've heard from him," he said. "Simon. My father, as you so cleverly deduced. He was supposed to send word when he arrived in Renalt—he didn't. Or at least he hasn't yet. And now we've been getting all sorts of troubling reports of political unrest . . ."

Frostily, I replied, "Tell me where Falada is, and I will divulge everything you want to know."

"She's safe. And now she'll remain safe in my protection."

"It's funny how, often, when someone says they want to protect you, they actually mean they want to control you."

"It must be terrible, having people care about your well-being."

"I'm being held against my will in an empty alley of a heathen city. Obviously, that's not a problem anymore."

"Heathen city." Zan rubbed the spot just below his lip. "Because Renalt is so civilized, right? If someone so much as breathes the wrong way, you just kill them. It's all very organized, I'm told." He saw my expression darken. "Oh, that hits close to home, doesn't it?"

"Let me go. I'm not going to tell you anything—" But I was cut off midsentence by the deep clang of a bell, not far away. Zan gave a start, and when the bell tolled again, Nathaniel raced toward us from around the corner.

"Forest Gate," he said.

Zan replied, "I know." He swore.

"Is that supposed to mean something?" I asked.

"The bell at the gate tolls for only two reasons: an army is approaching, or there's royalty coming."

Ah. It seemed as if Toris, Lisette, and Conrad had finally arrived.

Nathaniel asked, "What about the king?"

"He's having one of his parties at the Stein and Flagon tonight. Find one of the captains—they'll retrieve him."

Nathaniel was already sprinting away when Zan took me by the arm. "Come on."

We were closer to the second gate than I imagined. Two quick turns and we were out among a gathering crowd. Zan and I found a place to stand along the edge of the road next to a line of thorny hedges, waiting like spectators at a spring parade.

This road was a main highway, an unbroken stretch that began beneath this gate and ran to the steps at the castle entrance. Lights had begun to go on in the windows above me, and it wasn't long before people were pouring from their houses to see what the noise was about.

Beneath the gate, which bore the marble likenesses of three towering women, the portcullis was raised, and three figures, quite small in the distance, stepped forward onto the border, all holding one of Simon's stolen invitations ahead of them.

It went much faster for them than it seemed to have gone for me. A red flash that turned to blue and then disappeared, and they were all inside, panting and heaving but otherwise no worse for wear. I strained to get a better look at the last little figure on the left, his hair shining like burnished gold.

I was overcome with anxious fear. Was Conrad all right? Was he hurt? Did the passage across the wall make him sick? Was he scared?

Two horses carrying men in formal guards' uniforms came thundering down the road from the castle, and the crowd split to receive them. "Good," Zan said under his breath, "Nathaniel got to the captain in time." I stared at him for a second—in my worry about Conrad, I'd almost forgotten he was there.

When the riders reached the gate, the tolling bell stopped its mournful call and an expectant hush settled across the uneasy city.

The two guards, having spoken to the gatekeeper, turned and reined their horses into an escort position as the three travelers remounted their own horses, the man on one and the girl and child on the other. All of them were bedraggled and stained with the marks of hard travel.

"Make way!" the castle riders called. "Make way for the princess of Renalt!"

I shuddered, feeling suddenly vulnerable, exposed. Lisette, Toris, and Conrad and their castle escorts were coming fast now, the beat of their horses' hooves resounding on Achlev's ancient cobblestone. They couldn't learn that I was here. Toris would kill me if he saw me; I was certain of it.

With mere seconds to go before they thundered past, I yanked Zan behind the hedge and threw myself into his arms, using him like a shield so that even if the branches did not hide me, his body would.

Zan stared down at me in astonished alarm as I huddled against him, using the pinpricks of blood I could feel beading up from bramble scratches to cast a feverish spell. *We are not here, we are unseen . . .*

Despite the thorns and the awkwardness of being so intimately clasped in a strange girl's arms, Zan did not attempt to disentangle himself from me until the riders were long out of sight. Slowly, I regained enough of my sense to lift my wary gaze to his. My spell waned to a whisper and died on my lips as he searched my face with a new awareness, confounded and cautious, as if I'd transformed from damsel to dragon in front of his eyes.

Zan asked quietly, "Anything you want to tell me now?"

"Yes," I answered, surprising us both.

Then, in sudden panic, I gave him a swift kick to the shin and a hard shove from the hedge and tore out the other way, too fast for him to follow.

13

I didn't sleep much that night or the next. I did drift off for a few hours on the back stoop of a tavern but was woken up by a bucketful of frigid water when the proprietor discovered me. "No place for your sort here," he said, spitting a mouthful of tobacco juice at my feet. "This is a respectable establishment."

I slogged the roads of Achlev, waiting for my clothes to dry—wishing I'd taken Zan's money and hating myself for it—and felt my hopes diminishing. I'd vowed to bring Toris down and rescue my brother, but now that I was lost in this mazelike city, I wondered if such a thing was even possible. I was helpless, without even the most basic tools for survival: food and shelter. I couldn't gain those without money, and the only way to get money was to earn it or steal it. My first attempt at picking a pocket, however, won me only a welt across my back from an old woman's cane. I quickly abandoned all ideas about a life of thievery and decided to look for work.

The problem was, I had no skill with which I could acquire employment. I could not sew or cook or clean or serve. I slowed down in front of a brothel or two, considering the possibilities, but even there I had no experience to speak of and little to recommend me, as I was over-endowed in angles and under-endowed in curves. Ultimately I decided against it, but I did wonder how long I'd have to sleep in the streets before I found myself on the brothel doorstep again, and what was the likelihood of finding patrons who were really into elbows and knees? I was still looking back at one when I stumbled into something that gave a small squeak.

"Watch it, lady!" a little girl cried, and I realized I was being glared at by three children holding hands, forming a protective ring around three round stones. Another little boy was sitting gleefully on one of the stones, having broken through their circle to claim it. The children scrambled to get to the other two, but one girl was left standing and pouting.

"Not fair," one of the girls said to the boy. "You didn't break our wall. She did."

"I'm sorry," I said. "I didn't mean to interrupt your game."

"Doesn't matter how the wall gets broken," the boy said. "You're still it."

The children reassembled themselves into a new ring as I moved past them. Their singsong chant followed me to the edge of the square.

It begins with three dead white ponies,
Then a maid, a mother, a crone,
Then upon a bed of red rosies,
Bleed three fallen kings who leave three empty thrones.

They shrieked and giggled as they battled to keep their wall intact from the invading child and protect their stony seats.

When I could no longer hear them playing, I found myself standing at the door of a shop with dark windows on a less-frequented corner of the street. Above it an apothecary's sign hung on creaking hinges. The glass was too cloudy to see into the building, but painted on the window was SAHLMA SALAZAR: HEALER, MAKER OF POTIONS. PREFERRED HERBALIST OF THE DE ACHLEV FAMILY.

My skin crawled at the sight of the place, but what other choice did I have? This was the one field in which I might actually be of some assistance, and she was associated with the royal family. It gave me a small twinge of hope, despite the apprehension digging into my stomach like the claws of a startled cat.

A bell tinkled above the door as I entered the dim building, but the white-bonneted lady behind the counter did not acknowledge me. She was already immersed in a heated conversation with a woman offering a handful of coins—Renaltan gold marks, from the look of them. "Please," the woman begged. "This is all I have. You must help us."

"And what am I to do with those worthless hunks of metal? I told you, three *Achlevan* crowns. Now go on. I've got other customers."

The woman left in tears.

Sahlma was small in stature, but she loomed over her shop like a storm cloud. The shop itself was gloomy and cluttered, with cobwebs gathering in the corners, and the smell of herbs in the air was overwhelmed by a tang of decay. "Well," she barked from beneath her bonnet, "what is it you need today?"

I stuttered, "I—I just came in to see . . . to ask . . . if you were looking for any help . . ."

"Help?" She guffawed, which sent her into a spasm of painful-sounding coughs. "No, I don't need any help. If you aren't buying anything, then you can be on your way." A man had come in behind me, and she was already waving him over.

"Wait!" I twisted my hands on the counter. "I'm really good with herbs. I know all the varieties and can make concoctions for you, and assist you in whatever you might need. And in your poor health, couldn't you use an extra pair of hands?"

She glared at me. "My health is fine." Several more hacking coughs suggested otherwise, but she continued, "Why would I pay someone else to bungle what I can do perfectly well myself?" She began taking down several herbs for the other order. I recognized them: belladonna, jimson weed, henbane. Powerful sedatives of dubious reputation, all. I tried not to think about it.

"But maybe you wouldn't even have to pay me," I continued distractedly. "I just need a place to stay and perhaps something to eat. I could work just for that."

"Well, if that's all you need, there's a whorehouse about two buildings down from here. Not one of the real discerning fancy ones, either." She looked me up and down. "I'm sure they could find *some* use for you."

The other customer's attention was on me now too, a leering smile spreading across his face as if he were pondering what those uses might be. I took a step back and tried to look busy fiddling inside my pack. I'd wait until he was gone to needle her more.

A cool gust of air brushed my arms, and I whirled around, full of dread, expecting to find the Harbinger. Instead, I saw the timid eye of a little boy peering at me from behind a door frame. A small red cap sat askew on his head, soft curls sticking out from beneath it.

"Well, hello there," I said, kneeling.

He ducked away, but I could still see his little hands. After a second, he peeked out at me again.

"Don't be afraid," I said. "I won't hurt you."

Wrapping up the man's order, Sahlma barked, "Who are you talking to now, girl?"

"The little boy," I said, standing. "He's hiding, though. Is he shy?"

She glared at me and thrust the parcel into the customer's hands. "There are no children allowed in this shop."

"He's not yours? A grandson or something? He's very sweet. Dark curls and this little red cap . . ."

The color was gone from Sahlma's face. "Get out," she said.

"But . . . I just . . ."

"Get *out*," she said again.

"No, listen. I know I can be of some help—"

"Out!" she roared.

I tripped down the steps of the apothecary, followed closely by the cloud of her wrath and the man with a bag full of sedatives. I ducked behind a nearby merchant's stall, watching as he scanned the street. When he didn't find me, he seemed to give up and move on.

Even when I stepped from my hiding place and the man was definitely gone, I couldn't shake the feeling that I was still being watched. That's when I saw the little boy again.

He was standing in the upper window of the apothecary shop, cap still sitting crookedly on his dark curls. The entire right side of his face was covered in bruises, and long purple welts were ringing the gray skin of his neck. He pressed his small hands against the window, and we regarded each other for several long minutes before he turned and disappeared.

✴

That evening I sold the mermaid charm to a woman in a market booth for a pouch of six gold coins, a mostly burnt chicken leg, and a cup of ale, only to have her laughingly steal the coin purse back an hour later while I was busy being sick into the gutter from the tainted meat. When the painful spasms of my stomach finally subsided, it was dark again. Blearily, I dragged myself to my feet and forced myself to keep going, if only to avoid the temptation to lie down somewhere and be done with it. Simon and my mother were still bound to me. While it would have been noble to say that it was their lives I was motivated to preserve, at that point I was more moved by the idea that my dying would be futile, so why bother?

I was somewhere in the tavern district, on the south side of the castle between High Gate and Forest Gate, when the prickly feeling of being observed returned. There were several times I had to stop and look around, convinced that someone was following not too far behind me.

"Who's there?" I called, but no one answered.

A few minutes later, I heard another sound, this one unmistakable: a footstep that wasn't mine, on the cobblestones behind me. It wasn't the Harbinger, either—the Harbinger never made noise.

A man streaked out from a dim alley. Before I had time to yell, he locked his arms around me.

"Come now, love," he said, wrapping his fingers around my throat. "Don't make this difficult."

It was the man from the apothecary's shop. A second man circled— I was outnumbered. "Let . . . let me . . . g-go—" I stammered, but the grip on my throat tightened, cutting off my air.

He leaned his cheek against my hair, his breath hot on my neck. "That's it," he said. "Just relax."

"Make it fast," the other whined.

He kept his right hand clamped on my neck but loosened the other, and I heard the sound of him undoing the buckle of his belt. In one fluid motion, I threw my head back against his nose and stomped hard on his foot—a method I'd seen Kellan use in sparring matches at the barracks. The man released me with a yelp, giving me enough freedom to drive my knee between the legs of the second man. That one collapsed like a puppet with severed strings, moaning on the dank alley floor.

I tried to run, but I didn't make it far. The first man grabbed my hair and used it to yank me back. He slammed his fist into my jaw, caus-ing my head to bounce off the alley wall with a sickening crack. The world was spinning now, and the single gas lamp at the mouth of the alley became a blurry streak as he picked me up just to strike me again.

"You want to do it this way, eh?" Drawing a red-smeared knife from his belt, he said, "I *was* going to be gentle," as if that was a kind-ness I no longer deserved.

"What's it like to be so disgusting that you have to beat a woman half to death before she'll notice you?" I asked.

His lip curled and he lunged with his knife, just as I hoped he would. But I was too weak and dizzy; I miscalculated his swiftness and my slowness, and instead of dodging his knife completely, I felt it glide across my ribs as I tried to dart away.

I screamed as he threw me violently down to the stones, trying even then to crawl away one-handed, my other arm wrapped around the cut in my side, which was radiating with pain. He grabbed my ankle and dragged me back. *"Bitch."*

I hurt everywhere, every organ and limb singing louder and louder in an unrelenting chorus of agony. And the blood—it was seeping between my fingers now, staining them red. All I could see was the light from the lamp and the pulsing cobweb of veins in my eyes. All I could hear was the pounding of my heartbeat and the distant sound of my name.

Emilie! Emilie!

But it wasn't my name, not really. I was not Emilie. Emilie had burned. Burned because of me. I saw her in the bobbing glow of the gas lamp, screaming as she was consumed by the Tribunal's bonfire.

No. I wasn't certain if I said it in my head or aloud as I reached my blood-soaked hand to the lantern light. *Not her.*

The man slammed me over and climbed on top of me, still fighting to get his buckle undone. His face morphed in the lantern light, rearranging his features into a more familiar configuration.

"You killed Kellan," I told Toris. "I'll kill you." Rage and anger pulled tight in my core until, suddenly, it snapped. I cried out at the flooding fire inside me. I put my bloody hands on either side of his face and let go.

His skin began to blister and crackle where my fingers left bloodied prints. He scrambled back, clawing at his cheeks and eyes as the heat spread quickly into flame and the flame blazed into a conflagration.

I felt a pair of arms lift me free of the fire, and I struggled against them.

"Emilie! It's me!" Zan said. "I won't hurt you. Stop! It's all right. It's all right."

"All right?" I echoed.

I didn't know what that meant anymore.

Nathaniel had the second man cornered. He landed hard strikes on the villain's chin and then his chest, knocking the knife from his hand. He pushed him up against the wall, arm across his windpipe, before that man's skin also started to smoke.

"Bleeding stars," Nathaniel swore, jumping back.

"You're safe now," Zan said again, hand on my cheek. "You can stop. They can't hurt you."

His words were like cool water to a fire. When I looked again, it wasn't Toris writhing on the ground with charred clothes and bubbled skin but the stranger who'd attacked me. Behind him the other man was sobbing like a child, staring at the blisters disfiguring his arms and hands.

"Take them to the gate and toss them out," Zan ordered Nathaniel. Then he added coldly, "Your welcome in this city will be revoked. Set foot inside these walls again, you'll burn. Inside first, then out, and in such pain you'll *wish* she had finished you here."

If more was said, I didn't hear it. With the last of my energy spent, I felt myself falling, my vision blurring into blackness.

14

Heavens above. Is this the girl? What happened?

We found her in the tavern district.

Put her here. Quickly. Help me get this dress off. What of her attackers?

They've been removed from Achlev.

How many?

Two. One of them had this on him.

Stars, Zan. This is coated in bloodleaf. If she got cut with this, I don't know if there's anything I can do . . .

You have to try. Do whatever it takes. We need her.

I woke to brimming sun and sweet smells in a room painted with yellow flowers.

A woman was at the hearth. "You're awake. I honestly wasn't sure it was possible." She placed a mug of steaming broth in my hands. "Drink up. You'll feel better once you've got something in your stomach."

She had a cheery, doe-like beauty—pink cheeks and soft brown eyes, framed by a wealth of chestnut hair. I guessed she was probably three or four years older than me, though she was several inches shorter. When she turned, her round profile revealed that she was with child, and pretty far along. Despite that, she moved around the room with dainty authority, unbothered by her pregnant condition. "I'm Kate," she said. "Nathaniel's wife."

"Rosemary," I said, my voice barely coming out as a whisper. I moved the mug in a small circle, watching the liquid swirl inside it.

"Zan told me your name was Emilie," she said in surprise.

"No. I mean, yes. It is Emilie. But there's rosemary in the broth."

"Right." She smiled. "I like it because it calms the nerves," she said. "I add it to everything. Not much, but a little." She gave the pot on the stove another stir, then tapped the spoon on the side.

"Zan brought me here?"

"Don't you remember?"

"I . . ." I swallowed, a vague echo in my ears: *We need her. We need her.* "No," I said. In my cup, the liquid's surface was undulating in tiny peaks and valleys, disturbed by the shaking of my hands.

Kate took pity on me. "Yes. Zan brought you here." She gently took the cup from my hands. "You're very lucky, you know. You almost didn't survive."

"I heal fast."

"Well, the cuts were one thing. I stitched you up as best I could, but I'm a seamstress, not a surgeon. I did a much better job on the tear in your cloak. And being poisoned by bloodleaf . . . it must be the Empyrea's will that you're still here. I swear, that's the only sensible explanation."

"The knife was poisoned?" My mind was whirring. Bloodleaf?

Did the bloodcloth save me? Even now, was someone else dead in my stead? "My bag," I barked suddenly, desperately. "Where is my bag? I need my bag." I tried to stand.

"No, no, no, don't get up. It's right here. See?"

I snatched it from her, and when my trembling hands couldn't get the flap open, I turned it upside down and emptied the entire thing onto her floor while Kate watched, slightly agape. Dropping to my knees, I sifted through my paltry belongings until I found the square of silk. I almost cried with relief when I saw that of the three drops, only Kellan's was faded, and less so than I remembered. The other two were still a deep, dark red.

It was easier to clean up the mess than it was to make it; my hands were already steadier. The last thing I put away was the charm bracelet, from which hung a single remaining charm, the winged horse. I held it out to Kate.

"What's this for?"

"It's for your help. Please take it, and I'll go."

Her eyebrows lifted. "I can't let you do that."

"I have to pay you somehow. I know it isn't much, but—"

"No, I mean . . . I can't let you go." She gave a frustrated grumble. "Zan will be by shortly—he's been coming about every other hour to see how you're doing. He wants to talk to you. I told him that, if by some miracle you did wake up, I'd keep you here until he came back so he could at least try. I *didn't* tell him you wouldn't punch him in the face. I think he's earned it, taking your horse like he did."

In spite of everything, I found myself smiling. "I already did hit him once," I said. "But it was more of a really hard shove."

"Did you, now? He has that effect on people. I've gotten a few over on him myself. Mostly when we were children, but still. It counts."

"That's because you've always been a bully."

I hadn't heard Zan arrive, but there he was in the doorway, leaning a shoulder against the frame.

"And where's my husband?" Kate asked. "You've got him doing your dirty work again, no doubt. If I have to clean blood out of any more of his shirts . . ."

"You know it's never *his* blood on his shirts."

"And that's supposed to make it better?"

He shrugged. "Yes, a little."

She put her hands on her hips. "I still don't like it."

"Don't worry; tonight it's nothing dangerous. He's making my excuses to the king about why I won't be attending the Petitioner's Day banquets."

"Not dangerous?" Kate snorted. "That's only 'not dangerous' because he's telling Domhnall what he wants to hear." She leaned over to me and said in a conspiratorial whisper, "Zan's not really welcomed at any courtly dealings. They used to try to get him to be involved, but he made himself a terrible nuisance and blundered everything he touched until no one could stand it anymore and they quit asking him to come. And that's really saying something, considering *Domhnall* is king."

"It was a calculated effort," Zan said. "I did it to gain the freedom I needed to get real work done, unhindered by courtly politics and the irrational whims of that very stable genius."

"Of course it was," Kate said sweetly. But Zan didn't answer; his attention had turned to me.

I did not look up as he approached me, choosing instead to stare at his boots through the escaped tendrils of my hair. On our last encounter, I'd been deliriously burning two deviant brutes half to death. The time before that, I'd dragged him into a hedge and draped myself all over him like a lovesick lunatic. At this point I could go dance a naked jig in the town square and my humiliation could not be more complete.

Still, I was intensely aware of his proximity now. Those seconds together in the rose hedge had shifted something fundamental between us, exposing a strange and unsettling connection we'd been oblivious to before. Zan came to a stop a margin closer than should have been comfortable for our limited acquaintance, as if he sensed the connection too and was now testing its borders.

Determined not to be cowed by him or my own newfound curiosity in him, I forced myself to look him full-on in the face. He reached toward my cheek but paused a mere fraction before touching my skin.

"You're not going to kick me again, are you?" he asked.

"I'm still deciding," I answered.

Accepting the possible consequences, he tucked my hair back before crooking a finger beneath my chin, moving my face gently to the side so he could survey the bruises along my cheekbone and my swollen lip.

Pursing his lips, he asked, "I know you've been through a lot, but do you feel well enough to take a walk? There's something I'd like to show you."

✳

Moving was much more difficult than I anticipated, but Zan tried to be patient, retaining his air of casual uncaring but still putting his arm around my shoulders to help me when I winced or gasped as we picked over the rough terrain. And it was rough; we left Kate's house by the back door, skirting past an old hut and a small pond where a dozen geese watched us with lazy disinterest. The environment was quite different from the center of the city. Old King Achlev had wanted to make his wall into a perfect circle, and that meant enclosing parts of the cliffs and forest and mountain.

"Where are we going?" I asked, looking up at the towering pines.

"Not long now," he replied, helping me down into a depression that must have been left by a creek on its way to the fjord, before it was dammed to make the pond.

"That's not an answer."

"Look." He parted some tall reeds and pointed to the underside of the bridge.

"I don't see—"

He moved me two feet forward, and an opening came into view. It was little more than three feet high, framed into a square by old timbers. Probably some kind of defunct culvert. "It requires a slight change of perspective to find it," he said, ducking inside and motioning me to follow.

The interior of the passage was dark and musty, smelling strongly of mold and muddy soil. "After the wall was erected, a system of canals was built under the city to irrigate the vegetation growing on the inside of the wall. As the city grew, the earliest system was no longer sufficient, so three hundred or so years ago they blocked off some of the old water lines and built newer, stronger ones. Watch your head there. When I was a kid, I spent a lot of time reading old books from the archives, and I came across the plans for the old system."

"That's what this is? Some old canal?"

"Yes. This is one of the better ones. Most are collapsed or flooded, and impassable. This way."

The passage forked, one side slanting off sharply to the right, the other carrying on straight forward. We took the right passage, which seemed to descend for a long while before angling back up and winding in a narrow circle. Then, with little warning, we stepped out into the light.

We'd come to a rocky inlet. The water lapped moodily against the shore, sheltered by an overhanging outcrop of stone. In the distant stretch across the fjord, I could see the third of Achlev's gates, topped with three crowned figures. King's Gate.

Zan was already going up the rocks, but slowly; they were slick with water and very steep. I followed him, the stitches in my side pulling painfully. From the top, he helped me onto the last big step and then up over the ledge.

We were at the base of a standalone tower, separate from the castle and taller than its turrets by half. It stood in isolation on the edge of the water, cloaked in a thatch of vine that snaked all the way to the pinnacle; it took a second glance to discern that it was, indeed, made of stone and was not a massive structure of greenery that grew tower-shaped on its own.

I toed the vine at my feet. "Is this . . . ?"

"Bloodleaf," Zan said. "Yes. Best not to get any closer. Most people won't come near here because of it."

"What is this place?"

"A monument," Zan said. "To Aren. Do you know who that is?"

I thought of Toris's surprise at the Harbinger in the Ebonwilde. He'd called her Aren. I'd been too distraught to consider it then, but was it possible that the Harbinger and the fabled queen were one and the same? "Yes. I do. She was a high mage and the queen of Renalt. She and her brothers were casting a spell when Achlev killed her . . ."

"This is the site of the spell," he said, "but in our legends it was Cael who killed Aren. They were closing a gateway between the material and spectral planes when he heard a voice from the other side, an enchanting voice that convinced him to kill his sister to stop the spell." He turned his chin up, wind whipping his hair around the cut of his patrician profile, stark against a gray sky. "Achlev was a feral mage, but his true gift was transfiguration, not healing. He used every ounce of his magic to stop Cael and save Aren, but it didn't work. Full of guilt at his failure, he constructed this tower in her memory, and then built the city and the wall to protect it."

"In all of our stories, Cael died trying to save Aren from Achlev, and the Empyrea brought him back to life to serve as her messenger."

Zan scoffed. "Do you really think that if the Empyrea was to grant immortality to one person in all of human history, she would choose the man who would someday found the Tribunal? No, if I have to blame one of the brothers for what happened that day, I'm going to go with the one who made a career of murder afterward."

In Renalt the Empyrea was both the benevolent creator of our spirits and the vengeful decider of our fates. It never occurred to me to consider how contradictory each version was to the other. I struggled to reconcile with this new idea, even as I was relieved by it. "I've never thought of it that way," I murmured. "My whole life, I just assumed . . ."

"That the Goddess supposedly responsible for making you who you are despised you for it?" Zan paused, giving me an assessing stare, and I had the distinct impression that he could see into me. Through me. Like I was little more than a glass case, with every cast-off thought and childish emotion cluttering my shelves on clear display. "It's not hard to guess why you're here, Emilie. Especially now that the princess and prince of Renalt have recounted the Tribunal's attempt to dethrone your queen. The city of Achlev has ever been a place of refuge for people targeted by that organization. Most are not endowed with any special gifts, magic or otherwise; they come simply because the mere *suspicion* of witchcraft in Renalt is enough to warrant investigation and execution. The princess seems to be one of these unfortunate few; it's obvious she has no real talent for magic, no matter what the Tribunal has insinuated." He stopped. "But you do."

I closed my eyes.

"You worked in the castle, didn't you? That's how you met Simon. And that's why you didn't want to be seen when the Princess Aurelia and Prince Conrad went by; you knew they'd probably recognize you, and that frightened you."

This was my chance. I could tell him everything. My hands were clammy, my heart pounding. Zan could bring my case to Valentin —they were cousins, after all. I could let it all out right now. My story was on the tip of my tongue. I simply had to open my mouth and speak it. I could tell him my real name, tell him about Toris's betrayal, about Conrad, Lisette . . .

Lisette. If I revealed her now, what would be done to her? She'd committed treason of the highest order, but she seemed to think she was doing the right thing, protecting Conrad and Valentin . . . from me. I remembered her bright eyes when she was ten years old, clutching my letters from Achlev's prince. She was the one who'd answered them, not me. With her golden hair and bright blue eyes, she resembled Conrad more than I did. There was a chance that, if I did confess my identity, they wouldn't believe me. I could be punished, jailed, hauled off into a gibbet just for the insinuation that Lisette was an impostor.

And if they did believe me, then Lisette could face as much or worse. Despite everything that had happened between us, I could not forget that for the last seven years, she could have borne witness to my witchcraft and didn't.

I realized Zan was watching me, waiting for a response. I swallowed and commanded my hammering heart to be still. "How are they?" I asked. "The prince and . . . the princess?"

"They've been through an ordeal, to be sure. But they rely very heavily on each other. The princess is very protective of him, and he adores her. It's almost enough to make me wish I had a sibling."

"Be glad you don't," I said, feeling an ache in my stomach that had nothing to do with the wound in my side.

"Do you?"

"A brother," I answered. "I'm afraid we didn't part on very good terms. I'm pretty sure he hates me now."

"Because you're a witch?" My eyes darted to his, and he continued. "You fled Renalt not because you were afraid of being *accused* of being a witch, like the princess. You fled because you *are* one. Twice now I've seen you use magic. You almost killed two men with nothing but blood and your bare hands."

"Are you going to have me arrested? Send me back to Renalt? Please," I said, my voice cracking. "Please don't." *I can't leave my brother here alone, even if he's safe with Lisette. Even if he hates me.*

"That's not what I brought you here for."

"Then what *did* you bring me here for?"

"Look."

He drew my attention across the wild garden and sweeping stone terraces adorning the base of the castle to a stretch of tall grass in the northwestern quadrant of the grounds, where several horses were grazing. As I watched, a mare of brilliant white broke into a gleeful gallop across the open space, head high and mane flying.

"I can't let you take her," he said. "And I'm sorry for that. But I wanted you to see her. You can come visit her whenever you like. Take the passageway. The grounds are fortified to keep intruders out, but you should be able to come and go through the tunnel without trouble. I should warn you that Princess Aurelia and Prince Conrad are installed in the west wing of the castle, so you might want to avoid that area if you prefer not to run into them." He stopped. "I'm not going to just parade Falada around, like you accused me of doing. That isn't why I needed her."

"Why, then? What good is she to you, if not for that?"

Taking a deep breath, he said, "That's just it. She does no good for me at all. And if it wasn't for you, I'd probably have already killed her."

I recoiled, dumbstruck. "What can you possibly mean?"

"Let's get out of this wind," he said, "and I'll tell you."

15

The storm came on quickly. In the minutes it took for us to walk from the tower and across the terraces, the sky outside of Achlev had turned from gray to slate to billowing black. The clouds could not cross the barrier, but the wind did; as Zan led me up to the top of the castle wall, I lost the scarf that covered my hair and now the tendrils were whipping my face and arms like lashes.

We took shelter in an empty lookout enclosure just as a flash of lightning streaked across the sky and struck the outstretched hand of one of the marble kings at King's Gate. In an instant the bolt shot through the statue and into the wall, splitting into a million tiny streaks of blue-white light that ricocheted across the invisible barrier above the stone, crossing and recrossing one another as they circled the city in a cylinder of light that led straight up into the sky.

"How is this possible? How was it done?" I asked breathlessly.

"Blood and sacrifice," Zan answered. "As it is with all power." Raggedly, he said, "This is why Falada is important."

"You want to *kill* her . . . because of wind?"

"Yes. No. I mean . . . not exactly. Six weeks ago we would have been watching the storm out there with the sun beaming down on us and blue sky above."

"What changed?"

"Simon Silvis," he said, "my *father,* is the only known blood mage of real power left in Achleva. Before he left to attend the princess on her journey, he had been worried for a while that there was a plot in the works against the kingdom and wanted to go investigate some of his suspicions on his way to Renalt, taking a longer route that ran up the coast, giving him time to do some digging as he went. The king had been adamantly against such a journey before, so when Simon got the go-ahead this time, he left in hurry. He was supposed to send word when he arrived safely, but he never did. I wasn't sure that he had even made it there in one piece until you told me so."

"Have you heard anything else?" I asked intently. "Anything at all about him, or the queen, or the state of Renalt?"

"Not much more than what the princess herself relayed. Just that he's being held in Syric with the queen, as political prisoners of the Tribunal. I'm relieved that he's unharmed, out of danger . . . but because he's not *here,* we are not. Several days ago we woke up to frost in Achlev. It was on our windows, encrusting the leaves and trees. Everything sparkled."

"Frost? What's so dangerous about—"

"It was the first time since the wall went up that the temperature within Achlev had ever fallen below freezing. It was the most beautiful and troubling thing I had ever seen. Two days after that, we woke up to wind." He leaned against the battlements, facing the wind. "The changes seemed to have no correlation except one: on each of the nights before these climate shifts, a horse was found slaughtered in the streets. Different ages, different owners, but Empyreans both times."

"I don't understand."

"Do you know what ley lines are?"

I shook my head. I'd seen them mentioned, once or twice, in the scraps I collected over the years, but I'd never found any substantial description or definition.

"The old writings state that when the Empyrea left her home among the stars and gave up her wings to run free across the land for one night, the paths she ran were lit with her white fire, and even after she returned to her place in the sky, the fire remained and became the ley lines. They are, essentially, rivers of energy.

"When Achlev built his wall, he harnessed those rivers of energy and rerouted them into a perfect circle, then pinned them there by erecting three gates. Each of the three gates was spelled with three drops of blood from three symbolic donors, and each of the spells was sealed and rendered indestructible with the donors' eventual deaths. High Gate—"

"Three white horses."

He nodded. "Forest Gate: a maid, a mother, and a crone. And King's Gate: three of royal Achlevan blood."

I remembered the children's rhyme I'd heard in the square. *It begins with three dead white ponies . . .*

"You've seen what the wall does—it doesn't just repel the energy that comes up against it, it absorbs it. Now, imagine the power of every storm, every thorn, every marauding invader for five hundred years, still carried inside the wall. What happens when such a wall comes down?"

The breath came out of me in a rush. "Cataclysm."

"Annihilation. Likely, the entire city would be leveled. There would be casualties—death on an unthinkable scale." His eyes were dark. "And someone who knows how the wall went up is now going to a very great effort to bring it down, using sacrificial stand-ins for the figures that helped erect it."

It couldn't be Toris, I thought—he was busy at the time, whistling irritating folk songs and plotting my demise.

Zan let out a slow breath. "The original spells were each done in ten-day stretches over the course of a month, in concert with the moon's phases, beginning with a new moon and ending with a black moon. The gates can be brought down only by undoing the spells the same way, beginning with a new moon and ending with a black moon." He cleared his throat. "*This* month began with a new moon and ends with a black moon. Only one more Empyrean sacrifice is needed to destroy the seal at High Gate, and if my calculations are correct, it must be done before the tenth day of the waxing moon cycle."

I stepped back. "That gives you two days. That's why you wanted Falada. So that she wouldn't fall into the hands of the person trying to break the spells."

"This whole thing would have been much easier if you'd just sold her to me like I wanted."

"But then you wouldn't have known about my . . . my . . . *ability.*" It wasn't the right word, but *magic* still felt unnatural and shameful somehow. "That's why you are telling me all this. Why you showed me Falada and the passage, why you haven't just put her down to keep someone else from doing it for you. You need blood magic to fix the damage that's already been done, maybe even find out who is doing it, and with Simon gone . . ."

"There's only you. When you cast that spell in the hedge, I felt hope—real hope—for the first time since that frosty morning eight days ago. I scoured the city looking for you afterward, because you're right. We *need* you. Black moons are relatively rare—only happening every few years. If you and I can keep the next sequential sacrifice from being completed on the timeline, it will be a while before another black moon enables them to try again. Enough time to find and punish the perpetrator and undo whatever damage he's done."

"But . . . but . . ." I sputtered, "surely there are more people who can do this than just me."

"There could be. But after the demise of the Assembly, those who have the talent for blood magic don't know they do, or deliberately choose not to practice." He took my hand and turned it over, revealing the wealth of tiny cuts in various stages of healing. "I know it's painful. I wouldn't ask you—or anyone—to do it if I weren't so afraid of what will happen to my people if the wall goes down." He placed his other hand on top of mine, obscuring the cuts from view. "It isn't an easy gift you have, even here in Achleva. But it *is* a gift. Think what you can do, how many lives you can save."

The last time I was told I'd been given a gift, Emilie was burning to death on the stake. I stared at his hands on mine. "I've never been taught or trained. You saw what I did to those men. I don't know how to control it. What you're asking . . . it could be dangerous. I could make things worse."

His gaze was intent. "You could have killed them both—no one would have blamed you—but you let them live."

"I stopped only because you shook me out of it. There have been other times when I thought I was doing something good, only to find out later that what I'd done had . . . had hurt other people. Innocent people."

"I'll be with you every step of the way this time, too."

"And what if you're the one I hurt? What if you *die?*"

He stifled a snort, as if the idea that I could be dangerous was inherently funny. "If I die, then I die. It's a risk I'm willing to take to keep that wall standing and the people inside it safe." His mouth quirked to the side. "I would like to add that if I don't *have* to die, I'd prefer not to."

"I make no promises." I looked to the sky and shook my head. "Why does this great responsibility fall to you? Should not the king and prince be involved?"

"The king doesn't want to hear problems, only praise. And the prince . . ." He looked into the distance. "The prince is a coward. Spends all his time hiding from the world, too feeble and ineffectual to be of any real use to anybody."

Simon had spoken so highly of Valentin, Zan's critique seemed especially sharp. "Do you hate him so much?"

Zan's eyes softened, just a little. "I don't hate him, not really. He means well. He's just weak."

I sighed. I was caving. "I'd need to see whatever records you have of the original spells, just to give me somewhere to start."

"I'll get you to the castle library as soon as I can arrange it. I swear to you, if you help me do this, I will return the favor to you tenfold. Whatever you wish. I will find your family in Renalt, and I will retrieve them on a galleon ship and bring them here to be regaled with tales of your heroism. If you want your weight in gold, I will have it . . . melted into a sculpture of your likeness, with opals for eyes, rolled into the top of the eye sockets. Yes, just like that." Quieter, he said. "Whatever you ask. Please."

He was still holding my hand.

"And if all I wanted was to tell you something secret, something important, and have you believe me, would you do that, too? Could you promise me?" I imagined how that conversation would go: *Hello, Zan. Surprise! I'm the real Renaltan princess. Please don't execute Lisette; she only committed a little bit of treason.*

Slowly, he said, "Yes. I think I could."

If I meant to combat Toris and save my family's rule, I'd need enough clout in Achleva to convince them to join me in my fight against the Tribunal. This could be my best—perhaps *only*—way to acquire it.

"All right," I said. "I'll help you."

✳

That night, after Kate and Nathaniel were asleep, I donned Kellan's blue cloak and crept out, retracing the steps to Zan's passage. The storm had dashed itself to pieces on Achlev's invisible barrier, and when I broke from the tunnel onto the shore, the still fjord and sky were both a glittering cauldron of stars, one above and one below, making it hard to say which was reflecting the other. The castle windows were dark, and as I approached the western side, I wondered if any of them belonged to my brother. I knew he'd be long asleep, but I looked up wistfully, hoping to catch a glimpse of him.

I crept across the quiet terrace gardens and into the midnight fields on the other side. Falada whinnied at me as I approached, and I patted her head fondly. "Hello, my sweet," I said, mimicking the way Kellan used to speak to her. "You thought I forgot about you, didn't you? But how could I forget such a pretty horse as you?"

She nickered in reply, and I ran one hand down her sleek face while I pressed my nails into a half-healed cut on the other, wincing as it reopened and let out a tiny bead of blood. "I don't know what I'm doing," I confessed to her as I let three small drops fall onto her forehead. "But I need to practice, and this seems like a good place to start." I placed my hand over the blood and closed my eyes, searching inside myself; I knew the feel of magic well enough now to recognize its presence, like a constant low heat radiating from somewhere inside me. In order to access and direct it, however, I had to discover the source of it—I had to find the coals.

After several fruitless minutes, I felt my frustration growing. "What am I thinking?" I asked aloud. "How am I going to help Zan if I can't even do this?"

She gave a placid whinny, as if providing me with an obvious and sensible answer. "I'm very sorry, Falada. I'm not Kellan. I don't speak your language." I reached into my pocket and removed the bloodcloth.

His faded drop of blood seemed darker somehow—a trick of the light. When I touched it, sadness welled up in my center, pushing into the dark corners inside me; I could feel it in my every cell, from my crown to toes and into my fingertips.

I closed my eyes and placed my hand on Falada again, this time focusing the power with words. *"Tu es autem nox atra." Where there is white, they'll see only night.* Then I opened my eyes.

In Falada's place stood a night-black mare. It was a rough illusion; if I squinted just the right way, I could see her true color layered underneath. But anyone passing by would never look twice. The relief I felt was immediate and immense; Falada would come to no harm now that no one could tell that she had ever been an Empyrean.

I brushed her gleaming black coat for a while, whispering sweet things to her and periodically slipping her pieces of the carrot I'd pocketed from dinner at Kate and Nathaniel's table. She kept looking over my shoulder, as if waiting for someone.

"I know," I said. "I miss him too."

But she wasn't anticipating Kellan; she was watching the Harbinger, who was standing in the circle of bloodleaf with her back to me, facing the base of the tower.

When I ventured into the perimeter of the creeping bloodleaf vine, my shoe snagged on one of the twisting tendrils and it snapped, oozing a viscous, black-red sap onto my foot and hem. I brushed it furiously away, unsure of whether the poison could be absorbed through the skin or if it had to be ingested or enter the body through a wound to work its evil. I went forward with extra care, though each step crushed more of the red-shot leaves and left behind a bloody stain in the shape of my footprint.

Bloodleaf was a ground-cover vine, but here it had coiled into the stones and climbed to the highest point of the tower. There was no door—or if there was, it was impossible to find beneath the thick tangle of leaves. It must have been growing there for a very long time, because the new growth of the vine was laid over a brittle skeleton cage of long-dead shoots.

I picked my way to the ledge overlooking the fjord, where I experienced a familiar pricking on the back of my neck, starting at the nape and running down to the tops of my shoulders. The Harbinger was still facing the tower, staring up at the spire.

I took a step toward her. "What do you want from me? Why have you brought me here? How does Toris know you?" I gulped. "You used to show yourself only when someone was about to die. Is that still true? Is someone going to die?"

She was stock-still, save for the drag of her hair in an invisible wind, blowing in the opposite direction of the cold gust at my back.

"Aren?" I asked, trying her name aloud for the first time. She turned at the sound of it, and I had to stifle a scream.

It wasn't the Harbinger at all but the spirit of another woman entirely, one whose visage was so bloodied and broken as to be rendered completely unrecognizable. She gave me a long, assessing stare, then shambled on oddly angled bones straight into the bloodleaf thicket and disappeared, as if she'd dissolved into the tower itself.

16

"You should have seen it," Kate said, laughing as we walked the bustling market district the next morning. "Nathaniel looked like a big startled bear, standing there staring at his empty hands, the fish lifted right out of his grasp and up into the trees above him."

She'd invited me to come along while she delivered finished sewing commissions to customers closer to the center of the city, and had spent the entire early morning animatedly recounting the story of how she and Nathaniel met. Though I still felt shy around her, I was rapt. "*That's* when you fell in love with him? When a little boy hooked his fish and pulled it up into a tree?"

"Well, not at that *exact* moment," she replied amiably. "Nathaniel chased the thief back to his home, hollering the entire way. He was all set to box the boy's ears, too, when he caught him, but that's when he saw the family waiting for him; a mother was bedridden and sick, and there were two younger siblings who'd been without food for days. Needless to say, Nathaniel and I did not retrieve the stolen fish. It was cold beans for us that night."

"So that was it, then. It was when he gave your dinner away."

She pursed her lips and shook her head. "Not then either, really. But after that, we stopped at that house every time we passed, leaving baskets full of fish on the doorstep. Also milk, cheese, bread . . . Nathaniel paid for all of it with his own wages. He did it for weeks, until the mother was well again and could go back into the village for work. And somewhere along the line, back and forth between my fiancé's holdings and my family home, I fell in love with Nathaniel. My escort. My fiancé's best worker, his 'most valuable asset.' I was the daughter of an Achlevan lord, and Nathaniel was the son of a traveling swordsmith. Our paths never should have crossed. But once I *knew* him, I wanted him, and I decided I'd do whatever was necessary to keep him. If that meant leaving my old life behind—so be it. So one day, on my way to my fiancé's, I asked him to take me to the nearest Empyrean sanctorium and marry me instead." She smiled at the memory. "We just walked away from our old lives and never looked back. We came here, and Nathaniel started working with Zan while I took on mending and sewing projects to help us get by. And now this." She smiled blissfully down at her round stomach. "This isn't the life I imagined for myself as a little girl. It's so much better."

"How did your fiancé react?"

"With great relief, actually. I liked him very much—it's hard *not* to like him—but there was never anything more than friendship between us. The union would have been a savvy one, in terms of position and property, but I'm afraid Dedrick would have found matrimony incredibly tedious. He enjoys conquest. Commitment? Not so much." She laughed fondly. "We're both better off. We exchanged a couple of letters after I left, and he said as much himself."

"And you haven't seen your family once since then?"

"Can't say it's much of a loss." She played with the end of her braid as we walked. "The only one I miss is my mother. She and I were close."

After Kate delivered her last project, we walked for a while among the spice vendors. Strings of garlic cloves and garlands of thyme and rosemary sprigs draped across their booths like necklaces on a fine lady. "It's Petitioner's Day," Kate said. "The king gives audience to his people in public court once every month or so, hearing grievances, delivering sentences, conveying proclamations. We'll have to hurry. Zan said to have you back by the midafternoon. That'll be harder to do once the trials begin."

We'd come to the main square, which was swarming with people. Several men were taking seats on the platform constructed at the foot of the immense castle steps. "Are those the lords?"

"Yes. See that short, round one in the purple brocade? That is Baron Ingram. And the one with the silver hair? Castillion. To his left is Ramos. Then there is Achebe. And over there is Lim, and—" She stopped before naming the young man on the farthest end. He was blandly handsome, with a charming smile on his face.

"Who is that?" I asked.

"The fiancé I told you about? That's him. Dedrick Corvalis."

On the high platform, the king was in place upon the heavy velvet chair that had been dragged out to serve as his throne. Far behind him I could make out the shining waterfall of golden hair that could be nobody but Lisette. Beside her sat Conrad, looking every bit a prince. He was wearing a trim white coat with gold buttons meant to look like medals. His back was straight, his hands folded tightly in his lap. I could tell he was trying desperately to keep from squirming. I felt a pang; he needed a toy to fiddle with, like the ones I used to give him to help him stay calm and alleviate his distress.

Toris loomed over them both, dressed like a Renaltan lieutenant. There was a bitter taste on my tongue; it was Kellan's spare uniform he wore, missing only the cloak. I wondered if he'd stolen Kellan's name as well. Hearing him referred to as *Lieutenant Greythorne* might be more than I could take.

To Kate, I asked, "And which one is Prince Valentin?"

She shot me a sidelong glance. "None of them. He doesn't come to these things. He's never liked being in front of a crowd."

It seemed a common trait among princes, I mused. But at least Conrad was out here *trying* to do his duty.

The king rose. "Good people," he began, his teeth stark white against his ruddy skin. "It is written in our laws and traditions that the king must regularly hold audience with his people so that you may bring your grievances and lay them before him to mediate and so that he may hear the charges against imprisoned accused and grant fair judgment upon them. Today is that day. Come, petitioners. Speak, and your beloved king will hear you."

Kate snorted and said under her breath, "He thinks if he tells everyone enough times that they love him, it must be true. I'm surprised he hasn't issued a decree about it yet. Stars above, he is the worst kind of idiot."

"What kind of idiot is the worst kind?" I asked.

"The kind whose wholehearted, foundational belief is that he's a genius." She tipped her head toward a nearby wall where Domhnall's notices were tacked one on top of another, several layers deep. I squinted to read the most recent of them:

It is hereby decreed that the third day of the third week of each month, the Castle de Achlev will be opened to Lords and Citizens wishing to express their love and thanks to King Domhnall de Achlev, whose tireless efforts on Achleva's behalf have led to increased prosperity, wealth, and happiness among all inhabitants . . .

"The worst part is," Kate continued, "that he's too stupid to know when he's being manipulated. The lords fawn over him, reinforcing his delusions of grandeur, and he signs any law they put in front of him. Like this, see?" She pointed to the stand, where a young man's case was being heard. "That's a lord's nephew. He was caught doing something unspeakable, but his family is wealthy. Watch."

As the vile details of his charges were being read, the young man remained unperturbed. When it was finished, a woman stepped forward. "I am Sahlma Salazar, a royally sanctioned healer here in Achleva. On request of this man's family, I have done a full review of his health and have found it to be woefully compromised." She gave a hard, racking cough; it seemed her own health was also woefully compromised. "I regret to inform the king that the subject is too ill to stand trial at this time and recommend that he be committed to the care of his family until his health has returned."

"Which will be never, of course," Kate said under her breath. "A year or two ago, a real petition went before the king, asking that he grant sick, imprisoned criminals access to healers. It was meant to save the lives of the poor, who were dying before they could come to trial for trivial crimes—stealing bread, inability to pay a landlord, that sort of thing. Domhnall issued one of his glorious decrees just as he was asked, but with the addendum that the prisoner must provide payment for the healer. And so *this* is what we ended up with: the poor still can't afford to be treated for their illnesses and they still die, but now the wealthy can buy their way out of crimes. All they have to do is pay a healer to give false testimony and then pay Domhnall to accept it."

We moved on through the crowd while the king agreed to Sahlma's recommendation, and two more cases were pleaded and dismissed before we got halfway across the square. A third defendant was on the stage now, shuffling forward with irons on his wrists and ankles.

"I know that man," I said, surprised. "He was the one who brought Zan to me in the traveler's camps."

"Raymond Thackery," said the king, "you have been accused of forging royal documents and using them to smuggle the uninvited across the wall, thus sullying our great city with the worst of the undesirable: vagrants, beggars, whores—"

Thackery scoffed. "Since when did you have a problem with whores, Majesty?"

The king's face turned from red to purple. "Do you deny these charges, Mr. Thackery?"

"I do indeed," Thackery said. "If they was not born here or invited by royalty, they would not have got in, simple as that. *Thus*"— he grinned at borrowing the king's own word—"it ain't smugglin'."

"Then please, Mr. Thackery, tell us which person of royal lineage is unlawfully providing you with these invitations."

"Lots of possibilities, right? I bet you've got little bastards crawlin' all over the city, haven't ye? But no, I won't give ye a name. What I'm doin' ain't unlawful." He rolled from his heels to his toes and back again with an air of pride. "And the identities of my business associates is confidential. You know better'n most, I never outed you for all those opium deliveries, now, did I?" His grin widened.

"I will hear no more!" the king roared. "How dare you level these false accusations at me?"

"False accusations, Majesty?" Raymond did not seem to understand the trouble he was in. Or if he did, he'd given himself over to his fate and was determined to cause as much chaos as possible. "Facts is facts. Wishin' 'em false and declarin' 'em fake don't make it so." He raised his hand. "I swear, if you let me go, I won't tell 'em about the pantsless parties you host once a month at the Stein and Flagon, either."

The king spat out, "Raymond Thackery, you are hereby condemned: forty days in the gibbets for your treacherous falsehoods." He seemed to have forgotten all about the smuggling charge. To the guards, he said, "Take him."

"Forty days? My ol' friend Gilroy got fifty! Come on, you gotta at least give me as much as him!"

Under her breath, Kate said, "Most don't last ten."

I stopped to watch, mesmerized and horrified as they gagged Thackery and dragged him to a waiting cage of iron at the wall. They clapped him in, one guard attaching the gibbet to a chain while another, waiting above on the parapet, cranked a pulley and the cage began to rise.

I hoped, for his sake, that Ray did not end up like Gilroy. To die in the gibbets would be terrible; to have your spirit trapped there with your moldering remains would be a misery almost unfathomable.

I never thought I'd view the Tribunal's executions — hangings, beheadings, burnings — as merciful.

17

When we returned, Zan was waiting impatiently, shifting from foot to foot on Kate's doorstep. "You're late," he said crossly.

"Not true," Kate said, "and you know it." Hands on her hips, she added, "Did you do what I asked?"

He gave an impertinent shrug and a half nod.

Delighted, Kate grabbed my hand and pulled me down the walk. "This way," she said.

We didn't have to go far; Kate led me to the hut behind her house, the one next to the goose pond. We waited while Zan worked the lock of the hut with a rusty key, and when the door finally opened, it did so with a groan.

"Zan, you were supposed to *clean* it first," Kate said, swiping her finger across a dirty table.

"I did."

Kate pursed her lips. "I suppose this is what I get for assuming cleaning is something you'd know how to do." She turned to me. "Do you like it? I know it's small—I've only ever used it as an extra place to store my dried herbs and extra bottles of tonics and preserves.

I'm sorry it's such a mess—that's what we get for letting Zan draw here unsupervised—but it's not *terrible,* right?"

It was dim, the only light coming from one grimy back window. There was a stone fireplace with a hook for a kettle, a small table and rickety chair. The walls were lined with shelves, mostly containing rows of colored bottles and jars of herbs, but two or three were completely crammed with papers and pencils and charcoal sticks of varying lengths. I lifted a sheet of paper from a stack and had to turn it twice to make sense of it. At first glance it looked like a mess of furious black charcoal marks zigging and zagging in no meaningful pattern. But as I looked at it more closely, an image began to emerge from the chaos. It was a detailed study of a bird's wing, I realized, but it was so unlike the fussy, meticulous renderings that populated books and paintings that I wondered if I'd ever actually *seen* a bird before. This was less a catalogue of traits—feather, beak, bone, breast—and more an encapsulation of all the joy and terror of flight. It was breathtaking.

The paper was tugged out of my hands mid-stare. Zan added it to a stack he was hastily trying to straighten before giving up and roughly shoving it out of sight. Sheepishly, he said, "Just make a pile in the corner there. I'll come collect everything later."

I turned back to the sparsely equipped room. "I love everything about this," I said happily as I lowered myself onto the single cot set up in the corner. It creaked mightily in protest. "But I have no money to pay rent."

Zan started to say something, but Kate gave him a pointed glare before smiling sweetly at me. "No rent is needed. Zan will cover it with the money he owes you for borrowing your horse. Won't you, Zan?"

He gave a tightlipped nod. "Of course."

"And he's going to pay you a wage," Kate added.

"Yes, but not until after—"

"A daily wage. With a bonus when the work is done."

I tilted my head. "A gold statue in my likeness, I was told."

"It will be erected in the town square the next day," Zan said, beleaguered. "On my honor."

"Don't let him sculpt it himself," Kate said. "His drawings are all right if you know what you're looking at first, but his sculptures . . ." She cringed and shook her head.

"Can we go now?" Zan said, sounding snippy.

Kate had already grabbed a broom. "Would you, please? It looks like I have some work to do."

✦

"Were all those drawings really yours?" I asked as Zan helped me down into the culvert. "You don't look like an artist."

He gave me a sideways glance. "You don't look like a blood mage, and yet . . ." Inside the passage now, Zan was setting the pace, which could only be called a meander. "I got very sick when I was a child, had to spend a lot of time indoors; my mother started me drawing to stave off boredom. But I got sicker. Even lost my eyesight for a while. Shortly after that, I lost my mother."

"I'm sorry," I said. "Was she sick too?"

"Sick of caring for me, maybe." He paused, trying to be delicate, but I knew what he was trying to say. "I was ill constantly. It took a toll. Don't look at me like that. It was a long time ago." He waved me forward at the fork. "This way now."

Instead of taking the turn out toward the tower, we continued straight, up a slightly ascending slope. He maintained his unhurried pace.

"You don't have to go so slow for me today," I said. "I heal very quickly." I put a hand to my injured side. "I hardly feel it anymore."

"Who said I was going slow for you?" he asked.

The new alley came to an abrupt end beneath a square drawn in dim light. A trapdoor. Zan gave it a tug, and the hatch swung down, a frayed rope ladder along with it. He went up first and then steadied me as I climbed after him.

I wanted to ask him more about his drawings, but he put his finger to his lips as a warning to keep quiet while he reset the door and the ladder. We were in a cellar, surrounded on all sides by barrels of ale and shelves lined with bottles of wine. Outside the cellar room, sad cries echoed around the stone chambers. "The dungeon is that way," he said quietly, lips close to my ear. "It always sounds like this on Petitioner's Day." He cast his eyes around the corner. "It's clear. Let's go."

The grandiosity of the castle did not end at its façade; the interior was just as intricately decorated, if not more. Polished timber buttresses soared into vaulted ceilings decorated with intricate floral reliefs. Everything was painstakingly carved and painted with rich, heady colors. Gold, burgundy, lapis, purple . . . it was hard to tear my eyes away.

There was a distant rumble of voices and music from somewhere in the heart of the castle—the Petitioner's Day banquet was being prepared, Zan said—but the halls were largely empty. When a servant, on his way to some task or another, did hasten past, Zan ducked into a pocket of shadows and pulled me in with him before we could be seen. "Why are you sneaking around?" I hissed. "Isn't this your home?"

When the coast was clear, he replied, "I find it advantageous to keep my comings and goings to myself; there are too many people who think they know better than I how I should use my time."

I understood that notion all too well. I'd spent my whole life doing the same.

The library, when we finally came to it, was an enormous circular room, two stories high, with a sweeping balcony on the top level. The tiles beneath our feet were black-and-white marble, and dangling from the pinnacle of the ceiling was a chandelier of crystal stars that clinked and turned in a slow orbit around a shimmering blown-glass moon.

And there were books. Everywhere, books.

"Blood of the Founder," I breathed. "This is incredible."

"You don't have libraries in Renalt?"

"Not like this," I said. "There's only one book they want us to worry about: the Founder's Book of Commands."

"Explains why Prince Conrad loves this room so much. He spends much of his free time here. Drags his sister with him, too. This afternoon I wasn't sure they'd leave in time for me to bring you today."

"Oh?" I said, trying not to sound overly interested. "And what books did he want to look at?"

"Books on pirates, treasure hunts. Things like that."

My feelings were all mixed up: I wasn't sure if I should be happy that Conrad was reading about pirates and that Lisette was taking good care of him or jealous that she was doing so at my expense. "You were with them?"

"Some of the afternoon, before they were called away to watch the Petitioner's Day spectacle. I know you're wary of Aurelia, Emilie, and I respect your decision to keep your presence here a secret, but I don't think you have anything to fear. She seems lovely."

I immediately imagined him drawing her with those decisive charcoal strokes, to commit her beauty to his memory. I'm ashamed to say that the rush of renewed distaste I had for Lisette at that moment had little to do with Conrad. "I'm sure it looks that way," I said curtly, "but looks can be deceiving, can't they?"

"You tell me," he said, but before I could ask him what he meant, he turned lazily on his heel and I had no choice but to follow him. He led me to a sheltered corner of the library, where a cushioned window seat beckoned, a pile of books beside it.

"I made good use of my time this morning."

Vitesio's *Compendium de Magia*. Wilstine's *Essays on Blood Magic Theory*. There was even an anthology on the uses of feral magic for increasing crop yields—soybeans included—alongside dozens of other texts and histories, all in pristine condition.

"I may cry," I said, reverently touching the bindings.

"Please don't," Zan said. "Many of those books were brought here after the Assembly of Mages was dismantled. They're very valuable. I don't want tears all over them, wrinkling the pages and running the ink. You can find references to Achlev's spells here"—he lifted a book and placed it in a new pile—"here, and here. I'm still trying to find his original writings, but you can use these to get started."

Zan left me there to immerse myself in the materials while he went off on his errand. I settled myself into cushions with the volumes on my lap, eager to read from books left uncensored. But I had turned only to the first page when I heard voices nearby.

"Do hurry," a girl said. "The banquet will begin soon, and we can't be late. It's just a toy—is it really that important? And are you certain you left it here, and not in the Great Hall?"

"I know it was in here. I had it by the window."

My eyes tracked to the other side of the seat. Sure enough, a small object was resting there: a metal figurine with shifting pieces, small enough to hide in the palm of a hand. I knew it immediately; I'd used it as a prize for one of the seek-and-find games I played with Conrad, something to help him sit still and calm during the most tedious of his princely tasks. I didn't know he still possessed it, much less that he had carried it with him all the way from Renalt—I'd never seen him take it out during the journey, not once. But there it sat on the library seat, left behind mid-transformation, halfway between a hound and a hare.

I grabbed it and scrambled to my feet, but it was too late. Conrad had turned the corner and was blinking at me with round, saucer-shaped eyes. We regarded each other for a heavy minute before I slowly turned the remaining pieces—*click, twist, click*—and handed it back to him, a fully formed hare. He took it soundlessly.

"Well?" Lisette asked from the other side of the library. "Did you find it?"

I waited, heart pounding, for his response. With one word he could condemn me.

Finally, he said over his shoulder, "Yes, I've got it. I'm coming."

I peered through a bookshelf as he bounded back to Lisette. She ruffled his hair. "You'd lose your mind if it weren't locked up in that silly head of yours," she said, smiling as they left together.

He didn't look back.

✳

That night, beneath the last waxing crescent before the first quarter, I snuck back to the castle grounds and over to the west side. If Conrad's bedroom was in this wing, he'd have a decent view of these gardens from his window. I pulled the ribbon from my hair—blue, one of Kate's hand-me-downs—and knotted it tightly around a branch of a rosebush. Then I dropped to my knees and dug a small hole in the dirt just below it, praying that he remembered our old game. *Yellow for up, blue for down, red for north, green for south . . .*

When the hole was big enough, I dropped the winged-horse charm in and covered it up. I hoped it was enough to convey my message:

I'm right here, little brother. I didn't abandon you. Don't be afraid.

18

As darkness fell the next day, Zan met me at my hut. He had a sack on his back and a lantern in hand; I came with nothing but a few scribbled notes and my fluttering heart. "I got what you asked for from Falada, and saw what you did for her," he said. "She's unrecognizable."

"I needed to practice. Seemed like a good place to start."

"Do you think you're ready for this?"

"Not at all," I replied. "But do I have another choice?"

"Not at all," he echoed with a coy smile.

Tonight was the night. We were going to strengthen High Gate by installing Falada as a symbolic replacement for one of the Empyreans that had already been lost. Using the records of how the original rituals were done, I had pieced together a new spell that would bandage the hemorrhaging seal. I would have liked more time, but tonight was the tenth day of the month. The blood mage doing this would have to act now or not at all.

We hiked through the heavy woods along the old creek bed until we came to the foot of the wall. "There are some stairs over here somewhere," he said, walking alongside the stone. "Nobody uses them. Here."

Zan was right; there was a very narrow staircase, no more than two feet wide, that blended into the wall when viewed from the base. He started up them first, taking them one at a time.

I was beginning to feel the anxiety creep in. What if I was wrong? What if I couldn't do what needed to be done after all? I wanted to hurry, to get on with it, but I was stuck behind Zan on the stairs, and he, strangely enough, appeared to be in no rush. "You seem to know a lot of hidden avenues," I commented.

"I spend much of my time figuring out how to avoid human interaction. I explore a lot."

"That's hard to believe," I said dryly. "You have such a way with people."

At the top, the wall was six feet across, the flat width of the walk enclosed by battlements. There were wisps of ancient shades at the crenels, soldiers launching phantom arrows into a phantom army below. I tried not to step on any of the faint spirits littering the walk as we followed the wall north through the steepest ascent. We stopped often for Zan to complain that I was going too fast and that I might reopen the wound in my side—concerned, of course, because he wanted me to bleed only when necessary.

The far eastern stretch of the wall was built right into the mountainside, and the trees thinned as the wall climbed, built no longer on soil but on solid bedrock. The moon was showing through high clouds, incised down the center, a perfect half-cut of dark and light. A low rumble began to grow, and I felt a soft vibration in the stone beneath my feet.

"What's that sound?" I asked.

"Take a look for yourself." He leaned over the edge of the inside battlement and pointed down.

For a twenty-foot stretch, the wall lined up perfectly with the sheer cliff's edge to create a dizzying height. Directly below us a torrent of water was roaring down the side of the rock and disappearing into the dark swath of woods at the base. The soft lights of the city twinkled beyond. The only thing that stood taller than us was the bleak and lonesome tower. I felt my heart quicken.

"Achlev knew that building the wall would keep out the rain, but he didn't want to completely deprive us of fresh runoff. And the gates had to remain the only entrances, so . . . he bored into the rock itself. Holes large enough to let the water through but too small to compromise the sturdiness of the mountain or allow for human trespassers to get by. So, what do you think?"

We'd decided it was too dangerous to do such a big spell under High Gate itself, with so many people around, and I suggested that we use the portion of the wall least likely to have any witnesses. But now, looking down from the harrowing height, I wondered if I would have been better off braving an audience.

I gulped and nodded. "It will have to do."

Zan shrugged off his pack and took out the ingredients for the spell: chalk. A bowl. A lantern. And last, a lock of Falada's mane, silver-white again now that it had been excised from the rest of her and my spell of disguise.

Zan took up the chalk and began drawing the three-pointed knot—a triquetra, I now knew, courtesy of the complete *Compendium*—on the stone with a quick, confident hand. When he was done, I slipped off my shoes and stepped into the center barefoot, careful not to scuff his lines.

Taking a deep breath, I said, "I'll need a knife."

"I've got that taken care of." Zan extracted what looked like a miniature dagger from his breastcoat pocket; from pommel to point, the knife was exactly the length of my hand. The inscriptions on the sheath were indecipherable, but I recognized another triquetra in the center of the patterns. He pulled back the sheath, and I was surprised to find that it was a glass blade, not a metal one.

"It's luneocite," Zan explained. "Ground into sand and heated like glass. Unlike glass, however"—he took the blade and struck it against the stone wall with a resonant *ting!*—"once cooled, luneocite can't be broken." He handed it back to me. "They used to be given to the Assembly's triumvirate. This one belonged to Achlev himself. I thought that, if we're going to reinforce his spells, it couldn't hurt to use his knife to do it."

"It's sharp," I said, touching my finger to the point. A pinprick of blood beaded up from the surface. "Very sharp."

"It is," he said, taking a handkerchief out to dab at my fingertip. "So be careful."

"Careful?" I scoffed. "In a few minutes I'm going to draw a lot more blood than that."

"Exactly." He smirked. "We need your blood. Try not to waste it. Here. Let me."

He took the knife and held it longways across my palm, the clear blade glinting in the spare moonlight, scattering bits of light across my skin like a constellation. "You've been doing this wrong," he said. "You're cutting too deep, too wide, and in places more likely to scar, or reopen. Do it like this instead."

He made a quick flicking motion, to demonstrate, before giving the knife back to me. Looking up from behind his hair, he said, "I grew up watching Simon do it." He paused. "It's painful, what you do. I know it. Believe me when I say, I would never ask it of you if I didn't think it was worth it. You're saving lives, Emilie. My people's lives."

Our eyes met. "I understand," I answered honestly. "I understand completely." Then I made the cut, lightly and carefully, just as Zan had shown me, feeling the pain and power grow as the blood welled up and drowned the light from the knife.

Zan gently removed the knife from my right hand and replaced it with the bowl, guiding my bleeding fist over it. When the first drop struck the metal, it reverberated inside me like the clang of a bell. At the second, the sound became a wail. At the third, it became a screaming pitch so high and so piercing that I thought my cells might burst from it. But through the knifing pain, Zan's voice was clear and cool. "Last chance to back out. Are you certain you're ready? That you've got this right?"

"I scoured those books. This is how Achlev did it. I'm certain of it."

He nodded. "How's it feel to save the world?"

Nervously, I said, "I'll let you know. Read the incantation I gave you word for word, pausing so I can repeat each line." Wilstine may not have needed incantations, but I didn't want to take any chances. "At the end, light the blood and hair in the bowl."

He lit a match and read the first line. *"'Divinum empyrea deducet me.'"* *Divine Empyrea, guide me.*

"'Divinum empyrea deducet me.'"

He hovered the match over the bowl. *"'Hic unionem terram caelum mare.'"* *Here at the union of land, sky, and sea.*

"'Hic unionem terram caelum mare.'" Heat was spreading from the bowl into my fingertips, where it morphed into pinpricks scouring the underside of my skin. Inside the bowl, the blood had begun to form a circle around the lock of Falada's mane.

"Keep going," Zan said. *"'Nos venimus ad te dedi te in similitudinem.'"* *We come to thee with an offer in thy likeness.*

"'Nos venimus ad te dedi te in similitudinem.'" The pinpricks were like sharp pieces of glass hurtling through my veins, around and around in my head, down my throat, in and out of the valves of my heart before screaming down my legs and out the bottoms of my feet, into the wall. And then, expansion. It was like I grew outside of my skin and bones and existed instead as a circle of light.

"'Magnifico nomen tuum, et faciem tuam ad quaerendam.'" *Thy name to extol and thy favor to seek.*

I could barely form the words. I had little awareness left of myself. It was hard to know which parts I needed to move—I had no sense of mouth or lips or tongue with which to speak. Wind was whipping around the wall like a hurricane; I borrowed it. I bent the air to form the required sounds. *Magnifico nomen tuum, et faciem tuam ad quaerendam.* It wasn't my voice but the melancholy whistle of the wind.

Zan dropped the match into the bowl, lighting the contents inside with a whoosh and a flash. In that instant I felt the power of the white-hot fire rise and join the wind, swirling into a burning column, carving a circle in the sky.

And then I saw them: the ley lines.

The world outside of Achlev was covered with dazzling streaks of white light. Right, left, back across . . . they wove like a net over the earth, everywhere except within Achlev's Wall, around which they spun and spun . . . but even as I watched, the lines began to slowly dim; the wind began to wane.

"Don't stop," Zan commanded.

The blood in the bowl consumed Falada's mane, turning the fire from gold to silver. I saw a vision of her, riding free across a great, misty moor. I felt her fierce pride, her exuberant joy, her wild passion. It was as if she knew that if she chose it, she could run fast enough to fly and join the goddess in the sky. She was Empyrean. She was magic. And she was going to give me everything I needed. Because she loved me. She trusted me. She didn't use words, but I knew she was telling me that she wanted to help me, because Kellan would have wanted her to help me.

But then the fire sputtered. "Wait! Wait!" I begged. "I'm not done! Not yet!" I stepped out of the triquetra, chasing after the diminishing vision.

"What are you doing?" Zan asked as I dropped the bowl and spilled blood and ash in a line across the chalk drawing. "Wait, Emilie. Don't!"

"I heal too fast," I said in a daze, trying to hold on to the silver fire as it ebbed away. "The pain isn't enough."

All those other times I'd experimented with magic, it wasn't pain I used to make it work. What had Simon said? *Blood magic is rooted in emotion: the faster your heart beats, the faster your blood pumps.* At home I never used magic without being terrified that the Tribunal would somehow find out. When I rescued my pregnant mother, I'd done so out of sheer desperation. When I'd burned my assailants in the streets of Achlev, it was to end their savage assault on my person. Out loud, I breathed, "Fear. I need to feel fear."

I pushed Zan aside and ran for the battlement, clawing at the top of the merlon and hoisting myself upon it. Broken mortar crunched under my bare feet, and a few loose pieces of gravel tumbled into the yawning void below. I leaned out over the edge, remembering what it felt like to watch Kellan slip from my hands to his death, and my heart lurched into an angry, drumming rhythm. If I fell, I would die —but my life wasn't the one I feared to lose. The only way I could be frightened enough to finish this was to put the lives tied to mine on the line. I lifted my hand one more time and let the blood fall directly onto the battlement stone.

It worked, but I knew it would not be for long. Frantically, I reached across the void to where Falada was waiting for me. She bent her head and put her beautiful white muzzle into my bleeding palm. "Thank you," I told her, drawing the silver light of her spirit into my hands. I took only what I needed and held it inside, letting it circulate and expand. Then I stretched my awareness and again found the fissure in the wall, and I salved it with Falada's silver spirit. *Almost there!*

I thought, but the fire began to fade again. My body was stopping the flow of my blood, and with it my access to the magic inside the wall—I was clotting, binding, healing myself. I needed to be more scared. I leaned even farther out, standing on my toes . . .

"Emilie!" Zan said, catching my hand as I teetered there. "Emilie, don't. It's dangerous. Don't!" He gave me an angry pull, and I tumbled from the edge into his waiting arms.

I was shuddering. I was covered in blood. But I'd failed. Failed.

"Are you all right?" His white collar was askew, his hair tangled, his eyes as dark as the black woods themselves. We stared at each other. And slowly, I lifted my bloodstained fingertips to his face, resting them softly against the line of his jaw. There was no sound.

"Not afraid of anything, are you?" Toris had asked me at the banquet in Syric. *Everything,* I'd thought. *"Not anything,"* I'd said.

Not afraid of anything, are you? I heard him ask again, an echo.

Yes, I answered.

Zan.

I'm afraid of Zan.

Everything slowed, stopped. We were alone in that fragile moment, suspended together in magic and light.

Then I closed my eyes and let go.

The last bit of power burst from me in a wave, rippling across the wall and filling the cracks like salve in a wound. When it was done, I collapsed into Zan's arms. The magic was gone, leaving me empty and deflated and cold. And yet, as we held each other in breathless bewilderment, I was certain I'd never felt more alive.

19

I barely remembered getting home; the spell had sapped my strength completely. The only thing I could recall was the sound of Zan's soft encouragement to put one foot in front of the other. "I can't carry you," he said, though the words were fuzzy in my memory. "Please, Emilie. Keep going. We have to do this together."

The next morning I woke in my cot to a chorus of soft, syncopated taps that grew into a murmur. It was a familiar, comforting sound, and I drifted for a long while in the borderland between sleep and wakefulness, listening contentedly. Kate had done a goodly amount of work on my hut; the murky atmosphere and the smell of dust were gone, replaced by the scent of fresh garden flowers and rain-soaked pine.

It wasn't until a second noise—a hard, harsh pounding—interrupted the first that I shook off the last dregs of slumber. I sat up on my cot and saw that Zan was waking up too, rubbing his eyes as he pulled himself to his feet, papers scattering from his lap as he rose. It looked as if he'd fallen asleep while drawing by the hearth after helping me to bed. "What is *that?*" Zan asked in a creaky morning voice, dark circles under his eyes, soot stains on his fingers.

Thunk! Thunk! Thunk! I stumbled to the door and flung it open to find Nathaniel on the stoop, his clothes soaked through, rain slathering his hair onto his forehead.

Rain.

"Zan!" Nathaniel said breathlessly. "Zan! Is he here?"

"I'm here," Zan said from behind me. "What's the matt—" His eyes went wide and he pushed past me into the downpour, lifting his hands to catch the raindrops, his face a mixture of wonder and horror.

"You have to come with me now, right now," Nathaniel said urgently. "It's High Gate."

"Stay here," Zan ordered, slamming the door shut in my face. I stared, stunned, at the panel of wood for several long seconds before going for Kellan's cloak. I would not be left behind, not if something had gone wrong with the gate.

The entire city was pouring out of their houses to gawk and marvel at the downpour, whispering and pointing in a singular direction. Soon the three horses appeared above the rooftops, but their pristine marble was now marred with scorch marks. In the alleyway I spied the corpse of a silver-white stallion, an Empyrean, but one I did not know. I gaped at it. I'd used Falada to undo one of the two completed sacrifices. The death of one horse should not have been enough to cause this.

I felt a hand on my elbow and turned to find Kate, her heart-shaped face colored with concern beneath her dripping hood. "Emilie," she said gravely. "Don't go over there. I promise you, you don't want to see."

My lungs began to expand and collapse in rapid pace. I shook her off and pushed myself through the gathering crowd.

I knew that something terrible had happened—knew it in my bones—but nothing could have prepared me for the sight of it. Before I could stop myself, I let out a keening wail.

Nailed to the lintel above the portcullis was the head of a once-white horse. Her muzzle was curled back from her teeth, frozen forever in a contorted scream, while her beautiful mane was matted with blood into snake-like ropes. Her blood was splattered and smeared all across the marble, black burns streaking out from the stains like the feathery marks of a lightning strike. Blood and rain dripped from her lips, forming rivulets of red that outlined each cobblestone below. The spirits of the gate wandered listlessly beneath the grotesque spectacle, unmoved by death or downpour.

I hardly noticed Zan and Nathaniel making a beeline over to me, or Zan's attempts to quiet the awful sounds that were coming from my mouth. I couldn't look away. Falada was dead. *Dead.*

"Emilie, stop. Please. You're making a scene."

"Don't touch me."

"Emilie, just stop—"

"Don't *touch* me!"

Nathaniel scooped me up as easily as if I were a child throwing a tantrum. I fought against him, but the man must have been made of granite; he didn't seem to notice my struggle at all. When he set me down again, we were out from under watchful eyes. Kate and Zan were following close behind.

"How dare you," I said, quivering with rage.

Zan's face was a mask of calm, which infuriated me even more. "This is what we were trying to prevent, Emilie . . . Bleeding stars.

They must have realized, after they killed the one horse, what we'd done. And even though she was disguised, they could have cast a spell to see through it." He cursed again. "I'm sorry about your horse, but you have to understand we have much bigger problems now . . ."

"You're *sorry?*" Rain and tears were stinging my eyes.

"I'm upset too. We should have done it ourselves. At least then she could have gone humanely, but we failed—"

I lunged at him; I wasn't sure what I meant to do, but I didn't get close enough to find out before Nathaniel stepped in front of him. Impeded by the human barrier, I was forced to retreat, and I began stalking up and down on my side of the divide.

"*You* failed!" I futilely wiped my eyes on my soaked sleeve, chin quivering. "I almost killed myself working your spell because you said you'd protect her, and you didn't. I don't even know why I believed you; you can't even protect yourself. That's what Nathaniel is for, right? To make sure you never have to ruffle a hair on your head, never have to get your hands dirty."

Zan said in a quiet, dangerous voice, "Maybe you should go. Calm down, and we can talk again when you're back to your senses."

"Oh, I'll go," I said. "But this? This is over. I'm done with you."

"Emilie," Kate said, "wait!"

"If she wants to go," Zan said, "don't stop her."

✳

Back at the hut, emotions roiling, I slammed the door shut with a deafening crack and then collapsed against it as the expenditure of fury left emptiness and exhaustion in its place. My clothes were wet and cold, hanging heavy on my frame. I unlaced the ties of my bodice and dress and stripped it off, abandoning it where I stood, and moved toward the fire, wearing nothing but my white shift. I crouched, shivering, by the fire, and pushed the sodden lumps of hair from my eyes.

I was surrounded by the papers that had fallen from Zan's lap that morning. I gathered them together just to get them out of the way at first but found myself unable to set them aside unviewed. The first two were charcoal sketches of a twinkling city, as seen from our high vantage on the wall last night, captured effortlessly in Zan's bold, dramatic style. The third was of hands—my hands. In one there was a luneocite knife. In the other, nothing but black blood seeping between long, white fingers.

Letting go of the papers, I stared at them. Last night's cut had already knitted itself into a thin red weal. I closed my fingers into fists to hide the mark and the old, familiar shame. In my head I heard the distant echo of the Tribunal mob's fevered chants: *Witch! Witch! Witch!*

My focus caught on the corner of a new drawing that had shaken loose from the others when I dropped them. I plucked it from the pile and rose to my feet, feeling sick, wanting to strike the image from my mind forever and yet unable to look away.

The girl in the picture had wild hair flying around her face in a twisted halo, her eyes wide and staring, her mouth parted in what looked like a scream—of pain or ecstasy, I could not tell. The touches of beauty and elegance found in the detailed hand study were gone; in this rendering, the girl's fingers had become stiff and curled, like claws. Her cheeks and eye sockets were marked by cavernous shadows, hollowed by the tongues of flame from the blood and hair burning in the bowl.

No wonder, I thought. *No wonder they hate us. No wonder they burn us. No wonder the Empyrea wants to rid the earth of us.* This . . . this person . . . she was power and danger and death.

She was what Zan saw when he looked at me.

I cast the picture into the fire. While it smoked, I scrabbled on my knees for the other drawings, and then I burned them, too.

The fire roared in the grate, and my body flushed in the stifling heat, as if I and my effigy were inextricably bound and I, too, was being consumed by the flames. Desperate for air, I fled back out into the rain and then did not stop at the doorstep. Past the trees, the pond, down into the culvert and the passage beyond.

When I climbed up the rocks and out onto the field of bloodleaf, the Harbinger was already waiting for me. She knew I would come, the same way she seemed to know everything but what paths might actually *help* me.

"All these years I've let you guide me. I've put myself in danger to do as you bid me, and look where I am now. Just *look* at what's become of me. Is this what you wanted?"

She waited, wordless as ever.

"I'm sick of it. All of it. Of you, of magic, of death." I took out Achlev's luneocite knife and made a quick nick on my index finger. "I don't want you to visit me anymore," I said. "I don't want to see you following me. I'm done. *We're* done." I gathered every ounce of feeling I had left inside of me and let it loose at her. "Just . . . *be gone!*" I cried, and felt a strange, unsettling *snap*.

She stumbled backwards, as if I'd cast not words at her but weighty stones. She fell into the web of bloodleaf that encased the tower, and the vine reacted to her touch, snaking around her limbs and torso, up around her throat, and entwining itself in her hair. It enveloped her, it became her, until I could see nothing but her black-orb eyes, glowing darkly inside the tangle of red-shot vine.

And then she let out a silent scream as she and the bloodleaf turned to glittering orange ember and drifting ash, leaving a cavernous space in the hedge and revealing an ancient door beneath it.

I raised shaking fingers to the rusted iron inlay. It was a mess of swoops and swirls. There was a corroded lock set in the aged wood, but I didn't need a key; a soft push made the door give way. I took my first nervous step inside.

Rain was leaking through old cracks in the walls and spilling from thin lancet windows onto a mosaic of the triquetra knot.

At the foot of the stairs I saw her again, the ghost woman whose body was too broken to identify. She glanced at me over her shoulder and then moved up the stairs, revealing a painting behind her on the wall. Though age had worn much of it away, I could make out three figures: a woman between two men—one with dark hair standing in the light and one with light hair standing in the dark.

The paintings continued panel by panel, telling Aren's story alongside my ascent up the stairs. Black shadows slipped out from a tear in the barrier between the material and spectral planes, each one more grotesque and frightening than the last.

Aren and her brothers followed the ley lines to the spot, which sat in an ancient basin, next to a fjord, in the midst of a thatch of wild red roses. There they had joined hands to cast the spell that would seal up the hole forever.

As I neared the top of the tower, more and more of the panels were faded to obscurity. I could make nothing out until the second-to-last panel, which showed Cael with a knife in his hands and Aren dying in Achlev's arms. At first it looked as if Achlev was wrapping the rose vines around her, but a second glance showed me the truth—the vines were becoming part of her. As they overtook her, the red roses became pure white.

Instead of dying, she had been transformed into bloodleaf.

I was at the top of the tower now, looking up at an overhead door. Not unlike the entrance, it was aged and ineffectual. I pushed it open, emerging onto a platform in the rainy gray daylight.

I turned to find a huge sculpture of a woman, rimmed by a dim halo, looking down at me. A luneocite knife, not unlike the one I had in my pocket, was locked in her stony hands. I knew her face well now. My ancestress. The Harbinger. Aren.

I felt cold pricking along my arms in the dreary drizzle, and turned. The ghost woman was standing at the brink of the tower platform, beside the crumbling parapet. She reached out her hand; she wanted to show me how she'd died. Too tired be scared, I reached back.

More shocking than the cold was the jarring transition from day to night, from my perspective to hers in the last moments of her life. In this echo of the past, I had no eyes or ears of my own. I saw what she saw, I heard what she heard.

She was speaking to another woman in the same spot where we were now standing. "I can't watch him suffer anymore," she was saying.

"Every day he gets worse. I can feel him slipping away, Sahlma. And I can't let him go . . . I *won't* . . ."

Sahlma? I recognized her now, the healer from town. Younger, but with the same pernicious scowl. "Best to let nature take its course," Sahlma said. "Bloodleaf is both foul and fickle; even if I do manage to collect one of those petals—almost impossible to do; they disintegrate the moment you touch them—what if it doesn't work? Then you'll have died for nothing."

The woman was looking down now, and I could see a ring on each of her slender hands. One was a spread-winged raven, the Silvis signet. The other was a clear white stone, cut into a thousand triangular facets. "If I don't do it, then Zan will die." She looked up at Sahlma. "A mother should never have to be without her child." Then she slipped each of the rings off her fingers and placed them in the center of Sahlma's palm. Trembling, she said, "After you give him the petal and he's better, will you make sure he gets these? Will you tell him that I love him? *Promise* me."

"Don't do it, my lady. Don't."

She climbed onto the edge of the parapet and looked out across the expanse one last time. The city—the entire city—was built in the shape of the triquetra knot, I saw through her eyes. Each gate was a point. The lines of the city streets and the trees and the shape of the fjord all made up the curved swoops of the knot, contained within the circle of the great wall. We stood high above it all in the exact center, protected by the castle on one side and the fjord on the other.

Then she looked down at the carpet of bloodleaf far, far below. Taking a deep breath, she gave Sahlma one last look from over her shoulder and said, "Better hurry."

Then we turned and leaped over the side, she and I together.

But before I fell, two arms went around me, throwing me out of the vision and away from the ledge. I pitched backwards, screaming as I hurtled through the disintegrating door and down the stairs behind it, entangled with another body. I felt my ribs and head and arms and legs crack on the unforgiving stone until we crashed together onto a wide stair and slammed to a stop against the wall. I rolled over, dizzy with pain, and saw Zan.

His eyes were glassy, his face covered with a thin layer of sweat. He looked wild.

"Zan? What's going on? What—"

He was clutching his chest, each gasp a knife scraping against stone, sharp and metallic and desperate. "Don't. Jump. Please."

"What?" I looked from his shaking body to the square of light of the tower overlook, and knew. He'd saved me. And at great cost to himself.

"Zan? Zan!" Nathaniel was scrambling up the stairs behind Zan, frantic and stricken. "Is he all right? He saw you going up, and he ran. I tried to stop him, but he pushed me." Zan, trying to stand, had collapsed and was lying on his side, his breathing a piercing staccato. Nathaniel said, "It's his heart. I don't know what possessed him to — he knows his limits. He knew he couldn't make it all the way up here, or he'd be in trouble. He did it anyway."

Nathaniel put his arm under Zan's shoulder and lifted him. I was about to grab the other dangling arm when he seized my wrist and locked his terror-filled eyes on me.

"You're . . . bleeding," he said, wheezing. I looked at my hand, which sure enough was covered in blood seeping from a cut in my arm. And then, unthinking, I pressed my bloody palm to his cheek and told his pain, *Not there.* I addressed it the way I'd addressed the fire. All the books said that blood magic didn't lend itself to healing. But pain . . . it was universally agreed that blood magic could be fueled and funneled with pain. So even if I couldn't fix it, I could *use* it, couldn't I? I could maybe even move it.

I directed the pain inside myself. *Here,* I told it.

And suddenly I was seized by an agony the depths of which I could barely fathom, a weight in my chest, a vise on my ribs, fire in my brain. I was drowning. No air. No air. No way to scream my terror. No air.

I don't know how long we sat there: Zan writhing on the tower stairs and me bent over him in my sopping chemise, gripping his arms while I breathed in time with him. I felt the misery of his every attempted lungful, the tight shooting pain in every beat of his heart, and then . . . I took it from him. I took it into myself.

When finally, exhausted, he closed his eyes and his head lolled, I was released, gasping, still clutching his limp arm. I ducked beneath it; it was heavy on my shoulders.

"I think I've taken off some of the edge," I said, wheezing. "But we need to get him someplace warm and dry, give him something to help him breathe. Is there a healer in the castle?"

"We can't take him into the castle," Nathaniel said. "Being seen like this, in court, by the king—he would never allow it. He'd be furious."

"Not even to save his own stars-forsaken life?"

"Not even then."

I swore. Even unconscious, Zan was a pain in the ass. "I can do what needs to be done, I think, if we can get him to my hut."

We dragged his limp body between us, his feet thudding on every stair, and lurched from the door into the rain while I went back and forth between cursing his idiocy and praying for his full recovery. But then the thought of his coming out of this mess unscathed made me angry again, and the whole process would start over.

We slogged through the abandoned canals as the water rose to my waist, pushing on, paying close attention to the time between each of Zan's agonizing breaths.

At the hut we threw open the door and dumped Zan onto the cot. He moaned, on the edge of consciousness.

Nathaniel started toward him, but I held out a hand. "It's all right. Let him rest."

As I began to gather the things I needed for the potion, Nathaniel settled back against the door frame. "He hired me—at Kate's behest—to train him to fight. To help him get stronger, healthier. I taught him all I could, and he's come a long way. But some things can't be fixed, only adapted to." Gently, he added, "It's a hard thing for him, letting me handle what he physically cannot."

"I didn't know," I said. Those times I'd thought him nonchalant, slow . . . *That's what Nathaniel is for, right? To make sure you never have to ruffle a hair on your head.* I remembered my words this morning with growing regret.

"He didn't want you to know." Nathaniel sighed. "I feel useless, just standing here. Is there anything I can do to help?"

I rose to my feet, unsteady. I said tiredly, "Do you know what camphor is?"

"Yes," he said. "Kate distilled a batch not that long ago."

"Does she keep it in here?"

"No . . . it's stored in a closet in our kitchen."

"Can you retrieve some of it for me?"

"Yes," he said. "I'll be back soon."

I had everything else I needed. I remembered the pages from Onal's herbals well. *To ease breathing.* I wheezed as I collected all the required items; Zan's infirmity lingered in my lungs, too.

I put a kettle of water on the fire and started adding the ingredients from Kate's stores. Mint, tea leaves, turmeric, ginger. I breathed in deeply as I stirred. The relief, though small, was immediate.

As the mixture reached a boil, Zan began to waken "What is that smell?"

"It's medicine. It isn't quite perfect yet. Nathaniel went to go fetch another ingredient for me. But here." I ladled some of the mixture into a mug. "This will at least help, for now. And don't drink it. Breathe it."

He held the mug and let the steam rise into his face. "Are we going to talk about how you nearly jumped from the tower?"

"Are we going to talk about how you almost killed yourself trying to stop me?"

He scowled and looked back into his cup.

"I wasn't going to jump," I said.

"No? Then what *were* you doing?"

I hesitated. This was the same dilemma I faced over and over with Kellan: *Do I tell him, and have him doubt me? Or do I keep it to myself, another secret to guard, another brick in the divide between me and the people I care about?*

"I went to the tower, after what happened to Falada, to be alone. When I saw a way to get in, my curiosity overcame me." It wasn't enough of an explanation, and I knew it. I cast about for a piece of truth to reshape into a credible lie. "When I was up there," I said, "I saw the shape of the city—really saw it—for the first time. It was built in the shape of the Achlevan knot, with a gate at each of the points. It was beautiful. I . . . I climbed onto the battlement to get a better look."

"A half-decent map could have revealed the same thing. You didn't need—" He broke into a barking, rasping cough. I crouched next to him, ready to try the spell again, to transfer his suffering to myself, but he waved me off. When the coughing subsided, he said, "I never wanted you to see this."

"See what?"

"My weakness."

I paused, then went to the pot and began to stir it with violence before setting the ladle down with a sloppy clang. Then I clenched my fists and leaned against the table, unable to look at him.

"You're angry," he observed.

"What you have is an ailment. Not a weakness."

"It feels the same to me."

"When I think of weakness, I think of the weak-minded, the weak-willed, the cowardly. You are none of those things."

"I am all of those things."

"Stop," I begged. "What I said this morning . . . I just . . ."

He left the cot and came to lean against the table beside me, in the casual, careless way I knew now to be only a façade. He said, "Don't apologize. There is no part of this morning that I would wish to revisit, save for one thing. When you said you were done with me. Did you mean it?"

There was very little space between us.

"No," I breathed.

"Emilie," he said, "I should have died today, yet I am not dead. You did that, didn't you? You saved me."

"You saved me first," I whispered.

"Your eyes," he said, "they confound me. They're like a storm— gray, and then blue, and then silver—and always changing. There's something absolutely uncanny about them. About you."

But like a blow, I was confronted again with his depiction of me on the wall, casting a blood spell in nightmarish majesty. I was an ele-mental force, strange and devastating, beautiful as a bolt of lightning, terrible as the crack of thunder. *Uncanny,* I was. Inhuman.

I turned brusquely away from him, all the warmth between us instantly banished by a cold gust of air.

"I've got the camphor," Nathaniel said, banging through the doorway.

I dashed to take the jar from him and empty its contents into the pot over the fire, hoping that he wouldn't notice the deep blush that had started in my chest and was sweeping up my neck and into my cheeks.

Nathaniel glanced at Zan. "I see you're feeling better."

"Yes," Zan said, questioning eyes on me. "Much better, I think."

20

That evening, when I was alone again, the first thing I did was crack open the copy of the *Compendium* Zan let me take from the library. The day had left my feelings in an unruly tangle; now, whenever my thoughts began to drift, they invariably made their way back to Zan. His insufferable smile. His maddening, uncaring demeanor. His quick wit, his sharp tongue. His eyes.

To distract myself, I threw all my energy into a single, straightforward task: the identification of the blood mage who murdered Falada.

Despite the questionable place from which my motivation sprang, the goal was a worthy one. Now that High Gate's seal was broken, the clock for Forest Gate was ticking. If we didn't act soon, a maid, a mother, and a crone would meet the same fate as Falada. Zan believed these three sacrifices would be attempted in the span between the waxing and waning gibbous moons, the full moon marking the middle, the apex of the month. Ten days in total, but the attacks could begin anytime. We could not afford any delay.

I scoured the book back to front but saw nothing that might help until I turned to a section about scrying. *Farseeing,* it said on the top of the page. *Most easily practiced by feral or high mages. Blood magic is less precise and may return unsatisfactory results.*

It was the best option I could find, but my hopes to attempt it died quickly; this spell required a small personal token. I could use it to see someone far away, someone I knew, but it would not help me identify a stranger. I closed the book, frustrated, only to immediately open it again.

I could use it to see someone far away, someone I knew. I could use it to see my mother.

I needed her. I wanted to tell her everything. The fear, the hurt, the triumphs . . . the unexpected and complicated connection with an intriguing, infuriating boy with green eyes.

Following the instruction of the spell, I filled a copper bowl to the brim with water and let it settle until the surface was as smooth as glass. *Lay out the memento of the person you're trying to reach,* the book said. *A lock of hair, a handwriting sample, or a painting of their visage.*

I did have my wedding dress, sewn with my mother's own hand, but it was packed away, and I didn't want to be reminded that when all of this was over, if things went successfully, I'd still have to marry Zan's cousin. No, I'd use the bloodcloth. Kneeling, I held the folded square in one hand while I nicked a finger on the other and let the blood drip into the bowl.

Concentrate, the book directed, *and repeat the words: Indica mihi quem quaeritis.* Show me the one I seek.

"'*Indica mihi quem quaeritis,*'" I said as the droplets of my blood bloomed like roses in the water.

I clutched the bloodcloth and searched the water for some sign that it was working . . . anything . . .

When an image finally formed like an oily sheen on the surface, it was not my mother's face I saw but a man's. The spell had warned me that blood magic could return unsatisfactory results, but I was disappointed anyway. I squinted and leaned closer. It looked like . . .

I cried out in shock, knocking over the water bowl and breaking the vision.

The bowl had shown me the figure of a man, suspended in light, eyes closed, with wide green leaves dressing the wound on his naked torso where Toris had embedded his knife.

Trembling, I unfolded the bloodcloth.

After Kellan died, the circular drop of his blood had faded to almost nothing, but it had never totally disappeared. It was now almost as dark as the day he let it fall to tie his life to mine.

There were three bright drops of blood on the cloth. Three. Was it proof that somehow he'd toed the edge of death and come back from the brink?

Stars save me, I thought, astounded. *Kellan is alive.*

✳

I had to get a message back home to Renalt. Not to my mother, trapped as she was in the Tribunal's custody, but to the Greythorne estate. Kellan's family. They'd been kind to me when I was a child, and they were loyal to my mother and the crown.

And what was more, they'd have the resources and the reasons to find Kellan, if he was truly still alive and not a conjuring of my wild imagination, and ensure his safe return home.

Bringing anybody else into the knowledge of my identity could endanger them. It would have to be a stranger. Someone who didn't know me, someone who wouldn't question what I needed them to do or why I was asking them to do it. Someone who wouldn't think twice about going on a dangerous journey with nothing to go on besides my word.

In short, I needed to find someone who had nothing to lose.

I put on my blue cloak and swept the items on the table into my satchel before depositing a chunk of bread and a stoppered cruse of water alongside them. It was completely dark outside, but I found Zan's hidden stairs with ease, climbed them all the way to the top of the wall, and made my way down the walk. Not north this time but south, toward the gibbets. I passed Forest Gate first, skirting the narrow walkway at the base of the statue of the three women. This was the nearest I'd been to them, and they were even more stunning up close. The first was youthful and lithe, the second bore the soft curves and swelling stomach of a mother-to-be, and the last was knobby and bent with age, like a weathered tree.

The air was cool and clear now that the rain had finally stopped. Rainwater had collected in several places on the roads below, reflecting the waxing moon like scattered shards of a broken mirror. I was grateful for the damp smell left behind by the moisture; it covered up some of the stench of death that began to pervade the air as I came upon the gibbets.

The gibbets were spaced between High Gate and Forest Gate, hanging from hooked chains and spread every fifty feet. The first two housed men who were recently dead, men who'd probably been injured in the struggle to stick them in the gibbets. They'd bled out in their cages. The third gibbet held only bones and a hollow-eyed spirit that was slumped despondently among its remains. When it saw me, it threw itself against the bars, snarling and snapping its teeth, straining toward me with bony fingers. I shivered and passed it by.

At the fourth gibbet I slowed to a stop and leaned out over the notched battlement. I was greeted by the gaze of a living man. His mouth was still stuffed with the gag, but his eyes were bright. I tried to count how many days had gone by since Petitioner's Day. Two? Three?

"Ray? Raymond Thackery?" I said into the dark, and he slowly nodded.

"I have food and water. Without it, you'll die. You'll have another few days if you're lucky. Do you understand?"

A nod.

"I need a message delivered. To Renalt. It is of the utmost importance, and it requires absolute secrecy. There will be a great reward in it for you. A monetary reward as well as safety and asylum in Renalt. Do you understand the risks?"

A nod.

"Is this something you would be willing to do?"

Another nod.

"Good." I went to the pulley and turned the crank wheel. It creaked stubbornly as I reeled the gibbet in inch by inch, straining every muscle and dragging on the wheel with all of my weight. The heart and lung complaints I'd absorbed from Zan had long since subsided, but by the time the gibbet finally came swinging over the top of the battlement, I was sweating and panting anyway. Two more cranks, and it was to where I could reach it.

There was a lock on the gate, and Thackery watched as I jammed my little knife into it and worked the latch until it gave and the door swung free. He was trembling as I helped hoist him down. He sank against the battlement

I untied his gag. "Here," I said, unstopping the bottle of water to hand it to him. "Drink this. Careful, now. Careful."

"They will . . . will kill you . . . if they know you helped me." Thackery wheezed as he wiped the water from his mouth. "And it will be unpleasant. There's a reason folks don't just bust out every family member what gets hung up in a cage."

"I'm not afraid of the king."

Between gulps, he said, "The king is stupid, but he has a certain creativity when it comes to makin' folk suffer. And there are plenty o' people who exploit his stupidity and capitalize on his particular brand of creativity. Oughtta be afraid of them, too."

"Consider me warned." I gave him the bread next. "Eat slowly or you'll be sick."

Between large bites, he asked, "What message am I to carry, and to where?"

"Just this." I took out a paper, folded and sealed and addressed to Lord Fredrick Greythorne, Kellan's older brother. It recounted everything—what Toris had done in the woods, how Lisette was living in the castle under my name, how Conrad was unhurt but seemed to be going along with the charade. The last thing I included was my belief that Kellan had escaped, injured, and that he was probably recovering in one of the villages outside the Ebonwilde. I had signed it with my own name, marveling at how foreign it felt to use it.

If Fredrick could find Kellan, his story would corroborate my written account and provide proof of Toris's treachery. Likely, we could link his efforts to insinuate himself into Achleva with the Tribunal's takeover, and charge them all with treason. Mother could take back her crown, and then . . . they could come for Conrad and me. We'd be saved.

"You'll need to take this to Lord Fredrick Greythorne. Deliver it to him and no one else, understand me? His land is in the western Renaltan province. You'll save time if you go by boat and take port in Gaskin. From there it will be about four days' walk."

"One problem." Thackery stopped his ravenous chewing. "How am I going to pay for boat fare? They robbed me of everything when they took me. And how will I eat, for that matter? A man's got to eat."

I pursed my lips, wondering if I should remind him that up until five minutes ago he was going to starve to death in a gibbet. But I thought better of it and said instead, "Here. This should buy you boat fare and a little bit of food besides." It was the last of my treasures—the golden chain of my charm bracelet. Another piece of myself I was forced to surrender. "Don't stop. Don't dawdle. Time is of the essence. Now let's get you off this wall," I said. "Quickly, now, before anyone comes." I tried to help him to his feet, but he was too weak to stand.

"I can't help you . . . in the condition I'm in. I'd already be . . . dead if it wasn't for the rain. Sucked it out of the gag." He swallowed and said, "I'm useless to you, girl. Might as well put me back in the cage. Better that way. Gilroy would miss me too much, anyway."

"Quiet," I commanded. "I'll do no such thing."

I gave myself another little cut with the luneocite knife and then placed my hand in Thackery's. "Give it to me," I said, just like I had to Zan in the tower.

But with Zan I'd acted instinctively and emotionally. This was different. I did not know or care for this man. I could not make the same connection.

But I had to. Time was running out. This was my chance—probably my only chance—to undo some of what had been done to me. Anger and impatience bubbled inside. "*Give it to me,* damn it!"

It hit me like a blow. The nauseating hunger. The thirst. The weakness. I sucked in a hard breath and let go of him, breaking the connection.

"There," I mumbled, doubled over.

He straightened up. "What did you just do?"

"I made it so you . . . can get out of here." My voice was hoarse.

His eyes widened. "You're a—"

"Shut . . . up and get . . . out of here."

"What about—"

"I'll be . . . I'm fine. Do as I've . . . told you and *go.* Now!" I barked.

He bolted away, springing like a rabbit down the curve of the wall that led past the docks and onto King's Gate. I dragged myself to the battlements to try to watch him, but my vision was too affected; I lost track of him as soon as he passed High Gate. There was nothing more I could do; either he would make it to Renalt or he wouldn't. Either he would deliver my message or he wouldn't. There was no point in worrying now. It was done.

didn't make it home that night; I spent the hours between Thackery's release and daybreak stumbling, dizzy and drained, from street to street, every step an effort. At least the last time I'd been half-starved it had come upon me bit by bit, instead of hitting me like a sack of bricks, square in the stomach. By midmorning I had gone only as far as the city square.

Thackery's hunger was fading, but by now my own exhaustion was setting in. I was sagging against a pillar on the stoop of a textile shop to catch my breath when I heard an exclamation from behind me.

"Emilie?" Kate was exiting the shop, a basket full of cloth held in the crook of her elbow.

I turned and forced a smile. "Good morning," I said as cheerfully as I could muster.

She threaded her arm through mine. "I'm glad I've run into you! With the royal wedding so close now, I've got a pile of new orders for engagement-ball costumes. One woman is going as an owl, another—you won't believe this—as a tree. A *tree*. And not a good one, either, like a spruce or a weeping willow. No, she's going as a mulberry. Which I guess is pretty enough, with little berries and such, but we had a mulberry on our property when I was growing up, and it did the most unpleasant things to the birds who ate the berries . . ." She stopped. "Emilie, are you all right?"

I nodded weakly. "I'm fine," I said.

She looked like she didn't quite believe me, but continued, "Anyway, with the extra money from those commissions, I bought these"—she motioned to the fabric in her basket, delicate florals made of downy material—"so I can finally make a few things for the baby. Aren't they lovely?" She stroked the cloth dreamily. "Can you imagine a little dressing gown out of this? She'll look so sweet."

My vision was blurring a little, but I tried to ignore it the best I could. "She?"

"Oh, yes," Kate said, beaming at her belly. "She's a girl. I can feel it. Don't tell Nathaniel yet, but I want to name her Ella, after his mother."

We were approaching the lane to Kate's cottage now, and not a moment too soon; my strength was flagging. It was a struggle to comprehend what Kate was saying—I had to concentrate on each word.

At the end of the cottage walk, though, she came to a sudden halt. There was a man standing on her doorstep, fist raised as if to knock.

"Dedrick?"

The man whirled around, jaw dropping open. "Katherine? Is that really you?" Then he flew down the walk to sweep her into an enthusiastic hug.

"What are you doing here?" she asked with a broad smile. "It's been so long since our last letters, I can't believe you knew where to find me!"

"I was here for Petitioner's Day, but since it is so close to the prince's wedding date, I decided to extend my stay until after the engagement ball. That's why I'm here, actually. I've been inquiring about where to go for the best costume and came up with this address. I never *dreamed* you were the seamstress they were talking about." He took a step back. "Look at you. You're an absolute vision. How long do you have left?"

"Just a couple of weeks now," Kate said cheerfully.

"I always knew you'd make a lovely mother." He chuckled. "I imagined slightly different circumstances, of course." His eyes flicked to me, noticing me for the first time. I was puffing, my vision slowly darkening.

"Oh!" Kate said. "I forgot to introduce you. Dedrick, this is my friend Emilie. Emilie, this is Lord Dedrick Corvalis. My—"

"Friend," Dedrick said, bowing politely. "And former fiancé." He winked, then straightened up. He said, "Katherine, your friend doesn't look well. Maybe we should—"

That was when my legs gave out.

✳

"Lay her here, on this chaise."

Dedrick did as he was told and gently set me down, while Kate fluttered around me nervously, feeling the temperature of my forehead and prying my eyelids open to check the dilation of my pupils. I tried to swat her away. "Stop fussing. I'm fine. It was just a little dizzy spell, that's all."

"When was the last time you ate, my dear?" Dedrick asked with parent-like concern in his voice. He was even handsomer up close, with glossy brown hair, a smooth smile, and the barest hint of a dimple in his chin. He patted my bare hand with his gloved one.

"I'm fine," I insisted.

"I'll make sure she's cared for," Kate said. "And you'll have your costume by midafternoon tomorrow, on my honor." She paused. "Dedrick, I know we haven't spoken in person since . . . since . . ."

"Since you ran off with my right-hand man?" Dedrick gave a soft chuckle.

"Yes. That."

"I realized long ago that if I'd taken care of you better, escorted you myself, maybe it would have turned out differently. But I can't blame you for falling in love. I've done so myself. Hundreds of times."

She laughed lightly. "I've little doubt. Your reputation is renowned. You'd probably have made a terrible husband."

"Probably," he said, laughing with her, "but you would have made an excellent wife." I looked away as he fondly brushed her cheek. Kate's smile waned, and Dedrick quickly pulled his hand away, clearing his throat. "Your mother will be thrilled to know I've seen you. Can I let her know your happy news?"

"Will you?" Kate asked, eyes shining. "I'd love to see her again, even if nobody else wants to see me. Maybe after the baby is born . . ."

"Your mother misses you desperately," Dedrick said. "I'm sure that a reunion can be arranged."

He'd donned his hat and was at the door to leave when it swung open and Nathaniel, coming in from the other side, froze with his hand on the knob. The atmosphere immediately chilled.

"Dedrick," Nathaniel said, the word sounding more like an accusation than a salutation.

"Nathaniel," Dedrick replied. "So good to see you." He tipped his hat to Kate and looked around. "Lovely little house you've got here. Hope to see it again soon."

Nathaniel, occupying the whole of the doorway, did not move for Dedrick to get by, and their shoulders hit against each other heavily as Dedrick pushed past him. Dedrick gave one last salute over his shoulder. "Good day to you both."

When he was gone, Kate turned to her husband, seething. "What was *that?*" she demanded. "He was a guest—a client, actually. He came because he needed a seamstress for a costume; he didn't know he'd find me. Could you not muster a speck of civility?"

Nathaniel's voice was tight. "Do not let that man in my house again." I lay still as a stone, hoping they'd forget I was in the room. In fact, it seemed they already had.

"Your house? This is *our* house, Nathaniel. I can let in whomever I want. What has gotten into you?"

"Don't," Nathaniel said again, dangerously calm. "Do not disobey me, Kate. My word on this is final."

Kate opened her mouth and then closed it; I was certain that this was the first time Nathaniel had ever spoken to her in such a way. She might have cried, were she not so stunned.

Zan came in without so much as a knock. He marched across the room to slam a book open on the table, unaware of the tension he'd disrupted.

"I've done some more studying," he said. "And I think I've

pinpointed a way to get ahead of this. A way to discover, if not the perpetrator himself, the time and place of his next murder."

Kate took a deep breath and smoothed out her dress, avoiding Nathaniel's eyes. "And just how are you going to do that?"

He beckoned, and I got wearily to my feet to see what he had to show us. "Here. This is a volume on high magic. Back in the day, high mages lived and died by what they called the sight: visions from the Empyrea. Some were able to see pictures of the past; others, the present. And some—a very rare and special few—had the ability to see the future."

"That doesn't help us," Kate said. "Emilie's a blood mage."

"True," Zan said, "and blood magic doesn't work the same way as high magic does—she could chart star formations or stare at tea leaves all day and she still couldn't discern with any certainty what she might have for her next meal." His excitement was rising at the same pace as my dread. "But given the right circumstances, blood mages *can* speak to the dead."

For the second time that day, I saw stars dart across my vision, and I grabbed the edge of the table, wavering, desperate to keep from fainting again.

Zan's expression changed, noticing something other than his book for the first time since his arrival. "What's the matter with you?"

Kate pulled up a chair behind me and made me sit. "She's not feeling well today."

"No," I said tiredly. "What you want me to do? The answer is no."

"It might be our only option, Emilie. I don't want to see anyone die."

"Neither do I, so . . ."

"Think about it, Emilie." He was in earnest now. "There's at least one documented high mage whose ability was to see death before it happened. Aren."

"Lot of good it did her," Nathaniel muttered. "Wasn't very good at seeing her own, was she?"

Zan pulled something from his pocket and laid it in the center fold of the magic book: a spring of bloodleaf vine. Droplets of red sap leaked from the cut stem, staining the pages it rested on. "We have a piece of Aren right here, do we not? We can use it to call her back from the spectral plane and let Emilie ask her who will be sacrificed as the maid. If we know who the girl is, we can get to her first. We may even be able to use her to lure him to us."

"You want to use some poor girl as bait?" Kate asked, incredulous.

"Feel free to chime in if you have any better ideas."

I sat in silence, considering. I'd broken whatever bond existed between myself and the Harbinger. I'd cast her away. And now Zan wanted me to call her back. To deliberately subject myself to one of her terrible visions. The thought turned my stomach.

"You don't know what you're asking," I said softly, tracing with my fingertip the pattern of ruby-colored veins in the leaf.

"I'm asking you to just . . . try." He cocked his head. "You really don't look well. Worse than when I first met you, if that's even possible."

"All the more reason for you to leave her alone. She needs to eat, to rest . . ." Kate had him by the shirtsleeve, dragging him toward the door. "This can wait."

"No, he's right," I said, closing my eyes and thinking of Falada. "It can't wait. I have to at least try."

"Dim the lights," Zan said, hurrying before I could change my mind. "Cover the windows." He pulled every candle he could find from around the room and placed them into a haphazard collection at the center of the table. Then he struck a match, leaning in to touch it to each candlewick in turn. "Well, then," he said as the matchstick burned down to his fingertips, "let's get to it. Time to summon a queen."

The instructions seemed pretty straightforward. We were to all sit around the table, our hands clasped, while one of us—Zan—chalked the triquetra in the center of the table. "Each one of these points represents a plane from which mages draw their power." He touched each point in turn. "The spiritual, material, and spectral planes. Over each of these planes rules a deified iteration of the human life cycle: the maid, the mother, and the crone."

I looked up at him in surprise. I'd never heard this kind of lore; in Renalt the only deity we acknowledged was the Empyrea, ruler of the skies and souls. She would undoubtedly be the maidenly mascot of the spiritual plane, but what of the other two? I didn't have time to ponder; Zan was already moving on to the next phase of the séance.

"It is to the spectral plane that we wish to speak," he said, addressing the air. From across the table he gave me a nod.

I released Nathaniel and Kate's hands and took up the bowl in front of me, the sprig of bloodleaf waiting at the bottom. With a quick flick, I drew the barest amount of blood. The temperature in the room dropped instantly.

Zan, Nathaniel, and Kate exchanged glances.

"You can feel that?" I asked. Kate nodded, her breath white in the air. My ears had started ringing, just like they had during the blood-cloth ceremony.

"The words," Zan whispered. "You have to say them."

I gulped and let my blood drip onto the leaves of the bloodleaf, which seemed to curl around the drops and cradle them for a moment before they disappeared into the veiny surface, completely absorbed. The ringing in my ears intensified.

I read the script Zan gave me, my words barely a whisper. "Oh Aren! Spirit of the spectral plane, queen in life, and favored of the Empyrea, we summon thee." Then I repeated it in the old language: *"O Aren! Spiritu Dei spectris planum, regina, in vita. Favorite de empyrea, ut vocarent te."*

Please, Aren, I silently begged as shadows began to collect in the corners and an unnerving, scratchy whisper began to crawl into my ears, *come quickly.* Then I lit the contents of the bowl on fire. The bloodleaf seemed to hiss as it burned.

The shapes were growing larger and larger, amalgamations of darkness that were not human, not animal, not grass or rock or tree . . . they did not feel like spirits that had lived and passed on. Nor did they feel like death—they felt like whatever it was that cowered in death's darkest shadow.

"Emilie?" Zan was saying. "Are you doing this?"

The table was rocking violently beneath our clasped hands.

"Aren," I said aloud, squeezing my eyes shut. "Please, Aren, please. Merciful Empyrea, anyone. Please make this stop. Make it stop. Make it stop." When I received no answer, I reached for the magic set free when I drew my blood and struck out with it, wielding it like a weapon. *"Stop."* It was not an exhortation this time but a command.

Suddenly the whispering in my ears fell silent. The table grew still. The temperature of the air, already frigid, sank lower. When I opened my eyes, the shadows had disappeared and Zan, Nathaniel, and Kate were all staring at me open-mouthed. The candles were smoking; their flames had gone out.

Behind them stood the Harbinger.

She didn't look like she had before; she seemed more wan, more faded. The hollows in her eyes and beneath the bones of her cheeks were more pronounced, her hair more limp and snarled.

"She's here," I said softly. They stared at me; they couldn't see her.

"Ask her," Zan said. "Ask her our question. Who will become the first sacrifice of Forest Gate?"

Aren dragged herself closer and closer to me, reaching out those ice-cold fingers, creeping them into my hair, onto my cheek.

"Aren," I whispered. "Please. Show me the next sacrifice. Show me the maid."

She bent over and grabbed my face in both of her hands, wrenching it down until it was level with her own. The visions began in a chaotic tumult, rushing past in an incoherent, disorienting succession of flashes. I was a ship unmoored in a savage whirlpool, no place to go but into the depths.

"Tell us," Zan said earnestly. "What is she showing you? What do you see?"

"A . . . a party, I think. There are lights. Movement . . . dancing. The girl is waiting for someone outside. I see her dress . . . it's silver.

No, white. A man is coming. It's dark. He's tall. It's dark . . . I can't see his face." The images were coming faster and faster. "I . . . I don't know. There's a hand. Teeth. A knife. The chime of a clock. Fifteen minutes to midnight." I gasped violently. "Blood on hands. Blood in hair. A crack in an eye. Red. Red. Red."

"What does she look like? What is her name? Can you give us *anything?*"

I was wading through a nauseating avalanche of images and sounds. Music, screaming, blazing streaks of light, thousands of voices talking at the same time. I focused on the girl, separating her from the rest of the din. *She's waiting. She hears a sound. She's turning.*

Oh no.

I let out a wrenching cry, and the Harbinger released me, gone in the same instant. It was over.

Kate rose from her seat and began tearing open the curtains, drowning us in light, while Nathaniel furiously rubbed out the chalk triquetra. Zan knelt at my knee, trying to calm me with soft *sh sh sh's*. It took several hiccupping breaths before I found my voice again.

"I saw her," I said weakly. "I know who she is."

"Who?" Zan asked, searching my face.

"It's me. I'm the maid."

22

They were trying not to disturb me, to let me rest, but I could see them silhouetted in the doorway. I could hear their whispers.

"Nothing has changed," Nathaniel was saying. "In fact, we're in a stronger position now than we could have possibly hoped for—Emilie knows what's going on, she wants to help us, and we don't have to convince some other poor, scared girl to risk her life. She's capable, brave. Think of all of the things she's already had to do—"

"*Everything* has changed," Zan hissed. "Without her, we've got nothing."

Kate asked, "Have you told the king about all this? Surely, if he understood the danger, he'd take action. Postpone the wedding and all these silly parties and traditions, maybe even start evacuations."

"I tried to tell him," Zan said, "and he laughed at me." He ran his hand through his hair. "He made jokes about my intelligence and my 'girlish inclination toward hysterics.'"

Nathaniel said, "We can't dismiss the idea that he could be behind it himself . . ."

"He has no reason to bring down the wall; indeed, the King's Gate seal requires his death. And despite his overfondness for poppy and port, he does not seem in any rush to die. Even if he found a way around that detail, the landholding lords outside the city are growing more influential and powerful each day. If it wasn't for the protection of the wall, any number of them could simply decide they were tired of his leadership and launch an attempt for the throne. No, it is someone else. Likely someone with a grudge against the king."

"That doesn't narrow it down much," Kate said dryly.

"There is one way," Nathaniel said again. "Emilie could—"

"No." Zan's voice had gone flinty. "Out of the question."

"I agree with Nathaniel," I said from the doorway. "We cannot exempt ourselves from the consequences everyone else has to abide by." It was a saying I'd learned from my father. *That's not leadership,* he used to say. *That's despotism.* "You wanted a girl to use as bait. Well, now you've got one."

"And what happens if you die?"

"Then I die," I said, shrugging in that same flippant way he had before the night on the wall.

"You are not expendable."

"Everyone is expendable." The rest I'd taken while they debated had almost erased the last remnants of Thackery's condition and allowed me to come to terms with what I'd seen in Aren's vision. I was feeling myself again—stubborn, determined, and somehow perpetually annoyed at Zan. To Kate I said, "I'm going to need a costume for the ball."

She looked at me wearily. "I'm not sure there's time. I've got a few other orders, and to make a dress from scratch . . ."

"I saw the dress I wear, and I already have it. It's one of mine. You don't need to start from nothing." I saw the ball again in my mind's eye. "You just need to make it shine."

★

An hour later I sat on the edge of Kate's bed with a well-wrapped parcel on my lap, carefully pulling the ties while Kate watched with skeptical interest, one eyebrow up. She'd only ever seen me in plain homespun, not even nice enough to wear to pray at an Empyrean altar, let alone to attend Achleva's grandest costume ball.

But then I pulled the parcel's last tie, and the silken fabric spilled out and fanned all around me.

Kate gasped. "Stars above! Where did you get this?"

"It was supposed to be my wedding dress," I said.

"Wedding dress? Are you getting married?"

"I'm not," I said carefully. "Not anymore. I don't think."

She raised an eyebrow, but when I had nothing more to add, she said, "You certainly are full of mysteries, Emilie." She turned back to the dress. "It does need some work." She lifted it to spin it in a circle. "But I think I can do it. Just add something here, and take this up here . . ."

Nathaniel poked his head into the room. "There's been a report of a prisoner escaping his gibbet," he said. "Zan has asked me to go see what I can find out. I probably won't be back until late."

Kate's gaze did not move from the dress, and she didn't offer a reply. Nathaniel didn't wait for one either. He left.

"Are you two all right?" I asked when he was gone.

"He doesn't trust me, Emilie." She looked away; she was still hurting. "He's never talked like that to me before. Never."

"He was in the wrong," I said. "But I'm sure it will work itself out."

She pasted a bright smile on her face, a poor cover. "I'm sure you're right."

✳

Kate had lied about her skill with a needle. She wasn't good; she was incredible. Instead of adding the missing sleeve—a piece of which had become my bloodcloth—she finished the bodice without it, so that it cut in a fierce diagonal across my chest and joined the single remaining sleeve at my collarbone with a delicate swoop, like the shape of a furled wing. All in less than a day.

In fact, the entire dress had taken on a decidedly birdlike quality; Kate had embroidered the ivy into soft, silver feathers that danced with a swish of the skirt. And she'd crafted a matching mask to go with it, made from intricately braided threads of silver curved up at my cheekbones like the silhouette of a bird in flight. From one angle, the dress glimmered gold, from another, it shone with silver, and the tiny crystals sparkled white with every slight movement. It was moonlight, starlight, and sunlight, all woven into one. And after Kate was done dressing my hair and dusting my face with pearlescent powder, I became a creature as unworldly as my costume.

One of the more practical adjustments Kate made to the dress was the inclusion of pockets, which enabled me to carry my luneocite knife undetected without having to stuff it into my bodice—a profoundly uncomfortable way to carry a weapon. It bolstered me to have a blade so close at hand.

When my transformation was complete, Kate sat back to admire her work. "What do you think?" I asked, masking my nervousness with flippancy. "Do I look murderable?"

"Very murderable," she replied with approval. "Everyone there is going to want to murder you."

The canal passage was still too flooded to use; I'd have to make my entrance through the front door, with all the other partygoers. Kate, who'd lost an entire night of sleep working on costumes, insisted on walking with me up to the front steps anyway.

"Zan left me with some instructions for you," she said. "The Great Hall will be where the royals are installed, receiving their guests. He was very specific: Don't go there. Keep to the terraces, where most of the festivities will be taking place. If someone asks who you are, say you're the great-niece of Baron Percival. His siblings were very prolific—even he doesn't know how many great-nieces and nephews there are. Keep a low profile as much as you can, but stay where there are people until midnight. That's when Zan will meet you. But don't look for him; he'll come to you. Nathaniel will be watching the entrances and exits if you need him." She hugged me. "Also, don't die. You're not allowed to die."

"That was Zan's rule?"

"Mine, but it is the most important. Now, off you go."

Every lantern was lit for the event, and the normally gloomy castle glowed spectacularly. I donned my mask and, gathering my skirts and my courage, made my way up the granite staircase toward the doors, which were flung open in golden welcome, framing the glittering display of the party within.

Inside, my fears of being noticed subsided; as beautiful as my dress was, it didn't stand out among so much of the spectacular. In the first ten feet from the entrance, I passed a woman resplendent in the colors of a peacock, a man with the sleek black coat of a feral cat, and a lady wearing the jewel-studded skull of what might have once been a bear.

Growing up, I'd attended balls on occasion: mostly stuffy, mirthless affairs, where people danced with stiff arms and a wide berth between partners. A Renaltan ball could never be too celebratory, lest it risk drawing rebuke from the Tribunal. Hedonism was only one step away from witchcraft in the eyes of the magistrates.

This was so completely unlike that. The air was humming with a jubilant energy. Everyone on the floor was dancing close together; those on the outskirts were laughing and eating with buoyant enthusiasm. One table was piled with meat: boar, pheasant, duck; another was heavily laden with decadent desserts and exotic fruits. Serving girls in pristine white smocks lined each table. I knew I was not supposed to enter the Great Hall, but I couldn't stop myself from standing outside of it to watch the merriment. Would it have been like this if the party was for me? If I was the one they were celebrating, and not Lisette?

Lisette was impossible to miss, standing at the front and smiling proudly at the attendees like a shepherd over a flock of exemplary sheep. She was wearing a dress of gossamer and shards of colored glass, made to look like butterfly wings. Beside her, my brother sat in furry breeches, a floppy set of rabbit ears dangling in front of his eyes. He looked healthy and well, despite being deathly embarrassed. I almost laughed out loud, seeing him shrink into the chair, completely mortified, but I was heartened by the sight of him fidgeting with a little metal figurine in his lap. Someday, I decided, I'd have this scene painted. And then I'd wrap it extravagantly and give it to him as a birthday present. Or perhaps I'd save it until his coronation or wedding day and present it to him with all of Renalt watching.

The thought of a wedding brought me back to myself; standing beside Lisette, leaning heavily on Conrad's high-backed chair, was a man in a feathered mask. His costume, too, was red and birdlike; it was obviously crafted to look majestic and mighty, but the hunch of his shoulders and the way he kept his head bowed made him look more farcical than fierce. Valentin, I guessed. The ineffectual, sickly prince. My once-betrothed. I should have been eager to finally get a look at him, but I was unsettled instead; I had a quest to fulfill, and I didn't want to acknowledge that it wouldn't be Zan waiting for me at the end of it.

Just then I felt a hand on my arm, and I turned to face a man wearing the mask of a wolf. He held up one hand, inviting me to dance, and I hesitantly took it.

"I thought you weren't going to get dressed up," I said as he placed a hand on the small of my back.

In response, he gave me a twirl, my dress breaking into a thousand gleaming sparkles in the light as I spun.

When he pulled me back in, I felt my heart quicken at the intensity of his embrace. His arms were strong, and they guided me with ease away from the crowd. We moved toward the terraces as we danced, away from the commotion of the hall.

The garden terraces were transformed into something out of a dream—a fairy tale come to life. Globes with tiny candles were strung across the canopy, and colored ribbons drifted in the breeze. On the perimeter, tables had been laid out with pastries and tarts and spears of fruit cut into stars. He pulled me into a darkened corner, away from the eyes of the other guests.

Alone with him now, my breath hitched as I tentatively lifted his mask, nervous but eager to find Zan's sardonic smile hidden behind the canine teeth.

Teeth. I'd seen those teeth in my vision.

But just as the mask was about to come off in my hands, the wolf's eyes flashed and his hand closed around my throat.

"Toris." I choked.

He let the empty-eyed mask drop. "You foolish girl. Always so reckless. Did you think I wouldn't recognize the dress Genevieve toiled over for months?"

"Let me go!"

His hand tightened around my neck. "Where is the vial?"

"I don't know what you're—" I couldn't finish; he squeezed harder, cutting off my air.

"My relic," he said. "The blood of the Founder. Where *is* it?"

I gagged and spluttered as stars began to dance underneath my eyelids. He relaxed his grip just long enough for me to say, coughing, "I don't have it."

"What have you done with it?"

"I've hidden it," I lied, "and I've spelled it. If I die, it will be destroyed." He let go of my throat.

"You think you can play this game, girl?"

"I've been playing a long, long time." My hand had closed around the knife in my pocket.

"The quickest way to lose is to underestimate your opponent."

"Exactly," I said, and I slashed across his costume with my knife.

The fabric split open, revealing unblemished skin beneath. I went to strike again, but his hand came up to block me; the knife went straight through his palm and out the other side. I could feel the scrape of his bones against the blade as it went by, but when I pulled it back, it came out clean.

"There's no blood," I said, confounded. "You're not bleeding."

He sprang at me, grabbing my hair to yank me close, tearing the pins painfully away from my head. He laid his knife against my throat, rage in his bulging eyes. Flecks of spittle were gathering at the corners of his lips, which were curled back over his teeth in a savage contortion, mirroring the wolf mask. There was something about his face that was *wrong*, like a puzzle that had been taken apart and put back together with some of the pieces switched.

The desire to rend me limb from limb was stalking behind his eyes. Powerful. Primal. But I'd seen the silhouette of the man who'd killed me in Aren's vision, and it wasn't Toris. The attacker was too tall, too reedy to be him.

"If you kill me," I rasped, "you will never get your relic back."

With an angry growl, he shoved me to the ground.

I regained my breath in hard, barking gasps while struggling to my feet. He stalked away, clutching his bloodless wound as he went.

"Emilie?"

Zan was standing among the tall garden grasses, dressed in his typical linen shirt, long leather jacket, and breeches. "No costume for you, then?" I tried to sound unruffled, but my hoarse voice betrayed me.

"You didn't stay inside," he said accusingly. "I panicked when I couldn't find you. You weren't supposed to come out here alone."

"You're not my guard, Zan. You're not my governess. I don't need you to hover over me."

"No? Because your own account of what is supposed to happen tonight says otherwise."

"And if I'm supposed to accomplish your goals for tonight, I need you to *step back*." I knew it was not Zan's fault that I'd mistaken Toris for him and let myself be led so stupidly into danger, but I was angry at him anyway, because of how much I *wanted* it to be him. How confounding it was when it wasn't. My throat still ached from Toris's fingers, but my pride had taken the more grievous injury.

"I'm supposed to stand idly by while you let yourself get sacrificed?" Zan's black eyebrows were drawn down into an angry V.

"Your plan, not mine." I looked at the clock looming over the glass terrace doors. "It's almost time."

I was turning on my heel when Zan grabbed my arm. "I was wrong."

"What?" I was startled; Zan didn't seem capable of such an admission.

"You're not bait. No one should be bait. I should never have suggested such a thing. I was wrong."

I blinked up at him as he continued, "I hate using you. I hate seeing you in pain, knowing I'm the one who put you up to it. If it weren't for the wall, if it weren't for a lot of things—"

Above us the clock began to chime.

"Midnight," I gasped, pulling away. I raced toward the terraces, knowing that, with his heart, he could not follow. I made a sharp skidding turn and found myself in the exact location of my vision, directly under the clock tower. *How appropriate,* I thought darkly. *What better location to execute a witch?*

I saw him at that moment, twenty feet ahead: a man dressed in the costume of a third-century Renaltan cavalier, dyed black instead of blue. He was hunched over, back to me, alone in the moonlight.

No, not alone. He was crouched over a girl. A servant girl, from the look of her. One of the many who'd been manning the banquet tables, wearing those gleaming white aprons.

Only hers was not so white anymore. She was gagging and spluttering thick blood all over the front of it.

Red. Red. Red.

"Nihil nunc salvet te." The man's voice was low and liquid, like oil.

A flash of a knife.

The twelfth toll of the clock.

Streaks of blistering light above, and a scream.

My scream.

He plunged the knife into her chest.

I dove at him, brandishing my own tiny knife like a saber, inflicting a good-size slash on his forearm before he knocked my knife away. His face was a blank black mask, and I knew at once that he was costumed as the horseman of the Ebonwilde, a faceless executioner in Renaltan lore. I swiped at his expressionless mask with my fingers curled into claws, leaving red trails across his ear and neck. The mask wouldn't budge. I snarled like a rabid dog until he struck a blow to my temple with the hilt of his knife: a glass knife, a mirror to mine. I saw swirling stars for a moment, but my mask took most of the blow, cracking across the right side.

Crack in the eye.

I lunged again, this time from below, aiming for his midsection. The force of my tackle knocked him off balance; he fell with me against the terrace stones, hitting his back against the edge of a stair with a heavy crack, emitting a gruff cry of pain from behind the mask. I wondered if he'd broken his spine until he threw me off him with a roar. I tripped on the girl's body and found myself falling, entangled in her lifeless limbs, down the stairs. After rolling to a stop at the bottom, I climbed out from under the glassy-eyed corpse, sobbing.

Blood on my hands.

The man vanished into the shadows.

I'd made a mistake. I'd misidentified the maid, and this girl had died for it.

Zan and Nathaniel reached me at the same time, with Zan breathlessly pulling me to my feet and then into his arms. With my head tucked under his chin, he shouted to Nathaniel, "He went that way! He can't be far. *Find him.*"

23

The girl was named Molly. She was a server from the kitchen. She'd snuck from her post at the party to rendezvous with a secret beau; indeed, she'd gotten the job in the castle in an effort to be closer to him. The other girls all said that she'd never told them his name, and now she never could.

The man's trail was cold. He was a blood mage, after all, and probably used his wound to render himself invisible, as I had done so many times. If I'd obtained a sample of his blood, even just a drop, I might have been able to locate him, but the scene was a gruesome one. There was no way of knowing which blood, if any, was his.

News of the brutality of the girl's death was overshadowed, however, by another peculiar happening: inside the city, everything green was turning slowly to brown. Roses rotted on the vine, the woods were carpeted with fallen needles of now-skeletal evergreens . . . and the terrace gardens, which had been a sight of wild magnificence at the masquerade, now lay wilted and ruined. The smell of decay hung low over the city, permeating everything; it was impossible to escape it. The only thing that still seemed to flourish was the carpet of bloodleaf around the tower.

The bruise on my temple was an unpleasant purple, but it could have been much worse if the mask hadn't absorbed most of the blow. As Zan was eager to remind me, I was lucky.

It didn't feel like luck.

The next morning I found Nathaniel, Kate, and Zan gathered around Kate's table in silence, a melancholic mood pervading the air. *"Nihil nunc salvet te,"* I said.

Zan said, "You're supposed to be resting."

"I've rested long enough. I'm done resting." I repeated, *"Nihil nunc salvet te.* Do you know what that means?"

"'Nothing can save you now,'" Zan replied in a low voice. "Why—"

"It's part of the Tribunal execution script," I said. "They say it before they hang people." I gulped. While they all grimaced, I continued, "He said it to her, last night, before he killed her. For the Tribunal, the phrase is ceremonial. But this felt like a spell. A consecration, even." I paused. "I knew, once he drew her blood and said it, that nothing could be done for her."

Kate patted my hand. "What a terrible thing to witness."

"I've never seen that phrase mentioned in Achlev's writings or in any of the spell books. Only in Renalt, and only from the Tribunal."

Skeptically, Zan said, "You think this has something to do with the Tribunal? But they don't use magic. They hate magic. They want to destroy magic. This person wants to unleash it in monstrous proportions."

"You're probably right," I said. "It was just a thought. It's just that we have so little to go on, and so little time . . ."

"Less time than we thought, even," Nathaniel said.

"What do you mean?"

"You should be the one to tell her," he said to Zan.

I frowned. "Tell me what?"

Zan's lips were set in an unhappy line. "The king was very upset about how his party last night was so rudely interrupted. Never mind that a girl lost her life." He shifted in his chair. "Combined with his disappointment that a prisoner escaped his gibbets, his spirits have been very low. So he's decided to raise them the only way he knows how: by lavishing himself with leisure activities. This time he's decided to take Prince Conrad and Princess Aurelia on a grand old hunt."

My jaw dropped. "The plants are rotting. People are being murdered, and he's going hunting?"

"Usually when he gets this way, I'm glad," Zan said. "If he's gone, he can't do any damage at home." He was avoiding my eyes. "But this time he's decided that every lord and lady must go with him. Myself included."

"Everyone? The prince too?"

Zan shot a look at Nathaniel and Kate. Hastily, he said, "Him too."

"You're not serious," I said. I struggled to formulate a better response. All I could come up with was "When?"

"We leave tomorrow. Before sundown," Nathaniel said.

"You're going too?"

Kate said flatly, "I told him to." There was still something cold in the way she and Nathaniel were acting toward each other. Nathaniel did not comment; he looked the other way. "Zan needs him," she said curtly.

"You can't go," I said bleakly. "Tell Domhnall no. We need you here. *I* need you here."

Zan cleared his throat. "Can we talk? Maybe . . . outside?"

I followed him, arms crossed.

Alone on the stoop, Zan said, "Emilie, I know it's bad timing, and I don't expect you to understand—"

"Good. That's good. Because I *don't*."

"This is what my king has commanded—"

"Your king is a feckless half-wit."

"That doesn't make him any less a king."

"Doesn't it? I thought you were loyal to Achleva."

"I am. That is why I have to obey the rule of its monarch."

I heard the echo of my father's voice alongside my own. "Kings do not rule; they serve. The people do not swear fealty to a king, but he to them."

"Damn it, Emilie, I have no *choice*."

"Look around you, Zan." I motioned to the decaying mulch of Kate's garden that only yesterday had been populated with cheerful yellow flowers. "If obeying Domhnall means letting his people suffer, or putting them in danger, you have only one choice."

"And what is that?"

"Disobey Domhnall. *Resist*."

"You don't understand."

"I understand. We're in it up to our necks here, and you're going to take a vacation. You're running away when you need to stay and put up a fight."

"Like you did, with the Tribunal?"

I said dangerously, "You have no *idea* what you're talking about."

He was inches from my face. "Neither do you."

"Good luck on your hunt." I ended the conversation with the slam of the door.

✳

Kate kept herself occupied with sewing projects while I buried myself in books to distract from Nathaniel's movements around the house as he packed for the hunt, but though I was turning pages, I absorbed little of what I was reading. After I watched Kate sew and unpick the same seam three times, I suspected she was similarly agitated.

Shortly after midday, Nathaniel stopped just outside the sitting room, bag in hand. "I'm going now," he said. His eyes were fixed to the wall, as if he were addressing it instead of us.

When Kate did not respond, he picked up his satchel and moved for the door, his broad shoulders sagging just a little bit lower than usual.

Kate closed her book and rose from the table. "Wait," she said, taking his large hand in her small one. "Be careful."

His expression softened. "I'll be back soon."

She nodded and put her hand on her belly. "We'll be waiting."

✳

Nathaniel's departure left Kate feeling drained; I felt comfortable letting her stay in the house alone only after she promised to try to sleep. She'd extracted a similar promise from me, too, but I had no intention of keeping it. I tried to convince myself that maybe it was better this way. Maybe with Zan gone, I could go back to worrying about my own problems instead of being constantly distracted by his.

The first thing I needed to take care of was the Founder's blood relic. Toris had tipped his hand when my threat to destroy it caused him to retreat. I'd insinuated that I'd spelled the relic and hidden it, and that's what I decided to spend my time accomplishing. Better late than never, after all.

I thought of a half dozen places to hide it, but none of them felt right—that one was too close to home; wouldn't want Toris to track it back to Nathaniel and Kate. That one was too open; it could be too easily glimpsed by a passerby. Burying it wouldn't work, because what if an animal found it? Keeping it on my person at all times seemed like a good option . . . except that if Toris ever searched me and found it, I'd be dead on the spot.

Over and over, the thought that kept coming back to me was: Aren.

She had frightened Toris in the Ebonwilde. Her tower was protected by bloodleaf; no self-preserving individual would cross it willingly. And as my fluency in magic grew, so did my awareness of its currents. At the exact center of the city, the tower acted almost like an anchor to the ley lines rerouted into the wall. I was drawn to it.

The flooded canal passage had mostly drained in the days since High Gate fell, leaving behind a thick layer of mud and debris. I slogged through it, falling a few times, and ascended the tower stairs soaked and feeling sorry for myself.

It didn't take long to find a brick loose enough to remove and replace with the vial concealed behind it; indeed, it seemed as if the structure was still standing only because of luck or magic, or a combination of both. The brick I chose was on the pedestal just below Aren's left heel. I could have used a brick in the front, but it seemed somehow unfair to make her watch over the blood of the brother who'd killed her. I didn't spell it, either; I was tired, and my hands hurt—they were never without a new cut, no matter how quickly I healed—and I felt certain that if I did, it would somehow go awry, just like everything else.

Just as I was rising from my knees to brush the dirt and chips of mortar off my dress, I heard the sound of trumpets in the distance. I leaned out from the tower battlement in time to see the king's hunting party exiting through Forest Gate, blue Achlevan pennants streaming. It was a collection of lords and ladies dressed in costumes nearly as fine—and absurd—as the masquerade. A half dozen sleek hounds ran alongside the parade, barking for joy and nipping at the horses' heels. I caught sight of Lisette and Conrad's matching golden heads just as they disappeared under the gate. Behind them, about three riders back, rode Nathaniel and Zan.

I wanted to be angry, but standing there so far above the rest of the world, watching Zan blindly following the whims of his worthless king, I felt only sorry. For him, for the city he was neglecting, and for myself, because he cared so little for my good opinion when I would have moved mountains to earn his. Until this, at least.

I was retreating from the tower's edge when I saw it: a tiny scrap of red, fluttering in the breeze, bright against the wilted, brown garden. It wasn't smart to go gallivanting across the castle grounds in the middle of the day, but once I'd seen it, I couldn't stop myself. I flew down the stairs and raced across the bloodleaf to where I'd spotted that flash of red.

Sure enough, it was a ribbon tied to the hand of an impish garden figurine. *Red for north.*

I untied the ribbon and walked a few paces toward the fjord but had to stop at the terrace ledge. Leaning over, I peeked down and saw a rock, mostly hidden by rotted bushes, that had been laid on top of something white. A small paper box. I opened it quickly and was stunned to pull out Conrad's figurine, carefully twisted into the shape of a swan.

I searched my pockets, but I already knew I had nothing left to give him; nevertheless, the thought of stopping our game was intolerable. As much as I wanted to keep this token from him, I couldn't. I couldn't keep standing out in the wide open, either. So I turned the pieces one, two, three more times, until the animal I was holding was not a graceful swan but a noble stag. I traded the red ribbon for the one I'd come wearing—lavender—and left it under the rock. Then I moved east and hid the box under the overhang of one terrace stone and another.

All the way home, I let my hair fly free as I cradled that red ribbon as if it was the most precious thing in the world. Because to me it was.

24

The next morning I found Kate in the rocking chair next to her bedroom window, humming a sad, pretty lullaby in time to the in-and-out motions of her needle as she rocked. She paused to hold up her project—a lovely little dress—to admire. "Not bad," she said. To her belly, she added, "What do you think, my girl?"

I knocked softly on the door frame to let her know I was there. "With all the flower dresses you've made, what will your baby wear if it's a boy?"

"Flower dresses, of course," Kate said, smiling widely. "A baby doesn't care what it wears, and I've put too much work into them not to use them. Besides, I'd never want my boy to grow up thinking he couldn't love flowers." She pointed her needle at me. "But still . . . she's a girl, and until she's born, no one will be able to tell me otherwise."

"What does Nathaniel think of the prospect?"

Her smile dimmed. "I haven't told him."

Carefully, I asked, "How bad is it, really?"

"Bad. I made Dedrick's costume—how could I not? It was a

simple design, and he paid quite a lot for it. But Nathaniel was here when he came by to get it before the ball. It didn't go well."

"And now he's off chasing bunnies in the forest with Domhnall."

"He didn't want to go; I could tell," she said miserably. "But I didn't want to stop him."

"But why? It looked like you had a moment, right before he left . . . Maybe if he had stayed you could have—"

"This is why." She pulled a note from her pocket. "Dedrick sent me this yesterday. My mother is coming into town at his behest. He has arranged for me to see her, first thing tomorrow morning. She believes she's been invited to see a property my father is considering purchasing. I'm going to be waiting there, as a surprise. If Nathaniel knew . . ." She picked at the untrimmed threads on the baby's dress, shrugging.

Something about the subterfuge felt wrong, but who was I to judge? They all thought my name was Emilie.

I said, "It's only been a few weeks since I last saw my mother— and we did not part on the best of terms, either—but I'd give anything to talk to her. If I knew I could see her, I'd defy anyone who tried to stop me." I folded my arms. "So I understand how you feel. But it shouldn't be a secret. Nathaniel doesn't have to like it, but I do think that he should know."

"You sound like my mother," Kate said wryly. "You should come meet her. I think you'd get along."

"If she's at all like you, it would be hard not to. But Zan said Molly used to work in the fish market on the waterfront before getting hired in the castle. Maybe someone there could tell me more about her 'beau.' Might even be able to get a name."

"No magic this time? No séance?"

I shook my head. "The only thing I've been able to achieve with magic is to make things worse." I looked at my hands, dotted with tiny cuts in various stages of healing. "I'm going to try another way."

"Dedrick has a home on the waterfront. It's where I'm going to meet my mother tomorrow." She brightened. "We can walk there together."

✳

We left at the break of dawn, watching the sun send streaks of soft pink across the sky as it rose. It was almost enough to distract from the muck left from the dead plants. The sour-sweet stench of rot hung over the entire city.

As we approached the waterfront, Kate said, "Keep alert. In this district, it's easy to leave with empty pockets without spending a single copper."

Here the scent of decay was overpowered by the smells of fish and unwashed bodies and other, less pleasant aromas. The shouts of haggard, sea-weathered sailors intermingled with the cry of gulls circling above. Kate pointed to a building on the eastern side, a manor of glass and gold, that overlooked the docks like a smug emperor. "There's Dedrick's place." She fidgeted nervously. "Time to go. How do I look?"

"Beautiful," I said gently. "But your mother won't care. She'll just be happy to see you."

Kate gave me a quick hug. "Wish me luck."

"Good luck!" I said, but she'd already disappeared into the crowd.

I approached a stall constructed of gray timbers and old tin, near the ghost of a hard-bitten woman whose expression was a mixture of wary suspicion and open hostility. Small wonder: the back of her head was caved in. She sat on a barrel like a gargoyle, while a girl—a real girl, of flesh and blood—manned a display of buckets filled with drooping flowers nearby. I approached cautiously from the angle farthest from the ghost; that was one death I preferred not to see.

"Lovely day, is it not?" I asked the girl.

She gave me a nervous smile. "Perfect day for a daisy, mum, if I do say so meself."

"So it is. I'll take a few." I gave her two silvers—almost the entirety of my wages from Zan.

She gaped. "No, mum, I can't accept this. Not for flowers two steps from bein' compost, curse this blight."

"Keep it," I said. "What's your name?"

"Elizabeth," she said hesitantly. "Most call me Beth."

"Beth, I'm trying to find out more about a girl named Molly. She was a housemaid at the castle, and"—I cleared my throat—"she recently passed. Did you know her?"

Beth's expression clouded over. "I knew Molly. She used to sell chocolate and candy from that stall over there." She pointed across the way. "She was nice. I'm real sorry about what happened to her."

"They said she got her job as a housemaid to get closer to a man she'd been seeing."

"I don't know much about that," Beth said. "I didn't know her all that well. We was just friendly."

"You never saw a man frequent her stall?"

"All sorts of men hung around her stall, miss. It's the way o' the docks. Girls like me learn quick how to handle it." She flashed a gnarly-looking knife tucked into her apron pocket. "Men don't learn as quick. Takes a few pokes before they get that flowers is the only thing I be sellin' here." She paused. "Molly was of a softer spirit. She wasn't so tough as me. Sold more on account of it, I think. But at what cost?"

"What do you mean?"

Beth fiddled with the coins. "Nothin', mum. Just that Molly might still be 'ere if she was better at tellin' the difference between the sheep and the wolves dressed up in their clothing."

"Beth," I said slowly, "is there something else you want to tell me?"

She shook her head, maybe a little too quickly. "No. No, mum. Just a little advice, maybe. Fish ain't been so plentiful as of late, so the fishermen are all in foul temper today. Best steer clear if you want to keep that skip in your step." She tucked the coins away in her dress. "With the exception of Firth, o' course. He's in a fine mood. Caught himself a fugitive last night. There'll be a bit o' gold in his future, mark it."

"A fugitive?" I asked.

"That man that escaped from the king's gibbets," she said. "First one ever. Poor bugger didn't get far, though. Firth found 'is body floatin' in the water down by the next port. They'll be bringing it up this way soon, if you want a look."

"Thank you," I managed.

The din of the docks, the smells, the bright light of midday, my happy feeling at finding Conrad's toy . . . all were suddenly dimmed and deadened.

I thanked Beth again and stumbled into the narrow alley between two dockside buildings, where I wrapped my arms around myself. *It isn't Thackery,* I told myself. *It can't be Thackery.*

But it was Thackery.

I knew it before the body was paraded past like a prize buck, because his spirit preceded it, dripping and bloated, midsection punctured a half dozen times. Thackery was dead, and with him my last hopes of rescue. We regarded each other for a split second, and then he grabbed me. My shriek was lost in the sounds of the dock.

He'd been camped out in the woods. Someone had been following him. He'd heard the breaking twigs, the breathing, and whirled around and around trying to catch a glimpse. I could hear the faintest whisper, *I am unseen. I am unseen.*

When his follower finally showed himself, it was to press a luneocite knife into Thackery's ribs from behind. Hot breath on his neck. An oily voice saying, "This is your last chance to save your life, old man. The king wants to know who has been selling you those invitations. Was it the same person who let you out of your cage?"

"I can't say," Thackery gasped as the knife pressed deeper, breaking his skin.

"Does the king have a bastard somewhere? A child no one but you knows about? Answer!"

Despite all, Thackery chuckled. "Everyone knows the king is as sterile as a ball o' cotton. Only reason he had the one kid he got is because 'is wife asked the Assembly to use magic to help her conceive. Took the work of the whole lot of 'em, too, I'm told."

"You're useless," the man said, and pushed his knife the rest of the way in.

Thackery fell and rolled over, throat filling up with blood. The man nudged him with his boot and leaned down close.

"Send my regards to the other side," he said, before stabbing him with his luneocite knife again, and again, and again . . .

I came out of the horrid vision with tears running down my face.

Thackery was already gone. He'd done what he meant to do. He'd shown me what he wanted me to see.

The face of his killer. Dedrick Corvalis.

I dropped my half-dead flowers and ran.

✳

The manor was built dockside, but it was cut off from the teeming life that pervaded the rest of the pier. I ducked under a gate, struck by the emptiness. There were no people here, none. No servants or sailors or sound but the hollow *thunk thunk* of my shoes on the pier's timbers.

I let myself inside, thankful it wasn't locked. The house was a maze of golden chandeliers and marble columns but empty of furniture. "Kate?" I called softly, timidly, and the sound ricocheted around in the vaulted rafters. When it faded, I heard another sound: voices, a man and a woman.

She's up there, I thought, and I dashed toward the grand, circling staircase, taking the steps two at a time before stumbling breathlessly out onto the top floor.

I landed in a huge antechamber painted to the ceiling with a depiction of a terrifying, fiery-winged Empyrea descending from the heavens and touching down to earth. Fire and water and stone and storm and forest were shown to be colliding around her, while streaks of blue-white light jigged out from the collision point. This was a sanctorium, not unlike the one back home in Renalt.

Beneath the monstrous illustration there was a door.

It was dark, but there was still enough light to see that the entire left wall was made of ruched velvet curtains. I could hear voices on the other side.

"The crown jewel of the whole place, where a lovely, pious woman can come to rest and restore her spirit, basking in the light of the great Empyrea. This is the part of the house I'll miss the most."

"You saved the best of the tour for last, I see," I heard Kate reply. "Your home is very impressive. I can hardly believe you've sold it when you seem to love it so much."

"I wanted to collect the proceeds of my investment before property value declines within the city." A soft chuckle. "I have reason to believe that such a downturn is imminent."

"Always one step ahead, predicting the future," Kate said with a polite laugh. "Do you also happen to know when my mother will arrive?"

I peeked through a break in two panels to see Kate and Corvalis alone in the enormous inner sanctuary. It was at least six times larger than the one back home in Renalt. He took her hand and pressed it to his lips as her smile froze on her face.

"Now that we're in the confessional, I have a confession to make, dear Katherine. Your mother isn't coming today. I'm sorry. Something came up for her, and she wasn't able to make it."

"Oh," Kate said, visibly deflating. "Well, thank you for the tour of your lovely home. I'd probably better go."

"Back to a husband who mistreats you?"

"Excuse me?"

"I've seen it, Katherine. Firsthand. The irreverent way he speaks to you, the way he lords himself over you. Not to mention how he's forced you into subservience, working for others when it should be you going to balls, so the rest of the world can marvel at your beauty." He stroked her cheek. "It is my greatest folly, letting you get away."

"I'm sorry, Dedrick," Kate said, "if I've given you the wrong impression—"

"It would be easy to undo," he continued as if he hadn't heard her. "The marriage, so obviously performed under duress, can be annulled. And as for the whelp, no one of importance even knows about it. Once it has been delivered, it can be given to a decent, Empyrea-fearing family somewhere, or to an orphanage—"

Kate hit him, her hand whipping so fast across his face that it knocked his head to the side, revealing a series of scratches under his hair, by his ear. The ones *I'd* given him just after he'd killed Molly.

He touched a hand to his lip, and it came away with blood. "Don't be stupid, Katherine. I'm trying to save you. To give you a chance. A lesser man wouldn't even *consider* taking up with you now."

She raised her hand to strike him again, but he grabbed it before she could land the blow. His handsome face was drawn into a sullen pout. "Oh, Katherine. You're breaking my heart."

He pulled her against his chest and took out his luneocite knife, nicking his own hand with it before pressing it against her neck. I grabbed the object nearest me—a vase—and dashed from my hiding place. But I was fast enough only to hear him say, "Know that I never wanted this for you. *Nihil nunc salvet te.*"

I slammed the vase full-force against the back of his skull. Crystalline shards fell with Dedrick to the ground. My hand hurt; the force of the blow had reopened some of my cuts. Kate was holding her hand against her neck, eyes terrified.

Dedrick was on all fours, trying to crawl over to us. His eyes were blazing with a malevolent fire. He grabbed at my skirt, and I brought my foot down hard on his left arm, the one I'd cut the last time I'd faced him. He cried out, but I'd already moved to his other side, laying him out flat with a kick to the back he'd bruised on the terrace stones.

"Come on!" I shouted, pulling Kate to the door and slamming it tight behind us.

Kate was shaking, but she brought a candelabra to me and I drove the metal shafts into the handle to jam it.

Behind the door, Dedrick was laughing softly. Almost politely. "You don't know what's coming," he said. "You don't know what will happen when I get out of here."

Kate shrank away, and I slammed my hands against the wood. "You aren't getting out of here, you dog. The next time you leave this room it will be in *chains*."

The words surged from me, and with them, magic. What had Simon said back in Renalt, hidden away in the sanctuary? *Over time, and with practice, the more instinctual and accessible magic becomes.*

When I stepped back, my bloody handprint remained on the door like a promise.

25

he baby," Kate said. "I think she's coming now." Tears were streaming down her face.

"We're almost home," I said. "Can you make it?"

She took a long, deep breath. "I don't know. I think so."

"Do you have a midwife I can fetch?"

"No," she said, her face contorting with pain as a contraction took hold of her. "Nathaniel's sister is a midwife, but she lives days away. She was going to come next week." She opened her eyes. "There's just you."

It can't be just me, I thought but didn't say aloud. I'd helped Onal a few times when I was younger, but these were not normal circumstances. I also didn't want to mention the wound on her neck. It was small, but it still hadn't stopped bleeding.

I got her up the walk and helped settle her onto the bed. "I sent him away," she said between contractions. "Nathaniel tried to warn me against speaking to Dedrick, and I sent him away."

"This isn't your fault," I reassured her. "I'll go to town, see if I can find a midwife or a healer." Kate kept her sewing money in a can on the kitchen shelf, and I emptied it into my pockets.

"Please don't go," Kate begged, sweat standing out on her forehead. "I don't want to be alone."

"I won't be long," I promised. "Everything will be fine. I swear."

✳

In the evening light, the windows of Sahlma's apothecary were empty and forbidding, but I rapped on the door anyway. Three, four, five times. I paused, then three times more. "Open the door!" I shouted. "Please!" I didn't want to be here again, but I'd left Kate in too much of a hurry, neglecting to ask her for a name or address of someone qualified who could help. Sahlma was the only one I knew of.

It was a sour face that greeted me when the door finally came ajar, but it grew sourer still when I took down my hood and she saw that it was me. "Stupid wench," she said angrily. "You dare come back here and disturb my peace again?"

"I need your help!"

"Go away." She tried to shut the door in my face, but I slammed my hands against it before it could meet the frame.

"Don't!" I said frantically, pushing past her. "Hear me out! Please! I can pay." I took out Kate's coins and slammed them onto the counter. "I have a friend. She's about to have a baby, but it's too early and"—I swallowed hard against the lump that was burning in my throat like a coal—"she was hurt by a wicked man and now she's bleeding and bleeding and it won't stop. She's going to have this baby, and soon, and she or her baby could die unless you help me." I knew the truth of it as I said it; even with help, Kate's chances were grim.

Nihil nunc salvet te.

"Be gone," Sahlma said with a cough. "And take your coins and your troubles with you."

I said through gritted teeth, "Please. What about the baby? A mother should never have to be without her child."

It was what Zan's mother had said to Sahlma, right before she jumped.

She reeled back as if she recognized the words, but only for a second. "Get out."

A small, gray face peeked out at me from behind her skirts. "Who is the little boy in the cap?" I asked, gently assessing the similarities between his young, spectral face and her weathered, aged one. "He's your son, isn't he?"

The little boy in the cap watched me, waiting.

Sahlma's hand lashed my face. I could feel the sting of each one of her fingers on my lips, but I kept going. "You are the way you are because of him, aren't you? Because you lost him."

Her hand slowly lowered. "How do you . . . ?"

"I can see him. He's right here with us, right now as we speak."

Her voice began to shake. "You're trying to manipulate me." Her lips curled down in rage. "How dare you? How dare you use the memory of my son in such a way?"

I steeled myself. "I am not lying."

All my life I'd been terrified of their touches, to see their horrific tales play out in front of my eyes. But I knelt down and held my hand to him. He stepped out from behind her skirts and looked from my outstretched hand to my face, as if asking for permission. I gave a slight nod, and he placed his small, pale fingers in mine.

It was like plunging my arm into an ice-ridden river. I gulped at the shock of his cold touch, but I didn't let go.

Flashes of words and pictures and memories flew around my head like snow in a flurry. I told her, "He was named after your favorite bird. A . . . a kestrel. He'd always find a stick to carry when you'd walk from town to town, looking for work as a maid. Sometimes you had to take other work to buy him food. You'd make him wait outside in the street so he couldn't hear what was happening to you, but he could hear. You hardly ate much; you gave what you could to him and put a little money aside—to take him on a boat ride, you said. He loved boats. You'd walk past the docks with him every day and compare the ships in the harbor—the colors and sizes—and talk about which one you'd take him on when you had enough money saved up."

Tears were shining in her eyes. Her hands were twisted up in her apron, which she knotted and pressed against her mouth, dampening her shrill wail of grief.

My entire arm was becoming a block of ice, but I held on. "Your husband was often gone for months, but he always found you when his funds ran dry. The last time, he stole the money for your boat ride and wasted it on bad bets. When Kestrel found out, he cried. But the crying just upset *him*. He tried to make Kestrel quit crying." Breathless horror was suffocating me; I didn't want to see this. "And he . . . and he—"

"Stop," Sahlma begged. "Please stop."

Tears were running down my face as Kestrel's story flew past my eyes. "Stars. Oh, merciful Empyrea. I'm sorry. I am so sorry." I closed my eyes. "You buried him in the forest," I said shakily. "You planted a sapling on the spot. And then you went back to the man who took your little boy from you and you hit him on the back of the head with a rock while he was sleeping. You were about to hit him again when you saw the patch of bloodleaf under the bridge . . . and then you dragged him to it, dumped him on it, and then you slit his throat and pushed his body into the river below. Then you went back with the petals . . . you dug up the tree . . . you tried . . ." I looked up at her through bleary eyes, unable to finish.

Sahlma pressed both hands to her face and sobbed.

Kestrel waited calmly while I collected myself. "Your son . . . he wants you to know that he doesn't blame you, even though you blame yourself. He loves you. He doesn't want you to be sad anymore."

The boy nodded and withdrew his hand. My arm fell to my side. I couldn't move it. I clutched it with my other hand and staggered to my feet.

"I'm sorry," I whispered. "I'll go."

"Wait," she said. "I did collect bloodleaf petals that day. Two of them. One I used . . . you saw how. The second, I sold to buy my education as a healer. I wanted to help people like me . . . but time and circumstance has a way of beating the idealism out of a person." She wiped at her puffy face with the back of her age-spotted hand. "I'll help you, if I can. Show me the way."

*

It was dark when Sahlma and I rushed across the cottage threshold. We could hear Kate's wrenching cries before we even reached the walk. We found her kneeling at the side of her bed, bent over in excruciating pain.

Sahlma got right to work, rolling up her sleeves. "Water. Now."

I hastily filled a basin and rushed in with it, water slopping over the sides as I set it next to the bed. "It's bad, isn't it?" Kate asked.

"You're going to be fine," I said reassuringly before shooting a worried look at Sahlma, who said nothing.

Kate was racked with another hard contraction, tendons standing out against her skin as she struggled through it. The bloodstain on the gauze pressed against the cut on her neck began to spread further across the white plane. The wound still had not clotted.

"It won't be long now," Sahlma said, furrows deepening above her brows.

Kate labored through the waning hours of the night, growing ever weaker.

Near morning Kate gave one final, shuddering push, and the child was born. A little girl.

"Look, Kate!" I said. "You were right. A girl."

"She's alive," Sahlma said, looking wan and sad. "But she's small, and not breathing well."

Tears shone in Kate's eyes. "Can I hold her?"

Sahlma wrapped the baby up and passed her to me. I paused to pull the fabric away from her face. It was round and perfect, with sweet, tawny cheeks and a little bit of dark, curly hair crowning her head. Her eyelids flickered open and she began mewling weakly. Her eyes, I could tell, would be deep brown. Just like her father's.

Kate took her in shaking arms. "We did it, my girl. We did it."

I stumbled, numb, into the kitchen, while Sahlma did her best to stanch Kate's bleeding. I made myself as busy as possible, straightening what was already straightened, cleaning what was already clean. Kate's half-finished work was everywhere: a pie, ready to be baked. A bundle of fresh firewood in the hearth, ready to be set alight. A basket full of half-made baby clothes next to the chair. I lifted the first dress and stared at it, dazed, wishing I could finish it for her but knowing I'd never do it justice. When I went to lay it back in the basket, I felt a sharp sting on the tip of my forefinger.

Bleeding stars, I thought. I'd pricked myself.

It wasn't much, just a tiny drop of blood, no bigger than the head of the pin that caused it. But it was the last straw. The numbness with which I'd been holding myself together was gone. Kneeling over Kate's sewing basket, I cracked.

Zan, Nathaniel, I cried out in my thoughts as the blood drop fell, *come back. Kate needs you. I need you. Come back.*

✸

Sahlma's efforts had been in vain, I could see that. Kate was still bleeding. If the Empyrea had been merciful, Kate would have been allowed the kindness of unconsciousness—but her eyes were clear and full of sharp anguish as she lay holding her child's tiny, failing body under her chin. She was stroking the back of her baby's delicate hand, singing a broken lullaby.

"Kate." My tears were flowing freely now.

She turned her sorrowful face to me and said, "How can I bear it? How?"

"I don't know." And I backed out of the room, letting her be alone with her little girl for whatever time they had left together.

Sahlma was washing the blood from her hands in the next room, her face sagging and sallow. "A shame," she said. "A stars-forsaken shame." More softly, she said, "No mother should be without her child."

"You did your best," I said dully. "But please tell me . . . is there any hope for Kate?"

"No," Sahlma said, rising. "There's nothing within the laws of nature that can possibly save either of them now."

My heart sank, but Sahlma continued, "I think, however, there's a solution outside of the laws of nature." She reached inside her pocket and brought out a medicine dropper capsule.

"What is that?"

"It's bloodleaf petal potion," she said.

My heart quickened. Nearly incoherent with hope, I asked, "What? Where did you come by . . . *how?*"

"There was another time. Another mother, like her, wanted to save her child, took her own life to do it. I managed only one petal that time. I should have given the whole thing to the child, but I had realized, not long before, that there was something wrong inside me. A cancer. And I . . . and I . . . I didn't want to die. So I distilled the petal into a serum. I gave the little boy just enough to get him past the worst of his illness, and then I kept the rest for myself. I've extended my life with it, drop by drop, for almost twelve years now, assuaging my guilt by telling myself that if it wasn't for me, he'd have died anyway." She placed the capsule in my hands. "Even still, all night, I've been hoping I wouldn't have to use it. Arguing with myself against just giving it away to a stranger, but I think . . . I think it may be time to finally let go. There are two, maybe three drops left. Enough for one of them at least."

"You're making the choice to die?"

"Better to choose it for myself than to have it chosen for me." Her eyes were glistening. "I've done many things of which I am not proud. I knew that someday, if my son was waiting on the other side, I'd have to make an accounting to him, and I couldn't bear the thought. But now I'm not afraid anymore, and I think I've put off our reunion long enough." She gathered her things. "A mother should never have to be without her child."

26

When Sahlma was gone, I returned to the bedroom. Kate turned her tear-stained face to me as I entered.

"I keep praying to the Empyrea that this isn't real. I'll do anything she asks. I just want my baby to live, Emilie."

I pulled out Sahlma's capsule. "I might have an answer," I said gently. "It's a potion made from a bloodleaf flower. There's only a drop or two left. We can give one to each of you. It's our best chance now."

She kissed her baby and held her closer. "I don't want it. Give it all to her."

"Think of Nathaniel. He needs you. Please, Kate. Take it."

"He's stronger than I am. He always has been. He will heal, and live a good life. But if I take some, and she dies, I won't be able to live with myself."

"If you don't take it . . ." I trailed off. I didn't know how to tell her.

"I'm not a fool, Emilie. I know what Dedrick said to me. *'Nihil nunc salvet te.'* I know what it means. What if I take it, and you lose us both anyway? This way, I can die knowing I did everything I could for her."

I took a deep breath and nodded slowly. My heart was too sore to try to argue. *A mother should never have to be without her child.* "Then, here. Give her to me."

With the baby in my lap, I opened the vial and held the dropper above the infant's parted lips.

One, two. Two drops.

Nothing happened.

This was madness. What had I just done?

Live, I willed the child. *Live.*

I handed the baby back to Kate, unable to speak.

"Look," she said.

I watched in wonder as warmth began to spread again over the baby's arms, and legs, and down her torso, and to her toes. Two rosy circles began to form on her gray cheeks. And then she gave a sigh.

Then eyelids fluttered. She opened her eyes.

"Hello, love," Kate said with joy.

✳

I didn't realize I'd drifted off until I blinked groggily at the sight of Kate standing by the baby's cradle, gazing down at her. It was not yet daybreak; the full moon was shining through the window.

"You shouldn't be up," I said, forcing myself tiredly to my feet, shivering involuntarily. There was a chill in the early-morning air. "Let me help. You just rest. Kate?"

She turned and gave me a soft, sad smile. I stopped in my tracks.

Kate's body was lying still in the bed beside the cradle. The baby was sleeping soundly, tiny chest rising and falling.

"No. No . . . Kate!" I sobbed.

She placed a reassuring hand on my arm. Her touch was cold. The last few moments of her life drifted past my eyes like a breeze on the first breath of spring. She'd been watching her daughter sleep, joyfully cataloguing every precious detail: hair, hands, cheeks, toes. When death came, it was soft and sweet, like sleep. She died at peace, knowing her daughter would live.

"I'll take care of her," I whispered. "I'll watch over her for you. Whatever is in my power to do, I'll do."

She nodded and then she was gone. Forest Gate's "mother" sacrifice was complete. An unearthly fog rose and roiled against the window, swallowing the full moon whole. In an instant the landscape became an ocean of white.

✳

I didn't get to mourn long before my cries were interrupted by the baby's. I'd promised Kate I'd care for the child, so I dried my tears and went to work. I bathed and dressed her while she watched me with a wide, unfathomable gaze. Her eyes were the color of soft feathers: light gray and silvery brown, and alarmingly clear.

When she looked at me, it felt as if she was asking me a question to which I had no answer.

With no mother to feed her, I managed as best I could with a clean cloth dipped into a bowl of goat's milk, mumbling a haphazard spell to make the poor offering softer on her stomach, sweeter to the taste, and more nourishing. I had no way to tell if it worked, but she sucked the soaked corner until the bowl was mostly empty before falling asleep in my arms.

She was still slumbering when I heard the first sounds of hurried footsteps on the path outside. It was now coming on nightfall again; I'd spent almost a day in silence, just me and the baby. In the thick fog, it had begun to feel like we were the only two people left in the world.

I heard the door open. "Hello?" Nathaniel's voice came from the kitchen. "Kate?"

"Emilie's not at her hut," Zan said. "Maybe Kate will know . . ."

Nathaniel froze at the entrance of the bedroom, gazing at Kate, soundless and still.

"I am so sorry," I whispered, rising from the rocking chair.

I'd cleaned the room well; there was no evidence remaining of the difficult night, of the toil and torment that Kate had gone through. She lay on pristine white sheets, her beautiful hair still braided and coiled softly around her face. Her eyes were closed, her expression serene.

Nathaniel collapsed beside her, took her hand and pressed it to his lips. His shoulders shook, but he made no sound.

Zan, who had come in behind him, lowered his head and gripped the back of a chair.

It was nothing more than a brightening at first, like when thin clouds drift past the sun. Then the brightness collected into a shape. Kate knelt and touched Nathaniel's face with hands made of feathery light and air. He didn't react; he couldn't feel her touch. She looked up at me for help.

"Nathaniel," I ventured, the sound of my voice rippling through the deep darkness of his grief like a pebble in a still pool. He did not acknowledge me, so I spoke again. "Nathaniel."

Kate crossed to me and I held out my hand. She took it for the second time, and the cold drifted across my skin in delicate curling spirals, like frost on a winter windowpane.

Tell him that I'm sorry.

"Kate wanted you to know that she is sorry." I swallowed hard.

Tell him that I love him.

I took a quavering breath. "She said that she loves you."

Nathaniel raised his head to look at me with reddened, swollen eyes.

Tell him that I'll be happy.

"She said that she'll be happy."

And I want him to be happy.

"She wants you to be happy, too." I held the small, bundled baby out to him and said slowly, "She had to make a choice to save the baby. And she . . . she was at peace with the choice."

I approached him with the baby and laid her in his arms. Kate followed, misty eyes inscrutable as she watched him gingerly cradle her.

I remembered what Kate told me outside the fabric shop. "Her name is Ella," I said.

"That was my mother's name," he said, wiping his eyes. "I always thought Kate didn't like it. She looks like Kate, doesn't she?" he said, and then he smiled.

"She does," I said. "She's part of you both."

"Arielle Katherine. I'll probably be terrible at this. I didn't expect be doing this alone. But I promise, I will love you every day of your life. I swear it, I swear it. I will give you the love she wanted to give and can't."

Kate let go of my hand and went to them, placing an airy kiss on Nathaniel's lips and then another on Arielle's downy hair. Then she faded away. But though she was gone, her light lingered.

Zan came to stand beside me and laced his fingers into mine. The frost of Kate's touch melted at his. I looked down at our entwined hands and then up to his face. He said, almost inaudibly, "I heard you call for me. We got here as soon as we could." He closed his eyes. "I never should have left. I am so sorry. I am so very sorry."

I nodded mutely and we went back to watching Nathaniel gaze at his newborn daughter, clinging to her like he was a drowning sailor and she was his rope back to life.

✶

We gathered again at dusk on the foggy shore of the fjord to say one last goodbye to Kate. She lay on a raft Nathaniel had made of willow and rowan, with lavender at her feet and a laurel on her brow. There were few words said between us, and no one made a solemn address—none of us had it in us. What could we say that would make this better?

Nathaniel raised the torch to the funeral pyre, his other hand clutching their baby tight to his chest. Zan helped him push the raft from the shore, and we watched it float away with her, sending up sparks like red stars until it disappeared into the mist.

27

The next night Zan stood in front of my door, vacillating between knocking and walking away. He seemed to have chosen the latter only to turn and find me on the path behind him. After explaining everything that happened with Kate, Zan had gone to see what could be done to bring Dedrick Corvalis to justice, leaving me to spend the day helping Nathaniel change and dress Ella, then feed her with my spelled milk and rock her until they both fell asleep. I slowed to a stop.

"I probably shouldn't be here," he stated. "I know I shouldn't bother you. But it's been a very hard day and I didn't know where else I could go." He looked up at me through his dark hair. "This is where I always used to come when I needed someplace quiet. To think, and to draw."

I said, "Don't let me stop you." I went to the door and opened it, stepping aside to let him in.

It was awkward and quiet at first, as he settled into the chair with his paper and charcoal and I stoked up the fire and filled the kettle for tea. But the uneasiness abated quickly, and we were soon well absorbed in our endeavors—him, sketching; me, raptly watching him sketch.

We both jumped when the teakettle began to sing.

I poured two cups, keeping one for myself and setting the other on the table beside him. "Can I see?" I asked.

He nodded and sat back in his chair. I shyly leaned over his shoulder to peer at his work and immediately felt my breath catch.

It was a picture of Kate laughing, pulled from some bright place in his memory. A clear and vivid portrait, full of life and color—a feat, considering it was rendered in black and white.

When I was able to find my voice, I said, "I know the custom here is to burn the dead, and that we gave her a proper sendoff . . . but there's a part of me that thinks that she"—I flushed, swallowing the hard lump in my throat—"that she deserves something *more*. Something to mark her passage. To remember her by." I forced a tinny laugh. "It's the Renaltan in me, I guess. In Renalt, a headstone is almost like a trophy for virtue. The bigger, the better." I tapped the side of my teacup. "She deserves a monument. You know what I mean?"

"I do." Zan regarded me for a long minute before standing. "Are you up for a walk?"

✷

I followed him past the culvert tunnel and into the trees beyond. The terrain was rocky and rising sharply and our trail virtually indiscernible under the fog that had settled low and thick. Zan moved confidently forward, however, easily winding his way through the forest of evergreens turned brown. Looking up at the trees, he broke the silence. "You know, if it wasn't for all this"— he waved at the skeletal canopy—"I'd actually want the wall to come down."

"You want to leave Achlev open? So just anybody can come and go as they please?"

"Yes," he answered. "Imagine how different Achlev would be without it—think of all the art and thought and innovation we've missed out on because of it."

"And danger," I said. "A wall is protection, too."

"And yet, the greatest threat this city has ever faced came from within, not from without."

"Is it done, then?" I ventured. "Was Dedrick arrested?"

"Most of the guards had gone with the king to hunt, but I was able to recruit—which is to say, bribe—a few of those who remained. When they went to retrieve him, he was still in the sanctorium, just like you said he'd be. Your spell held true; they couldn't get him out until he was good and chained. He's being held in the dungeons tonight. I plan to question him tomorrow. If I have my way, he won't make it to the next Petitioner's Day. Whoa, there."

The toe of my shoe had caught on a gnarly root, but Zan caught my hand before I fell. He eyed a new red-dotted bandage around my palm.

"Casting spells without me?" he asked.

"Are you going tell me that I shouldn't?"

"I know better than to tell you what to do and what not to do."

"It was for Nathaniel and Ella," I said. "It wasn't a spell, exactly," I said. "It was more like . . . like a prayer. For them to find peace now that Kate is in the arms of the Empyrea."

He agreed. "Let them have peace even if we cannot. I'll never forgive myself. For choosing to follow the king when I knew it was wrong."

"If there's blame to be had, I must share in it. I figured it out too late." I sighed. "I practically walked her to Dedrick's front door."

We stopped at an impression in the steep hillside, an opening like a cave. Ducking into it, he said, "We're here. Follow me."

It wasn't a cave after all, just a short, shallow walkway that quickly widened into a meadow sheltered on all sides by mountain stone, open to the sky. The fog swirled around my feet as I ventured into the moonlit circle. Everywhere I turned, there were markers standing like pylons in drifting eddies of fog. There was no pattern to the placement or materials used—some were stone, some moldering planks, and there were even a few roughly hewn statues. Still others were simply mounds, their adornments long lost to time. But unlike Renaltan graveyards, where spirits wait and wander among the ostentatious tombs, this place was quiet—no sounds or souls stirred.

"Nobody is buried here," I said, turning and turning again. No spirits meant there were no bodies. This was a place made to comfort the living, not to house the dead.

"That's true," he said. "On the old maps, this was called *ad sepulcrum domini quod perierat,* the Tomb of the Lost." He gazed across the fog-shrouded shrine. "The city of Achlev has always burned its dead. It's meant to hasten a person's spirit into the arms of the Empyrea, and it's considered a great honor to receive such a sendoff. But during the wars, there was not always a body to burn. For the noblest soldiers, a raft was burned empty. For the very poor, or the prisoners of war, or the ones who died by their own hands instead of the enemy's . . . there was simply nothing done or said to honor their life—imperfect as it may have been—or mark their passing. They were just . . . gone."

"The Lost," I said.

He nodded. "And to the bereaved, being unable to have their loved one acknowledged was unbearable. So they came here, made their own rituals of goodbye, placed their own markers to honor their dead. Often at night, often alone . . . always in secret."

"There are no names on any of these."

"To place an unsanctioned marker for the disfavored here—or anywhere inside the wall—could bring a great fine or worse. They left off names so that if this place was discovered, there was nothing that could be traced back to them, so they couldn't be punished for what might have been viewed as an act of rebellion."

"But the kings let the stones stay?"

"If they knew, they looked the other way. When the war eventually ended, so did this method of mourning the dead, and the custom became as lost as the people it was created to remember. And yet this place endures." He unfolded the portrait of Kate and handed it to me.

I found a nice spot near the edge of the hollow and knelt, laying Kate's picture down gently and carefully pinning it in place with a stone. Tendrils of mist curled and cradled it for several long moments before drifting back into place over the top of it. Kate's visage disappeared like the sun behind storm clouds.

Returning to my feet, I noticed another marker nearby. A thin slab of slate that had been placed upright into the ground so that it looked like a headstone. Scratched coarsely into it was the shape of a bird like the Silvis raven, but delicate and white. A dove.

The stone, unblemished, stood out from the rest. All the others had been in place for two hundred years at least, and even without rain or wind or snow, time had still taken a toll on them. Not this one, though; it was new in comparison.

"This one is yours, too," I said. "Isn't it?"

Softly, he replied, "I was sick when my mother died. Unconscious, near death myself. She took her own life, so she was not given an Achlevan funeral. She was buried in a shallow, unmarked grave in the forest outside the wall before I ever knew she was gone. To this day, I don't know where she rests." He took a deep breath. "She was everything that was good about my miserable childhood. She would draw with me, read with me, study maps with me. This was one of the last places we discovered together, before I was too sick to leave my bed."

I knelt next to the slate marker. The bird etching was rough, rudimentary. I swallowed, reaching to trace the grooves. "Who helped you place the stone? Was it Simon?"

"Simon was not always around. His duties as a blood mage often kept him away." He shook his head. "It was just me. I was seven."

"Seven," I repeated, imagining a little boy the same age as Conrad, devastated and weak from prolonged illness, wandering these woods, erecting this stone in this hidden hollow, then engraving it as best he could with small, frail hands. And he did it all alone. I could hardly bear the thought of it.

"She died because of me, because caring for me became too much for her to bear. This was the least I could do."

"Zan," I said, rising, "you're wrong about your mother."

"I know what you're going to say: I was just a child, it wasn't my fault . . ."

"No." I approached him carefully. "I have something . . . important . . . to tell you. It's going to sound insane, but it's true. You have to believe me."

"As I recall, that was your price for helping me with the wall. Since Corvalis is in custody, I suppose now is as good a time as ever for you to collect."

Words tumbled out, one on top of the other. "Most spirits move on immediately after death, but some linger in the border between. It's how we were able to call Aren to us, during the séance. The spirits that do delay their final passage . . . they want to be seen. And when they *are* seen, they want to tell their stories."

"What?" His eyebrows knitted together, and a bemused smile crossed his lips.

"I know all this because *I* see them. Because it's *me* they want to communicate with. I don't know why . . . but the dead have been as much a part of my life as the living, for as long as I can remember."

His smile slowly faded.

"I saw her, Zan. Your mother. I saw her at the tower. Her spirit. That day you went up the tower after me . . . I was there only because she wanted me to follow her. She wanted to show me how she died."

He looked away sharply. I continued, as gently as possible, "I relived her last moments. She was with a healer from the village,

Sahlma. She was talking about her son, who was ill. She knew he did not have long to live, and she couldn't bear losing him. And so . . . and so . . . she took matters into her own hands. She *did* jump from the tower, but not because she wanted to die. She jumped so that her blood would spill onto the bloodleaf below. So that Sahlma could collect the bloodleaf flower petals and use them to save her son. You."

He fell back a step, his hand balled into a fist over his heart. He was trying to keep his breathing steady and regular; I could almost keep time by his breaths. *One, in. Two, out. Three, in. Four, out* . . . I placed a hand on his arm, and when his eyes flicked up to mine, they had lost all traces of their cynical glint.

"She wasn't abandoning you," I said from my heart. "She loved you. She died for the mere *hope* that she could create the petals that could be used to save your life. She had to decide between herself and you. She chose you."

He put both hands in his hair and turned his back to me. I could feel a shift in him as he rearranged the narrative of his life. His mother had saved him. It didn't change the loss—nothing ever would—but the light in which he viewed her death had been altered irrevocably.

"Zan?" I asked, wanting to reach out to him but too nervous to try. "Are you all right?"

He took a long, deep breath. "No," he said, "and . . . yes." A crooked pillar was jutting from the fog, and he fell back against it as if suddenly exhausted, but his eyes were alive with emotion, somewhere in the realm between relief and regret.

I approached him timidly. "You believe me? You don't think me mad?"

"With all the astonishing things I've seen since meeting you, you could tell me that you were the Empyrea herself and I would believe it."

I didn't move; I barely dared to breathe. Remembering his fearsome depiction of me on the wall, I said, "I'm just a girl, Zan, figuring things out as I go along. I'm just as lost and confused and lonely as everyone else."

"Lost? No." He took my hands in his. "Confused . . . I'd never guess it. Lonely?" He leaned his forehead against mine and said softly, "Not if I can help it."

We were so close. I could feel the break of his breath across my cheek, soft and slow. I looked up at him, heart racing as he bent his face to meet mine.

And then the ground lurched beneath us.

He pulled me tight to him as the column he'd been leaning on shook loose and fell, breaking into jagged chunks. Beneath our feet, the earth heaved while the stones high above groaned and rained dust and stinging gravel down upon our heads. I clung to Zan's hands, and we ran through the maelstrom to the hollow's stooped entrance. Rocks began to fall, closing in the narrow way behind us.

On the other side, pine needles transformed into projectiles and sliced through the air like arrows on an undulating battlefield. Ahead of us, the trunk of a giant spruce snapped and moaned as it splintered at its base and fell across our path. We couldn't go forward. We couldn't go backwards. I could taste panic on my tongue, sharp and sour, like blood and bile.

Zan pulled me down against the side of the fallen tree and curled his body over mine, shielding me from debris as the ground gave one last great shudder and then, at last, lay still.

He got to his feet first, then quietly helped me to mine. The fog was gone, seemingly swallowed up into the shaking earth. Only dust remained; when it finally settled, it revealed an almost unrecognizable landscape. Tumbled rocks, broken trees, and several plumes of smoke rising from the heart of the city beyond, silhouetted by the first weak rays of a grim sun rising.

"No," Zan murmured in shock. "We stopped him. It was over. This can't be."

But we both knew the truth: this was the sign of the death of the crone. The seal at Forest Gate had fallen.

✳

It took us most of the night to pick our way through the disarray in the forest. We used the culvert passage to make it into the castle, but we could hear distant shouts coming from the city even through those subterranean walls. When we emerged on the other side, the first light of morning was breaking.

Zan had me wait in the storage room, in the mess of broken bottles and overturned casks, while he went to question the guard nearest the entrance of the dungeon cells.

"I'll not ask again," he was saying, his voice carrying a dangerous edge. "I left you here last night. I paid you well. Now tell me the truth: between then and now, have you let anybody in there with him? Has anybody gone out?"

"I told you, no," the guard muttered. "Ain't nobody gone in or out all night. Not even when it felt like the whole castle was shakin' apart."

He paused. "Well, except for his physician is all. Court-granted physician. He asked for an evaluation; I couldn't deny 'im. You know the rules. King's decree. He's got more 'n enough in his coffers to pay the fee."

"Zan," I said, emerging from the storage room.

"Emilie," he said firmly, "you're supposed to stay—"

"It's Sahlma," I said sadly, lifting a shaking finger to point at the woman waiting for us at the top of the stairs to the cells. Blood stained her white smock, soaking into the white ties of her bonnet, but Zan could not see her.

I followed Sahlma's spirit into the depths of the dungeons, with Zan close behind. The cells in Renalt were made to hold witches: iron bars, low ceilings, thumbnail-size windows that let in sickly strings of light. But however dark and sad the dungeons were in Renalt, these were worse. There were no windows, no light, and no sound except for the slow *drip drip drip* from somewhere deep in the belly of the cavern. And the smell . . . the stenches of decay and vomit and urine mingled to form an unholy brume that curled into my nostrils and clung to my skin.

Sahlma stopped at the last door. I knew what was waiting behind it; I could see the marks of it well enough on her spirit. I nodded to her, whispering, "We'll see justice done. Go now. Kestrel waits for you." A tender, hopeful smile crossed her lips, and then she was gone.

Zan undid the latch. The door swung open to reveal Dedrick Corvalis, sitting languidly against the wall, hands covered in blood past his wrists, a lazy smile playing at the corners of his mouth.

"Finally," he said. "I've been calling for hours. My physician attacked me. I was forced to defend myself . . . I'm afraid I've made a terrible mess."

Sahlma's body was lying in a crumpled pile in the corner.

Nihil nunc salvet te.

A faint tremor—an aftershock—sent tiny ripples across the pool of blood. When it stopped, Dedrick grinned. "Strange weather we're having," he said conversationally. Then, "I require some water. And a fresh set of clothes. Can't go to my trial looking like this." He lifted his hands and gave a little laugh.

"Trial?" Zan said. "Your trial will happen when *I* make it happen."

"That's where you're wrong, my dear boy," Corvalis said, sneering. "The king will be overseeing my prosecution. As luck would have it, he's come home from his hunting trip early. I've been assured that the trial will take place without delay."

My face blanched—I'd been operating on the belief that Conrad's distance from the city, out with the hunting party, would have kept him out of the quake's range. I hoped, if he had experienced it, that he was all right.

Dedrick was still talking. "We're great friends, the king and I. I'm sure he'll see that I get justice for this wholly wrongful imprisonment. I bet his guards will be down to get me any minute." He cocked his head, listening as the sound of boots on the stairs echoed down the chamber. "Ah. Here they come now."

Zan and I dove into another cell before the approaching guards saw us.

"What do we do now?" I whispered.

"I'm going to see what can be done here to stop this. I need you to go and get Nathaniel and meet me back at the castle stairs. Tell him to be ready to testify."

I nodded, moving to the other wall to watch for an opening to escape through, knife poised to cast the invisibility spell if there wasn't one. "Be careful," I said, stealing one last reassuring glance at him before plunging down the hall.

Behind me, the guards were gathering outside of Corvalis's cell. I could hear him laughing at their arrival. "Gentlemen!" he said with welcoming gusto. "It's about time."

28

It wasn't until Nathaniel opened the door that I realized how, even now, I expected Kate to be standing there, smiling brightly and welcoming me in to taste-test whatever she had cooking on the fire. Nathaniel offered no such cheer; his shoulders were bent, while weary lines flanked either side of his mouth. He stepped aside to show me the interior of the cottage: books shaken from their shelves, broken crockery on the floor, furniture sitting at odd angles. Another after-shock rumbled through the floor, rattling the windows.

Nathaniel said, "Another seal broken. Another gate down. How, if Dedrick Corvalis is imprisoned?"

"It was Sahlma," I said. "Corvalis called for a physician to evaluate him in his cell." I swallowed, remembering her corpse cast off in the cell corner while Dedrick preened. "The king is forcing an early trial, Nathaniel. Today. Zan wants you to be ready to testify—"

Nathaniel always had an intimidating presence about him—stern, quiet, looming. But today red heat was simmering underneath his skin and I wondered if I hadn't mistaken a volcano for a mountain. "No," he said quietly.

There was a mewling cry from the other room, and Nathaniel rushed to scoop up his daughter. I followed him hesitantly. A pack stood at the foot of the bed. "Are you going somewhere?"

"Yes," Nathaniel said. "My wife is dead. The city is falling apart around us. I have a child I can barely feed, or dress, or put to sleep . . . My sister has two babies of her own. She'll know what to do."

"What about Zan?"

"What *about* Zan?" Nathaniel barked. He took a deep breath. "Zan tried to help us; it's true. But it doesn't change the fact that if it wasn't for him, my wife would still be here."

I balked. "Kate isn't here because of the man who's about to go to trial!"

"Stay away from Zan, Emilie. Trust me on this. He can't be with you. And if he was remotely worthy of you, he would have told you that himself." He wrapped Ella in one of Kate's handmade blankets and laid her on the bed while he closed the pack and slung it over his back.

"I don't know what you mean."

"You will soon enough." Nathaniel hoisted Ella, who seemed like a tiny doll in his brawny brown arms.

"If you want someone to blame, blame me!" I cried. "I'm the one who couldn't stop the seals from being undone. I'm the one who didn't stop Kate from going to see Dedrick, and I'm the one who couldn't save her afterward."

He was already headed out the door. Without looking back, he said, "I have a boat to catch."

★

The avenues were cluttered with broken timbers and crumbled stone, while distraught and confused people were picking through the debris in the morning light, trying to assess the damage. In the distance, the women of the Forest Gate statue were broken and blackened, large chunks of marble blocking the exit.

And all the while the king's guards were erecting the Petitioner's Day platform on the castle stairs. Though it wasn't Petitioner's Day, Dedrick Corvalis, it seemed, was too important to languish in the dungeon for another month. Just as he'd said, the king intended to try him immediately. If news of his arrest hadn't spread so quickly, I wondered if he would have faced a trial at all.

I found Zan in the crowd that was gathering to watch. "Where's Nathaniel?" he asked.

I shook my head. "He wouldn't come. He's taking Ella to his sister's house." I cleared my throat. "He blames you for what happened to Kate, but he's wrong."

Grimly, he said, "He's not wrong."

"He also told me to stay away from you. Is he right about that, too?"

Zan jerked his head away to avoid my eyes. "You should."

"Are you going to tell me why?"

He said coolly, "Not if I can help it." With a jolt, I remembered our near kiss before the earth started shaking. Could that have been only a few hours ago? I was formulating a reply when he said, "Look, the doors are opening."

We pushed into the throng, trying to get as close to the front as possible. I caught an elbow in my ribs and felt hard boot heels come down on my toes; showers of spittle rained down on me from the mouths of angry men, who were shouting profanity at Dedrick. He was now gagged but smiling at his audience from the top platform step. Behind him, guards were hastily arranging a chair to accommodate the king's hefty rump.

"I've read the charges against this man, as outlined in his arresting documents," the king said. "Who will speak against him? Who?"

We were almost to the front; I could see the whites of Dedrick's eyes.

"I will!" came a small but determined voice.

"Then speak," the king directed.

It was Beth, the girl from the flower stall. She ascended the stairs with the skittishness of a mouse, casting quick glances between the glowering king and the grinning accused—but was doing her best to keep her back straight and her voice steady. "My name is Beth Taylor, sir. Molly Cartwright, the girl what got killed at your ball, was my friend. She was sweet, and a little bit naïve. She had lots of men at her candy cart, but there was only one she took a real likin' to." She fiddled with her skirt. "She was in love—she talked about it all the time. Someone important had an understanding with her. That he loved her and wanted to marry her. She never said his name, but I knew. I wanted to tell someone, but I didn't dare. Corvalis is the lord what owns the stall I rent to sell m'flowers. I was afraid that if I spoke against him, I'd lose my only way of makin' money that wasn't stealin' or whorin.' Beggin' your pardon, sir," she said as she curtsied shyly at the king, "for the coarse language."

"Do you have any evidence of this assertion?" the king asked equably.

"Nothing beyond me own guesses."

"Guesses are not enough to convict a man. You are dismissed." He waved his hand at the girl as the crowd booed.

Zan emitted a low noise that might have been a growl. His body, close to mine, was taut with tension.

The king said, "Is there anyone else who can provide testimony of Baron Corvalis's supposed crimes?"

"Anyone who ever lived in his horrible tenements!" shouted a voice.

"Anyone he ever cheated out of fair wages!" shouted another.

"I will." The voice was clear and calm, and it cut across the cacophony like the tone of a bell. Nathaniel, head high, climbed the steps to the stage. I grasped Zan's arm.

"What is that?" the king asked, sneering at the baby in Nathaniel's arms. "Get rid of that."

Beth was descending the stairs, and Nathaniel handed Ella to her before taking his place to testify.

"State your name," the king said.

"You know me, Majesty."

"I said, state your name."

He turned to the crowd and spoke louder. "My name is Nathaniel Gardner. I was born into humble circumstances, but my wife was not. Her name, before marrying me, was Katherine Morais, daughter of Baron Morais, and she was originally betrothed to Dedrick Corvalis. She died as the result of his treachery two days ago, but that is not why I'm here to testify." He looked down at his hands, as if in shame. "I worked for Dedrick Corvalis for years before I met Katherine. I moved up the ranks in his hired guard, until I became one of his most trusted employees. Such a title was no honor, though, sir, because I had to do terrible things to achieve such a position. Corvalis was always very good at convincing people he was the perfect lord: polite, dedicated, with excellent sense in trade. But it was all for show. In truth, he was cruel and conniving. If he wanted a piece of land, he'd have me jump the man who owned it, break his legs so he couldn't work it anymore, and then he'd buy up the property when the owner could no longer afford to keep it."

"That doesn't sound like murder, Mr. Gardner," the king said. "That sounds like you committed assault—a punishable offense—and are now using it as a way to frame your dead wife's former fiancé."

"There's more. Dedrick Corvalis wanted to expand his trading operations to Renalt. He wanted to have already established the trade routes before Renalt and Achleva became official allies. He went there several times, meeting with those he saw as having the most power in Renalt: magistrates of the Tribunal. I was never allowed into those meetings, nor did I ever see the men of the Tribunal he spoke to, but it was not long before the Corvalis coffers were overflowing with Renaltan gold—far more than could have been gained through any trade deals alone."

The king was radiating animosity now, and Nathaniel seemed to be sweating from the heat of it. He swallowed. "His father, Francis Corvalis, found out about his son's activities. He did not approve and ordered him to stop. Days later Francis Corvalis died under mysterious circumstances."

"You're saying Dedrick Corvalis killed his father?"

"I'm saying," Nathaniel said, "that my employer asked me to gather several sprigs of bloodleaf from the forest—he was very specific about it; he did not want it purchased from an apothecary who might keep a record of it—and less than a day later, his father was dead. I never told my wife." Nathaniel wrung his hands. "I didn't want her to know about what I'd done in Corvalis's service. I was a coward, and now I've lost her because of it."

"But no personal witness?" King Domhnall said. "More hearsay." He stood up. "Can anyone out there give me a firsthand account of this man's supposed crimes?"

The mob was chanting *Guilty! Guilty! Guilty!*

"Why are none of the king's guards speaking up? They saw what happened this morning! Where are they? Zan?" I looked around, finding myself alone in the throng. "Zan!"

"Well, then," the king was saying, "with no real evidence to discuss and no firsthand witnesses of quality to testify against you, Baron Dedrick Corvalis, the crown has no choice but to—"

"I will speak against him." Zan appeared on the stairs, climbing each with a carefully measured slowness to, I knew, control his heart rate and his breathing. He kept his head high as he addressed the king. "Would you like me to state my name for the crowd, Father?"

Realization struck me like a thunderclap. Every nerve revolted; I was numb.

King Domhnall's jaw tightened. "It is required by royal court for all witnesses to state their name."

Zan placed a hand on Nathaniel's shoulder and gave him a slight nod. Then he turned. "My name," he declared to the now-silent mass, "is Prince Valentin Alexander de Achlev. I am the one who had this man arrested and imprisoned." He was standing erect, but I could see his hands shaking.

All around me, I heard whispers. *The prince? The prince. The prince. The prince.*

"I do not bring hypotheticals or suppositions or presumptions to place before this court today, but a firsthand witness. This morning, this very morning, I went to question Dedrick Corvalis in his cell and found him there, covered head to toe in blood that was not his. He had with him the body of a healer by the name of Sahlma Salazar. A woman who has long rendered assistance unto the people of this city. He called her to examine him, as per his rights by your decree, and when she came to his cell to do her duty, he attacked her. He cut her throat. He shed her blood"—he lifted Dedrick's hands—"blood you can *still see* under his fingernails! And the earth shook because, with her death, the three seals of Forest Gate were undone. He's been working against you all this time, Father. Against Achleva itself. The proof of that is all around us. Collapsed roofs. Fallen houses. Damage to structures nearly as old as the wall itself."

Zan is the prince, I thought. I asked myself, *How could I not know?*

And then I asked, *Didn't I?*

I closed my eyes, only opening them when I heard him speak again. His voice. Zan's voice. The prince's voice.

"Corvalis murdered Sahlma Salazar in cold blood as part of an effort to destroy the wall, the structure that has guaranteed our city's survival and prosperity for centuries. There are others who would stand with me in this assertion, but there should be no need, my dear

Lord King. For I am the prince of this realm, and my word, under testimony this day, is irrefutable."

The smile in Dedrick's eyes was gone. In its place, hatred. Raw, burning hatred.

The king was tapping his fingers in an out-of-rhythm pattern on the carven arm of his chair. He stood up. "Very well. It seems, given this new testimony, that the crown must convict you, Baron Dedrick Corvalis, for the death of Sahlma Salazar. Your sentence, sir, to be delivered immediately, is forfeiture of your title and your property, and exile from Achleva."

The crowd ignited, pushing forward and screaming in protest.

"No!" Zan said, even as the king turned his back on it all. "Our laws dictate that murder and treason must be rewarded in kind—and this man has committed three at least, and perhaps more that we do not yet know of. The people of Achleva demand justice! Answers! Will you rob them of it?"

The king whirled on his son, eyes bulging, his sword sliding out of its scabbard with a metallic *shink!* He held it aloft, the point at Zan's heart. "You dare to contradict your king, boy?"

Don't falter, I thought. I willed him courage. *Be strong.*

Zan did not flinch. The crowd roared for him, and he slowly lifted a hand in response. He was not the sickly prince anymore. In an instant, he had transformed into someone else, accessing some reservoir of power inside him that he'd never touched before. He was an opaque glass lamp that had suddenly been lit from within, and all I could see was the fire inside.

"He betrayed *you*," Zan said quietly. "Don't you want to know why?"

The king lowered his sword. "The sentence has changed," he announced. "The punishment is death."

Dedrick knew the end was near. He was gibbering and giggling now; manic, high-pitched squeals came from behind his gag.

"I think he wants to say something," Zan said. "Undo his gag; let him testify on his own behalf."

But Domhnall did not wait. He laid his sword across the man's throat and sliced. The crowd gasped; the king had become executioner.

Dedrick's body fell sideways and lay there, bleeding, at Zan's feet.

29

The king's guards made a show of escorting Zan from the platform with deference, but I could see the roughness with which they handled him. I was about to follow after him when Nathaniel clapped his hand on my shoulder. "Not that way."

Ella was sleeping on his chest, held fast by fabric wrapped over his shoulders and around his waist. Sheltered next to his heartbeat, she was blissfully unaware of the tumult that surrounded her.

"What will they do to Zan?" I asked fearfully as Nathaniel led me out of the uproar. Someone had pulled Dedrick's body from the platform, and it was now bobbing above the crowd, passed from hand to hand, like a grotesque marionette. When it came to executions, Renalt and Achleva weren't really all that different. Delighting in death spectacles seemed to be an ugly trait of humanity rather than nationality.

"I don't know," Nathaniel said. "Domhnall hates him. He always has. Zan was sickly from the start; Domhnall resented that his only son was so small and frail. Used to beat him savagely. An attempt to toughen him up."

I remembered the words he'd used to describe the prince: *Weak. Feeble. Ineffectual . . .* He'd been talking about himself. Repeating the lies and insults he'd heard so often, he'd come to believe them. I could hardly process the horror of it. I'd felt so sorry for myself growing up, but I'd been gifted with a mother and father who loved me, whose single-minded purpose was to protect me. I ached for Zan. For the little boy he used to be. For the childhood he didn't get to have.

Nathaniel ducked through one side door of the castle and then another, and I followed him. The route led out into a long-unused sitting room, crowded with stacked chairs and cobweb-laden shelves. The only break in the dust was a well-trodden path zigzagging through the maze. "What is this?" I asked.

"Zan knows all the back ways and passages in the castle. He's been coming and going unnoticed since he was a kid. This one leads out to the top of a stairway that ends at a short hallway. Follow the hallway to its end; that's where you'll find his private rooms. That's where they'll probably keep him while the king decides what to do with him, but they only ever post a guard at the bottom of the stairs, so it is unlikely they'll see you."

"Aren't you coming with me?"

"I can't," Nathaniel said, looking conflicted. "When Kate found out she was expecting, I made a promise to her that our child would always come first. I've got to get Ella out of here. I can't wait, not even for Zan."

I nodded. "I understand. Zan will, too."

Nathaniel hugged me roughly; it was like being embraced by a bear. "I plan to camp tonight just off the southwest road outside of

High Gate, and tomorrow set off for Ingram. My sister is a midwife there. Her name is Thalia. If you need to find me, that's where I'll be."

"Empyrea keep you," I said, tears starting from my eyes.

"And you," he replied, his own eyes moist. Then he gave me a nod and left the way he came.

I followed Nathaniel's directions to the letter, pausing from time to time as guards and courtiers went by but otherwise unimpeded. I tried to practice what I was going to say as I went. *I'm the real princess, Zan. I'm Aurelia. We're supposed to be together. We were always supposed to be together.*

A painted portrait of a woman was hung on the wall opposite Zan's door. She wore a simple but elegant dress, with very few ornaments save for a ring set with a clear white jewel on her left hand and a raven ring on her right. She had hair like a raven's wing, too, and wide green eyes; her beauty was marred only by a furrow in her brow and hard lines of worry on each side of her mouth. Simon's sister. The late queen of Achleva, I knew now. It wasn't his father Zan took after; it was his mother. *Queen Irena Silvis de Achlev,* the nameplate read. I paused beneath her portrait to thank her, silently, for saving his life.

The door to his room was not locked. It swung open with the barest turn of the knob.

Zan was sitting in a darkened corner, head in his hands. I tried not to stare, but I could hardly help myself; I had never allowed myself to *look* at him before, to admit to myself how much I truly *wanted* him, and now that I could, I was like a souse having a first draft after long and torturous sobriety. I wanted to drink him in, every part of him: the way his hair, always askew, fell to perfectly frame his right eye and hide his left. The shape of his shoulders beneath his white linen shirt. The angles of his cheekbones, the trim cut of his waist . . .

"Zan?" I said, finding my voice.

He looked up with a start, and for a minute I wondered if I'd made a mistake coming here uninvited. What if I guessed wrong about how he felt? What if he didn't care who I really was? What if he didn't care much about me at all?

"I'm sorry that I—" I began, but had to stop when he crossed the room, closing the gap between us in one stride, and crushed his mouth against mine. Wonder and doubt collided inside me like two errant stars that, on impact, burst into a cloud of fire and dust.

The kiss softened, and I pulled reluctantly away. "Are you all right?" I murmured into his shoulder. He smelled like cedar and fog, like autumn hearth fires and rain on the windowsill.

His cut-glass mouth formed a sad smile. "I'm fine," he said tiredly. "Emilie. You must think . . ."

"I'm not angry that you didn't tell me who you are." I rested a hand on his arm. "Honestly, I probably should have figured it out sooner. It's just that you look so much like Simon . . ."

"It was easy to pretend that Simon was my father. It was something I've always wished were true. But I shouldn't have misled you. I didn't know that you would turn out to be . . . *you*."

My eyes drifted from his lips down to the hollow of his collarbone, where I became fixated on the soft thrum of his heartbeat beneath his skin.

"Emilie," he said with a soft urgency that drew my eyes back up to his, "the things I've done today, I can't undo. There will be consequences for my open defiance at the trial. The guards will be coming to get me soon, so that the king—my real father—can decide what to do with me. You have to be gone before then. If he knows about you, I've no doubt he will use you to hurt me."

"Wait! Just wait. Your father . . . Corvalis was a close confidant of his, correct? And Nathaniel said that while he was still working with him, he began some kind of alliance with the Tribunal in Renalt, right?"

"Yes . . ." Zan said slowly.

"Corvalis was also after the name of the person providing Thackery with invitations. He was almost *desperate* to hear that it was some other child that King Domhnall might have fathered. What if *he* has been behind all of this? Your father."

"King's Gate's seal requires the deaths of three Achlevan royals. He wouldn't—"

"Zan, he's looking for more royals. Could he be on the hunt for his own replacement in the line of sacrifices?"

Zan stepped back, as if stunned. "The monarchy's power in Achleva has been waning for generations. The landholding lords, should they decide to unite, would be able to overthrow him with ease. But the alliance between Renalt and Achleva . . ."

". . . is worthless if the Renaltan monarchy is also in its last days."

"My father has always been a gambler; he must have looked over his odds and decided to back the strongest horse: the Tribunal."

"And the first thing the Tribunal would want to do, if aligned with the Achlevan king, is to take down the magical wall that keeps wayward witches like myself out of their hands."

Outside his bedroom door came the sound of several sets of boots on the floor. "Here," Zan said urgently, pushing me behind his wardrobe door, "hide!"

"No, wait! There's more I have to tell you! Zan—"

He kissed me again, fervent and fierce. "I know what I have to do now," he said. "And I'm likely to face exile for it." There was a heavy knock on the door. "I don't know where I'll go, but . . . will you come? Will you come with me, Emilie?"

"I will," I said breathlessly. "I'm with you."

He pressed a hard kiss into my forehead, eyes closed tight, as another, harder knock thudded against his door. "Pack whatever you need. Meet me at midnight," he said, taking my hands. "On the wall, by the waterfall. The site of our first spell."

When he pulled away, he left something in my grasp. A ring. I recognized it immediately. It was his mother's.

"Prince Valentin," a gruff voice said through the door, "you're wanted in the Great Hall."

I watched through the crack between the wardrobe hinges as they burst through the door and flooded into the room, wrestling him to the ground and pinning his arms behind him while his face once again became a mask of sardonic calm.

"Boys, boys," he said glibly, face half-pressed into the floor, "if you rip me limb from limb now, my father will be very angry that you deprived him of the opportunity."

My fingers curled against the door. I could feel the magic pressing against each tip, eager to be let loose, ready to destroy them all for daring to lay a hand on him. But Zan had warned me against making myself known, so I hung back until they'd hauled him out of sight. Then I made a quick nick on my palm and stepped out from my hiding place. *"Ego invisibilia,"* I whispered. "I am unseen."

I slipped in step behind them, and none of them seemed to be the wiser.

Inside the Great Hall, the king—Zan's father! I was still reeling at the revelation—stalked across his throne room, face purple with rage, kicking down anything in his path. "How dare you?" he spluttered. "You little bastard. Dedrick Corvalis was like a *son* to me!"

The guards released Zan at Domhnall's feet. Zan reflexively cringed, but after a few moments of measured counting—*one, in, two, out, three, in, four, out*—he was able to control his breathing and his fear, and he straightened to his full height. It seemed to surprise the king to have his son suddenly looking down on him.

"You know, Father," Zan said, "despite everything . . . I never thought it could be you."

"I don't know what you're talking about."

Zan continued as if he hadn't heard him. "I told myself it wasn't possible, since finishing the job would likely kill you, too. And if you are good at anything, it's saving your own skin. But now I understand why you insisted so doggedly that I go with you on your asinine little hunting expedition, *just after* I told you everything I knew about what was happening with the wall: you wanted to prevent further meddling in your operation, didn't you? That explains why you were so adamant about keeping my marriage date within the month of the black moon; on the day we're married, the princess, too, will be eligible for sacrifice. It helps, I suppose, that all the landholding lords would likely be attending the wedding, so we can all die together."

Sweat was collecting in beads on Domhnall's ruddy forehead. Zan continued, "You try to hide behind your brutality and extravagance; you put on a good show. But you're scared. Your power is dissolving, and you feared it was only a matter of time before someone came and took it from you."

"Like you?" he asked with a sneer. But there was fear burning on the edges of his voice.

Zan went on: "The answer was simple: find a strong ally, one who would let you keep your crown and title if you followed their orders. Dedrick Corvalis brokered the deal with the Tribunal, didn't he? Did you promise him, once I was dead, that he'd be your heir? Did he already know blood magic before you reached that deal with our enemies, or did he learn it afterward, solely for the purpose of bringing down the wall?"

"You're speaking nonsense."

"Am I?" Zan roared. "I know, I know. I'm a disgrace! A nuisance! You're ashamed to call me your son. I've heard it all before, Father. But you know what? I *agree* with you. I *don't* deserve to be called your son."

Zan stalked to the Great Hall doors and threw them open, and I continued my whispered chant, *"Ego invisiblia." I am unseen* . . .

"Call the Princess Aurelia and her guard to me," Zan told the guards waiting in the corridor. "And call a scribe."

They arrived in minutes, Lisette fluttering like a nervous butterfly,

Toris prowling behind her like a hound on the scent of a kill. "What is this about?" she asked.

Zan spoke not to her directly but to the gathered audience as a whole. "Let it be written today that I, Prince Valentin, have formally refused to wed Princess Aurelia of Renalt." There was a collective gasp; Lisette's mouth fell agape. "In recognition that this is an act of defiance against the orders of the king and a criminal breach of the treaty between our kingdoms, the Prince Valentin has voluntarily accepted the punishment of exile, until the matter can be peacefully resolved through negotiation with the crown of Renalt. If such an agreement cannot be made, Prince Valentin hereby abdicates all claims on the Achlevan throne."

"Negotiation?" Toris barked. "There can be no negotiation. This is an act of war."

"So be it," Zan said. "Achlev's Wall, however embattled, still stands, and our city remains safe. Better this path than the one that would have it fall and all my people with it."

Toris's eyes glittered. I knew then that he was a part of all this, probably from the very beginning. If his daughter married Zan and then died alongside her husband and father-in-law, without heirs, there would be only one person left in line to assume the Achlevan throne: Toris himself.

"Go to your exile, coward," King Domhnall hissed. "So that I can be rid of you. Just as your mother wanted to be rid of you . . ."

"My mother," Zan thundered, "*loved* me. She gave up her life so that I could have mine. And you know what? For the first time in my life, I'm *glad*. I'm glad that because of her sacrifice, I now have the chance to look you in the face and tell you that as long as I live, you will not win."

I slipped out before any more was said; I had an appointment to keep.

Zan's kisses lingered on my lips. Waterfall. Midnight.

30

I had not returned to my hut since Forest Gate had fallen, and the earthquake had left it in a shambles. It was as if someone had lifted the structure and vigorously shaken it. The window was dashed to pieces, the brick fireplace was nothing more than a pile of rubble, and bits of broken tonic and herbal bottles covered the scene like colored glass confetti.

I searched the mess by candlelight, finding Kellan's blue cloak first, then my empty satchel. Beneath it lay the ribbon-tied parcel that held my wedding dress. I pulled the ribbon and watched it flutter out one last time, marveling at how faint the bloodstains were, and how very like Kate it was to attempt to clean it. She was always trying to save the unsavable.

I kept the black ribbon from the parcel—it could still prove useful in communicating with Conrad—and laid the dress out in the center of the pile of debris I'd once called my home. Then I tossed my candle onto it and watched it go up in flame.

The fire spread rapidly, climbing up the curtains and into the thatch roof in a matter of minutes. I watched it start to cave from several yards away, with a near-empty satchel on my shoulder and Kellan's cloak on my back. But despite the heat from the burning hut and the warmth of the cloak, cold crept slowly up my neck and across my limbs. A feeling of dread came over me as a mist began to form between me and the fire, knitting itself together in slow, fitful lurches. The cold deepened.

When the apparition was fully formed, she was almost unrecognizable — a haggard shade of herself.

"No, Aren. Not now. Please, not right now." I begged her. "It's almost over. Dedrick is dead; the collusion between Domhnall and the Tribunal has been uncovered. I'm going to get my brother, and then he and I will escape with Zan . . ." I twisted Zan's ring around my finger. "We've almost won. If someone is going to die, I don't want to see it. Please don't . . ."

She dragged herself closer, clamping her frigid, bony fingers around my wrist like iron shackles, sucking every last scrap of warmth from me and plunging me headfirst into a sputtering, shifting vision.

An exchange of rings.

The flash of a knife.

A girl in a swirling snowstorm, sobbing — me. Leaning over the broken body of the boy I so desperately loved.

Blood on the snow.

My head on his chest. A ring on his finger, his ring on mine. His dark, dark hair stark against the terrible white storm.

Blood on the snow. His blood.

"*No,*" I said, tearing my hand away. The storm and the snow and the blood disappeared. "I've been misled by your visions before. I won't let you take this—take *him*—from me." I tried to dismiss her with a decisive turn on my heel.

I didn't get far. The ground groaned and convulsed beneath me, forcing me to my knees. Another aftershock, timed as if to remind me of my insignificance. When it stopped, Aren was advancing on me again. I shrank from her expanding shadow. Gone was the regal queen I'd grown up with; in her place loomed a twisted wraith, an unholy amalgamation of vein and vine and bone. She reached through the black ribbons of her hair with thorny fingertips, which skittered spider-like across my cheek and around my skull. When she had my head cradled in her hands, she drove her thumbs into my eyes.

I cried out, first from cold and pain and then in anguish as she forced me to watch it all again. Over and over. *Rings. Knife. Death. Rings. Knife. Death.*

Blood on the snow.

Blood on the snow.

Blood on the snow.

Firebird.

It was just a fleeting glimpse, a mere flash in the procession of more frightening pictures, but it was unmistakable: at his death, Zan is wearing my charm.

I hardly noticed when Aren removed her spiny thumbs from my eye sockets and withdrew; the awful images continued their cavalcade without her. I slumped where she left me, racked by full-body shivers despite the waves of heat rippling from my hut.

She wanted me to see, and now I could see nothing else. When I tried to imagine Zan's eyes now, there was no more green clarity to them; they were vacant and staring. I couldn't think of his lips without envisioning them blue and breathless and cold. I wouldn't be able touch him again without revisiting the way his body looked as I knelt over it in grief. I'd burned my hut to raze my past, but as it was eaten away by flame, it was my future I saw crumbling in the embers. My future with Zan.

Blood on the snow.

Aren had made her message clear.

Leave him, or he dies.

✳

I waited on the wall for three hours, pacing and practicing what I was going to say, but when I turned and finally saw Zan approaching me in the dark, lit by a shard of moonlight, my composure cracked.

"This is where I first knew I loved you," he said as he drew near. "Watching the lengths you went to for my people, for *me* . . . feeling the strength of your spirit in that spell . . . How could I not?" He reached out and tucked a stray lock of hair behind my ear. "I never dared to let myself hope that you might . . . that you could ever possibly . . ." He trailed off, flushing.

Stars save me. I wanted to kiss him, cling to him, melt into him and into this wall and become stone so I'd never have to let him go. But the minute I let those thoughts into my mind, I was confronted again by gruesome images of his death.

So instead of leaning into his touch or returning his confession with one of my own, I pushed every ounce of emotion into the coil inside me. It twisted and tightened, so taut now that if I so much as breathed wrong, it would snap and I'd shatter, torn apart from the inside.

"Emilie?" Zan asked.

"My name is not Emilie," I said emotionlessly, not daring to look at him. "My name is Aurelia."

"What?" He stepped back, as stunned as if I'd slapped him.

"Emilie is the name of a girl I knew in Renalt. And the Aurelia you know . . . her name is actually Lisette. We've been friends since we were small. I used to read your letters to her and we'd laugh at them. Made it something of a game. Whatever responses you got back from them, they were all from her. She thought it was great fun. We both did."

"I don't understand." Zan leaned heavily against the battlements.

"I never wanted to come to Achleva," I said, pinning my lies to a plausible truth. "I resented being wed, without my consent, to a man rumored to be afflicted with such a wide variety of infirmities. So I came up with a plan to make it so I didn't have to." I could hear Zan's breathing become more painful and labored, and I almost lost my nerve. To keep from faltering, I plunged forward. "I offered to pay Lisette to take my place. I arranged everything. She wasn't too keen at first, but the amount I offered was substantial, and the prospect of becoming a queen was quite appealing as well."

"Why are you telling me this?" Zan demanded. "Why now?"

"Things didn't go quite as I planned," I continued. "I didn't count on the Tribunal's takeover. That made things a little more difficult. I didn't expect to have to bring my little brother along, either. He believes that I'm an Achlevan spy and that he's helping Lisette uncover my treachery, poor thing."

"Was any of it real?"

"I have grown . . . fond . . . of you. And I thought, when we talked this afternoon, that maybe I could make it work after all . . . but then I followed you into the hall and hid. I heard everything that was said there, and I . . . I just can't." I thrust his mother's ring back into his hands. "You and your father are the only Achlevan royals left, which means the instant you marry someone—anyone—she becomes a target to bring down the wall. It's a risk I can't afford." I thought of the rings Aren showed me. "In fact, you should just never marry at all. If you die without blood heirs, the wall will stand forever." *And you will live a long, full life.*

"You think I should die alone?" Zan was so astounded, he almost sounded amused. Then his expression changed. "No." He came to me suddenly, putting both hands on my face, eyes feverish. "Emilie, Aurelia . . . whoever you are . . . I love you. And despite everything you've told me, I think you love me, too. Please, *please* say you do."

Oh, Empyrea! I cast the most fervid prayer of my life into the heavens. *Help me!*

I said, "I can't." I put my hands over his and pulled them gently down from my cheeks. "Nathaniel is camping tonight just off the southwest road toward Ingram. I think it would be wise for you to meet up with him. Maybe you can stay in Ingram for a while until you—"

My fingers grazed something at his wrist. I yanked up his sleeve, revealing a leather cuff. My firebird charm was sewn into the band like a talisman, exactly as Aren had shown me.

My breath caught. "Take it off."

"What? No—"

"Take it *off!"* I snarled as I tried to wrench it off myself, fingers curled into claws.

He snapped his arm back, scrutinizing my face with disbelief and something akin to grief as the impact of my revelations finally landed. The Emilie he cared about didn't even exist.

Wordlessly, he retrieved a piece of paper from his pocket and thrust it into my hands before he turned and was gone.

I waited until he was out of sight and then opened it carefully, heart in my throat.

It was a sketch of a girl absorbed in a spell book, one hand propped under her chin, the other turning a page. The drawing was in Zan's dark, expressive strokes, and details were spare, but there was a sweetness to the curve of her neck, the delicate turn of her wrist. This was not the towering, terrifying witch of his other drawing. The subject here was just a normal girl in a quiet moment, as seen through the eyes of someone who loved her.

I sank to the stones and buried my head in my arms, my devastation complete.

✳

I put one foot in front of the other. It was all I could do. I'd burned down my hut and my connection to Zan. Kate was dead and Nathaniel was gone and the last deaths required to bring down the wall were stayed, hopefully forever. There was nothing left for me in Achleva. I had only one objective now: retrieve my brother. Once he was safe, I would be able to return with single-minded focus to destroying the Tribunal. If I had to face my own oblivion to do it . . . well, all the better.

I went to the castle the usual way, past my smoldering hut and down the passage to the tower, where the water was still ankle-deep from all the rain. I had to put my hands against the walls to keep from falling in a few places, cringing at the slimy film now covering them. After climbing up from the alcove opening, I was surprised to find someone standing a little farther down on the rocky shore, staring out toward King's Gate. It was too late to try to conceal my passing; the figure turned at the sound of my footfalls.

I shrieked and lost my footing when I saw his face, narrowly catching myself by snagging a bloodleaf vine before I could go over the edge and onto the rocks below.

King Domhnall was dead.

The spirit watched me climb back up with a snarl curled permanently into his lips, his throat hanging open below it, blood spilled all down the front of his golden doublet. I treaded carefully toward him; his was an ugly soul in life, warped by rage and greed. Dying did not seem to leave him much improved.

I reached toward him, tentative and slow, but he didn't wait for me to gain the courage to touch him; he snatched my wrist in his fleshy paw, wrapping his cold and clammy fingers tight around my bones. I tumbled, headfirst, into the last moments of his mortality.

"The plan is still good," the king was saying. He was standing beneath the gate bearing the visage of his ancestors. "I've fulfilled my side of the bargain. No reason to deviate now."

"Still good?" Toris's lip twitched. "Our executioner is dead. The prince has broken the betrothal and resigned himself to exile. I don't know how things could possibly be worse. You've failed me, Domhnall. You almost had everything you wanted: forgiveness of your debts, freedom from your barons, and unquestioned rule over two kingdoms for the rest of your life." He shrugged. "Too bad your brother Victor isn't still alive. At least then I'd have another option."

"Another day, maybe two, is all I need. I heard a rumor about a kid in the Canina District. Pretty sure it's mine. I remember the mother—"

"We don't have two days to wait for you," Toris said. "The black moon is upon us. The deadline fast approaches."

"You don't have to kill me, Toris!"

Toris took him by his collar and said, "Ah, but I do. Because, you see, my mistress commands it." He drew his knife.

"I'll call my guards," the king blubbered. "They won't let you hurt me."

"Your guards?" Toris scoffed. "You pay them a few measly coppers and throw them a few scraps and think you can call them yours? If it weren't for my plentiful gold, they'd have long defected and you'd have had none. They are mine, and they have been for a very long time. They obey you only because *I* ordered them to. No one is here to help you, Domhnall. And quite frankly, you've worn on my patience long enough."

Domhnall tried to escape, but despite his size advantage, his fear made him clumsy. Toris had him quickly cornered. *"Nihil nunc salvet te,"* he said as he drew his knife—Dedrick's luneocite knife—and deftly sliced Domhnall's fleshy neck from one ear to the other. Then he shoved Domhnall over the edge of the wall and the king fell down, down, down through the mist, trailing blood, until he landed, splayed flat, against the water. It held him there on the surface, his eyes empty and staring, as the blood poured out around him in thin tendrils that grew and grew, lashing out across the water, turning it a milky, jewel-toned red, visible even in the dark.

With a cry, I tore my hands from Domhnall's grasp and ran to the beachside edge. The inky, midnight-blue fjord was gone. Instead, scarlet waves were lapping the rocky shore.

The first seal of King's Gate was broken. The king was dead, and where once was water, there was now only blood.

PART THREE

THE WALL
AND
THE TOWER

31

The tree I used to first communicate with Conrad was now little more than a mess of naked, thorny branches; it was still dark, so the black ribbon from my dress parcel hardly stood out against the dreary grays of the garden's squalid remains. I cast a sideways prayer to the Empyrea that my brother would see it anyway.

When I first heard the rustle nearby, I whirled around, expecting to find Aren. But it wasn't the Harbinger. It was Lisette.

"I thought it was you," she said. She was holding a pair of lace gloves in her hands, wringing them nervously.

"What do you want?"

"I want you to leave Conrad alone. Stop taunting him. Scaring him with your messages. He is a little boy, Aurelia. Just a little boy who doesn't deserve to be dragged into your conspiracies, your treachery—"

"*My* treachery?"

"I know you killed Kellan," she said, eyes shining. "I know everything. And it won't be long, mark my words, before you pay for what you've done. Father says we're very close to uncovering the entire thing and then this nightmare can finally be over."

She was scared; I could see that. She was scared of *me,* and she had come here to confront me because . . . she was trying to protect my brother.

"You have no idea," I muttered. "All this time . . . and you have no idea."

"No idea about what?"

"What has really been happening here. I didn't kill Kellan. He was my truest friend." I didn't dare give voice to the idea that he might still be alive; I'd been keeping that possibility safely tucked away in my mind. "Your father threatened that if I didn't give him the invitations to cross the wall, he'd kill him. I did what he asked," I said through my teeth, "and he killed him anyway."

"You're lying."

"I'm not."

"You and that Achlevan, Simon Silvis . . . you're in this together. You're trying to sabotage Achleva and Renalt. Your own mother—"

"Is being held hostage by the Tribunal under your father's direction!" Toris must have met Dedrick Corvalis through trade at the de Lena ports, just as Simon had been investigating. Toris recruited Dedrick, and then King Domhnall, into his plans. But even as the *how* was becoming clearer, the *why* was still a mystery. "All of this, every last detail, has been orchestrated by him, not me. Did you know, in the forest, he tried to kill me, too?"

"No. No. My father is a righteous man. None of this makes any sense—"

I grabbed her by her shoulders and looked directly into her pretty face. "We were friends once, you and I. You could have sent me to the gallows years ago, but you didn't. I think you knew, deep down inside, that I didn't deserve it. That I'm a good person, despite being born with magic in my veins."

She opened her mouth and then closed it again. I'd struck a nerve. "Think, Lisette. Think. If our friendship meant anything to you when we were little, I beg of you to listen to me now. Has there been nothing that your father has done over the last months . . . years! . . .that has given you pause? That has made you stop and question yourself, even just for a moment?" I let her go. "There has been, hasn't there?"

"No," she said quickly. "It's just me. I have a very active imagination, and Father says—"

"Your father is a liar and a traitor. You can't believe anything he has told you. Did you think that all of this was just some big charade? That you'd come here, strut around with my name, just for . . . what? To catch me in some treasonous act? Prove my disloyalty? No, he brought you here to marry the prince, Lisette. So that you both could be married, and then *murdered,* and bring down the wall with your deaths. That's what all of this is about. Everything. Toris de Lena will not stop until he's destroyed Achlev's wall, and the city with it."

"No, no—he would never! Why would he want that for me? I'm his daughter! Why not just let you marry the prince and then kill you instead?"

I took a step back. "Because I saw through him." He'd said as much in the Ebonwilde, when I'd tried to negotiate for Conrad. *Unlike you, he's proven himself valuably malleable.* "He didn't want to use me because he couldn't intimidate me. He couldn't control me." I'd never thought of it that way before. Toris removed me from his plans not because I was weak but because I was too strong to be controlled.

"And I'm a fool, is that it?"

"No," I said. "It's just as you said . . . you're his daughter. He was counting on your love for him to overcome any of your doubts. And can't you see? It worked."

She sniffed and turned her back on me. "He wasn't always like this, you know. When I was very little, he was affectionate, loving . . ."

"But the loss of your mother changed him. I know." I hated mentioning Camilla; I didn't want to remind Lisette whose fault her death was in the first place.

"What? No. They fought constantly before she died. She always said it was what he saw at the Assembly that changed him. He was there when it fell. He was the one who relayed the news back to Renalt."

"What was he there for, Lisette?" I asked urgently. "What did he see? What did he find?"

"I don't *know!*" she cried.

I placed a tentative hand on her shoulder. "I know you love Conrad. In many ways, you're a better sister to him than I ever was. Ever could be. Thank you, truly. But look around you. The king of Achleva is dead! The water is red with algae and dangerous to drink. Anything green in the city has rotted away. Something terrible is about to happen, and I must get Conrad away from it as soon as I can."

"All of this"—she waved her hand at the dead terrace garden

 302

and the crimson fjord—"is because of the wall? And for the wall to fall . . ."

It begins with three dead white ponies,

then a maid, a mother, a crone.

Then upon a bed of red rosies,

Bleed three fallen kings to leave three empty thrones . . .

"Three of Achlevan royalty will die."

"King Domhnall, me, and . . ."

"Valentin," I said, swallowing hard. "The prince."

She took a step back. His name had unnerved her.

"You can judge me for going along with this, for taking your place, but"—she gave a helpless shrug—"I love him, Aurelia. I've loved him since I was a little girl, reading his letters. I kept writing to him, too. I paid one of the castle messengers to deliver the letters to me instead of you. After my mother died, they were the only thing that kept me going." She dashed some tears from her eyes, sniffling. "I know it's stupid. It couldn't last forever, I knew that. But ever since we got here, he's hardly spoken to me. And . . . and . . ."

I surprised myself and hugged her. Maybe it was Kate's influence. Maybe it was that our long-lost friendship wasn't so lost after all. Maybe it was because I knew what it was like to love Zan and have to let him go. She returned my hug softly, almost shyly.

"I'm leaving today," I told her. "I want you and Conrad to come with me. We can all go back to Renalt and face the Tribunal together.

Since the Tribunal is orchestrating the destruction of the wall, once the Tribunal is gone, Zan—I mean, Valentin—will have nothing more to fear." I took down the black ribbon and gave it to her. "Give this to Conrad. He knows what it means."

She took it cautiously. "Do you know where he is now?" she asked. "Valentin?"

"Gone into exile," I said. "Safe, far away from the wall."

Even as I said it, from a distance there came the chime of a bell.

✳

I remembered what Zan had said: *The bell at the gate tolls for only two reasons: an army is approaching, or there's royalty coming.*

Lisette and I went together, shoving our way to the front of the angry crowd as three riders from the king's guard made their way sedately up the street from the gate. A man was stumbling behind them, tethered by ropes wrapped thickly around his wrists. Zan.

"They caught him!" someone near me shouted, celebrating. Behind me, epithets were being thrown in his direction. *King killer. Murderer. Betrayer. Destroyer.*

Zan was being cast as his father's assassin. Domhnall was a terrible king, but the people were scared and desperate for someone to blame for their suffering. Toris was feeding Zan to them like carrion to hungry wolves.

"Zan!" I cried, trying to break from the line to reach him. "Zan!"

Lisette tugged me back. "If my father sees you, he'll kill you," she hissed.

Hearing me call, he looked up, and my heart dropped at the sight of the dried blood caking his temple, the purple bruises marring his cheeks. His eyes were bright and angry, though, warning me away. I backed down, and Lisette and I fell into step with the mass as it moved toward the front steps of the castle, where Toris was waiting in full Tribunal regalia.

"Good people of Achleva!" he called with the same zest he used to always save for the most salacious witch executions. "Your great King Domhnall spent his life in your service, only to have it cut so short by the person he loved the most: his son. Prince Valentin has been doing everything in his power to destroy this sacred, ancient city, one murder at a time . . . even going so far as to frame and execute the innocent Dedrick Corvalis. But no more. His treachery has been dragged out into the light, and justice will soon be done!"

The crowd that had, only yesterday, cheered at Zan's defiance of the king now screamed their hate-filled belief that he'd murdered him. Blood magic be damned; this was what true power looked like. Toris could wield a mob like a weapon.

I was wrong to have ever counted being paraded through a crowd bent on my death as my greatest nightmare. In truth, helplessly standing witness as it happened to someone I loved was far, far worse.

"What do we do?" Lisette whispered.

"We get him out," I said. "We take him with us."

I couldn't watch Zan be dragged inside. Instead, I turned the force of my gaze to Toris, who was basking in the citizens' fear and anger like a snake in the sun. He gave a deep bow and, wearing a confident smile, retreated into the castle that was now all but his.

I began calculating all the many ways I would make him pay.

✳

Lisette was right: if Toris saw me, he'd kill me without hesitation. She, however, could move around inside undetected, so the task of surveillance fell to her. She was to observe everything she could about Zan's imprisonment: If he was in the dungeon, which cell? How many guards would we have to contend with? How often did they rotate shifts? She'd collect as much information as possible, anything we could use to our advantage, and bring it back to me. At dark, I'd retrieve Zan and meet her and Conrad at the tower, and we'd all leave the city together.

She was a reluctant spy; I was an anxious sentinel. We were both ill-suited to our roles but united in our cause: retrieve Zan, escape with Conrad. Rob Toris of his pawns and deny him his victory.

I had to wait out the day in the tower. I meant to go all the way to the top, to watch what was happening in the city from its highest vantage point, but I barely made it inside the door before my knees gave out. I crawled a few more feet before the days of accumulated exhaustion caught up with me. I slept for hours, curled up inside the mosaic triquetra, the tower's thousand stairs spiraling into infinity above me.

My dreams were troubling, full of unnatural shadows and beguiling whispers. *Help me,* they said. *Free me.* I saw myself from above, thrashing in my sleep as serpentine tendrils of smoke coiled around my limbs. *Let me out.* The whispers grew more insistent, transforming from a plea to a demand.

Let me out.

I woke in a panic and scrambled from the mosaic, pressing my sweat-soaked back against the cold stone wall. Just a bad dream, I reassured myself. An unfortunate side effect of a weary body and a wounded heart.

Still, I didn't want to spend another second in the tower.

I spent the rest of my vigil on the rocks below, watching boats—full of rich merchants, mostly—leave the docks across the water one by one, crossing beneath King's Gate and leaving the suffering city behind. The poor could not leave so easily; my father used to say that a hurricane was an annoyance to the rich, while a mere drop of rain was a catastrophe to the poor. I wondered what wisdom he'd have imparted now, if he hadn't died in the fire I'd sent to de Lena's pier. I needed guidance, now more than ever.

It was dark again when I heard a shuffle on the other side of the tower. I scrambled to my feet.

"Aurelia?"

"Where have you been?" I said frantically. "I've waited all day! We need to—"

I stopped. Lisette was standing behind Conrad, who was watching me with hesitant eyes. I tripped over my feet to get to him, grabbing him with both hands and pulling him into a fierce embrace even as I stumbled. I wasn't sure if I was laughing or crying or both, but I didn't care. He put his arms around me and hugged me back, and I buried my face in his hair.

"He said you killed Kellan. That you were trying to hurt Mother . . ."

"I didn't hurt Kellan. I would never have in a million years hurt Kellan or Mother or you or anybody. It was Toris. It was all Toris."

"Aurelia, I mean Lisette, has been taking care of me."

"I know! And she has been doing an excellent job. Look at you. You're growing up so quickly. Mother will be so proud."

"Look." He brought out the winged-horse charm I'd hidden for him. "I've taken really good care of it."

He tried to hand it back to me, but I shook my head. "You keep it. So the Empyrea can grant you good luck."

"I couldn't get to Valentin," Lisette said under her breath. "Not even close. I tried all day. They've got an entire floor closed off. At least ten guards at every exit. Father has it locked down."

I recalibrated my plans around this new information. "We'll have to make some kind of diversion. Start a fire or something. Wait till they go running—"

"We can't," she said, putting her hand on my arm. "There's more. I heard him talking to the guards. They're going to seal the gates shut tonight. No one will go in or out. We have to be out before they do." She glanced up at the castle behind her. "And before they know that we are gone." She swallowed. "I told Father I wasn't feeling well, that Conrad and I would retire early to our beds. I'm not sure he believed me, but I didn't know what else to do."

I nodded. "We'll get you two out before the gates close. Once you're safe, I'll come back for Zan. I'll find a way."

I went over the ledge first; then I helped lift Conrad down from the bottom. Lisette's boots were still hanging over the side when we began hearing shouts from above. "They must have already figured out we're not in our beds," she said as she touched her feet to the rocky ground of the inlet. "They're going to come after us."

"They won't find us," I said. "I promise. But you need to stay calm. For me, and for Conrad. Can you do that?"

She took a breath and nodded, and we had already gotten several feet into the tunnel when I remembered that I'd left the Founder's blood relic hidden under Aren's statue. I hadn't thought of it in days.

"Wait!" I said. "I have to go back; I forgot something—" But I was cut off by the sound of hoofbeats on the ground overhead.

"Whatever it is, you don't need it," Lisette said. "It's too late to get it now."

She was right. I *hated* when Lisette was right. I had to trust Aren to watch over the vial now.

I led the way, and we sloshed through the red-toned sludge that was coating the inside of the passage. With Conrad beside me, I was sharply aware of every serrated piece of rock underfoot, every slippery turn; I could hear the soft tones of Lisette's voice: "It's all right, little prince. Not long now." But the reassurances seemed more for her own benefit than for his; he was marching with a gusto that suggested he was enjoying himself.

When we got to the wall, our plans to scale it disintegrated and scattered like dust. Guards were stationed along the top of the wall now, each patrolling a section of one hundred feet. There was no way we could go up the staircase now; we couldn't leave the shelter of the trees without risking being seen. We were forced to retreat, scurrying like rats into the city's maze of alleys.

A crowd was gathering near the base of Forest Gate, its statues cleft and crumbling now that their magic seal was broken. Men were moving chunks of stone to clear the way for the portcullis to descend past the damage and close off the gate. Guards pressed the simmering mass of people back in a great half circle while they shouted their outrage at being denied exit.

"What are we going to do now?" Lisette asked. "There are guards everywhere! They are sure to see us." She shook her head. "My father will be so angry."

"They won't find us," I said. "We're going to get out. Can you trust me, just a little?" I didn't wait for them to answer before I drew my knife. "Give me your hands," I said.

"What?" Lisette said, recoiling. "No."

"Don't be afraid. Conrad, look." I pointed up to one of the guards on the wall. "He has a bow and arrow on his back. Can you tell? Yes, look closer. There it is." My brother squinted. "A bow and arrow is a weapon." I turned his face to me. "I am not a weapon. I am a *person*. Your sister." I turned to Lisette. "Your friend. And magic is as much a part of me as the prints on my fingers or the color of my eyes."

Conrad asked in a small voice, "Isn't magic dangerous?"

"Yes, it can be—the way a knife or a bow or a staff are dangerous. But I can control it, and I will not let anything happen to you. Understand? Not one thing." I cast a prayer to the stars that I could make good on that promise.

And there it was: the barest flicker of a smile. He held out his hand. He believed me.

I peered around the corner to survey the layout of Forest Gate. "If we come at it from the east side, we can cross there, see?"

"That's right out in the open," Lisette said. "They will catch us."

I took out my knife and drew it in a slim line across the very center of each of my hands. I could feel the magic immediately, drawing on my fear at crossing the wall and my elation as Conrad put his small hand in mine. I held out my other to Lisette. "Well?"

Reluctantly, she removed her glove and clasped my hand. "Walk slowly," I said. "Follow my lead. And whatever you do, don't let go."

Together we walked to the street while I murmured the spell under my breath, hoping that it would work as well for all of us as it had for just me so many times before. "*Nos sunt invisibiles.* We are unseen. *Non est hic nos esse.* We are not here. *Sunt invisibiles.* We are unseen . . ."

I could feel my magic wrapping around them in threads; I crossed it back and forth, weaving it like a net.

"Aurelia," Lisette said from the corner of her mouth as we moved toward the gate with aching slowness.

I couldn't stop. We were past the line of the crowd, too far out in the open now. "Aurelia!" Lisette said again, frantic this time. "Look!"

The men were finished clearing the rubble, and the portcullis had begun to move, creaking as it slowly descended, with six men cranking the chains on either side of it.

"We have to run!" Lisette said.

I shook my head furiously as I continued my chant. I could feel my blood flow slowing, the spell pulling up at the edges as I healed and clotted. I knew I wouldn't be able to hold the spell over them if they jarred or broke the blood connecting our hands. I quickened my pace, hoping to reach the portcullis before my blood flow stopped completely and I lost the spell altogether. Sweat was standing out on my forehead now from the strain. I had to keep my grip. I couldn't lose my control.

I had promised Conrad I wouldn't let anything happen to him.

We were getting close, but the iron teeth of the portcullis were coming down faster than we could cover ground. Tears were flowing freely out of my stinging eyes now, but I kept on. "*Sunt invisibiles.* We are unseen. *Non est hic nos esse.* We are not here. *Sunt invisibiles.* We are unseen . . ."

And then Lisette's hand broke from mine. The part of the spell that had been blanketing her snapped back into place over Conrad and me alone. Now fully visible in the center of the road, she let out a piercing scream.

"My kidnappers! They're getting away! Stop them! Stop them!"

She had betrayed us. She had convinced me of her innocence, conned me into bringing her into my plans, only to turn us over to the enemy. It was all for nothing.

But when I looked back over my shoulder and saw her, standing resolutely in the swarm of guards responding to her scream, she was not pointing to Conrad and me. She was pointing the other way. She had given up her own chance at freedom to draw them off, to allow Conrad and me to escape.

She mouthed *Go!* And we obeyed, surging forward—making sure to keep our hands connected and the spell intact—and ducking beneath the portcullis mere seconds before it fell the final feet and its teeth sank into the ground with a resonant clang.

32

Once we were a safe distance from the gate, I let the spell fall. I wasn't sure I had the strength to cast it again. Anyone who saw us out here would be able to identify us to possible pursuers with ease. And the campsites were especially populous tonight, full to the brim with city dwellers who must have gotten out before the entry and exit were barred and, confronted with the long roads and the endless Ebonwilde, chose to shelter on the outside of the wall for a while before facing it.

Conrad had not let go of my hand, and I did not dare let go of his, even to clean off the blood that was now half-dry and uncomfortably sticky. I didn't know quite what we would do; we couldn't just wander into the forest with no map, no guide, no plan. I didn't have Falada to carry me anymore, and the last time I'd seen Aren, she almost destroyed me.

Conrad was clinging to my skirt. "I'm hungry," he said. "And it smells bad here. And I miss Lisette. Is she coming soon?"

I knelt beside him. "No, little brother. I don't think she is coming with us anymore. She did a very brave thing back there, helping us get across the wall before it closed. Can you be brave, just like her?"

"I *am* brave, Aurelia," he said a little crossly, but he hugged me anyway. I closed my eyes and squeezed him back, as tight as I could. "I have a friend out here somewhere. If we can find him, he can help keep us safe. But until then, we have to blend in. Keep your head covered and your eyes down, and follow my directions to the letter. Understand?"

In response, he pulled his hood down over his hair.

We made our path by skirting the edges of the travelers' camps, close enough to the firelight to scan the faces of the people huddled around them, far enough to keep our own obscured by shadow. No one gave us a second glance; they were displaced and scared, victims of circumstances they could not have predicted, that they could not have controlled. But these were the fortunate ones; how many more were stuck inside the city, unprepared for what might come?

There were shouts in the distance behind us—guards raiding the camps. From over my shoulder, I watched as one of them accosted a girl not far from my own age, forcing her to her knees and cuffing her when she cried. They ripped off her cloak and then spat on her when it was discerned that she was not the girl they were looking for. Me.

We hurried forward, but the awful smell intensified, and I looked up to see the spirit of Thackery's old friend Gilroy still sitting glumly in his gibbet. Aha. I knew where we were, and I tugged Conrad with me toward Thackery's old encampment, which was now occupied by a man with patchy whiskers and ruddy cheeks.

This time Darwyn didn't see me coming. I had my knife pressed into his back before he could scramble up from the fire. "Take what you want, sir," he mumbled, hurriedly emptying his pockets. A few copper coins, a half-eaten apple, a misshapen brass ring, and a hardened hunk of cheese scattered across the dirt as I forced him to his feet.

"I don't want your scraps," I said icily.

At the sound of my voice, he exclaimed, "Wait! I ain't gonna be robbed by no girl—"

"Quiet," I snarled, moving the knife to his neck. He stiffened, hands up. "Listen carefully. My brother and I are going to hide in Thackery's stable. If men come looking for us, you will do everything in your power to steer them away."

"Or what?" he asked, a bit too surly for a man with a knife to his neck.

Whip-fast, I nicked a finger and let the blood drop fall in front of his eyes. "Uro," I said. Burn. And the blood turned into a streak of fire that burst into three-foot flames the instant it hit the ground. I closed my hand and the fire went out.

Darwyn was trembling. "There was two men what came through here a couple weeks ago, chattering about some blood witch . . . Their faces . . . cracked . . . scarred . . . unrecognizable."

"Do as I command," I said, moving the knife away from his neck now that I'd made my point clear. "Or it won't be your face that I burn into something unrecognizable."

"But what would be worse than—" Then it dawned on him. "Oh."

The guards were only a few camps away now. Darwyn ushered us into the stable. "Ray has a little hidey-hole in there," he said. "He didn't think no one knew about it, but I did. After Ray was gone, Empyrea keep 'im, I moved all my good stuff into it. Just in time, too. When my ol' lady Erdie left me, she took everything she could get 'er filthy scheming hands on. But I was one step ahead." He grinned, pleased with himself, until he saw my flat expression and his smile disappeared. He moved aside a big pile of hay in the empty first stall, revealing a plank in the ground. He lifted it and motioned us over. "In here."

Darwyn's hidden "good stuff" was liquor in a surprising quantity; the hole was several feet deep and ran the length of the stable, but it was full to capacity with bottles of spirits. I climbed in the hole first, settling in between a jug of ale and some bottles of rum, then brought Conrad down to sit on my lap. The whole space left for us wasn't more than four feet by four feet; it was a tight fit.

Conrad was trying to peer through the cracks to see what might be happening above, but I pulled him back, pressing a finger to my lips.

It was just a matter of moments before we heard the voices outside our hiding place. The words were muffled through the straw and the wood plank, but we could still make out the string of uncouth exclamations Darwyn was letting loose on the soldiers as they started throwing things around the camp. Then they opened the stall door.

Darwyn said, "There's nothing in there but straw. See for yourself if you like."

We jumped as the man began stabbing his sword into the hay, shaking dirt down into our eyes with each jab.

"See?" Darwyn said. "Nothin'. And I don't suppose the lot of ye are planning to pay for all the damage you've done?"

A guard's voice answered gruffly, "Out of our way, old man. Men! Next camp!"

We stayed down in that hole most of the night, long after it might have been safe to emerge.

When we finally swung the trapdoor open, the movement dislodged a bundle of documents that had been tucked between one of the boards: Thackery's invitations for crossing the wall, written in Zan's own hand. I gathered them up and stowed them inside my mostly empty satchel, next to the bloodcloth. From the corner of my eye, however, I saw something glint in the space behind where the invitations had been stashed. I pushed my fingers between the boards and came back with something incredible: the topaz gryphon I'd given to Thackery that first night in Achleva. I clutched it, thanking Thackery and the Empyrea for returning it to me.

Darwyn was pounding on the stable door. "Best be coming out now, girl. Someone's here for you."

I put Conrad behind me and readied my knife. If I couldn't get close enough for a good shot at whoever it was waiting outside the stable, I'd use magic. I'd get us out of here, one way or another. I'd burn and pillage and destroy anything or anybody that stood in my way.

I kicked open the door. Then, stunned, I said, *"Nathaniel?"*

"Emilie, it *is* you! I heard the guards looking . . . I thought it might be, but I had to be sure . . ."

Darwyn's hands were up; Nathaniel had his neck in the crook of his arm, poised to give it a quick twist if the man put up a fight. Grumpily, Darwyn said, "Of *course* you two would know each other."

"What are you doing here?" I asked, putting my knife away. "Where's Ella?"

Nathaniel nodded to a bundle of blankets close by, where Ella was staring wide-eyed up at the gibbet where Gilroy's ghost seemed to be playing a game with her. He would peer out, wiggle his fingers until she gurgled at him, pull back for a moment, then peek out again. "I was at another camp, procuring horses for us, when they got Zan. There are guards everywhere, watching everything, so I haven't been able to get back into the city to find him. And then I heard some talk about a girl who appeared out of thin air outside the wall after the gates closed, and she matched your description, so I followed your tracks here . . ." He paused. "Is that Prince Conrad? Emilie, did you *kidnap* Prince Conrad?"

"No, of course not! He's my—"

"I'm her brother," Conrad supplied, peeking out from behind my skirt.

Nathaniel gaped.

"Too tight," Darwyn said in a strangled voice. "Too tight!"

"Oh," Nathaniel said, sheepishly releasing him from the headlock. "Sorry."

"Bunch of stars-forsaken loons," Darwyn muttered, rubbing his sore neck. "The whole lot of ye."

★

Despite Darwyn's fierce objections at being made to leave, Nathaniel secured a place for him in one of the refugee trains heading out. He carried as many bottles of his booze as he could fit into his bag and grumbled ferociously at having to leave the rest behind, but he went. Nathaniel gave him a coin for his trouble. He was kinder than I would have been; Darwyn did help us, true, but only because he feared for his extremities. In my opinion, keeping all his parts attached should have been payment enough.

Nathaniel knew of a good place to camp a couple of miles south of the wall, by the River Sentis. With the roads now overwhelmed by travelers, his options had dwindled. His plan was to bypass most of the slow caravans by cutting through the Ebonwilde and meeting the road again several leagues past the junctions from Achlev to Ingram, Castillion, and Achebe.

"Maybe by then," he said, one hand on the reins, the other cradling Ella's sling, "many will have split off to head toward Castillion and Achebe, or Aylward farther west, and the road will be clearer." He looked at Conrad, sitting in the front of the saddle on the horse that had been meant for Zan, dozing against my chest. "What are you going to do?"

"I'm going to make sure Conrad is secure, and then I'm going back for Zan." The sound of his name left my stomach in a twist. "I'm going to get him out. Once that's done, I can worry about everything else."

Nathaniel was staring a little. "I'm sorry," he said. "I still can't quite comprehend that *you're* the Renaltan princess."

"Believe me, you are far from alone."

Nathaniel reined his horse in. "Stop. Do you hear that?"

"The river?" I asked, but he'd already dismounted and was leading his horse quietly through the undergrowth.

"Wake up, Conrad," I whispered as I softly shook my brother from his doze.

He stirred, rubbing his eyes. "Where are we?"

"I don't know," I said. Ahead, Nathaniel put his finger to his lips. *Shhhh*. I dismounted but let Conrad stay in the saddle as I brought our roan up next to Nathaniel's bay mare.

Nathaniel pointed. "Look, there. In the valley."

The first things I saw were blue flags emblazoned with the silhouette of a white winged horse: the standard of Renalt. Beneath the pennants stood a cluster of tents and dozens of horses, all bearing the regalia of the Renaltan military.

"Are they friends or foes?" Nathaniel asked.

"In Renalt it's always hard to know." I squinted while I scanned the encampment, then gasped. "There."

Beneath one of the blue flags waved a smaller white one, bearing the circular, spread-branched hawthorn seal of the Greythorne family.

I leaped back onto the horse behind Conrad and snapped the reins. With my heart pounding in time to his hoofbeats, we sailed down the embankment toward the camp. I had no backup plan, no strategy for escape if these soldiers had come at Toris's behest. My only thoughts were of a white flag and a hawthorn tree.

The soldiers saw us coming. By the time we reached the encampment, the men in blue uniforms were lined up in a defensive formation, swords drawn.

"Halt!" one of them cried as we approached. "State your name and your business."

Head high, I said, "I am Aurelia, princess of Renalt. I bring with me my brother, Conrad, high prince and future king of Renalt." Nathaniel cantered in behind us. "And Nathaniel Gardner, our valued ally and friend."

A murmur went up among the men as Conrad and I were scrutinized. We were dirty and disheveled, with bags under our eyes and little bits of straw stuck in our clothes. I didn't blame them for doubting our claim.

"Can anyone here speak to the truth of her words?" the man asked.

Suddenly a voice rang out from behind the line. "She is who she says! I can testify on her behalf! I'll vouch for her, and I'll stand with her, and I'll fight anyone who gets in my way."

"Kellan?" I asked, hardly daring to breathe.

He pushed his way out of the crowd. "As I always have. And always will."

✴

In the largest tent, a makeshift table was made from a scavenged flat-topped stone. Not everyone could fit inside, so half the men stayed outside, on guard, and the other half lined the inside of the canvas.

Kellan's explanations were hasty: after he'd fallen into the river, his memories were vague, little more than impressions of washing ashore, then being moved, and careful hands dressing his wounds. He was still in the haze of fever when his brother, Fredrick, found him delivered to the Greythorne estate's front door with no sign of his benefactor. Just Kellan and, in the distance, a watchful yellow-eyed fox.

Wisely, Fredrick kept Kellan's sudden appearance a secret. He ministered to his younger brother himself, keeping vigil by his bed for two days, until the fever finally broke. Finally lucid, Kellan was able to relay what had happened to us in the woods at Toris's hands. In turn, Fredrick's news of the queen in the capital was equally perplexing: it seemed that though my mother had been taken as a royal hostage in Syric, the Tribunal had then made no further moves to consolidate their power. But something was simmering; everyone knew it. The only question was: What was stopping them? What were they waiting for?

I provided that answer. The Tribunal was waiting for Toris to destroy Achlev's Wall.

What they had planned after that, I hoped we wouldn't have to find out.

Now, inside the tent, Fredrick Greythorne was standing behind Kellan, dressed in the livery of their family. He looked like Kellan in nearly every way except the hair; where Kellan had a wealth of tight, corkscrew curls, Fredrick kept his hair closely shorn, skimming his deep brown skin, but not so close that he could hide the hints of iron gray at his temples. He was fifteen years Kellan's senior, and watching him made it easy to imagine how Kellan would look fifteen years from now: handsome, with a wide, well-cut jaw and fine, crinkly lines around his mouth and eyes.

It had been Kellan's idea to infiltrate Syric and rescue the queen, and Fredrick's plan that had made it happen.

"My mother is free?" I asked, jubilant for the first time in what felt like years. "Where is she? How was it done?"

Kellan was slowly pacing; it was clear from his movements that he was still feeling the effects of his injuries. "The castle was completely

 322

locked down. The Tribunal was in total control, and even though they maintained that the queen was in good health, Onal was the only person Simon allowed to go in and out of the room, to bring them food and the like."

"And the Tribunal clerics let her?"

"She's a harmless old woman. What was she going to do?"

I nodded. "So they were all scared of her."

"Terrified."

Fredrick said, "We went to Onal first, and used her to pass messages to your mother and Simon, make plans. Then I went secretly to my old comrades in the guard and recruited anyone still loyal to the queen. We didn't have as much force as we would have liked, which made storming the castle impossible. So we had to be furtive and use our only real advantage: Simon. We drugged their night guards and dragged them into the room, where Simon created an illusion to make them look like himself and the queen."

"And that worked?"

Kellan said, "It got us out. I'd hate to know what kind of punishments those two had to face when the rest of the Tribunal figured out they weren't their actual prisoners." His wide grin said otherwise. "We'd have been sunk without Simon. After we broke them from the room, he made himself and the queen virtually invisible until we were out of the city. It was the damnedest thing."

"I can't imagine," I said dryly.

Fredrick picked the story up where Kellan left off. "The Tribunal didn't realize she was missing until well into the next day. By then we were halfway to the port at Hallet."

"But the Tribunal still holds Syric?"

"They do. We've gotten the queen to safety; she's with a regiment of soldiers at the Silvis family's holding halfway up the fjord. We wanted her to start making plans for our next move to regain the capital, but all she can think about is you and your brother."

"And what about Simon?" I asked. "Is he all right?"

"You can ask him yourself," Kellan replied. "He's with Onal right now, two tents down. So is Conrad and your friend with the baby."

I raced in the direction he'd pointed me, and when I located the right tent, I tossed the flap aside to find Conrad on a stool with a miserable look on his face. Onal stood behind him, tugging a comb through the knots in his curly locks. She didn't even glance up before saying crossly to me, "Look at this mess. You couldn't have wiped some of the smudges off his face before bringing him in front of an entire troop of soldiers? He's supposed to lead them one day, Aurelia. He can't command their respect when he looks like he rolled around in a trash heap all day."

I threw my arms around her bony shoulders, and she patted my back in a rare display of fondness before saying, "I sure hope your stink doesn't get into my clothing, young lady. I'd prefer not to smell like a cesspool."

"How is my mother?" I asked, pulling away.

"She's well." I turned to the new voice coming from the other corner of the tent. Simon was sitting back against a pallet, next to Nathaniel. He was rocking a sleeping Ella and smiling, but he looked haggard and sallow, as if he'd aged years in the weeks since I saw him last. "My family's property isn't large, but it's well secured. She's more than safe there until we return. Until then, she sends her love to you both."

"What happened to you?" I asked, aghast.

"Aurelia!" Onal chided. "Where are your manners?"

"Bleeding oneself daily does take its toll," he said, and I nodded. Back in Renalt, I'd been so eager to learn blood magic, so dismissive of the pain and exhaustion, mental and physical, that would accompany it. I understood better now: the strongest magic requires the greatest sacrifice.

Simon carefully shifted Ella back to Nathaniel. "It was a good thing Lord and Lieutenant Greythorne acted when they did; I'm not sure how much longer I could have lasted. And the Tribunal were like wolves outside a farm gate, licking their chops and waiting for their first chance to get in."

"You are not out of the woods yet," Onal said, turning her attention back to Conrad's hair. "That's why I had to come along on this little jaunt: to make sure he didn't die on the way here." She gave him a sideways glance. "Though he'd be doing better if he just took my concoctions without constantly complaining like a dumb baby."

Sorry, I mouthed to Simon. Onal's concoctions were notoriously potent in efficacy and rank in flavor.

"I'm glad you're both here," I said. "There's a lot I need to tell you all and very little time in which to do it." I looked over my shoulder at Kellan, who was waiting quietly for me by the door flap. "I'll need all the support I can get."

✳

In a private tent, Onal provided me with a bucket of frigid water and orders to scrub myself clean ("Down to the bone, if that's what is necessary to get that smell off of you"), then left me alone while she took my tattered clothing away.

I doused myself with water and soap, chattering with cold, resisting the temptation to be hasty by telling myself I couldn't rescue Zan smelling like I'd climbed out of a swamp. "If you burned my dress," I said when Onal returned several minutes later, "I'll have nothing else to wear."

"Nonsense," she said, brandishing an entire uniform made up of pieces borrowed from women of the guard. I got into the breeches well enough myself but required her help with the tunic. Lifting it over my head, she had a good look at the plentiful bruises and scars I'd acquired over the last weeks. Sighing, she said, "If your mother knew what you've been through, her heart would surely break in two."

I wanted to say that I was fine, that I'd made it through unscathed, but I couldn't. I was changed in vast, irreversible ways.

When she was finished helping me resettle my cloak back over my shoulders, she handed me a weathered hand mirror to hold while she brushed and plaited my hair down the side.

I couldn't remember the last time I'd taken a good look in the mirror. I wanted to think that, after all of this, I'd be able to look at my reflection and see some new strength written there, or some beauty brought to the surface through adversity, but I looked the same as I always had. Ashy blond hair, pale cheeks, and eyes like silver saucers—too big and too strange for the rest of my face.

"Onal," I said thoughtfully as she wove my hair with her long, nimble brown fingers. "Nathaniel's daughter, Ella . . . did you take a look at her?"

"I did. Perfectly healthy babe, if a little small."

"She was a little early, you know, so tiny and precious. But she had these beautiful brown eyes."

"That's nice," Onal said absently.

I continued, "After Ella was born, both mother and babe were in a bad way, and the woman acting as midwife gave me a potion she'd distilled from bloodleaf flower."

Onal's hands grew still. She was listening intently now. "Even so, Kate—my friend—wouldn't take the potion herself, and insisted that I give it to the child instead. I respected her wish." I felt my throat constrict. "Ella woke from the very brink of death, Onal. But afterward her eyes were different, more silver. Like they are now." Without looking up, I asked, "What color were my eyes before you gave bloodleaf flower to me?"

There was a long pause.

"I don't know," Onal said quietly. "You never opened them before you received it."

33

The king and queen had tried for several years to conceive, and when they did, they were elated. But—as was by then tradition—they chose not to reveal their joy to the public until after the birth. Arrangements were made. If the baby was a boy, the birth would be celebrated throughout the land for weeks. If it was a girl, she would be spirited away in the night, given to a family somewhere far away, and the kingdom would never even know she existed. They were more than prepared for either outcome."

Onal sighed and sat down beside me. "But then the babe arrived, so silent and still. They had been ready to send her off, knowing that she'd live a full and happy life, but this was a parting they had not considered. Such sorrow I've never seen, before or since. So I went to my stillroom. I'd kept my three preserved bloodleaf petals secret and safe for nearly thirty-five years by then. I knew it was pointless to waste one, that in the face of death they are useless . . . but if you had seen their faces . . . ." She shook her head. "So I took that little babe in my arms, and I parted her tiny, blue little lips and pressed that petal onto her tongue . . . and then she opened her eyes. *You* opened your eyes. And they looked just like they do now.

"After that, your mother and father could not be parted from you. They saw the miracle of your life as a sign that you were meant for a greater purpose. They reached out to the king and queen of Achleva, who sent Simon to us as a liaison. The arrangements began for your wedding, though you were only a few weeks old. But what happened with you made me too confident. I wasted another petal on your father, after the fire—as you well know, it did not work."

"Why did it work on me, then?"

"I don't know. But you've always had a healing touch, not to mention how quickly you heal yourself. I've often wondered if those anomalies were just *you,* or residual effects of being given the bloodleaf flower before you took a living breath."

"All this time, why did no one ever tell me? I've gone my whole life thinking—"

"We told you what we thought you needed to know. Don't glower. And don't slump—you'll look like a potato. Now listen to me, Aurelia. All of your adversities have shaped you into who you needed to be to get through all of this. Be thankful that you're strong enough."

"Am I?"

"Well, you're not dead yet. So for now, let's assume you are."

✳

It was dark again when I emerged from the tent in Renaltan uniform. All the guards were gathered on the grass, waiting for me to speak.

I positioned myself at the head of the gathering, and Kellan took his place behind me, just the same as always. I gave him a quick glance, still marveling that he was alive. That he was *here*. Catching my eyes, he gave me a slight, reassuring nod.

I wasn't quite sure of my phrasing, but I began anyway. "Men and women of the guard. On behalf of my brother and myself, I thank you for your loyalty to our mother, Queen Genevieve, and to our monarchy."

Some of their faces I recognized from past hurts; the group was populated with soldiers who had ignored me, or whispered about me as I passed. One or two of them I'd even seen in the crowd at executions, chanting and screaming. But I could not criticize them for prejudices I, too, once held against myself. The past was irrelevant; they were here now, on Achleva's doorstep, ready to fight. For my mother, yes, but also for me.

I cleared my throat. "For centuries we've seen Achleva as our enemy. Hundreds and thousands of Renaltan lives were lost as we tried and failed to penetrate Achlev's Wall, all on the word of one man: the Tribunal's founder, Cael. Senseless, useless deaths," I said, "pursuant of a single man's agenda of revenge. The same man who created the organization that, for five hundred years, has kept Renaltans obedient and afraid. Obedient to his statutes, afraid of one another." I remembered what Zan said, that *the greatest threat this city has ever faced came from within, not from without.* "But the truth is this: Achleva is not our enemy. It never has been. Our true oppressor is, and has always been, the man we call the Founder . . . his teachings, his Tribunal, and now his self-appointed successor: Toris de Lena."

My voice grew stronger. "Toris is even now enacting a plan years in the making . . . an effort to destroy the sovereignties of two nations and bring them both under the Tribunal's complete control. In mere weeks he has displaced our queen, kidnapped our future king, and begun a sequence of destruction within Achleva that has culminated in regicide: King Domhnall is dead at Toris's hands."

I heard several gasps.

I continued, "As upsetting as it is, Domhnall's death was not Toris's end game; rather, it was just another necessary step toward a larger goal. Toris is trying to bring down Achlev's Wall. And when it falls, the lines of power Achlev used to construct it—the ley lines—will snap back to their original paths, bringing five centuries of suppressed calamity in their wake." I lifted my chin. "Already there are signs of the coming danger: the water is bad, the plants are dead, the ground has been shaking, and Toris has barred the citizens from leaving. Without intervention, the wall won't even have to fall before everyone inside it starves to death."

I took a deep breath. "The wall's protective magic is held in place by the three gates, each requiring three sacrifices to break its three seals. High Gate and Forest Gate have already fallen; King's Gate is the last remaining, and King Domhnall's death has already broken the first seal. Two more of the royal line must be sacrificed to finish the job. Zan—Prince Valentin, I mean—is the sole heir remaining. He now stands as the last obstacle between Toris and his totalitarian objectives."

Fredrick spoke up. "But if there are three seals to be broken by

Achlev's bloodline, and there is only one descendant left, how can the wall possibly fail?"

"Marriage," Simon spoke up. "The Achlevan marriage ritual is a blood-binding ceremony. It makes the two participants essentially of one blood. The only way for the prince to ensure that the wall will stand forever is for him to die without marrying or siring an heir."

Cold fear stole over me. *Oh merciful stars above.* Lisette was still in the city. Lisette, who had been Toris's choice for Zan's bride from the very beginning.

"Our mission is threefold," I managed to say steadily. "Evacuate the innocent citizens of Achlev, retrieve Prince Valentin and secure his safety, and apprehend Toris de Lena and bring him back to Renalt to face justice." My voice dropped. "If we fail, there will be many thousands of innocent Achlevans who die as a result. And that's just the immediate cost; imagine a future where the Tribunal rules and reigns with absolute power and impunity." A weighty hush fell; it was a grim prospect, even to those who had never before questioned the Tribunal. "We simply cannot fail."

Simon rose to his feet, still looking frail. "I thank you, Princess, for trying to help us . . . but the fact remains: those of Renaltan blood cannot enter the city uninvited, and such a thing requires the willing blood of a living direct descendant of Achlev. My sister was the queen, but I have no blood ties to the throne, so I cannot do it. How can you save the city if none of you can cross the wall?"

I motioned to Onal, who had been waiting on the sideline, a stack of folded paper in her hands.

"I have these," I said. "Invitations issued by Prince Valentin and sealed by his willing blood. There are only nine. As I have already been through, we'll have ten total in our party. It isn't much, but it will have to be enough."

Onal walked slowly in front of the group, so they could all see what I was talking about.

"I will lead these nine into the city, while the rest of you will be divided into two groups, one to be stationed at High Gate, led by Fredrick, and one at Forest Gate, led by Nathaniel. Fredrick and his company will create a diversion that draws the guards from their posts, allowing me and my nine to cross undetected."

"What kind of diversion?" Fredrick asked.

"I happen to know where you can find a sizable store of bottled liquor on the outside of the wall near High Gate. Add a little fire . . ."

Fredrick nodded. "We can make some noise."

"Try to keep your firebombs aimed at the wall, not past it. Don't want to burn Achlev down before we save it. My group will work from the inside to get the gates open and go after Toris and the prince. As soon as the portcullises are raised, the companies at Forest and High Gates will assist in evacuations from the outside. And when that is done, I want you and all of the evacuees to *get clear of the city immediately.* After that, make your way back to the Silvis holding to rendezvous with the queen. Is that understood? Now," I said, squaring my shoulders, "this is the time to choose: Who among you is brave enough to follow me across the wall? For Renalt, for Achleva, and for the unnamed number of those who've gone before?"

And to my everlasting surprise and gratitude, they all, one by one, rose to their feet.

★

It was quickly settled: Kellan and eight of his best fellows would go with me into the city, while Onal and Simon would take Ella and Conrad and journey immediately to the Silvis holding to reunite with the waiting queen. The rest of the soldiers were divided evenly between High Gate and Forest Gate. King's Gate was on the water, so the plan was, after we freed Zan and Lisette and arrested Toris, we would acquire a boat at the docks and exit that way, taking along any straggling refugees we came across in the interim.

"I wish I could go with you," Simon told me as we made the final preparations.

"You're not well," I said sympathetically. "And I am familiar enough with the layout of the city now. We will be fine without you, and I will be able to rest knowing that you are watching over Conrad."

He patted my hand and surveyed its scars—far more plentiful than they had been before. "It shames me to learn that Dedrick Corvalis was to blame for much of this."

"What shame could you deserve?" I asked, startled. "It's not your fault."

"I tried teaching him for a while, when he was a young boy, but even then I glimpsed an uncomfortable way about him that put me ill at ease, and I ended our studies. Maybe if I'd given him the education he needed, I could have shaped him. Prevented all this . . ." Simon stopped with a shake of his head, his hand going to the chain around his neck. It was a habit—hadn't he done the same thing back in Ren-alt? But this time I noticed what it was he was clutching.

A vial of blood.

"Simon," I said, "what is *that?*"

"It's a tradition in the old Order of Blood Magic. When a blood mage moves from novice to master, he saves a little bit of his blood in a vial like this, so that even after he's gone, some of his essence—his magic—is preserved. The vial is made of luneocite glass." He pulled the chain out from under his shirt so I could take a closer look. "It's almost like leaving one final spell."

My thoughts were whirring like the gears in a clock. "And the luneocite . . . is what keeps it that way?"

"Oh yes. Luneocite is Empyrea-given. And the Empyrea is the creator and conservator of life. This blood belongs to Domhnall's brother, Victor de Achlev, a gifted blood mage and the best man I ever knew. My partner. He died with many of our friends and colleagues at the Assembly"—here Simon's expression became soft and sad—"but he gave it to me to carry long before his death, so that I'd have a piece of him with me always."

"Simon," I said urgently. "I think I must ask of you a great, great favor."

34

We waited within the tree line, a hundred feet from the camps along the wall, now mostly abandoned; anyone with sense had long gone.

I'd drawn a map to Darwyn's cache of alcohol for Fredrick and his men. From the cover of the woods, we watched the guards patrolling the top of the wall and waited for signs that Fredrick was putting the bounty to good use.

Kellan was on one knee to steady his spyglass. "No sign yet."

I paced the ranks.

"Be calm," Kellan said under his breath. "They take their cues from you. If you're confident, so will they be."

"I'm worried," I said. "It's taking too long. And who knows what could happen to—"

"To Zan?" Kellan finished.

I looked at my hands. "Yes. Kellan, listen. I haven't gotten a chance yet to thank you for coming back for me. And to tell you that I am so sorry about Falada. She served me well until the end."

"Then she did what I could not do."

"Kellan, don't—"

He collapsed the spyglass. "I was given one charge: to keep you safe. And at the very first test, I failed you. I'm no longer worthy to be your protector."

I studied his face. It was still handsome, despite a few new scars and deepened shadows beneath his eyes. "I don't *need* a protector, Kellan. I can take care of myself," I said, and knew at once that it was both true and likely difficult for Kellan to come to terms with. "I need a friend and ally. In return I can offer unending aggravation. If you're interested in that sort of thing." I gave a wry shrug. "It's a much better deal, really. You should take it."

He smiled, just a little. "Do I have to keep getting stabbed all the time?"

"I can't say you won't," I said. "Hope that's not a deal breaker. Here," I said, placing a small object in his hand. "I want you to have this."

He looked at it, puzzled. "A charm from your bracelet?"

"The gryphon is noble and loyal," I said. "This one was lost to me for a while. But somehow, miraculously, I got it back." I cleared my throat. "It seems appropriate that you have it."

He closed his fingers over the gryphon, but before he could reply, there were sounds farther down the wall—shouts and crashes. Kellan lifted the glass and turned to scan the wall again. "That's it. Our cue."

Toris's guards stationed on the wall all started running toward High Gate.

"Let's go," Kellan said.

All ten of us rushed across the open space and stopped at the foot of the wall to secure their grappling ropes to their hooks.

"Do you all have your invitations with you?" I asked. "Bring them out. Since you can't climb and hold the invitations, it is my recommendation that you put it somewhere secure, and touching your skin."

As I went from soldier to soldier, I continued, "Even with the weakening of the wall, crossing will likely be extremely unpleasant. Which means you don't want it to catch you while you're still on the rope. I will go up first, so that I can steady Kellan from above. Then we, in turn, will steady two more of you as you go up, and so on until we're all past the border."

"You ready?" Kellan asked, and I set my jaw and gave him a determined nod. He and the others gave their rope-threaded hooks several synchronized swings, and they all flew high over the wall and caught. Kellan tugged on the rope to make sure it was stable, securing one end around me and knotting the other around himself. With him anchoring and belaying me from below, I was hoisted up and over the battlements with little difficulty. Then I gave Kellan the all-clear signal; it was time for him to follow me up.

He had made it two-thirds of the way up the rope when the lines from the invitation's bloodmark began branching up his neck like lightning. He cried out, and I yelled, "Don't let go! You have to get over. Don't stop. Come on!"

Somehow he managed to climb the rest of the way, even as the searing lines of magic traveled under his skin and into his blood. I pulled him over and held him as he thrashed in pain. When it was over, he lay prostrate on the wall's walk, breathing heavily. "I thought being stabbed and falling off a cliff was unpleasant. I was wrong."

"We've got to help the others," I said.

The next two cadets had a similar experience to Kellan's, but the third began convulsing before he even made it halfway up.

"Hang in there, Warren!" Kellan called. "Keep going!"

The cadet lasted for another fifteen feet before the pain became too much and he let go with a scream, landing with a sickeningly liquid thud on the ground below.

I wanted to look away, but I forced myself to bear witness to his death — he was one of my soldiers, here at my request. I owed him that dignity. His spirit materialized beside his body, and looked up at me on the wall. "Thank you for your service, Lieutenant Warren," I whispered. "I won't forget your sacrifice."

He gave me a ghostly salute and was gone.

The remaining six soldiers stared at their fallen friend with grim faces.

"There's got to be a way," I said. "There's got to be a way to make it easier."

As I drew my knife, Kellan said, "What are you doing?"

"Whatever I can," I replied, before drawing a quick line across both of my palms. I felt the magic inside me stir. "Tell them to climb. All of them. I'm not sure how long I'll be able to do this."

"Do what?" he asked, but I had already knelt and pressed my palms to the stone of the wall.

The magical current whirring in an endless loop inside the wall seemed to eddy at my touch, humming as if it recognized me. I allowed the magic passage through me, as if I were just another part of the conduit, and began to stretch my perception to where my soldiers were ascending. There I pulled back on the current, letting the magic part and swirl around them, like rocks in a river stream. It strained against my hold, and I began to sweat and pant with the exertion.

"Hurry!" I said as prickling numbness spread from my fingertips up into my arms. "I can't hold it much longer."

And then Kellan said, "They're here! They're all up!" And I let go. The magic I'd redirected snapped back into place, and all six of the soldiers were knocked to their knees, writhing in agony as it scorched their insides with vengeance.

"I'm sorry," I said as they slowly came out of it. "I know it's terrible. But at least you made it over first. At least you didn't fall."

"Warren was a brave man and a good lieutenant," Kellan said to the rest. "He died in service to the princess, which means he died in service of the queen. May the Empyrea keep him."

"Empyrea keep him," the others intoned.

When we made it off the wall and into the city, everything was eerily quiet. "Where is everyone?" one of the soldiers asked.

"They hold their public events in the square by the castle," I said. "That's where they'll be."

We zigzagged through the abandoned streets, listening as the sound of the crowd grew from a buzz to a murmur to a loud hum. We approached the square from the east, keeping to the alleys to stay hidden from the guards. Swords drawn, they had formed lines on each side of the square, penning the people within it like cattle.

Kellan motioned to a ladder on the back of one of the buildings. We climbed it and scrambled across the sloping roof to view the scene from behind the peak.

At first I couldn't make sense of it. Zan and Lisette were facing each other, holding their bleeding hands together. Toris was standing behind them, clutching his beloved Book of Commands. And that's when I understood.

This was a wedding, and the entire city had been invited to watch.

Toris's voice was loud enough to carry across the square. "It is by the authority given me as a magistrate of the Great Tribunal—"

"I won't do it," Zan declared.

". . . that I do bring this man and this woman together now to join them as one in name, blood, bone, and purpose. Do you, Lisette de Lena, take this man, Valentin Alexander, as your husband, willingly, now and forevermore?"

"Wai—" I tried to cry out, but Kellan clapped his hand over my mouth.

"Don't." Zan closed his eyes, shaking his head. "Don't say it."

Quaveringly, she said, "Yes."

Toris turned to Zan. "And do you, Valentin Alexander, take this woman, Lisette de Lena, as your wife, willingly, now and forevermore?"

"No." His voice was loud.

"Say yes, boy," Toris commanded. "Say yes now, or regret it."

I struggled against Kellan's grasp. He put his finger to his lips and pointed to the Achlevan guards on the ground. To my horror, I saw that every single one of them had a citizen under his arm, swords drawn.

"*No,*" Zan declared, more vehemently.

Toris turned his attention to the crowd.

"How many people do you think are here today? Several

thousand, I'd say." He gave a nod to the guards lined up on the stairs. Each one moved into the gathering and picked someone out at random, ripping them from their families and dragging them back up the stairs. An elderly woman, a middle-aged father, a youth with the first shadow of a beard . . . The guards returned to their stations to stand at attention, swords held at a perfect perpendicular to each person's neck. Toris's hand hovered in the heavy air for several tense moments, as if he were an orchestra conductor extending the last note for a little too long. And then he let his hand fall. In perfect synchronicity, the guards moved their swords across each victim's neck with all the practiced elegance of musicians in a murderous symphony.

Order in all things.

The exodus of nearly a dozen spirits at once hit me like a wave; I felt their passing from the material to the spectral planes in the vibration of my bones. It made my sight blur, my ears ring, caused hazy shapes to form just outside the edges of my vision while whispery words circled me like vultures. *Let me out. Let me out. Let me out.* I pressed my hands against my ears. *Go away. Leave me alone.*

Kellan was shaking me. "Aurelia, snap out of it! Look at me. We have to do something!"

Through bleary eyes, I saw Toris calmly asking Zan again, "Valentin Alexander, do you take this woman, Lisette de Lena, as your wife, willingly, now and forevermore?"

"Stars forgive me," he said brokenly as Toris lifted his hand, ready to signal another slaughter. "Yes."

"Stop," I tried to yell, but my voice came out a crackling whisper.

"With the great Empyrea as witness above, your two lives are now entwined into one. Exchange the rings now, as king and queen."

This was the first image of Aren's last vision: the exchanging of the rings. I fought through the disorientation left by the bloodshed and climbed, unsteady, to the top of the roof. "Stop!" I yelled again, louder. I needed to draw blood, let the magic carry my voice. I cast around in the layers of my uniform to find my knife.

"It is done," Toris said triumphantly, snapping his book shut. "All these years, all these preparations, and just like that—it is done!"

"No power is worth killing your own child," Zan said. "May your remaining life be tormented by it."

Got it. My hand closed around the knife handle.

Lisette was crying. "Don't, Father. Please don't hurt me. You've gotten what you wanted. You have control of Achleva now—"

Toris turned a glassy stare on her. "I am *not* your father," he stated.

And with predatory dispassion, he drove his knife into her heart.

I screamed, drowned out by the shocked cries of the crowd. *Lisette*.

Zan had tried to pull her back into the safety of his arms, but there was nothing he could do. Blood swept across the bodice of her dress as he lowered her down, her hair fanning out on the stone steps, and she reached for him even as blood began to well up in her throat and drip from the corners of her lips. "I'm sorry," she said, choking, trying to return the wedding ring to Zan with bloody hands. "I never wanted to hurt you. I lo—" She sputtered blood. "I love—"

"It's all right," Zan reassured her. "Hush now, be still. I'm sorry, too. I'm so sorry."

"Nihil nunc salvet te," said Toris.

Zan laid a soft kiss on Lisette's brow. "Go in peace," he told her. "Empyrea keep you."

She closed her eyes.

The wind howled, and a pulse of light burst from her body and rolled like a shock wave through the air until it hit the wall's cylindrical shield and spread across it like an ulcerous cancer.

Lisette's spirit stood beside her body, staring sadly down at it. *Don't linger here,* I thought. *Find serenity in the arms of the Empyrea, my friend.* She gave a slight nod, as if she had heard me, and then walked slowly, gracefully up the stairs toward the castle, fading away a little more with each step. She was gone before she reached the top.

"The queen of Achleva is dead!" Toris announced, smiling. "Long live the queen!"

35

oris!" My voice cut across the square like the fall of a scythe. I'd drawn a drop of blood and sent the resulting magic out in waves, not as heat or fire but as sound. I climbed to the high peak of the roof and stood like a pillar against the wind as the clouds went black and began to churn in circular rotation, lightning crackling in their angry depths.

Toris, who had been advancing on Zan, his knife still slick with Lisette's blood, snapped his head toward me. His guards, too, began to surge in our direction as I defiantly raised a vial of blood into the air.

"Have you been looking for this?" I trumpeted. I pulled the stopper from Victor de Achlev's blood vial. "The blood of the Founder. The last remnants of Cael's essence. His magic. If those guards come any closer, I will spill every last drop."

Toris froze. When his men did not, I let a single drop fall.

He screeched, *"Halt!"*

I lifted my voice. "I have what you want. You have what I want. I suggest a trade."

On his knees, Zan wore an expression of naked emotion; hope, fear, and fury fought side by side with a longing so keen and clear, it nearly broke me. Toris yanked him to his feet. "I would request we begin our negotiations inside. Will you join me in the Great Hall, dear Princess?"

I did not respond. Instead, I tipped the vial of blood a second time.

"All right," he said testily. "We can negotiate here."

"If you want this blood returned to you, you must first open the gates," I said. "Let these people evacuate the city. You and I both know that you kept them inside only to motivate Prince Valentin to marry Lisette. Their purpose has been served. Let them go."

Toris waved off the guards, and they stepped aside to allow people to pass, though nobody moved. Then he cocked his head to the right, anticipating my follow-up demand for Zan's release. He knew I would ask; I knew he would refuse. If there was one thing to be said about Toris and me, it was that we understood each other.

"When the city is empty, I will exchange the Founder's blood for Prince Valentin. If any of these people are not allowed to go freely from the city, I will spill it. If any of your men harass any of mine, I will spill it. And if Valentin dies before I come to make the exchange and the wall comes down, I will die spilling it. Am I clear?"

"You've been making so very many demands, dear Princess. For this to be fair, I must be allowed to make some of my own." His voice lost its jovial lilt. "We'll meet at the top of the tower at dusk. Come alone. Come alone and I will accept the terms."

The Founder's actual blood was still hidden at the top of the tower. If I meant to barter for Zan's life, I'd need the real vial. "We are in agreement."

"No, Aurelia! Get out! Go!" Zan cried as Toris fastened his hands behind his back and yanked him to his feet. Then, with his luneocite knife still poised at his neck, Toris withdrew toward the castle.

"The tower!" Toris said before he disappeared, with Zan, behind the great castle doors. "Before night falls."

I turned and bellowed, "Open the gates!" As I said it, a bolt of lightning sailed down and struck a high, steepled window less than a block behind me. In little more than a second, the aged timber lit up like a torch.

The crowd became a stampede as lightning struck again. And again. Wails of fear and frustration were drowned out by the ear-splitting blasts of thunder. A number of Toris's implacable guards tried to funnel the furor toward the gates and were quickly trampled underfoot.

"We've got to get down there!" Kellan said as sparks flew past our faces and landed by our feet. My soldiers and I scrambled over the roof's edge to the ladder and onto the ground just as the thatching began to smolder. The alley was narrow but provided a thin window to the forested mountains of Achlev's eastern segment. The mountains were shimmering with heat as the fire advanced across them in delicate, curling patterns, like red-gold glitter trimming black net lace. I marveled at how swiftly it had begun.

"Cover your face!" Kellan demanded. "Don't breathe the smoke!"

We combed the streets, sounding the alarm and searching for stragglers. Those who couldn't make it to High or Forest Gates we brought with us as we headed to the docks even as great arcs of lightning were striking at increasingly short intervals. I found myself counting the seconds, knowing that my chances of saving Zan and the spaces between each strike were dwindling at the same exponential rate.

We were a hundred feet from the pier when lightning struck the mast of a moored battleship, igniting the black powder of its cannons, and the entire thing went up like a great ball of fire, showering us with burning ash and dust. We rushed the final distance only to find that the pier was gone and the churning water was polluted with debris: shattered planks and scraps of canvas and bits of tattered clothing. The last large piece of the ship's hull was still on fire on top of the water, scattering orange light across the red waves. There were bodies in the water, too — people who'd been on the pier, waiting to board and get themselves to safety and never had the chance.

I gripped Kellan's sleeve. He said, "These remaining boats have taken too much damage. They won't get to the gate before they sink."

"There's a private pier not far from here," I said. "The Corvalis pier. There were plenty of boats there."

"Some of these people are still alive!" one of my soldiers shouted. "Look!"

Kellan was a good swimmer; he and his men dove into the water to drag some of those farther out back to safety, while I and the other refugees scuttled around the edge, pulling out those who could swim on their own. Person after sodden person, we lugged and yanked, slipping on slick timbers and straining every muscle. For some of them, it was too late. The waterfront was choked with surprised, despondent spirits watching their bodies sink into the depths.

"We have to go," Kellan said, hauling up one of the last survivors and climbing out. "The storm is getting worse. If we wait any longer, we won't be getting out."

"The boats I told you about are that way. " I pointed. "Get everyone there as fast as you can."

"You're staying?" He asked. "You're still going to the tower?"

"I'm going for Zan," I said. I would not leave the city again without him.

I expected Kellan to object, to plead for me to listen to reason and head for safety while I still could. He didn't. Instead, he turned and began barking orders. "Move out! We're heading west, to the ships at the Corvalis pier!" He moved to the head of the group, giving me one last nod from over his shoulder before leading them out of sight.

I ran alongside the waterfront road toward the castle. Above the rooftops, the Corvalis house was bowing beneath the assault of the wind as weblike fractures spread across the great, ostentatious windows. I could hear the snap and pop of the glass even over the roar of the storm. There was no chance Kellan would be able to get all those people onto a ship and out of port before it gave way.

I careened to the left, dragging out my knife as I sprinted for a better view, leaping over chunks of stone and brick as they tumbled from caving buildings. From atop the remains of a demolished sanctorium, I made a clumsy cut just as the first glass splinters of the Corvalis manor were giving way.

"*Sile!*" I cried, flinging magic out in bolts as the windows began to burst. *Be still.*

Thousands of knifelike glass shards froze where they were,

scintillating as they hung in the air, reflecting fragments of lightning and fire.

I could feel every sliver straining against me as I held them in arrest, groaning with the exertion.

Please, I silently begged. *Hurry!*

And then I saw it: the mast of a schooner, pulling away from the pier.

The glass began to quaver in the air, thousands and thousands of glittering pieces juddering against my hold. My ears were ringing, my hands shaking from the strain, but I hung on until the ship was clear of the waterfront and halfway to King's Gate.

Tears pricking my eyes, I watched it diminish. "Empyrea keep you," I whispered.

Then I let go.

36

The tower was the center of it all.

To get to it, I pushed through mighty wind, over bucking earth and surging tide. I was lashed by rain mixed with glass, scraped by the tumbling rocks of the falling terraces, and scratched to shreds by thorns of the plants grown rampant and ravenous. Lightning-strike fires were scavenging the roof the castle, and burning ash was flung into the black sky, as if the stars themselves had turned to fire. Once on top of the bloodleaf field, I could make out several places where the leaves had been crushed by footsteps, though most of the brackish sap had already been washed away in the rain and red waves crashing on the rocks.

Inside the tower, however, all was eerily quiet.

One step, then another. Up, up, up, alone save for the howl of the wind and the painted figures on the wall, telling the tragic story of those doomed siblings who started this all. Achlev. Aren. Cael. I lingered at the last panels for a moment, gazing at their inscrutable faces. Then I steeled myself, ready to put an end to the sequence they'd put into motion all those years earlier.

This is it, I thought, armed with Victor de Achlev's vial of blood in one hand, my luneocite knife in the other. Then I pushed the door free and strode out onto the tower's open pinnacle.

Outside, the firestorm was raging, whipped by the circulating wind into a cylinder of flame. The city below was completely engulfed, the scorched streets standing out like a black triquetra-shaped brand against the blaze. Above my head, however, hung a perfect circle of star-studded sky, the eye of the storm. Marking its center was a dim void: the black moon.

"So glad you could make it, Princess."

Toris had Zan forced to his knees, still bound and gagged. They were surrounded by a thatch of bloodleaf that had grown voraciously, clawing into any crack in the mortar, any imperfection in the stone. I took one step toward them, then another. Zan watched my approach with heavy, feverish eyes, shaking his head as if to say *You shouldn't have come.*

Toris tapped his knife on Zan's shoulder. "I think the prince here was hoping you'd renege on our bargain." He laughed. "He must not know you at all."

"We had an agreement. I've come to deliver my end of the deal."

"Would it surprise you to know that I never had any intention of delivering mine?"

"Not in the least."

"I can't finish my business until the last gate has fallen, and for that to happen, the prince has to die. There is no other way."

"So what purpose does *this* serve in your scheme?" I lifted the vial and unstopped the top. "Why do you need this blood so very badly?" I gave it a lazy little swirl. "The blood of our most revered Founder. It's supposed to be just a symbol, and yet . . ." I tipped it and let a splash of blood fall out onto the tower stones. "You treat it like it has a greater importance."

Toris's eyes were locked onto the vial. "Do that again and I'll kill him."

"You just told me you would kill him no matter what." I tipped the vial and spilled the blood again but more liberally this time, a long, thread-like stream. "I want to hurt you, Toris, for what you've done. To me, to my country, to everyone I love." My eyes flicked back to Zan, who was struggling to breathe against the gag. "If this is how it must be done, so be it."

"Stop!" Toris demanded, eyes bulging. "You don't know what you're doing!"

"Tell me," I said. "Tell me why this blood is so important to you." I tipped it again and let it splatter on the ground. A third of it gone. A half. Two-thirds . . .

"It's *mine!*" Toris barked. Through his teeth he said, "So help me, if you spill even one more drop . . ." He lifted Zan's chin with the point of his knife, and a bead of blood slid down the edge and onto Toris's hands. His knife was luneocite glass, twin to my own, the one that had once belonged to Achlev himself.

That's when I knew.

Toris's visage was little more than an illusory overlay, like the one I'd used to make Falada's white coat seem black. A simple trick that, once seen, could not be unseen. I circled him in astonishment, staring at a truth that was simultaneously incredible and intolerable, extraordinary and obscene.

"I see you," I whispered. "I know who you are now. Who you *really* are."

His eyes were no longer brown but a chilly cornflower blue, gleaming with a mixture of mirth and malevolence. Under my appraising stare, he regained some of his poise, straightening his clothes and procuring a white kerchief from his pocket to daintily clean the trickle of Zan's blood from his hands.

Order in all things. Was that not always his motto?

I might have laughed, had things been different.

Centuries had passed, and he still looked exactly like the man in the portrait hanging in Kings Hall in Renalt: chiseled jaw, sandy hair, lips pulled into a thin sneer.

The Founder himself. Cael.

"It's been five hundred years since you stood at this point, hasn't it?" I asked. "Stood here with your brother and your sister for a ritual of magic meant to seal up a rift. A dangerous hole between the spectral and material planes. But then, in the midst of it, you turned on Aren. You killed your sister. Why?"

"I had to take a life, so I took one. My mistake," he said, "was choosing Aren. She just happened to be standing closer, you see. Easier to grab. It should have been Achlev. All of this . . . this *mess*"—he motioned with flippant disdain at the fallen city, the raging storm—"could have been avoided if *he'd* been standing there instead of her . . ."

He shook his head. "So good at seeing death, she was, yet never saw her own."

"You were triumviri. A leader of your order. Sent to this spot to do something good. And instead you destroyed everything you ever loved."

He laughed. "Love is weakness. I lost nothing because I loved nothing."

My eyes slid to Zan, whose breathing was getting more and more rapid, more distressed. *How much easier would it be if I'd never met him?* I wondered. And then: *How much would I have lost if I hadn't?*

"And what," I asked, "did you have to gain?"

"Eternity," he said.

"This is what you wanted? To wear another man's face? To live another man's life? Forever?"

"Toris was a means to an end. Don't feel too bad for him, Princess; he knew what I was when he woke me. Luckily, he didn't live long enough to regret it."

"The Assembly," I said, remembering. "Lisette said he changed after he went to visit the Assembly. He went there as a historian. He came back as . . . you. You took his place. After you killed him."

"I've killed a great many people, my dear. Toris, Lisette. Your father. Her mother. All the fools who tried to keep me locked away at the Assembly. Soon enough it will be his turn." He motioned to Zan. "And then I'll get to you."

I eyed Victor de Achlev's blood. Toris—Cael—still didn't know it wasn't his.

"Five hundred years," I said. "It took five hundred years for you to get back here, to finish the job you botched. Because your brother saw what you did to Aren and tried to save her. He was a feral mage. He worked with nature, not with blood. So he used yours and left you with only this." I dangled the blood vial again. "How *unfortunate* for you."

"Achlev"—he spat out the name—"*wasted* my blood to make *this* monstrosity." He indicated the thatch of bloodleaf, crushing a shoot beneath his heel. "But while I do require blood to work magic, like you, and my own blood was singularly potent, it doesn't *have* to be my blood I use. I quickly found an excellent alternative source through the Tribunal." He grinned. "Of course, it was much more effective when the guillotine was our primary method of executing witches. Beheadings went out of vogue during my involuntary confinement at the Assembly. I've been pushing for the practice to make a comeback; I have to interrogate subjects for *days* to obtain a fraction of the blood I can get removing a head."

I closed my eyes. "All the countless people who have suffered and *died* to serve your vendetta against magic . . ."

"I have no vendetta against magic, only against those who might have more of it than I do. Achlev took mine, so I merely found a way to compensate for the loss. The Tribunal was my best idea. My greatest legacy," he said proudly.

"Destroying it will be mine."

"You're not going to make it from this tower, little girl. I need you to die so that I can finally open the rift and set my mistress free." He tilted his head. "Can't you hear the whispers? She's calling for you."

Come to me. Find me. Free me. The voice was soothing, comforting, cajoling, demanding . . . *Let me out.* I looked up at Cael, startled. He had his ear cocked to the wind, a smile playing on his lips, letting the silky whispers lull him into obedience.

"Everyone worships the Empyrea so blindly," he said, "never wondering about the *other* powers. There were always three of them, you know. One to rule the sky, the other the earth . . . But the last sister . . . she was given the refuse to rule over. The dead and the damned and the souls deemed too corrupt to be given life. They call her the crone, but they are wrong. She is perfect. She is beautiful. My mistress. The mistress of *all* blood mages, really. And she chose *me* that day, to do her work: Take a life. Open the portal. Set her free."

I was inching closer to him as he spoke. "Your mistress made you ageless, undying, just in time for Achlev to take all of your blood and stop your sacrifice. So you failed her, and then you fled, and he built this monument and the entire city and the wall to keep you from fulfilling your bargain with her for *five centuries*." I shrugged. "I can't imagine she is well pleased with your work."

He kicked Zan to his side and dove toward me but skidded to a halt as I hovered the vial over the abyss.

"Name your mistress," I said. "Name that dark force to whom you sold your soul."

"*Malefica.*" He spat out the name. He was so close, I could see the serpentine red vessels in his glassy eyes.

I said, "May you find joy in your reunion." And I threw the vial down. It fell with a clink, trailing an arc of blood behind it, rolling to a stop at the statue Aren's feet.

Cael let out an animal snarl and leaped after it, scraping his fingers across the splattered blood as if trying to gather it back into the vial. I flew past him and scrabbled to Zan, who was still lying on his side. As I worked my knife through the ropes binding him, the wind rose from a whistle to a scream and the tower swayed as a dozen funnel clouds spooled down from the sky to the ground. The air was hot and electric as the earth gave a deep, primal groan, and the three marble men at King's Gate splintered into pieces that tumbled into the roiling ruby water of the fjord.

It seemed that my gamble had paid off. Victor de Achlev's last remaining blood had worked in place of Zan's for the sacrifice. King's Gate was falling, and it was the last anchor; its loss catalyzed the wall's final decimation. All around the city the ancient, indestructible stones of Achlev's Wall began to shake and crumble. Below us the blue-white lines of magic seared across the black expanse, snapping back to their original course, one after another after another. I clutched Zan close as they intersected in the earth deep below us, a throbbing tangle of energy and light.

"I've got you," I murmured into Zan's shoulder. "We're going to make it out of this. We're . . ."

But Zan was slumping against me. When my hands came away from his back, they were red with his blood.

I let out a wrenched cry.

I was wrong. It was not Victor's blood that had broken King's Gate but Zan's. Cael had delivered his death strike before I ever arrived at the tower. Aren's final foretelling was coming true right in front of my eyes, and I was helpless to stop it.

"No," I begged, lowering him onto the bed of bloodleaf and tearing his gag away with my bloody fingers. "No." My voice was breaking. "Please, Zan. Don't go." I took out my knife and held it to my palm. "I can fix this," I said. "Like I did before. I can—"

"*Nihil nunc salvet te,*" Cael rasped from behind me.

A spidery blue light burst from Zan's body and spiraled into the clouds. Beneath him the bloodleaf vine was coiling, stretching, straining toward his trickling lifeblood while his spirit materialized above. I lifted my head from his prostrate body just in time to see his ghost glimmer and fade, as if swept away into the swirling storm.

I let out an angry sob, pressing my forehead to his chest and twisting his shirt in my fists. His hand fell limp to his side, and from his cold fingers tumbled his mother's ring. It fell onto the blanket of bloodleaf just as the first tiny, white petals began to unfurl.

Blood on the snow.

I reached for the ring and stood up to slip it onto my finger, now filled with a terrible calm.

Cael was amused. "Well played," he said. "Using someone else's blood. But I got you one better, didn't I?"

The last king of Achleva had fallen, and with his death the final seal holding the wall's magic into place gave way, and the plane of the spell cracked into tiny, jagged shards. Above us the black moon oversaw it all, a portal into darkness itself.

I turned to Cael, knife in hand.

He tilted his head. "Your weapon is useless against me, girl."

"It's not for you," I said.

Sorrow and rage burgeoned inside my body, corrosive and

catastrophic. I wrapped my fingers around the glass blade and gave a quick, searing yank. Then I fell to my knees and pressed my hands against the stone, feeding the energy of my loss into the tower and deep into the power below, letting it expand and grow until I was not simply me; I was the tower. I was the storm. The magic. The bloodleaf.

Then I lunged and closed my bloody fingers around Cael's neck. The force of my grip sent him reeling, slipping in Victor de Achlev's blood and falling backwards against the bloodleaf-ridden battlement. He was stunned for a moment, before throwing his head back to laugh.

When the first vine of bloodleaf wrapped around his throat, the laughing came to an abrupt stop. "You can't hurt me," he said as more vines encircled his arms, his legs. "I cannot die."

"I don't want you to die," I said. "I want you to suffer."

I clenched my fists, and the bloodleaf tightened in response. Lines of red were spreading from the veins of the leaves across his skin, leaving black trails behind them, like the spirits of Achlev's gates.

"My mistress will destroy you," he said, choking. "She is angry, she is wrathful, she does not forgive—"

"Nor do I," I said as I unleashed the last of my magic into the vines holding him.

The bloodleaf absorbed him, consumed him, *became* him. It ate away his body, separating cell from cell, until he was nothing but a pile of blackened leaves and thorns that fell into dust, whipped away on the wind.

"Nihil nunc salvet te," I said, and sank to my knees.

37

When I gathered enough strength to reopen my eyes, it was to a world of white.

The Harbinger was watching me.

I blinked. No, not the Harbinger herself. The image reflecting in the stain was not flesh and blood or spirit. It was Aren's statue. I pushed myself away from it and then saw *him*.

Prostrate on the bloodleaf lay Zan.

Blood on the snow.

But of course, it wasn't snow, I now knew. He was lying motionless on a bed of drifting white petals. His eyes were closed, one arm bent beneath his dark head.

I sobbed as I knelt beside him and tried to gather him into my arms, hating how chilly his skin was, how blue his lips were.

This was it—Aren's vision made real. Zan was gone. Dead and gone and cold, and here I was, surrounded by bloodleaf flower when it was already too late to use it.

Then a single petal floated down and landed on Zan's lips, as fragile as a frond of frost at the break of day. I stared at it there and remembered: Had not bloodleaf flower overcome death before? Had I not gone to the other side and come back myself?

Ever so carefully, I brought my lips within an inch of Zan's and let out a slow, soft breath into his mouth, sending the petal fluttering between his parted lips, where it dissolved and disappeared.

Nothing happened.

I rose and slammed my fist into the foot of Aren's statue, violently resentful of her impervious, stony expression high above me. I hit and punched and kicked at it until my knuckles were torn and bloody.

"How dare you?" I screamed. "How dare you show me his death and not show me how to stop it! What was it for, Aren? What was it all for? Why was I saved? Why preserve my life and guide my path if you were only ever leading me to *this?*" I dragged my sleeve across my burning eyes and running nose. "Bring him back!" I screamed at Aren. At the wind. At the stars. I sank down beside him and buried my face into his chest. "Please," I begged. "Please bring him back."

And then I smelled it—roses. Not the tainted, coppery smell of bloodleaf but the smell of fresh roses on a spring day. Light spilled all around me, and I lifted my heavy head to peer over my shoulder.

There she was. Not the haggard wraith I'd seen last, nor the slit-throat spirit that had haunted my periphery since childhood. Aren was the way she must have looked in life—luminous and lovely, with violet eyes and straight, silken hair the color of cinnamon. She crossed the tower to me, reaching out to take my ruined hands into hers, her skin soft and unblemished. Her touch wasn't cold.

She closed her eyes, and I was spun into a new vision. This was not a death of the future; it was one of the past.

She showed me her brothers. How handsome. How doting. How, even as a child, she'd felt the stirrings of a sacred healing power and had visions of the future—the power to see death and circumvent it. She showed me how, under the Empyrea's direction, she rose in the ranks of her order at the Assembly, married the Renaltan king, and bore a son, only to have the Empyrea whisper of another hallowed path: There was a rift between planes. An unwilling sacrifice would lay it open, but if she gave up her life willingly during the spell, she could close it forever.

She went into the spell having already consumed the poison that would take her life, content with her fate, until her brother Cael, enticed by the Malefica's whispers, turned on her.

She showed me how dark and brooding Achlev, unknowing of the Empyrea's designs, could not let her die. She showed me how he used the blade of her luneocite knife from the botched ritual to catch three drops of her blood and embedded them within it, preserving a tiny spark of her spirit as he tried unsuccessfully to save her life, too . . .

I saw him build the tower and the statue. I saw him place the luneocite knife in her marble hands. I saw him construct his wall and the arduous lengths he went to to spell it and strengthen it, spending every last ounce of his living breath making sure that his brother, now far away, could never come and finish the evil he had started.

Aren, bereft and bodiless, watched her family suffer and survive without her. She watched them go to war in her name. She spent the centuries feeling every death her poisoned blood wrought through the bloodleaf, her only solace the few lives that were spared from the bloodleaf petals. And she was connected to them all—she felt every life that was saved, every life that was lost.

The last thing she showed me was a tiny newborn baby whose parents had given her a bloodleaf petal in hopes that she would live. Aren, watching her descendants mourn, was moved by their love and grief, reminded of her own son who grew up without her. The little girl needed a spark of life, so Aren gave her what was left of hers. The moment I took my first breath was the moment the last three drops of her blood were finally spent. She took her last steps into death and sent my spirit back into the world of the living.

She and I were tethered together after that, my spirit fueling hers, giving her enough energy to show me her visions. When I cast her away at the tower, I'd snapped our bond and she'd begun to waste away, just like the other spirits trapped in the borderlands between the material and spectral planes. Until now, in this place, when the portals to the spiritual, material, and spectral planes aligned for the first time in five hundred years, finally free of Achlev's Wall.

She released my hands. "Do you understand?" she asked in a sweet, sad voice.

"Yes," I breathed.

And then she was gone.

I had everything I needed. Three pieces of purest luneocite: Achlev's knife, which had become my own, the knife Cael had left behind, and the one I climbed to retrieve from statue Aren's hands. I placed them at each point of the triangle: Cael's next to the black stain left by his disintegrated body, Aren's at the feet of her statue, and Achlev's next to the spill of Victor de Achlev's blood from the vial.

Then I pulled the brick from beneath Aren's feet and retrieved the true vial of the Founder's blood I had hidden there.

"The blood of Victor," I said, tracing the three-point knot into the stain of his blood as bloodleaf blossoms — tiny copies of the symbol — fell and dissolved into it. "Descendant of Achlev."

I moved to the next point in the triangle. I emptied the Founder's blood vial onto the black smear left by his disintegrated body. Then I traced the knot into it as well. "The blood of Cael," I said.

Last, I pressed my own bloodied hand beside Aren's knife and repeated the process. "The blood of Aurelia, descendant of Aren."

This was the original point of convergence between creation, growth, and death. Long ago, Aren, Achlev, and Cael began a ritual on this spot to close a tear between the planes. With their blood now back in place, it fell to me to give their spell a definitive end.

Cael had wanted to widen the tear, Aren had wanted to close it, and Achlev had tried to protect it when neither of them succeeded. It was my choice now which effort would finally win, but I no longer cared about their ancient agendas. This was my life, and there was only one thing left in the world that I wanted.

Carefully, I pulled Zan's body into the center of the points and, kneeling, opened his shirt so I could place my hands on his skin. Then I closed my eyes and tried to imagine the barrier that separated us, the curtain that stood between my spirit and his — the place in which, for nearly five hundred years, Aren had lived in limbo, unable to move forward or backwards. I imagined it as a thin gauze — flimsy. Insubstantial. Behind it, another world.

I saw everything. The knots, the connections both minuscule and massive. The patterns in the stars and in the roots and limbs of trees and the ley lines and in the cobwebby network of vessels that carried blood from heart to head and hands and lungs and round and round and back again. I saw the three points of Achlev's gates and the three-petaled bloodleaf flower and the three round circles of red on the bloodcloth. And in the center of it all, it was just Zan and me.

It was time to cast a spell. The final spell.

I could feel the pulse of magic deep within the earth, thrumming like a beating heart.

I concentrated on the flow of blood within my own veins, until my awareness expanded to the *other* connections hidden within them —the crisscrossing course of vitality, of life force, that pushed the blood down the channel in the first place. Then I let that power seep out from my hands and into Zan's chest, traveling the circuits inside him. It was a call to arms; I sent my life force marching through his body, leading his stagnant blood back into motion, ordering his heart to pump and pump again, commanding his lungs to stretch and release, stretch and release . . . but his body would never do this on its own if the wound in his back remained, so I took his wound on myself. His skin knitted together even as mine came apart.

There was only one more thing left to do: retrieve his spirit.

It wasn't hard to find death; hadn't I always had one foot planted in it?

It wasn't a great beyond, like I'd always imagined—it was just like the world of the living, seen through a looking glass. Two sides of a coin. The same but not the same.

It was cold in death. Not a winter's cold, where warmth can be attained by striking a match or huddling beneath a heavy cloak. This was the cold of a place where warmth simply did not exist. I didn't have to go far, however; Zan was right there, blinking at me as if I'd materialized out of thin air. Perhaps I had.

"You," he said in surprise.

I ached at the sight of him looking so alive. "I should have told you," I said stumblingly, "on the wall that night. I should have told you what you were to me. I should have given you the truth."

He touched his hand to my cheek, letting his thumb rest on my bottom lip. I couldn't feel it physically—in here, I couldn't feel anything—but whatever bits of light and noise that made up my unruly spirit surged under his touch.

"Then tell me now." His voice was soft. "Before I have to go. What am I to you, Aurelia?"

I said, "Everything."

And then I took the tattered threads of my soul and knotted them tightly around his. When I knew I had him secure, I pushed him over the border and stepped into his place on the other side. My death, as Aren's was meant to all those years before, would finalize the spell and heal this gap forever. I saw just a flash before the border sealed up—Zan's eyes as they fluttered open.

Aren had given up her last spark of life to save mine; now I had done the same for Zan, exchanging my own life for his. My death, in this place and on this day, would fulfill Aren's mission and keep the Malefica sealed in her kingdom down below. It was my choice, and I was at peace with it.

"Aurelia?"

I whirled around, startled. "Mother? What are you—"

"Look at you," she said wonderingly. She was standing on the wrong side of the border. On the side of death. "So beautiful and strong."

"No, Mother. No. You're not supposed to be here."

"Of course I'm supposed to be here," she said. "Did you forget the bloodcloth spell? *Three lives now tied to one, bound by blood, by blood undone.*"

"This can't be happening," I frantically stammered. "It's *my* life I meant to sacrifice. Not yours, Mother. This isn't what I wanted to do."

"My sweet girl," she said. And she put her arms around me and held me while I remembered all the times I'd treated her ill, punishing her for what was wrong with my life when everything she'd ever done was to ensure that I'd have one. "You wanted to save someone you love, I understand. So do I, dear one. So do I."

She stroked my hair as I clung to her, crying because I'd never get to smell the rosemary soap she used in her hair again and she'd never get to chastise me for all the stupid, reckless things I'd done in Achleva, and because she was here only because I forgot that if I died, someone else would die in my place.

"Mama," I cried, "I'm so, so sorry. I love you."

She smiled, her hand on my cheek. "I know, love. I always knew. Go now and live."

38

A lick of flame formed from smoke and silence. I watched it curiously as it glimmered and grew, forming wide, outstretched wings and great clawing talons. A bird of golden fire. It glittered orange and red, yellow and red, orange and red.

I blinked and attempted to focus on the bird that was dancing and twisting in front of my eyes. It wasn't a real phoenix, no. It was small and made of gold and gemstones, and it dangled from a leather cuff. Zan's cuff, around Zan's wrist.

Zan. I tried to sit up, but I cried out in pain. My body creaked when I moved, as if I'd been left too long in the rain and had begun to rust. And my back—it was slick with blood. My blood, from the wound I'd taken from Zan and made into my own.

"Aurelia?" he whispered, hands in my hair.

I reached for him, and he wrapped me up into his arms and buried his face in my neck, half in relief, half in disbelief. "This isn't real," he said.

"You're here," I said. "It worked."

My happiness was short-lived. I pulled my bloodcloth from my pocket and stared at it, whipping in the wind. The first drop of blood—my mother's drop of blood—was gone completely, erased as if it had never been. It wasn't a dream or some terrible hallucination. Everything was real, and that meant—

"My mother. Merciful stars, she's dead. She's *dead,* Zan. And it's my fault."

He held me tighter, murmuring soft, comforting words against my temple, into my ear. He, too, knew what it was like to lose a mother.

We spent two days in Aren's tower as the storm seethed around us and the fire raged below, passing stories of our childhoods back and forth and huddling together for comfort. Zan worried constantly that if he let me close my eyes for more than a minute, I wouldn't open them up again. "I won't let go," I reassured him. "I refuse to let go."

Dying once had cost me my mother. I couldn't let Simon or Kellan face the same fate. I used thoughts of our loved ones as a ward to keep death away.

The storm broke in the middle of the night, and we woke to the sight of sails on the fjord below. The ship was flying two flags: one, the raven of the Silvis family; the other, the Renaltan royal arms.

We descended the tower stairs a final time, and I ran my fingers across the stones painted with Aren's story. *Goodbye,* I thought, though I knew she would not hear; having passed the weight of her calling on to me, she was in the Empyrea's care now.

The ship was waiting for us just outside the rubble of the castle's shoreline. We emerged from the tower to the sound of cheers; a dozen guards were leaning over the sides of the ship, lowering a plank ladder and jubilantly shouting, "They're here! They're alive!"

Kellan was the first to greet us, offering an arm to help Zan climb over the edge before they both turned to hoist me over together. "Why are you here?" I asked him as he took in our sad states. "It's a risk to sail through this wreckage when you had no proof we'd survived."

He gave me a wan smile. "I'm still alive," he said. "That was proof enough. Besides, I had no choice. Orders of the king."

"Aurelia?"

I turned to see a small form silhouetted in the doorway of the captain's cabin. Conrad was wearing a new brocade suit, with our family's crest on the breast. On a chain around his neck, he wore our mother's signet ring; his fingers were still too small to wear it on his hand. Next to the ring hung a diamond-and-opal winged horse.

I tried not to cry when he buried himself in my arms; he was the king now, and I didn't want to embarrass him with my tears. "Mama's dead," he said in a small voice.

"I know," I said, swallowing the hard knot in my throat, "and I'm sorry. I'm *so* sorry. But look at you! I've never seen a nobler king. She would be so proud of you. I know I am."

He said, "Aurelia, I don't think I'm ready. I'm scared."

"Don't be. Toris is gone, and the Tribunal will fold without him. You'll be the *first* king in five hundred years to rule without their influence. Imagine what you'll be able to do! It'll be hard, of course, but you'll have me to help you. Mother told me to protect you, little brother, and I will. And look." I pointed at the ruins of Achlev. "I lived through *that*. It turns out, I'm very hard to kill."

He nodded, reassured, and straightened his kingly shoulders before scampering off to order Kellan, at the helm, to take us home—no matter that the location of "home" was still rather unclear to us all.

I turned my attention to Achleva, giving it one last look as we sailed away. Buildings had collapsed; many had burned. The fjord, returned again to a crystal blue, had risen and flooded the streets; entire neighborhoods had been washed into oblivion. And the castle was nothing more than a burned-out, hulking shell. Achlev's Wall and the three towering gates were gone, as if they'd never existed.

And yet, even in its devastation, it was still beautiful—rough and also exquisite, like one of Zan's charcoal sketches. I was overwhelmed by the wonder and terror of it.

Zan came to stand with me as we watched the horizon diminish. "Cataclysm," I said.

"Annihilation," Zan replied. "And yet, we made it through. It's over."

I tried not to think about the relentless insistence in Malefica's whispers, *Let me out, let me out.* Zan was right, it *was* over. It was time to look forward, not back.

"Does that mean I get to collect my payment now?" I asked.

"If you still want your image in gold, you may be disappointed. I'm fresh out of gold."

"As I recall, my price was to tell you a secret and have you believe it, no matter what it is."

His green eyes had a new, golden glint despite the hazy light. "I'm listening."

I wound my hands into his dark hair, ignoring the lingering pain in my back, to lift my lips to his ear and murmur, "I think I might love you."

He gave me a smile I'd never seen on him before: bashful and crooked, and big enough to wrinkle the corners of his eyes. "I thought you were going to tell me a secret. I've known *that* for ages."

I laughed with tears in my eyes, and then I kissed him with all the force I could muster. It hurt—oh! How it hurt—but in that moment, caught between the ruined city and our unknown future, I felt my blood begin to stir with a new kind of magic.

"How is this possible?" Zan asked fervently, twining his fingers into mine. *"This?"*

"Blood and sacrifice," I said. "As it is with all power."

ACKNOWLEDGMENTS

With five wildly different versions written and queried over six excruciating years, I often joke that while *Bloodleaf* is a fairy tale, my path to publishing it was anything but. Though it might have been a long and sometimes bumpy road, I am so thankful for the people who saw me through it. The first on this list is my incredible agent, Pete Knapp. Your passion for this story and faith in my ability to tell it are the reason *Bloodleaf* is on the shelves instead of collecting dust in a trunk. I will be forever grateful for that query feedback giveaway that gave me just enough courage to click "send" one more time. And to the team at Park Literary, foreign rights rock stars Blair Wilson and Abby Koons, as well as Emily Sweet, Andrea Mai, Theresa Park, Alex Greene, and Emily Clagett: thank you all for your efforts on my behalf.

Huge thanks are also due to my fabulous editor, Cat Onder, whose visionary guidance brought *Bloodleaf* across the finish line with flying colors and rock 'n' roll flair. You helped me shine it into something I'm truly proud to send out into the world. To everyone at HMH Teen: I am so happy my book ended up in your capable hands. I know

I've got one hell of a team in my corner, and I'm thankful for that every single day.

To Mom and Dad: I am extremely fortunate to have been given parents like you. Your support and encouragement (and leniency when I stayed up to the wee hours reading every night) shaped me into who I am today. I'll always be glad you read all those sci-fi novels aloud to us—even if I might have preferred princesses to brainships (sorry, Dad!). I won't tell the others, but I know I'm your favorite daughter.

I must also thank my siblings: Carolanne, for the endless story-time phone calls and for not laughing when I said I was going to make *Bloodleaf*'s main deity a flying horse. Brandon, for always pushing me to think bigger and bolder . . . to make every scene a "wow" scene. Carma, for patiently reading every version of *Bloodleaf* (and there were SO MANY) and fangirling over it every time. Melody, for being my go-to design guru and for always having a good song to add to the inspiration playlist. Stacy, Katey, and Tiffany, for being constant, caring listeners and *Bloodleaf*'s best cheerleaders. Thank you all for the countless "clandestine" meetings over the years. I'd never have gotten this far without them (and you).

Stan, Paula, Logan, and Amy: I'm not sure how it happened, but I definitely hit the in-law lottery. We've depended on you a thousand times and you've come through for us in a thousand ways. I'm so proud to call you family.

Over the years, I was lucky to land in the classrooms of some extraordinary teachers who recognized my love of writing and enthusiastically encouraged me to nurture it: Mrs. Kaufman, who gave me an A+++ on a story about a girl saved from drowning by her trusty dog; Mrs. Lewis, who led the class in a round of applause when I got a five on the big state writing test; Mrs. Van Dyke, who taught me to never drop the baby; and Ms. Williams, who got special permission for me to go write novels in the computer lab each period after I went through all the creative writing courses my high school had to offer and registered for her class again anyway. Thank you all for your tireless work. It left a lasting impression on this student.

Additional thanks go to Kierstyn, who said the right thing at the right moment to get me pointed down the right path. To my early readers, Kenra, Camille, Danielle, and Jana: thank you so much for your ideas and your important feedback. To the makers and fellow fans of my favorite show, *12 Monkeys:* thanks for being a source of positive energy and inspiration and for teaching me that the right ending is the one you choose. And to my fellow debut authors of the Novel Nineteens: I am continually grateful for your camaraderie and support. I'm so proud to be numbered among such an extraordinary group of writers. Thanks to Billelis for bringing this beautiful cover to magical life. Laura Sebastian, Rebecca Ross, and Sarah Holland: I'll probably cry every time I re-read your kind words for the rest of forever. Thank you, times a million.

And lastly, to my little family . . . Jamison: your incisive mind and encyclopedic memory remind me to keep thinking deeper and building higher. Lincoln: your boundless enthusiasm and devilish charm keep me on my toes and ready for the next adventure. It's because of you both that I know exactly what lengths a mother will go to for her kids (but I'd rather not jump off a tower if I don't HAVE to—just saying).

And to my BFF, Keaton: thank you for the endless witticisms and word games and inside jokes and being proof that young love can last. Thanks for keeping me laughing and caffeinated and motivated to carry on writing even when it was hard and I wanted to give up. I don't know where I'd be without you, but it probably would have 100 percent less terrible puns, and that would not be okay.

I love you all. Thank you, again, for taking this journey with me.

THE MAGIC CONTINUES . . .

A *Bloodleaf* NOVEL

Greythorne

CRYSTAL SMITH

CONRAD COSTIN ALTENAR, EIGHT YEARS OLD AND THE ASCENDANT

king of Renalt, was humming to himself in time to the creaks and jolts of his carriage. It was an old Renaltan folk song, meant to be sung in a melancholic minor key: *Don't go, my child, to the Ebonwilde, / For there a witch resides . . .* Everyone knew the first verse, but he much preferred the lesser-known second, which described a phantom horseman:

> *Don't go, my child, to the Ebonwilde,*
> *For there a horseman rides.*
> *His stallion's mane is silver flame*
> *With night-black coals for eyes.*
> *Don't go, my child, to the Ebonwilde;*
> *Please stay here warm in bed.*
> *If you see him, child, in the Ebonwilde,*
> *You just might lose your head.*

As Conrad hummed, he fiddled with a new toy: a pointed puzzle box with nine sides and a series of intricate buttons and latches that had to be pressed and turned in just the right order to open a hidden compartment with a prize inside. It was from his sister, Aurelia, an early gift for his upcoming coronation, now only two days away. Convinced the box concealed candy, Conrad had been poring over it for the duration of his Renaltan tour. He wanted to have it figured out before the excursion reached its end, and though Greythorne—the final stop and chosen location to begin his coronation procession—was only a few miles away now, he was sure he could have the puzzle cracked and the candy consumed before they pulled onto the drive.

As he concentrated harder, his humming tapered off.

Push, turn, twist, twist, tap, and then . . .

Nothing.

"Bleeding stars," he cursed before glancing around the empty carriage to reassure himself that no one had heard. But his only companion was his own reflection, which gazed back at him from the mirrored panel on the other side of the carriage.

Onal, the crotchety old woman who'd spent the last five decades serving as the royal family's physician and most trusted adviser, always said foul language was a clear sign of a weak mind. It was something of a joke, however, as she possessed an impressive vocabulary of vulgarity of her own and made liberal use of it. But while *she* was above reproach—mostly because no one ever dared reproach her—his own behavior was being closely observed and chronicled. That's what this tour had been all about: showing the people of Renalt that their young king was capable and ready to lead. *They're looking for reasons to remove you,* Aurelia had warned at their parting. *Don't give them any.*

He wished that she could have accompanied him on this venture, though he knew it was better that she was keeping her distance. If he wanted the people to accept his rulings, they first had to accept his rule. Best not to remind them of his ties to a blood witch suspected of bringing down Achleva's capital.

Not that Aurelia was too frightened to face her detractors; she wasn't afraid of anything. Not intolerant townsfolk or falling cities or blood spells or being alone. Not even the dark.

He gulped and found himself moving the carriage curtain aside to peer up at the black clouds gathering in the sky above. A storm was coming and, on its heels, nightfall. He sent a mildly remorseful prayer up to the heavens: *Most Holy and Merciful Empyrea, I'm sorry for swearing again. Please let us arrive at Greythorne before it gets too dark.*

He didn't used to be afraid of the dark, but in the last months, it seemed like the blackest nights heralded the bleakest events. It was in the dark that Toris had tricked him into betraying Aurelia; it was in the dark that Lisette was torn from him, never to be seen again. And it was during the darkest night he ever knew—the night of the black moon—that his beloved mother took her last breath.

Nothing good ever happened in the dark.

A deep, rolling rumble of thunder rattled the floorboards, and the carriage suddenly slowed to a stop. There was a knock at the door. His appointed regent, Fredrick Greythorne, poked his head in and yelled over another slow groan from the sky, "A storm is coming, Majesty. This road has been known to flood in heavy rain."

Fredrick's brother and new captain of Conrad's personal guard, Kellan Greythorne, was waiting behind him. He said, "We can push through or find higher ground off the path until it blows over."

Conrad leaned out of the carriage. They'd come upon the hawthorn thickets that surrounded the Greythorne property. The journey was close to its end now, and how long could the storm last, anyway? Probably just a squall, summer's last fit of anger before handing over its post to autumn. It would probably tire itself out within the hour. The obvious choice would be to just pull off the road until it did, but they were so close to the welcoming fires of Greythorne, and it was going to be night soon.

"We keep going," Conrad stated. "We push through."

"As you wish," Fredrick said, exchanging glances with his brother, and Conrad could see that they'd both have preferred the other option. But their king had given an order.

The horses pounded the path at breakneck pace until the rain started falling, coming down in heavy sheets. The carriage squelched through mud that, in minutes, became a mire. Conrad, bracing himself in a corner, felt the whole contraption sinking lower and lower into the sludge as the noises outside grew louder, until the cries became shouts and the carriage stopped with a heaving lurch, sending him toppling.

Conrad scrambled back onto his seat, craning his neck to peek through the crack between the curtain and the window sash.

There was no one there.

The road was deserted, the horses and guards all gone. There was no rain, either; it was dry and quiet, with just the whisper of a slight wind across a hazy, red-tinged twilight.

"Hello?" Conrad called into the empty expanse, his voice trembling. "Anyone there? Fredrick?" He gulped. "Kellan?"

He wanted to retreat into the carriage, to huddle and hide until his men returned from . . . wherever they had gone. But what if something was wrong?

Aurelia would never cower in a carriage and wait to be rescued.

She'd be the first one on the ground, heading boldly toward the danger, letting nothing stand in her way.

If Aurelia could be brave, so could he.

He put one gold-slippered foot to the dirt, then the other, pulling his butter-colored brocade coat after him before abandoning it, disgruntled, on the floor of the carriage. If he was going to play the role of the hero, he didn't want to look like a foppish fool doing it. The pointed shoes and high silk stockings were embarrassing enough. He would have much preferred to save the day while wearing the sterling mail and cerulean cape of a Renaltan soldier, or the long, dark coat Zan used to wear that made him look baleful and brooding, but this would have to do.

Everything was unnervingly still, as if all the insects and animals were pausing to watch what he would do. He pulled the clear glass knife from its sheath—a luneocite blade that had also once belonged to Aurelia. He'd found it among her things and decided to make it his own; the knife was small and looked fragile, like Conrad himself, but it was actually sturdier than steel. Having it on his belt made him feel stronger, too.

Ahead on the road, he saw something move. A trick of the strange crimson light, he thought at first, but then it moved again.

He squinted. "Hello?" he asked the silence.

The figure seemed to form itself from silver smoke and murky shadow, beginning as a wispy outline but quickly coalescing into a substantial, looming shape that towered over him. Conrad's eyes widened, fingers becoming slick on the handle of his small knife as the shadow further sharpened, becoming not one entity but two.

He was face-to-face with the characters of his silly folk song: a gray-cloaked rider atop a ghostly horse.

If you see him, child, in the Ebonwilde, / You might just lose your head.

"Bleeding stars!" he yelped again, swiveling on the toes of his pointed shoes and diving into the shelter of the hawthorns lining the road.

The net of branches and their needle-like spines lashed his clothing as he plunged through them. He could hear hooves behind him, coming closer and closer with each passing second. The thick-woven thatch was nearly impenetrable even for his slight shape; it should have been impossible for anything larger. But when Conrad cast a glance over his shoulder, he saw the gray rider and his silver steed pass through the thicket like smoke through a sieve.

As he ran, the hawthorn changed form too; soon, the thicket became a hedge that parted before him, revealing a cobblestone path. He took one corner, then another. Right, then left, then right again. It was a maze — Greythorne's maze. And the horseman seemed to be herding him toward the old church enclosed in the heart of it. Outside the hedge, lights winked from the windows of the familiar estate, beckoning like beacons.

He dashed forward while the horseman followed, coming closer and closer. The bells in the church tower were chiming a discordant song as Conrad swiped at the thorny tangles standing between him and the safety of the sanctorium. He strained to remember the path Kellan had taught him, turning left, then right, left again, back and forth and around again, through the twists and spirals, losing ground every time he had to backtrack after a wrong turn.

They came to the center at the same time. The horse screamed and the rider reached out from the flying folds of his colorless cloak for Conrad as he scrambled for the sanctorium steps.

For a moment, all stopped. Both figures were crystallized where they stood for the space of one heartbeat, maybe two, before the church bells went silent and everything—the ground, the air, the fabric of reality—seemed to splinter apart in a searing flash and a roaring pulse of power.

✳

On the road into Greythorne, the rain ceased as abruptly as it started, and in the distance, the travelers could hear the bells of the Stella Regina beginning to chime the hour. Fredrick Greythorne checked in on his young charge to make sure he wouldn't be frightened by the violent lurching of the carriage as they pulled it from the mud. But when he opened the door, he found Conrad fast asleep inside, surrounded by a slew of crumpled waxed candy papers, his golden hair tousled into unkempt knots and his shoes and satin stockings in dirty tatters. He had drifted off to sleep clutching his strange, nine-sided puzzle box.

My opponent was a merchant of middle age by the name of Brom Baltus who had stopped at the Quiet Canary Tavern hoping to acquire some female company and play a couple of rounds of Betwixt and Between before hauling his goods—a cartload of apples, cheeses, and fine wines—the final stretch of his route. It was to his great misfortune that he sat down at the card table with me; when I was done with him, he'd be lucky to leave with enough coin left to hitch a ride home to his unhappy wife, let alone purchase an hour or two of a Canary girl's precious time. I'd have hated to rob them of good business, but from the smell of him, none of them were likely to mind.

Brom leaned forward to lay down his second-to-last play. His smug grin revealed a mouthful of tobacco-stained teeth. "Sad Tom," he said, pushing the card toward me. "Time to up your wager, miss, or call the game."

I frowned at the card and its depiction of a despondent, droopy-eyed lad clutching a withered four-petaled daisy. It was a surprisingly savvy move for a man who had accidentally singed his mustache trying to light his pipe not five minutes earlier. I'd already put down all the collateral I'd planned on staking—twelve gold crowns earned over two months of careful card-game conquests—and had little left with which to improve the pot. If I failed to provide Sad Tom with something to cheer him up, I'd lose all of it, and the cart of goods besides.

I hesitated only a moment before reaching into my pocket and retrieving the last thing of value left to my name: a fine white-gold ring set with an exquisite clear-cut stone. I hadn't worn it for months, but somehow I could not bring myself to lay it away in a jewelry box. Even now, as I placed it in the center of the table and the stone caught the candlelight and bounced it back in a thousand rainbow shards, I felt a keen sense of trepidation at the possibility of its loss. But I had plans to keep, costly plans, and Brom's goods would go a long way toward covering the costs.

"Finest Achlevan jewel crafting," I said. "Pure luneocite stone, skillfully cut and artfully set."

"And what makes you think it's worth—?"

"It used to belong to the late queen Irena de Achlev," I said. "It's engraved with her initials and the de Achlev seal." I steepled my fingers and leaned forward with a cocky tilt to my head, eyes still shrouded beneath my dark hood. "Imagine what the ladies at court in Syric would pay for such a souvenir."

Brom's eyes were gleaming—he knew exactly what kind of price it would fetch. Relics of the fallen de Achlev dynasty had become hot commodities among Syric's social elite. And to have belonged to the last queen . . . the ring was worth double the pile of coins on the table. I said calmly, "Surely Sad Tom is not so sad anymore?"

"Indeed not," the man said with a smirk. "Wager accepted. Make your next play, little miss."

Little miss. If a man had placed that selfsame wager, it would have been met with suspicion. This fool would have at least asked himself, *What kind of hand would warrant such an extravagant offer?* But because I was a woman, and a young one at that, Brom Baltus saw the move as a signal that he'd already gotten the better of me. That he'd forced me into a corner and I'd naively cast out my last line in desperation just to stay in the game.

What had Delphinia said? *You don't play the cards; you play the player.*

We were still two moves from the finale, but I had already won.

I waited for Brom to settle into his self-assuredness, using my next turn to play the Fanciful Blacksmith, resplendent in his great brown beard and frilly petticoats, hammering happily away at his forge. My opponent did just as I thought he would and mistook the balance card for a schism card and played Lady Loveless over the top of it. He sat back in his seat with a sneer, certain that he'd just secured his success.

"Lady Loveless has just sent your Blacksmith into the furnace," he said. "Time to pay up."

"Ah," I said, "but the Blacksmith stands on his own. He has no need for Lady Loveless's approval." I allowed myself a tiny hint of a smile. "Which means I have one more card to play."

I made a slow, deliberate show of turning over my last card, taking far more satisfaction than necessary in Brom's changing expression— disinterest followed closely by chagrin, shock, and dismay—as he realized what I'd done.

Staring up at him was the Two-Faced Queen.

The card depicted two versions of the same woman, one with night-dark hair against a snowy background, the other with ice-white hair against a deep black wood. They echoed each other in the exact same position, as if the line dividing them and bisecting the card was a mirror. And indeed, the card itself acted like a mirror, reflecting the players' own plays back onto them. My cards had all been balance cards, while his had been schism after schism. He had, in effect, annihilated himself.

I plucked the ring from atop the pile of coin and twirled it around my fingertips, allowing myself a single moment of melancholy before returning it to my pocket. "Now, then," I said, brusque and business-like, "where shall I collect my winnings?"